THE INVESTMENT

5-22-16

To: Joe & Margaret
Thank you for your friendship. GOD bless!
Bob Zinnecker
Psalm 42:11

ROBERT W. ZINNECKER

outskirtspress
DENVER, COLORADO

This is a work of fiction. The events and characters described herein are imaginary and are not intended to refer to specific places or living persons. The opinions expressed in this manuscript are solely the opinions of the author and do not represent the opinions or thoughts of the publisher. The author has represented and warranted full ownership and/or legal right to publish all the materials in this book.

The Investment
All Rights Reserved.
Copyright © 2016 Author Name
v3.0

Cover Photo © 2016 thinkstockphotos.com. All rights reserved - used with permission.

This book may not be reproduced, transmitted, or stored in whole or in part by any means, including graphic, electronic, or mechanical without the express written consent of the publisher except in the case of brief quotations embodied in critical articles and reviews.

Outskirts Press, Inc.
http://www.outskirtspress.com

ISBN: 978-1-4787-7588-1

Outskirts Press and the "OP" logo are trademarks belonging to Outskirts Press, Inc.

PRINTED IN THE UNITED STATES OF AMERICA

IN MEMORY

TESSA

(AKC: Oak Knoll Hidden Treasure)

January 6, 2001 – November 30, 2015

Acknowledgements

I am indebted to my family for their support and encouragement, in particular, my wife, Elaine, and my daughter, Karen, for their help in reviewing and editing the manuscript. I am also grateful to my friends and associates, Sarah Matthews, Susan Roberts and Dr. David Tweedie, DDS. Without their support and wise counsel this book could not have been published

Biblical Quotations

Biblical quotations are from the New American Standard Bible—Reference Edition—A.J. Holman Company—The Lockman Foundation 1975—All rights reserved.

Partial Cast of Characters

Many of the characters from *"Acquisition"* appear again in *"Sell Out"* and now in ***The Investment***. For those who haven't read *"Acquisition"* and/or *"Sell Out"*, as well as those who would like to re-acquaint themselves, you may find the following list helpful. You will meet new characters in *"**The Investment**"* and we hope you will find them equally interesting.

<u>**Bob Allison**</u>—CEO of Fairfield Communications, a Colorado Springs based telecommunications company. Fairfield has, in the past, attempted to acquire Tachyons, the company headed by Wilson McCann.

<u>**Stu Bailey**</u>—New York City merger and acquisition specialist who aided Wilson McCann in his failed attempt to save Dynacom, the telecommunication company where McCann was CEO, from being acquired by Legent over five years ago. He also helped to arrange for the financing of McCann's new company, Tachyons, a telecommunications company headquartered in the small town of Farnsworth in Michigan's "Thumb" area.

<u>**Donna Barnes**</u>—the love of Wilson McCann's life and mother of his son, J.W. Storey, who was born when she was a teenager and placed for adoption without McCann's knowledge. Donna died over five years ago while on a missionary trip to the Czech Republic. Before her death, she owned and operated the Barnes Loft, a department store in Farnsworth.

<u>**Meadow Lark "Lark" Bishop**</u>—named for the famous Harlem Globetrotter, "Lark" is a graduate of Coastal Carolina

University where he played basketball and is now the General Manager of Eastern European Christian Missions.

John Botek—Administrative Manager for Eastern European Christian Missions.

Ed Cantwell—Chief Operating Officer of Fairfield Communications.

Charles Corbin—former Chairman of Dynacom who sold it to Legent over the bitter objections of his hand-picked CEO, Wilson McCann.

Janice DeGroot—reporter for The Bay City Times and former native of Farnsworth. Janice covers the "Thumb" area of Michigan and won a journalism award for her coverage of the formation of Tachyons.

Mike Divell—former co-worker of Wilson McCann who now owns and operates MTD, an information technology consulting firm based in Atlanta, Georgia.

Ed Feldman—head of a New York City investment banking firm that holds the majority investment in Tachyons. He is the only member of Tachyons' board who is not a Christian.

Elmer Gabbard—Pastor of the Farnsworth Wesleyan Church. Rev. Gabbard suffered from Polio as a youth and wears a steel brace on one of his legs.

Kathy Garrety—Director of Human Resources for Tachyons.

Nick Hardesty—owns and operates a small auto repair business out of a large tool shed on McCann's farm and doubles as McCann's hired man. He takes care of McCann's farm during McCann's frequent absences.

Darcy Hardesty—Nick's wife who manages the Barnes Loft. As an unmarried pregnant teenager, she worked for Donna Barnes. She and Nick became Christians and were married. Upon Donna's death, she took over the management of the Barnes Loft through the assistance and support of

Wilson McCann and Fred Penay. Penay was, at the time, the President of the Farnsworth State Bank.

Fred and Ella Harms—Wilson McCann's deceased Aunt and Uncle. Fred and Ella owned the debt-ridden farm that McCann worked on during the summers of his high school and college years. McCann bought out the mortgage and moved to the farm over five years ago when Dynacom was acquired by Legent and he was ousted as CEO.

Charles Hastings—former pastor of the Farnsworth United Methodist Church who has since been relocated to a church in a Detroit suburb. Hastings was instrumental in leading Nick and Darcy Hardesty, Cindy Melzy, Wilson McCann and Sally McHugh to become Christians. His wife, **Dorothy** stepped in to help Sally McHugh run her diner when Sally took over the management of the Dunt Center for Wilson McCann.

Shirley Jacobs—CEO and Chairperson of Eastern European Christian Missions (EECM) headquartered in Weaverville, North Carolina. EECM was founded by Shirley's husband, James, a good friend of Charles Hastings. Charles and Wilson McCann are on EECM's board.

Jeanine—the harried Assistant to Stu Bailey. She owns a condo in the Bahamas but never gets to go there.

John King—retired Vice President of Legent, a large telecommunications firm. King was instrumental in the sale of telecommunications properties to Tachyons and is a member of Tachyons' Board. He lives in Savannah, Georgia.

Ted Lark—formerly Farnsworth Tele's information technology specialist, he is now Tachyons' Director of Information Technology.

Jim and Lona Marks—McCann's neighboring farm family and, together with their two children, they are among his closest friends. Jim and Lona are committed Christians. Jim works a good portion of McCann's farm.

Max—an investment counselor based in Chicago who handles all of McCann's investments and oversees his business ventures.

Wilson McCann—CEO of Tachyons. Tachyons has operations in Michigan, Wisconsin, Minnesota and Iowa. McCann, through his investment company, HHF also has investments in the Dunt Center, his farm and Tachyons.

Sally McHugh—deceased thrice married and thrice divorced manager of the Dunt Center in Farnsworth. Sally had owned the Farnsworth Diner. In her teens, Sally had a "summer fling" with Wilson McCann and remained an admirer. Because of McCann's influence, she became a Christian. She put together the designs for the remodeling of the Dunt Center, a former elementary school that became a combination community center, bed and breakfast facility and offices for a good portion of Tachyons headquarters staff. Sally died in a tragic automobile accident two years ago.

McIntyre—the burley Scotsman is a reformed alcoholic accountant who now drives a cattle truck for a feedlot operation in Hemlock, Michigan. McIntyre is responsible for having trained McCann in using his Border collie, Ted, to work with his cattle. McIntyre also brought McCann a new Border collie named Wink after Ted was shot by two drunken farmers. After Wink died from old age, McIntyre brought McCann a Shetland Sheepdog named Tessa. McIntyre is a man of deep faith with a practical approach to life who seems to appear at just the right time to help McCann.

Linda McCann—Wilson McCann's wife, formerly Linda McReedy. She is a brilliant team leader for Mike Divell's company. Linda led the conversion of EECM's Information

Technology systems over five years ago. She was a team leader at Tachyons for its process improvement project when she fell in love with, and married, Wilson McCann. Linda bears a striking resemblance to the 1950's movie star, Kim Novak.

Cindy Melzy—CEO of Triad, a New York City investment banking firm. Triad has minority investment in Tachyons. Cindy accepted Christ after conversations with Belle Warner. A divorced mother of one boy, Cindy is a good friend and admirer of Wilson McCann.

Fred Penay—retired former President of the Farnsworth State Bank. Other than Donna Barnes and her father, Penay was the only one to know about the delivery of her baby. Penay kept the secret for 24 years and was forced to introduce J.W. Storey to his biological father, Wilson McCann, over five years ago when J.W. came to Farnsworth, seeking to learn about his birth mother and father.

Al Prince—Linda McReedy's friend, confidant, and co-worker at Mike Divell's company. Once one of Linda's secret admirers, he is now happily married and living in St. Louis.

Tammie Ring—Administrative Assistant to Wilson McCann and mother of two. She is a committed Christian and member of the Farnsworth Wesleyan Church.

Jonathan "Jon" Sager, M.D.—Chief of Staff at the Farnsworth Hospital and Wilson McCann's personal doctor.

Malcolm Shaw—Chairman of the Board of Triad. Shaw is Cindy Melzy's mentor.

J.W. Storey—McCann's son. Born out of wed lock to Donna Barnes at age 18, J.W. was adopted by Frank and Francis Storey and was not told he was adopted or who his biological father and mother were until five years ago.

Donald Straylin—CEO of Straylin and Co. a Charlotte based investment banking firm that merged with Triad two years ago. His firm had been in business since before the great depression. Straylin and Co played a major role in the formation of Tachyons after meeting Wilson McCann and was one of Tachyons minority investors. Straylin is also on the Board of EECM.

Belle Warner—matriarch of the Warner family, the unofficial "first family" of Farnsworth. The Warner family owned the Farnsworth Telephone Coop. prior to its acquisition by Tachyons. Belle is a mentor to Wilson McCann and played a role in Cindy Melzy, McCann, and Linda McReedy becoming Christians. Belle's son, Doug, was President of the family owned company and is now the General Manager of a good portion of Tachyons' Michigan operation.

Phil Willard—owner of the Farnsworth Agway. Phil and his wife Martha are committed Christians. Phil was also county Republican Chairman for Tuscola County and was previously a board member of the Farnsworth Telephone Coop. A gregarious and wise man, Phil is a good influence on Wilson McCann.

Peter Zastrow former Russian Army Captain who came to the United States and amassed a fortune as the operator of the Black Bat hedge fund. Zastrow will use any means to eliminate those who get in his way. He is currently serving time in a minimum security prison in Marion, Illinois for securities fraud and conspiracy to commit murder.

Notes

The name "Mogollon" is pronounced "mug-ee-own"

The term "Aggregator" as used in this story describes a corporation which grows through the acquisition of other corporations and "aggregates" them into one consolidated enterprise.

The abbreviations CEO and COO stand for Chief Executive Officer and Chief Operating Officer.

Prologue

1970—Chicago, Illinois

He parked his battered pickup behind the diner on Chicago's south side. It was a 50's diner and, as he entered through the rear door, the McGuire Sisters were harmonizing on "*Sincerely*". B.J. was seated in a booth looking out on the street. He was dressed, as usual, in a maroon sport coat and maroon and white slacks. A wide white belt matched his white loafers. The collar of his pink shirt was outside the collar of his coat.

"Jimbo! How you doing man?" B.J. said loudly. "B.J" stood for Bennett Joseph but he didn't like to be called "Bennett" or "Ben" or "Benny" or "Joe" or "Joseph" so he was "B. J".

B.J. always called him "Jimbo". He had done so since they were in high school together. He didn't especially like the nickname. He preferred to be called "Jim" or at worst "James" but tolerated it because of their friendship. He figured that if his best friend could be "B.J." he could be "Jimbo" when they were together.

As he sat down, he put his hand in his jacket pocket. He could feel the envelope, thick with money, and wondered if he was doing the right thing.

B.J. saw him do it and smiled broadly. "Did you bring the money?"

"Yeah. Are you sure this will work?" he replied, putting his hands together on the table between them.

"Man, there is going to be an oil crisis like you won't believe in the next two years and they are going to have to do something about it. I'm telling you, they are going to have to get that oil out of Alaska and they are going to need a pipeline to do it. That's where you and I are gonna make a bundle!"

"It's all the money I've got, B.J. It's seven years of scrimping and saving and going without for the wife and my kid. I could take it and make a down payment on a house. I could get us out of that apartment. I could…"

B.J. raised his hand to stop him. "I know, man. But this kind of opportunity ain't coming along again. I've got the patent filing ready to go and my lawyer is drawing up the papers even as we speak. When those oil guys see the design, they are going to go nuts and you and I are going to be rich! You'll be able to buy two houses! Your boy will be able to go to Harvard if he wants to!"

"You're going to give me something in writing, right B.J.? Something that I can put in the box at the bank that shows I'm a partner, something that my wife and my boy will have if something should happen to me?" He tried to make his voice sound as forceful and businesslike as he could.

"You know it man! As soon as the papers are ready, I'll bring them to you and you sign them and we're partners! You trust me don't you?"

"Sure, it's just that…this is…this is all I have."

B.J.'s tone became somber. "I know, Jimbo. It's a big gamble and I wouldn't ask you to do it if I didn't really believe it will succeed. You're my best friend and I want you to have a part in this. You can trust me."

He handed over the envelope and they sat there drinking their coffee and talking about their future. A future filled with promise and excitement. As he drove back to the apartment, he knew he had taken a step forward that held the potential for both outstanding success and tragic failure. He attributed the tightness in his chest to the excitement that went with having taken that step.

Twenty four hours later, he would feel that same tightness as he operated the drill press in the plant where he worked. This time, it didn't go away. Three hours later, he was pronounced dead from a heart attack.

B. J. came to the funeral home to offer his condolences to the widow and her son. He didn't mention the envelope or the money it had contained. Jimbo's widow didn't know about any of it and what she didn't know wouldn't add to her misery.

Three years later, the Alaska pipeline began operation and B.J.'s design for its valves made him a multi millionaire.

In Chicago, Jimbo's widow continued to live in their small apartment and work at a law firm to earn enough to raise her now 10 year old son.

2010—Knoxville, TN

The black Escalade pulled slowly up to the curb and stopped. He reached for the pager in the console and turned it on. He looked out of the SUV's window at the house. It was a white Cape Cod with attractive landscaping on either side of the front porch. The sidewalk came down to the street. All it lacked was a picket fence to be the home they had talked and dreamed about forty six years ago.

"I'll page you when I'm ready to leave," he said to his driver.

"Yes sir, I'll be waiting down at that coffee shop we passed about a mile back," George replied.

George had been his driver for the past 20 years. He would make sure that George and his family were taken care of when he was gone. He opened the door and slowly got out. He would have to give up the Escalade before long. It was getting too difficult to get in and out. Another sacrifice he would have to make before…the end. He started up the walk.

Inside the house, she checked the mirror in the entrance hall one more time and looked out through the door as he came up the walk. Her heart beat just a little faster. He was just as tall as she remembered. The short dark hair had been replaced by a longer mane of gray. The glasses were the latest style. The jacket and trousers were as well. The shoes shone in the midday sun. What else would she have expected? He carried himself with the same ramrod stiffness that she remembered from that night so long ago when she broke his heart. She smoothed her skirt down over her hips and opened the door.

"Hello Ann," he said, gazing down at her. She was a foot shorter than he was. She was a little broader in the hips now than when they had parted so long ago. The smooth round face he remembered from their shared past had been altered by a few wrinkles. The hairstyle was the same, the glasses a little thicker. He had dreamed about this moment for so long, so very long.

"Hello Ben. Come in," she replied, stepping aside as he entered. She closed the door and turned to face him. She saw the look in his eyes and waited.

"It's so good to see you…I've thought about you often…I…" he began lamely.

"You too," she said, stepping forward and looking up at him.

"May I…may I?" he stammered.

"You want a hug? Sure, I'll give you a hug," she smiled up at him and they hugged awkwardly, her head against his chest, just as they had the first time, so long ago.

They stepped back and she led him into the small living room. Sunlight lit up the modest furnishings. She gestured to an easy chair in one corner of the room and he sat, taking in the pictures on a wall shelf opposite. There was one of Ann with her second husband and one of a younger woman who resembled Ann's first husband. He had both in a file folder in his office.

"Would you like some coffee? I just made some," she said, standing a few feet inside the arched doorway.

"That would be fine. Thank you."

She turned and he watched her go. His mind flashed back to that night in June so many years ago when she had turned and went into her parent's home. He had made it back to his car and driven home, his life forever changed.

They had met when he was a senior and she was a sophomore in high school. He had sent his best friend, Jimbo, to ask her if she would go out with him. She told Jimbo that he would have to ask her himself. He had stood outside the door to her Biology class, his heart beating wildly and waited while the teacher, irritated by the interruption, summoned her. She had come out into the hallway and waited while he stammered through his invitation. Her smile and perky "sure" in response had begun a four year relationship that ended when she handed back a diamond engagement ring and walked out of his life.

As he sat there in her home, he fought back the bitterness that had driven him for all these years. He was here to try to put that to rest.

She returned with two mugs and a cream and sugar set that didn't match and set them on the coffee table between them. She brought the coffee pot and poured the steaming black liquid into the mugs. She added cream and sugar to hers while he took his black. She sat opposite him, cradled her mug in both hands, and waited.

"This is a nice home. How long have you lived here?" he asked, knowing the answer. It was all in the folder. Her whole life laid out in black print on white paper with pictures and supporting documents. The product of one month of investigative work by a man he had paid $7,500.

There was the brief affair with a supervisor in the clothing store where she worked after graduation. There was the short lived marriage to an auto mechanic that had produced the young woman in the picture before ending in divorce. The daughter had died at age thirty six, childless but happily married to an insurance agent.

Ann's second marriage had lasted well into her fifties before her husband passed away, leaving her financially secure. The house was debt-free and, between Social Security, the pension payments from both of their working lives, and dividends from some small investments, she lived a comfortable but not extravagant life. He knew that she volunteered at the local shelter twice a week and was one of a group of women who gathered every two weeks to drink coffee, play cards and gossip. She didn't go to church and he wondered why. He knew that she took flowers from her garden to her second husband's grave each month during the summer. She did not visit her daughter's grave with the same frequency. Her relationships with her two younger brothers and a younger sister were good but distant. The affair at the clothing store had strained her family relationships.

She smiled at him before she answered. He was clearly out of place in this house. The carefully groomed appearance, the fashionable clothes, the expensive watch on his wrist all supported the air of power and influence that he carried. Yet, she sensed that underneath it all, there was the inner core of the good young man she had loved many years ago, the same good young man that she had deliberately hurt because she did not want to inflict an even greater wound.

"Thirty years. My second husband, Bill, and I bought it in 1980," she said, taking a sip from her mug.

"What did he do?" he asked, knowing the answer.

"He was an investment counselor with Edward Jones," she sipped again, eyeing him over the rim of her mug. She was content to let him lead the conversation. It was, after all, his idea to come here.

"I was thinking as I came up the walk about how this house is what we had talked about. Remember? A little white house with a picket fence, two kids and...," he didn't know what to say next.

She looked around the room. "The Cleaver family, Ward, June, Wally and 'the Beav'...you've gone a lot farther than that."

"It still sounds good to me," he said, looking into the green eyes behind the glasses.

"You never married?" She asked. She also knew the answer before it came. She had followed his career over the years. It wasn't in a folder or a scrap book but she knew the basic facts. He had finished college, taken a job as a manufacturer's rep and then hit it big. His invention had filled a need in the market at the right time and he had become a multi-millionaire over night. Now he was one of the richest men in the country if not the world.

She knew he lived in Chicago and was portrayed as a rich recluse, similar to Howard Hughes. But, as she looked across the room into his eyes, she sensed that there was something there that she didn't know, something dark and frightening.

"No, I guess I was too busy. And, I never found anyone who wanted a white house with a picket fence and two kids," he said, trying to make it sound light. It came out more seriously than he had intended.

She heard the message within the message and decided to push him a little just to get this moving along and get it over with. "Do you…did you…hate me?"

"No…never…I didn't understand…don't understand today…why…," he said, putting the mug down on the table and leaning forward in his chair.

"Ben, you had me on a pedestal. I wasn't Cinderella. I was one of the evil sisters. I had done, was doing, things that you didn't know about. I was nineteen years old and I knew that if we got married you would have eventually found out and you would have hated me. I couldn't do that to you."

"What you were doing…did it begin before we…before you…?" he asked. She could see the pain in his eyes. It was the look of the twenty one year old young man holding a diamond engagement ring standing on the sidewalk of her parents' home almost fifty years ago.

"It began just about the time we got engaged," she said quietly.

"He was old enough to be your father," he said it questioningly, not accusingly.

"Yes, and I wish it had never happened. It changed me forever." Her eyes didn't waiver as she said it. Then, it dawned on her. Her eyes glittered with disbelief. She rose, folded her arms across her chest and turned to the window, her back to him.

"You knew? You know...Ah! It all makes sense now! You have been digging around checking on me! You are some sort of stalker! I cannot believe this! This explains a call from my investment broker two weeks ago. She said someone was snooping around, asking questions! She thought I was thinking of changing to another firm! What were you doing? Trying to see how much money I do or don't have? God! I can't believe you. You and your money and your fame and your power! And you come to me now...for...for what?"

He looked at her helplessly, his hands outstretched, pleadingly. "Ann, I swear! I only wanted to.."

"To what? Rekindle an old romance that has been dead for almost fifty years? What?"

"I mean't...I mean no harm. I just wanted to see you...to see if you were okay to...I don't know what I wanted...I just..." he stammered into silence as she turned. He dropped his head into his hands.

She turned and took a deep breath as she looked down at him. In that moment she realized how badly she had hurt him that night so many years ago. She had thought she was saving him and now she realized that she had inflicted the most grievous of all possible wounds. She had destroyed a part of him, a good part. It had been replaced by a hardness of purpose that allowed no room for him to love again. In a corner of her heart that she had long been kept at bay, the spark of affection blossomed again.

"Ben, why did you ask to see me?" she asked, her voice soft and caring.

"I wanted to see you one more time before…before…" he stammered, looking out the window.

"Before what, Ben? What's going on?" There was a note of concern in her voice.

He took a deep breath, reached for the mug and took a long drink before replying.

"Before I die. I've been given six months to live."

"Oh my God!" She took off her glasses and laid them on the table and sat down. She wiped away the tears that had come so quickly. She was, once again, that little blonde teen-ager outside the Biology room door, looking up at the dark haired senior as he asked her for a date.

"I have an inoperable brain tumor. It's growing very fast. I'm sorry, I shouldn't have come. I'm a stupid old man who is living in the past these days more than in the present. I have no future. Do you want me to leave?"

She leaned back in her chair and looked up at the ceiling, trying to regain her composure. Memories, good and bad, flooded through her. The anger toward him that she had felt a moment ago was gone.

"No, I'm glad you came," as she said it, she tried to make it true. As she looked at him, it was true.

"Remember when we spent the night at my grandparents' farm and the thunder storm came through and the lights went out?" she asked, smiling.

He sat back, smiled back at her and let the memory roll over him. They had sat there in the dark together with only the light from the fireplace, holding hands and dreaming about the future. Ann's grandparents were away for the evening. They had the entire house to themselves. The joy of teen-age love filled their hearts. She had wanted to go into the bedroom and do it. But, he was not that kind of a boy. They had stayed in the living room before the fire and dreamed. The storm was so bad that her grandparents had invited him to stay until the next day. He had awakened that morning with

Ann kneeling beside the bed. He had dreamed of the day when he would find her next to him every morning. He had kicked himself for years afterward that he hadn't led her to the bedroom. Perhaps if he had they would have realized their dreams.

The barrier between them had been broken. They sat there, drinking their coffee in the sunlit room of the present while they revisited the brightness of their past. And, as they did so, he realized for the first time that this wonderful girl, now aged just as he was, had done him a great favor that, until now he had only thought of as a great disappointment. Finally, he glanced at his watch and realized that it was time for him to summon the Escalade. He pushed the button on the pager. A mile away, the big SUV rolled out of the coffee shop parking lot.

"I have to be going. It was kind of you to see me. Thank you," he said.

"Ben, I know that I hurt you. I'm so sorry. But you have turned out pretty well. Can I ask you a question?"

"Sure, fire away," he said, wonderingly.

"Have you ever betrayed someone…like I did?"

His mind traveled back over the years and landed in another place and another time. He felt, again, the pangs of guilt that had traveled with him for so long.

"Yes, someone close to me…just like you," he admitted, quietly.

She stood and came around the table. She knelt before him and looked deeply into his eyes.

"Make it right, Ben," she said softly.

"It may be too late but I promise you that I will try," he said as he wrapped his arms around her and buried his face in her hair. They remained there for a few moments before she pulled away and stood. He stood as well and turned toward the door. They moved toward the doorway, engaging in small talk. She slipped her hand into his and he squeezed it impulsively.

"I'm glad you came, Ben. Good luck and God bless," she said, as she opened the door, knowing that she would never see him again and feeling glad for the moment of seeing him now.

He looked up at the ceiling and struggled to keep his emotions under control.

"I've never loved anyone like I loved you," he said, looking down at her.

"Thank you for that," she said, not knowing what else to say.

The Escalade pulled up and sat idling as he brushed his lips against her cheek and walked out the door. She watched him go. It wasn't love she felt but a deep fondness for a time in her life that had been made special by a special person. He slowly got into the SUV and looked back through the window at her standing in the doorway of the white Cape Cod without the picket fence. As George pulled away from the curb, he vowed to do everything he could to correct the other great flaw in his past just as Ann had said.

(1)

Liam Colter stood in the shadows of the doorway next to the restaurant's entrance. One of Tazlov's contacts in the City of Chicago's Division of Electrical Operations had taken care of two street lights in front of the portion of the street. For twenty yards in either direction, the street was dark except for the light from the restaurant's windows and the headlights of passing cars.

He fingered the sap in his jacket pocket. It was like caressing an old friend. He had owned it since his IRA days. The flat leather pouch, filled with lead shot, encased a coiled spring that gave the weapon its "whip" for use in close quarters.

The door to the restaurant opened and the man he had been waiting for stepped out onto the sidewalk. Colter moved out of the doorway and followed him for about ten yards until the two of them were in the darkest part of the street. He reached out and touched the man's shoulder.

"A fine night it is for a bit of food and drink. I trust you enjoyed yours," he said quietly.

The man whirled to face him and brought up his arm to defend himself. But, as he was raising it, Colter brought the sap down on his forearm just above the wrist. The sound of the sap breaking bones was followed by the start of the man's scream. Colter clamped his left hand over the man's mouth, shoved him up against the wall of the building and brought the sap in hard to the side of his right knee. The man went down in a heap and lay there, moaning loudly.

"I trust your medical insurance, paid for, as you well know, by Mr. Zastrow's benevolence, will pay for setting your broken bones," Colter said quietly, as he knelt before the man. "I hope that it will not be necessary for us to call upon you again to remind you that any thoughts you might be having about talking to certain FBI agents would be dangerous to your life."

He stood, slipped the sap back into his jacket pocket and walked away into the darkness, leaving the man crumpled on the sidewalk.

An hour later, Colter entered the bar where he worked and called Tazlov.

"It's been taken care of. I doubt he will be of any further trouble to you," he said quietly. He didn't wait for a response as he knew there would be none.

In his suburban Chicago home, Tazlov put down the phone and checked his watch. He needed to get to his son's soccer game. Colter had done his usual efficient job. Tazlov would be using him again in the future. Of that he had no doubt.

The mid-September sun warmed the dinette area in the McCann home, situated on forty acres north and west of McCann's farm near the small village of Farnsworth in Michigan's Thumb area. The two year old ranch house sat on a slight rise. The floor to ceiling windows provided a panoramic view of the fields and a small stream below the house. McCann and his wife, Linda, had deliberately built the home so that the morning sunlight would bathe their morning meals and the evening sun would illuminate the living room which overlooked a ravine to the west of the home.

THE INVESTMENT

Wilson McCann poured a cup of coffee from the old aluminum percolator into a travel mug and replaced the mug's cover. The percolator seemed out of place in the modern kitchen.

"But", McCann thought idly, looking at the percolator, "it's part of my past and I don't want to part with it." McCann was the CEO of Tachyons, a telecommunications company headquartered in Farnsworth. The company, founded five years previously, operated in four Midwestern states

"We could get one of those new cup-at-a-time units," Linda said, as she entered the kitchen. Twelve years younger than McCann's 47, she still retained her movie star good looks. Many people thought she had a striking resemblance to Kim Novak, the 1950's star of such films as *Vertigo* and *Man with the Golden Arm*.

"It and the Ranger are all I have left of my life before you," McCann said, as he turned to face her. He let his gaze travel from her head to her toes. He still couldn't believe that she had agreed to be his wife two years ago.

He had first met Linda when she led the installation of a completely new information system at Eastern European Christian Missions in Weaverville, North Carolina in 2005. McCann was a newly appointed Board member at the ministry and had called on an old friend and former co-worker, Mike Divell, to re-vamp the outmoded systems EECM was using. Mike had worked with McCann at a telecommunications company named Dynacom, before it was taken over by Legent, another telecom firm. Mike had left Dynacom to form his own technology consulting company, MTD, headquartered in Atlanta, Georgia. Linda was one of Mike's team leaders based in St. Louis, Missouri. A year later, McCann had hired Mike's firm to take charge of improving Tachyons' information systems and installing new cloud-based technology. Linda was the team leader for the job.

A series of events, starting with the breakup of her ten year live in relationship with a professional football player had blossomed into a relationship when Linda crashed her rental car into the light pole on McCann's farm, a mile and a half away from their new home. Linda had given her life to Christ in the living room at the farm after talking with Belle Warner, Farnsworth's leading lady and the former owner of a local telecommunications company that was now a part of Tachyons. A trip to Estes Park, Colorado had brought McCann and Linda together for three days at her parents' lodge and McCann had proposed a week later. They were married in Estes Park in the fall and moved into their new home upon returning from their honeymoon.

Two years ago, the three primary investors in Tachyons had seriously considered an acquisition offer from Fairfield Communications, a Colorado based telecom "aggregator", but decided not to sell. They had backed McCann's expansion of the company into fiber optic networks in some of the Midwest's major metropolitan areas. The expansion had enhanced Tachyons' value as an acquisition target and Mogollon, a Phoenix based telecommunications company had recently submitted a new acquisition proposal.

If and when Mogollon took over, Kent Lister, Mogollon's CEO would make sure that McCann was finished at Tachyons. Mogollon would send in someone to run the former Tachyons operation. That person would oversee the eventual consolidation of Tachyons into Mogollon and the phase out of Farnsworth as Tachyons' corporate headquarters. The small community would continue to be the headquarters for the Michigan state operations but the present Tachyons operations in Iowa, Minnesota and Wisconsin would be managed from Mogollon's regional office in Minneapolis.

"You and your old coffee pot and pickup truck!" she said, as she walked across the room to where he stood. She put her arms around his neck and whispered.

"Like what you see?"

"Very much," he said as he kissed her. "But I'm still keeping the pot and the truck."

"Well, I still want a BMW," she said, as she moved away and poured a cup of coffee from the percolator.

"Then get one," he said, putting on his suit coat. He knew she had enough money from her last consulting job to buy one for cash but he hoped she would resist the temptation at least until Christmas. He was hoping to surprise her with a new BMW then.

"Maybe I will," she said, smiling. "But perhaps I should wait to see what the beef sells for and what the beet and bean crop does and what happens when Ed Feldman sells Tachyons out from under you."

McCann owned a one hundred acre farm. It had been his aunt and uncle's and he had worked for them during his summer vacations during high school and college. He had purchased the debt-ridden farm after they had passed away about five years ago. The farm was now worked by a neighbor, Jim Marks. Marks had planted navy beans and sugar beets the previous spring. McCann was feeding 50 head of beef cattle as well. Nick Hardesty, a young man whose wife, Darcy, ran a small clothing store in Farnsworth, took care of the buildings and grounds and rented the farmhouse for his family. A large tool shed on the farm had been converted into Nick's automotive repair shop. Their son, going on six, had just started the first grade.

Ed Feldman was Chairman of Tachyons' Board of Directors and the majority investor in the privately held company. Feldman had long felt that eventually Tachyons should be sold or merged with another telecommunications company. Only McCann's success in improving and expanding operations and the associated return on investment, as well as the continued support of the other investors through their representatives on the board, had prevented Feldman from accomplishing his objective.

Tomorrow, McCann would travel to Raleigh, North Carolina to make one last attempt to forestall the sale of Tachyons at the quarterly meeting of its Board of Directors. The next day would be spent with members of the board at a one day seminar at Campbell University's College of Law.

"It might be wise to wait. We might have to live off your earnings," he smiled as he turned toward the door.

She put down her coffee cup and moved to intercept him. When they both were home, it was a regular routine. They embraced and prayed together before he headed out the door. McCann had come to faith in Christ while burying his faithful dog, Ted, during a snowstorm five years ago. Ted's death was the final straw that brought him to his knees after losing his position as CEO of Dynacom, a large national telecommunications firm, the love of his life and his mother.

Prayer was the way they began and ended each day. Linda still traveled for MTD on projects overseas and in the U.S. They were hoping to have children and had agreed that if and when they did, Linda would be a full time mother.

"See ya later, alligator," McCann said, kissing her one last time and going out the door.

"Right back at ya," Linda responded as she closed the door.

McCann's 1984 Ranger pickup sat in the driveway. It had been his uncle's and he was sentimentally attached to it. Two years ago, Nick Hardesty had done a full restoral and the bright red machine that rolled out the drive was a sight to behold.

McCann drove for about a mile and turned down a narrow gravel road that led to his farm. He was feeling nostalgic and a stop at the farm always seemed to get his day started right.

He pulled in to the drive and drove slowly up the small rise. The house, a rambling two story, stood to the right of the drive which circled around past a granary and small shed and the big L-shaped barn. The ground fell off to the west of the farmstead and a big hip-roofed tool shed dominated the landscape to the right of the turn-around. He followed the drive to the crest of the hill next to the barn where it turned to complete its circle. He stopped, got out and walked to the fence at the crest of the hill.

He looked out over the fields to the west. In the distance, a wooded area rose up on the next range of hills. Below, next to the barn's lower level, several white faced steers stood next to a water tank in the barnyard. Two looked up at him while the others looked off to the east. Out in the field below the barnyard, more steers grazed in the early morning sunlight.

He stood there, the sun behind him, and reflected back over the years. He had first come here from his mother's apartment in Chicago over thirty years ago. The summers had been demanding. His uncle, Fred Harms, believed that hard work was good for man or boy. Under his Uncle's stern supervision, McCann had learned the basics of survival farming. He had still found time to sow his wild oats with the girls from the town. Twenty four years later, one of those wild oats came back into his life in the form of the son that he hadn't known about. J.W. Storey, the illegitimate son of McCann and Donna Barnes, had come to Farnsworth on Christmas Eve five years ago, looking for his biological father. Placed for adoption by the 18 year old Donna without McCann's knowledge, J.W. had not been told by his adoptive parents about circumstances of his birth. After both had passed away, the family attorney had given J.W. the links to his past.

Donna died accidentally while serving on a mission trip to the Czech Republic five years ago. She had loved McCann all her life but he hadn't returned that love until it was too late. The thought of Donna still brought sorrow but, at the same time, he praised God for bringing Linda into his life.

Now, as he stood there looking out over his fields, a great feeling of thankfulness rose up within him. God had truly blessed him. His walk with the Lord was a great source of comfort and confidence. His opportunities to witness to his faith were almost limitless. His Christian friends were a great source of support and guidance for him. Perhaps the Lord would answer his and Linda's prayers and grant them children. In the meantime, his only cause for concern was J.W. J.W., while continuing to forge a strong relationship with McCann, had continued to resist becoming a follower of Jesus Christ. McCann, Linda and others had made it a matter of prayer and McCann continued to trust that, someday, J.W. too would join in the faith.

He said a prayer of thanksgiving for the blessings he had received and asked for guidance for the day. Then, after taking one last look out over the fields he had worked in so many years ago, he turned and got back in the Ranger and drove slowly out the drive and headed for Farnsworth.

Nick Hardesty stood at the kitchen window inside the farmhouse and watched him go.

"Wils having his morning talk with God?" Darcy asked from the kitchen table where she was finishing her breakfast.

"Yes. He said one time that this is really home for him," Nick replied, turning to face his wife.

"He is such a good man. God has really blessed a lot of people through him," she said, rising to start clearing away the breakfast dishes.

"Including us," Nick replied. He thought back over the five years since he had first met Wilson McCann. He had just been fired from his job at a local auto dealer. Darcy was pregnant and they weren't married. Nick's father, a local insurance broker and community leader, wasn't happy with him. He had gotten word that McCann, the new owner of the Harms farm, might have work for him. McCann had put him to work painting all the buildings on the farm. A few weeks later, he and Darcy had walked down the aisle of the local Methodist church and given their lives to Christ. They were married a few weeks later and McCann had continued to find work for Nick at the farm. He had also arranged for Darcy, upon Donna Barnes' death, to take over the operation of the Barnes Loft, a local clothing store. The two teenagers, with a son on the way, had begun a successful walk with the Lord and a lot of support and help from Wilson McCann.

Neither McCann nor Nick had seen the small dark thundercloud that formed to the west. Slowly, it gathered force and soon its shadow covered the woods to the west of McCann's farm. As the west wind brought it eastward, its shadow began to spread over the farm and surrounding countryside. By the time it reached Farnsworth, a wind whipped rain slammed into everything in its path. It was an omen of things to come.

(2)

It had all gone downhill from the moment she walked into the restaurant and joined him at his corner table. He had known something was up when she sent him an e-mail at the office and asked him to meet her rather than walking down the hall from her office like she usually did. The fact that she hadn't offered to drive together was another tip-off that this was not their usual candle-lit dinner.

    J.W. Storey had been dating Traycee Morgan for over two years. She was the Office and Human Resources Manager at Trinity Technologies, a small software company supplying I.T. solutions to religious and non-profit organizations across the U.S. from its offices just north of Mountain View, California. J.W. was Director of Information Technology at Trinity. Traycee, twenty seven, five foot two with curly light blonde hair and flashing green eyes had just given him some very unsettling news.

    "Fresno? Sheesh! Who moves to Fresno?" he said, in an exasperated tone, as he put down the fork that he had been about to spear a grilled shrimp with.

    She picked at her Tilapia without eating any of it. Her meal was growing cold. She kept her eyes down while he fumed. Now she looked up and he saw the firmness in her gaze.

    "I guess I am," she said, quietly.

THE INVESTMENT

It felt like someone had stuck a knife in his heart.

"Traycee, please…marry me…I love you," he said quietly, leaning toward her across the table and reaching out for her hand. She sat back and dropped both hands into her lap.

"J.W., you know I love you too but I cannot marry you. We have been over this a lot in the last year."

He felt his blood pressure rise. They had, indeed, been over the subject of marriage many times in the past year. After they had been dating for a year, he had asked her to rent an apartment together. When she had resisted that, he had asked her to marry him. She had told him she could not. He had asked her again and again and the answer had not changed.

The issue was Traycee's Christian faith and J.W.'s lack of it. Traycee was a committed Christian. She and J.W. had gone to church together, read the Bible together, prayed together and discussed the issue of faith in Jesus Christ on many occasions over their two year relationship. J.W. remained unconvinced of the need to make a decision to ask Jesus to come into and take charge of his life. Traycee had made it clear that, without that decision, she would not marry him. She had not engaged in brow-beating him about his lack of a decision. That was what bothered him the most. She loved him. He knew that. He also knew that, tonight, they had reached a decision point in their relationship.

"I go to church. I read the Bible. I don't cheat on you. I don't lie, steal, or any of the stuff that other guys do. Please, Traycee! Don't do this!" His voice rose as he pleaded. A couple, two tables over, stopped talking and looked over at them. Traycee looked down, embarrassed, and held up her hand, palm toward him, bringing his outburst to an end. Without looking up, she spoke quietly.

"We'll always be friends. I'll stay in touch. I promise. But, I have to do this. I need some space and this is a good job and I'm going to take it. I'll let you know when I'm settled in," she said, as she looked up at him. For the first time that evening, he saw the trace of tears well up in her eyes. She quickly looked away and wiped the back of her hand across her eyes. When she looked at him, he saw that the resolve had returned to her face.

He sat back, defeated. "Have you told Ralph?" he asked. Ralph Cox was the President of Trinity Technologies and their boss.

"I told him this afternoon. He is bringing in a person from a HR services firm on Monday. Next week will be my last week."

"I leave on Sunday for Chicago and I'll probably be there most of the week. I planned to go up to Farnsworth to see Wils and Linda when I'm done there," he said, looking away.

"I start a week from Monday in Fresno. I'm going to room with one of my friends from college for the first month while I look for something. She works at the hospital in Fresno," Traycee replied, taking a final drink from her coffee. It too had gone cold. She would be the new Human Resources Director at a large surgical center in Fresno. It was a step up for Traycee and would provide an increased salary and benefit package as well as an excellent opportunity in the rapidly expanding health care field.

They made small talk for a few minutes and finally J.W. asked for the bill and paid it. They stood and walked together to their cars. They stood there in the fading light and held each other. Finally, she stepped away and got into her car and drove away. He watched her go and felt as though she was taking a piece of him with her.

It was a hot and humid day in Raleigh but inside the auditorium at Campbell University's law school the only heat was being generated by the speaker, a "born again" investment broker from Charlotte. Wilson McCann, Belle Warner, Cindy Melzy and Donald Straylin

THE INVESTMENT

sat in the fifth row from the stage. Straylin had made the arrangements for them to attend the one day seminar. This was the last speaker on the agenda. Straylin had left one seat empty between himself and Cindy as a symbolic gesture of the fact that Tachyon's largest investor, Ed Feldman, was not with them. The four who were represented forty five percent of the ownership of Tachyons. All of them had been instrumental in the creation of the firm and all of them shared a faith in Jesus Christ. Unfortunately, Feldman did not share that same faith or their view of the future for Tachyons. Within the next three months, Feldman would use his majority power to set in motion the sale of the company and Tachyons would cease to exist.

McCann, as CEO of Tachyons, had made a spirited presentation of his plans to continue to grow Tachyons and his optimistic view of the company's future at the Tachyons Board meeting on the previous day. Tachyons' rapidly growing Competitive Local Exchange Carrier (CLEC) operations in the suburbs of Des Moines, Iowa; Minneapolis-St. Paul, Minnesota; Madison, Wisconsin; and the Tri-Cities of Midland, Saginaw and Bay City, Michigan, had added over thirty thousand customers to Tachyons two hundred and fifty thousand land-line customers in the Midwest. At its current rate of expansion, Tachyons' CLEC and growing fiber optic based broad band networks would add another twenty thousand customers by year end. The operation would be cash flow positive by the end of the first quarter of the coming year.

Feldman had listened respectfully but, in the end, had advised the others that he intended to tender his investment in Tachyons to Mogollon, a Phoenix based "aggregator". He had recommended that the minority investors do the same. With majority control of Tachyons, Mogollon could impose its will and would move to consolidate the smaller company into its system. McCann would be replaced by a CEO from Mogollon and the inevitable pressure on the minority investors to sell their interests to Mogollon would begin. McCann knew that would happen within the next six to nine months. He had done his best and it had not been enough. But, as he sat there, he was not bothered by that fact.

Six years ago, McCann had been the CEO of Dynacom, a large telecommunications company headquartered in Chicago. Dynacom's Chairman and McCann's mentor, Charles Corbin, had sold the company to Legent, a Dallas based Telecommunications Company, over McCann's spirited resistance. McCann had retreated to his uncle's debt-ridden farm in Farnsworth and licked his wounds. During the ensuing six months, he had lost Donna Barnes, his mother and even his dog, a Border Collie named Ted. McCann had finally come to the realization that his priorities were wrong and, as he fell to his knees beside Ted's freshly dug grave during a snowstorm, he had accepted Jesus Christ as his personal savior and had turned his life over to Him.

Three years later, he renewed his commitment to love the Lord with all his heart, soul, strength and mind. He made and kept a commitment to Linda, who entered his life and became his wife. He had renewed his commitment to making Tachyons all that it could be.

The fact that Tachyons was now a viable acquisition for Mogollon was proof that McCann's business planning had succeeded. He had hoped that, if Tachyons were to be acquired, Fairfield Communications, a Colorado Springs telecommunications company led by his friend, Bob Allison, would be the successful bidder. Mogollon, however, had trumped Fairfield's bid.

McCann now lived his life by a different standard. He prayed for God's will in all things, loved his wife, the son he hadn't known until five years ago, and his friends and co-workers, while doing the best he could and leaving the rest to God. If Tachyons was to be acquired, he would look forward to what new opportunities God had for him.

The audience at Campbell this day was made up of Christian

executives from both the public and private sector. The speaker's topic was "Return on Investment" and he had carefully and forcefully developed his topic using the parable of the talents from the book of Matthew, chapter twenty five, verses fourteen through thirty, as his point of reference. Now, as he neared the conclusion of his talk, he paced back and forth across the stage, drawing ever nearer to his audience.

"So, what does an investor want from someone he invests in?" he asked loudly, looking out over his audience.

"A return on his investment!" someone about five rows behind McCann and off to his right called out.

"And.....?" the speaker questioned further.

"The return of his money!" someone else, off to McCann's left, responded.

"Exactly! That's what God wants too! God loves us and wants us to return that love to Him...and to others! And he expects us to spread His word to others. Don't bury His love within yourself... share it! Don't keep His message of grace, love and redemption to yourself! Share it! He has invested Christ's blood in each one of us. It's an investment far beyond description and words. Go out and try to love Him as much as He loves you. Go out and share the gospel message with everyone you meet! Let's pray."

The auditorium grew quiet as the speaker prayed. When he finished, several people went to the front to speak with him privately. McCann and the others stood and began a slow exit toward the rear of the auditorium.

"God wants His love back and a return on his investment," Cindy said, a smile on her pretty face.

"And Ed wants his money back and some return on it too," Straylin replied.

"He thinks he'll get it in Mogollon stock," McCann observed over his shoulder as he headed up the aisle toward the exit.

Belle Warner was in her 80's but still had the vitality and positive attitude of a much younger woman. Yet even Belle was in a somber mood as they walked out of the building and into the heat and humidity.

"I've heard that Mogollon is having a tough time digesting their latest acquisition. I've heard that they are having trouble integrating it into their information systems and they are having to spend an unexpected amount of money for outside consulting services. That will impact their earnings and that, in turn, will alarm their investors. They are carrying a lot of debt." she said as they walked toward the parking lot.

As usual, McCann was impressed with Belle's ability to stay informed about all of the various aspects of the world around her and in particular the telecommunications industry. Her past position as an industry leader in Michigan and national industry affairs, had given her many sources of information. It was obvious that she had continued to maintain those contacts even though she was, for all intents and purposes, retired from anything resembling active involvement in that industry other than her seat on Tachyons' board.

"There's not a lot more we can do," Cindy said quietly, her arm draped loosely around Belle's shoulders. Cindy, as CEO of Triad, an investment banking firm in New York City was especially close to Belle who had led her to faith in Christ during a time when Triad, Donald Straylin's firm, and McCann had been working to put the investment in Tachyons together. Straylin and Co. had merged with Triad during the nation's financial crisis in 2008.

Later, McCann and Belle drove to the airport to catch a flight back to Michigan. He thought about the speaker's message. His mind went back to the snowy day in December when he had fallen on his knees next to Ted's freshly dug grave and experienced the fullness of God's redeeming love for the first time. His memories rolled forward three years to a rocky outcropping near McGregor

Mountain at the edge of Colorado's Rocky Mountain National Park where he had made a commitment to love God with all his heart, mind, soul and strength without regard to the circumstances he found himself in. Whatever happened to Tachyons, he was determined to keep that commitment and to love God and share the message of the gospel whenever and wherever he could. He would leave his future in God's hands.

(3)

Labor Day was a two point day at the medium security prison located in Marion, Illinois, three hundred miles south of Peter Zastrow's former office in Chicago. Two points were deducted for holiday visits from Zastrow's twelve points per month allotment for visitors. Any other week day would have only resulted in one point being deducted. It was all irrelevant to Zastrow.

Zastrow, the former head of the Black Bat hedge fund and, prior to that, a Captain in the Russian Army, was in Marion for securities fraud and conspiracy to commit murder. He could apply for parole in thirteen years. He was convinced that it would be denied. He was also convinced that he would die in prison. In Zastrow's mind, his situation was, just like his son's suicide years ago, because of Wilson McCann. The fact that McCann had not been a party to his trial and conviction mattered little to Zastrow. McCann had been a witness at the trial of a woman, Sharon Wilder, whom Zastrow had employed, along with others, to do high tech espionage at companies Black Bat invested in, including Tachyons. Wilder and the others were now serving lesser terms in Arizona and New York.

He sat across the table from his guest, a well dressed, fair haired man about fifty years of age with an impassive face. They had talked for thirty minutes about the weather, the U.S. involvement in

Afghanistan, and the past they shared together. Thirty minutes of conversation in English about nothing important.

"убить его," Zastrow said quietly in Russian.

"Да, сэр," the fair haired man responded in the same language.

They spoke in English for another fifteen minutes about nothing in particular. The four words exchanged between them in Russian were what was important. They were the reason the fair haired man had traveled from Chicago on Labor Day to see his old comrade in arms.

An order had been given, an assignment would be carried out and a man would die.

While the fair haired man was returning to Chicago, another meeting was being conducted. The meeting place contrasted significantly ffrom the visitation area in Marion. The 5,700 square foot home in Glenview, Illinois was for sale at over $2 million. The man who owned it would be dead within a year according to his medical team. His visitor was a private investigator from a reputable Chicago firm. He had read through the file that lay on the coffee table between them and had surfed the Internet to gain additional information about the subject in the file. This was not the first assignment the old man had given him. He wondered, but did not have the nerve to ask, what had happened as a result of the previous one.

"So, you understand what I want done?" The old man said, leaning back on the sofa. He hadn't looked at the information that the investigator had brought with him. What he wanted to know couldn't be found there.

"Yes, I think I do. It's just that…it is a bit unusual…what you are asking me to do," the investigator said, leaning forward. He tried to keep his eyes off the file but failed. The older man watched his eyes, his face impassive.

"I want to know the man, not about the man," he said.

"Much has been written about him. It's not like he is unknown even if he does live on a farm in a small town. He has a reputation. What you see is often what you get," he said, trying to keep his tone respectful.

"The older man sighed. "Perhaps I should find someone else. I thought you did a good job on my other assignment, but, perhaps this one is outside of your skill set."

"No, we'll do it," the investigator said quickly.

"If you do it, you will do it the way I want it done," the older man said firmly.

"Correction, I will do it and it will be done the way you want it done."

"Good. I'll expect your first report in early December," The older man smiled for the first time.

The investigator picked up the file and stood. He reached down to shake the older man's hand and instead received a thick envelope.

Ben smiled up at him. "An 'off the books' advance on your expenses."

He left the home and drove for several blocks before stopping to open the envelope. It contained $100,000 in cash.

"Why?" "Why do it this way?" These thoughts ran through his mind as he drove back into Chicago. He hoped he would find the answers the following Monday in Farnsworth, Michigan.

Later that afternoon, two men hunched over a computer monitor in the security office at the prison in Marion. The one man, gray haired and wearing glasses, wisely leaned his head to the side of the monitor to be closer to the speakers. The other, head of the prison's security group, brought his face to within two inches of the screen in the hope that he too would hear more clearly.

THE INVESTMENT

The image before them was from the security camera in the visitation area of the prison. The image had been enhanced to show only Zastrow and his visitor. The sounds, however, were the buzz of several different conversations going on in the room plus the normal sounds of a large room, heating, the scrape of chairs on tile floors, and people walking back and forth and shifting in their seats.

"Play it again," the gray haired man muttered, bending closer to the speakers. The other moved the computer mouse and the screen refreshed again. This was the third time they had viewed it but they weren't looking any longer. They were listening. The gray haired man closed his eyes, blocking out the image but not the sound.

"Is that as loud as you can make it?" he asked, not opening his eyes.

"Yes," the other responded as the sounds began to fill the small office.

They listened in silence until what they wanted to hear had, once again, ended. The gray haired man opened his eyes and watched Zastrow's visitor lean back in his chair.

"You can stop it now," he said, rising from his chair and walking to the only window in the room. He looked out, thinking. The other man waited, expectantly.

"Tell me again who the guy is," he said, without turning from the window.

"One of Zastrow's henchmen, his name is Tazlov. He was in Zastrow's Russian army unit in Afghanistan and immigrated to the US years ago. From what we know, he plays the role of legitimate businessman. We think he is a possible 'enforcer' for Zastrow. Tazlov pays his bills, pays his taxes, loves his wife, goes to his kids' soccer games and lives in a middle income neighborhood outside of Chicago. From time to time, he disappears for a week or so. Those disappearances correspond to events in Zastrow's past that make him a suspect in some cold case files. The most recent was at the time of the disappearance of one of Zastrow's key lieutenants who was about to give evidence in a securities fraud investigation.

The reply was more than he had asked for and he frowned as if addressing an overzealous college student when he turned toward the other.

"But, he's Russian, right?"

"Yes. As I said…" the other began. The gray haired man raised his hand to stop him.

"They talked in English about nothing for the whole time they were together except for four words we can't understand. I think that those words were in Russian. If that is correct, and it's hard to hear them without further enhancement of the surveillance information, my interpretation is that Zastrow told this man, Tazlov, to kill someone and he agreed. I think you should send the file to the Feds and have them perform their magic on it and see if it bears me out."

"Thank you," the other said, rising and extending his hand.

The gray haired man shook it and left. He drove home and went back to preparing the lecture for his next class at the Russian, Eastern European and Eurasian Center at the University of Illinois in Champaign where he was a professor. As he worked, he paused briefly to consider what he had heard at the prison. He wondered who this man Zastrow wanted dead and what power he had over Tazlov to bend him to do his will. Concluding that it wasn't really his concern, he went back to his lecture notes.

After discussing the matter with the Warden by telephone, the prison's security man e-mailed the surveillance video to an FBI office in Chicago with a request for enhancement of audio during the segment containing the meeting between Peter Zastrow and Alexei Tazlov.

(4)

The name on his *TECHEXEC* business card and ID was Charlie Dumas. As he and his assistant drove down M-81 toward Farnsworth, he rehearsed his cover story again in his mind. He was Charlie Dumas from Waco, Texas. He had been hired as a freelance by one of the leading technology magazines in the US to do an article on Wilson McCann. If McCann bothered to call *TECHEXEC's* home office to check him out, the call would be directed to a certain Editor's office. The Editor had been given $5,000 to say that, indeed, Charlie Dumas was working under contract to do an article for the magazine. He was pretty confident that McCann wouldn't make the call since another of his contacts had already established his bona fides and set up the first interview.

The article would focus on McCann's life in the telecommunications industry. It would look at the "man behind the man in the headlines". It would be a story of McCann's rise to CEO of Dynacom, his failed battle to save it, his rise from the ashes of that defeat to found Tachyons in the small town of Farnsworth and the impending sale of that company to Mogollon Communications which was all but a "done deal" according to most reliable press accounts.

As background, Charlie would delve into McCann's family background as well as his youth and manhood. Charlie would meet McCann's beautiful wife, Linda, considered by many to be a "trophy wife". They would also meet McCann's illegitimate son, J.W. who had surfaced a little over five years ago, the product of a summer fling with a local girl when McCann was in his early 20's. Charlie would interview them all as well as friends and associates in Farnsworth, New York City, Chicago, and elsewhere. The interviews would all be filmed.

To add credibility, he was bringing Shelly Martinez, his "photojournalist" assistant. Shelly would film the interviews and take pictures at the appropriate times and disappear when told to do so. He would gather additional information by talking to employees and others "off the record". Shelly would keep her pretty dark eyes peeled for anything that he didn't pick up. Shelly had been part of his team in Chicago for eight years and he had been trying to get her to go out with him for the last five. Shelly was good at keeping her personal and business life separate and he was batting a big zero on the romantic front. She sat in the passenger's seat of the Buick, looking out at the flat Tuscola County landscape.

"So, tell me again why this guy wants us to do this?" she asked without turning.

"I don't have the foggiest," he replied, glancing at her. She was beautiful, even dressed as she was in a man's safari shirt, jeans and hiking shoes. Her long dark hair was pulled back in a pony tail and, in keeping with her assumed character, she wasn't wearing any makeup. A Cubs cap lay in her lap. When they arrived, she would put it on backwards and her character would be complete.

"Isn't he the same guy that you did the job for a couple of months ago?" She asked, turning toward him and favoring him with those flashing dark eyes. He felt the car start to wander and quickly turned the wheel to correct it. Shelly had that effect on him.

"Yes," he said, "I looked into an old teenage flame of his," he responded, not willing to share too much.

"And, what came of that?" She asked, turning her gaze to look at a big John Deere tractor working in a field.

"I've no idea," he said, honestly.

"This guy…he's dying, right?" she asked as a big tanker truck roared by, heading west.

"That's what I hear," he said, conversationally.

"So, why this sudden interest in this guy McCann and why are we doing all this cloak and dagger stuff?"

"Like I told you before, he wants us to tell him about the 'man within the man'. We're getting paid big money to do it and we'll do it his way," he said, as he slowed down and entered the village of Farnsworth.

"I don't get it," Shelly said, as she put on her Cubs cap.

Linda McCann, clad in a University of Michigan sweat suit, sat at one end of the dinette table and her husband sat at the other. She had worn the sweat suit to provoke a reaction from her husband and he didn't disappoint her as he spooned sugar into his coffee.

"Flying the family flag again, I see," he said, pretending an irritation that he really didn't feel.

Linda was the most beautiful woman in the world in his estimation. The Michigan themed suit was a birthday present from her father, a self proclaimed "Michigan Man", who had graduated from the University with an engineering degree. Quentin McReedy and his wife, Lucille, now ran the McReedy Lodge in Estes Park, Colorado. Quentin never tired of teasing McCann about the Michigan vs. Illinois rivalry in sports. McCann had graduated twenty five years ago from the University of Illinois.

"I could wear what I was wearing last night," Linda replied with a flash of her green eyes. She gave McCann a look that sent a clear message that he couldn't miss.

"I'd like that much better," he replied with a smile, leaning back and letting his eyes roam over his wife.

"It would only take me a minute to change," she said, putting her cup down and starting to push her chair back.

He put up his hand. "Stop! I have to go to work. I have the guy coming to do the *TechExec* interview."

"Hah! Called your bluff!" she grinned, picking up her cup again. Her face grew serious as she looked out the window. Winter was just around the corner. All of a sudden she felt a chill and it wasn't from the advance of the seasons.

"Is there no way to save Tachyons?" she said, without looking at him.

"None that I can see," McCann replied, looking down. A cloud crossed the sun and the intimate moment they had shared was lost. "I spoke to Stu and to Allison again and there is simply no new investment money available that would entice Feldman, and Fairfield can't up the ante."

Stu Bailey, a merger and acquisitions deal maker in New York City had assisted McCann in his failed bid to save Dynacom and had been instrumental in putting the deal together that resulted in the formation of Tachyons. In the following five years, he had helped McCann in several smaller telecom and fiber networking acquisitions. The nation's weak economic recovery since the financial disaster in 2008 had inhibited many sources of investment money in general. McCann knew that telecommunications was not high on many potential investor's lists.

Bob Allison, as CEO of Fairfield Communications, had made an offer for Tachyons two years ago but had withdrawn it when an insider trading scandal involving a man named Peter Zastrow had broken in the press. Zastrow was accused of securities fraud and conspiracy to commit the murder of Sharon Wilder. Sharon owned and operated a performance improvement firm that Tachyons had hired. Zastrow had been sentenced to thirty years in a medium security prison in Illinois. Wilder had been sentenced to five years in prison for furnishing insider information to Zastrow about Tachyons and other companies. Allison had made another run at Tachyons during the previous summer but Fairfield would not match the offer from Mogollon.

"I'll have to take some overseas projects for Mike to pay the utility bill," Linda said, trying to restore some of the light that had faded away. She was a project leader for MTD, an Atlanta based information technology consulting company headed by a former associate of McCann at Dynacom named Mike Divell. Since McCann and Linda's marriage two years ago, she had continued to work but had limited her projects to those which allowed her to spend as much time as possible here with McCann. She had made no secret of her desire, shared by her husband, to start a family and, at most, be a work from home mother and wife. Her failure to conceive was the only disappointment of their marriage. Earlier in the year they both had been assured by their doctors that there was no reason that they couldn't have children.

"By this time next year, you are going to be spending all your time changing diapers. You won't be going anywhere," McCann replied. He smiled when he said it but she sensed the seriousness behind the words. "I'll go to work for Jim and we'll add some dairy cattle and sell milk."

The sun came out from behind the cloud and she laughed out loud. Jim Marks and his wife Lona were their best friends. Jim owned two farms, one that adjoined McCann's farm and another adjacent to these forty acres. He farmed McCann's one hundred acre farm as well. Lona was Business Manager at the Dunt Center, a combination conference center, motel, day care and office complex in a renovated elementary school in Farnsworth that McCann had purchased with help from the Michigan Economic Development Corporation and investment by Donald Straylin, one of the minority investors in Tachyons.

"I'll open a roadside stand and sell butter," Linda said.

McCann rose and drained his coffee cup. She rose as well and he took her in his arms and buried his face in her hair. "You'll need to take that outfit off and dress like a farmer's wife if you do," he said squeezing her hard.

"Maybe I would sell more if I wore that I wore last night," she said with a smile, squeezing him back.

"No doubt about that!" he said, continuing to hold her close.

They had a few moments of prayer together and McCann released her and turned toward the door.

"I'll take this outfit off tonight and have something better to show you. Have fun with your interviewer," she said at the door as he headed out.

After she watched him go, she stepped back inside. Another cloud had shut off the sun's rays as she walked back into the kitchen. She leaned against the kitchen counter top, bowed her head and shut her eyes.

"Please Lord, help him get through this loss and continue to be your man in every way," she prayed quietly.

"Mr. Dumas and Miss Martinez are in the conference room. They've got a camera set up there. They say they want to talk to some of your staff as well," Tammie Ring, McCann's Administrative Assistant said as he walked in.

"Did they give you a schedule?" McCann asked, pausing at the doorway to his office.

"Talk to you and your staff today, talk to some of the community leaders tomorrow, and then a wrap up session the next day at your home with you and Linda," Tammie replied.

THE INVESTMENT

"Are they clear that there is to be no discussion with anyone but me about Mogollon or anything related to it?" he said.

"I think they understand that. You might want to reinforce it with them," She replied. He sensed something unsaid in the reply.

"What?" He asked. Tammie had been with him for all five years here at Tachyons. Not only was she his Assistant, she was, at times, his conscience, his big sister in the faith and, when he needed it, his supervisor.

She leaned back in her chair and twirled a pen in the air while she gathered her thoughts. "There's just something…I can't put my finger on it but…"

"What?" he said again, giving her his full attention.

She sat forward and put the pen on the pad in front of her. She looked up at him and he could see the seriousness in her eyes.

"There's something not right about this. I don't know what it is, but these two just don't ring true. I feel like they're after something that has nothing to do with you as CEO of Tachyons or the industry. I wish I knew why I feel this way. When I do, I'll tell you."

"Fair enough, keep your eyes peeled. It might not be a bad idea to clue Phil, Belle and Fred in on your thoughts. Don't say anything to any of the staff," he said, going into his office. Charlie Dumas was scheduled to talk to Phil Willard, owner of the Farnsworth Agway, Jim Marks, Belle Warner and Fred Penay, the retired former President of the local bank, about McCann and Tachyon's impact on the local community. McCann trusted all four completely. Once alerted to Tammie's concerns, they would be careful what they said.

He flipped through a few call back notes and checked his e-mail before walking down to the conference room. Dumas and Martinez were seated on opposite sides of the conference table. They were thumbing through information packets, provided by Tammie, that contained information on Tachyons, McCann and Farnsworth. A video camera on a tripod was behind Martinez and aimed at the vacant chair at the head of the table.

"Good morning," McCann said, extending his hand. Dumas rose and shook it. Martinez looked up and said "Hi" before standing and moving behind the camera.

"How would you like to do this?" McCann asked, dropping into the vacant chair. Dumas resumed his seat as well.

"I'd like to start by reviewing some of the information your assistant provided, just to get it into the record. Then, we can get into the personal stuff. I'd like to build the story about you, with the company and the community as the background. Sound okay to you?" Dumas replied as he pulled two sheets of information from the packet.

"Let's do it," McCann said, as a green light flashed on the camera.

Forty five minutes later, Dumas had finished asking questions about Tachyons and Farnsworth which dealt with employment, economic impact, network expansion and McCann's views on the current evolution of the industry and the economy. McCann couldn't help feeling that he could have given any answer and it would have been accepted. Dumas asked few follow-up questions but simply moved on to the next question. McCann began to feel that Tammie's instincts were correct.

"Need to take a break?" Dumas asked.

"No, that was pretty easy," McCann said, smiling. Dumas didn't react.

"Okay, let's get to the personal stuff," Dumas said, leaning back in his chair. He didn't look at the pad before him or at any other notes.

"Shoot," McCann said. He could sense that Shelly Martinez was zeroing in with the camera.

"Where were you born?" Dumas asked.

McCann immediately was on guard. This type of question had been fully covered in the biographical sketch that Tachyons' Public Relations Department had provided.

"Chicago."

"Who were your father and mother?"

McCann tensed. That information was not part of the biographical sketch.

"James and Ellen McCann."

"What did your father do?" Dumas rolled his pen between his fingers as he continued to sit back in his chair.

"He worked in a plant. My mother was a legal secretary," McCann replied.

Dumas leaned forward and looked at his pad. Somehow, McCann felt that he was doing it only for show.

"Your father died while you were young?"

"Yes, I was seven. He had a heart attack."

As he said it, McCann's thoughts went back forty years to a day he had stood beside his mother in the cold rain and watched as his father's coffin was lowered into the ground. He had leaned against his mother's legs and wept. He had never felt as alone as he had that day.

"Your mother was working then?" Dumas asked.

"No, she went back to work after my dad died," McCann replied, looking down at his hands. He could feel the camera on him.

"Did your father have any insurance or leave any kind of money to your mother?"

"No, nothing. I don't see what this has to do with what you are here for," McCann said, looking up. He needed to try to see where this was going.

Dumas put out his hand defensively. "I'm just trying to get a sense of the kind of childhood you had. I know this is a technology article but a lot of our readers are interested in the forces that shaped the industry leaders."

The response was too quick and too glib. It seemed as though Dumas had anticipated McCann's unease. He leaned back and said nothing.

Dumas cleared his throat and looked up at Shelly. Then he turned to McCann again.

"So, your mother went to work. Where did you live?"

"We had a two bedroom apartment. I stayed with a neighbor lady after school until my mother came home from work."

"She was a Legal Secretary. She must have worked late a lot," Dumas observed.

"She did."

"Were you alone a lot growing up?"

McCann looked away and took a deep breath before answering. "Yes."

"Did your father have a lot of friends? I mean, were there men who had been friends of your father that might have been a surrogate dad?" Dumas asked, looking at him intently.

"Most of my father's friends were men at the plant or one or two high school friends," McCann replied, wondering at the question.

"Your father went to high school in Chicago?"

"Yes."

"Did you ever meet any of his friends from high school?"

McCann leaned back in his chair. "I really don't see how this helps with an article," he said, watching Dumas to see how he responded.

"Sure, forget the question. I just was wondering…you see there were a couple of people from your dad's high school who went on to quite successful careers in business. I thought one of them might have been someone you knew or had influenced you in your career. How did you come to be in Farnsworth?" Dumas replied, looking down at his notes for the first time. McCann could see that he was trying to regain the offensive.

"My mother's brother owned a farm here and I worked here during the summers in high school and college."

"Were your mother and your uncle close?" Dumas asked.

"Not really. She just felt it would be an opportunity for me to get out of the city during the summer and learn to work," McCann replied, smiling at the thought of learning what work was under the watchful eye of Fred Harms. "Learn to work" was an understatement!

Dumas saw the smile and pounced.

"You didn't like your Uncle?"

McCann looked him in the eye. "My uncle believed in hard work and expected me to pull my weight. I worked for him for five summers and much of my work ethic was forged on the farm."

"What did you do for fun?" Dumas asked. He already knew the answer but wanted to see how McCann would answer.

McCann leaned back and smiled again. He knew where this part of the interview was headed. "Chased girls and partied."

"Anything serious?" Dumas asked.

"Look, I know that you know that I have a son that I didn't know about until five years ago. I got a girl pregnant and she gave the baby up for adoption without my knowledge. She died in an accident while in the Czech Republic just before I met our son for the first time."

"Did you love her?" Dumas asked.

"I didn't learn what real love was until a few years ago. Her name was Donna and I came to love her too late," McCann replied softly. Shelly Martinez looked away. The camera continued to roll.

"Any significant others from those years?" Dumas asked.

McCann tensed. It was time to see what this was really about. "Why do you need to know about my teen aged love life for this article?" he said tightly.

The man playing role of Charlie Dumas knew that it was time to pull the trigger on this interview and see what happened. He placed his pen carefully on his pad and swiveled his chair to face McCann.

"Look Mr. McCann, with all due respect, here's how I see it. You are a two-time loser as a CEO. You and I both know that, within the next year or so, Tachyons will be no more. You are one of the 'darlings of the industry' and you have this saintly reputation in this community as some sort of reformed sinner who is now a saint. But, you got a girl pregnant when she was eighteen, you played fast and loose with another girl who grew up, had three failed marriages and went back to work for you before dying in a car crash after a night at a bar trying to drown her sorrows because you were in Colorado romancing a Kim-Novak look-alike who is now your 'trophy wife'. You were mentored by Charles Corbin who had a reputation as a wheeler-dealer who cut corners to make a buck. Your company was the target of some crazed Russian ex-patriot hedge fund operator who had a personal vendetta against you because he says you caused his son's suicide. He is now in prison. He was being fed information from inside your company by a rather well endowed lady in a short skirt who apparently had her eyes set on some sort of romantic involvement with you. There are at least two businessmen on Main Street here in Farnsworth who say you cheated them out of their investment in the local telephone company by cozying up to the matron of Farnsworth's leading family who fell for your grandiose plans of an expanded company. Now, before I print one word of an article about you, I want to get behind the scenes and sort out what and who you are. Our readers, and those who will view the video associated with it, want to meet the man behind the 'tech exec'. Okay?"

Shelly Martinez 's face betrayed her shock at Dumas' rant. However, she kept her camera trained on McCann's face and it caught every bit of his reaction.

McCann fought down the urge to reach for Dumas' shirt-front and smash his fist into the reporter's face. He clamped his jaws together, closed his eyes and inwardly prayed for good judgment before he responded.

"Fair enough, Charlie. I spent the first forty years of my life living for myself. I didn't do anything dishonest but I didn't make any close friends. I suppose growing up mostly alone, without the influence of a father, turned me into a survivor. My highest priority was my own satisfaction as a teenager. I used others without regard to their feelings. When I started my career, I threw myself into it one hundred percent. I didn't care what it might cost me in terms of relationships or friendships. Dynacom became my obsession."

"When I lost it, I didn't know where to turn. I came here to try to find purpose for my life. Donna Barnes was running a local business. She had become a Christian and tried to persuade me to give my life to Jesus. I resisted it, while at the same time falling in love with her. When she died, it was just another part of me that I lost. Then, my mother died. We hadn't had much of a relationship due to my own self-centeredness. She had become a Christian too. My uncle and my aunt had become Christians. I found myself surrounded by a whole new set of people who had something that I didn't. Belle Warner was one of them. She helped me understand what was important in life and that God had a plan for my life. She believed in me. But I hurt her as well. Despite my attempts to do good for others, I seemed to hurt those I touched."

"Sally McHugh was one of those I hurt. She loved me. I didn't love her except as sort of a sister. She tried to fill the gap in my life but I wouldn't let her in. The same was true for Cindy Melzy at Triad, one of our investors. When Cindy found Christ after Belle witnessed to her, I still resisted God. When I came here, I found a dog named Ted in the hay mow at my uncle's farm that I had bought out of bankruptcy. He was almost dead. I nursed him back to health and he became my companion. When he was shot by a couple of drunken farmers, my world collapsed. The loss of the company that I had given my life to, the woman I loved, my mother and even my dog brought me to my knees and I begged for God's forgiveness. I found Christ and a whole new way of life."

"Tachyons came into being and I threw myself into running it. But, I maintained my new found faith. I had known Linda from previous work we had done together at a Christian ministry in North Carolina. Two years ago, her boy-friend ended a ten year live-in relationship and we were thrown together in a most unexpected way. Belle Warner led her to the Lord. We fell in love and she helped me realize that, although I was a Christian, I was not making and keeping a commitment to the Lord, those who cared for me, and my company."

"About that time, Fairfield made a bid for Tachyons and Peter Zastrow hatched his takeover attempt. His son had worked for Dynacom at one time and was let go in a force reduction in our Marketing department. He committed suicide. Zastrow blamed me as the CEO. He coerced Sharon Wilder into supplying him with inside information about Tachyons that she gathered by hacking into our information systems. When he realized his plan would fail, he hired a man to have her killed so she couldn't testify against him. The man he hired turned out to be a disguised FBI agent. You know the rest of that story."

"You can check with my neighbors, Jim and Lona Marks, about Sharon Wilder's attempts at romance and how I handled it. I'm sure you'll find it amusing! So, Charlie, I'm a sinner saved by God's grace. If you push George Whyte at the implement company and Joe Rambaugh at the Chrysler dealership hard enough, they'll tell you that they were more than adequately paid for their investments in Farnsworth Tele. They needed money and I supplied it."

McCann leaned back to catch his breath but had one more thought.

"Oh, I should add that I agree with you that Linda is, indeed, a 'trophy wife'! I love her more than anyone else in this world along with my son, J.W. I'm still learning how to be a father to a grown man but we are making progress and I hope to use my newfound knowledge to good advantage in the future."

Dumas looked at Martinez and nodded. The light on the camera turned red.

THE INVESTMENT

"I think we've done enough for today," he said, extending his hand. "Thank you for your time."

McCann's thoughts were still in turmoil as he walked back to his office. Tammie looked up and then followed him to the door.

"How'd it go?" she asked, tentatively.

McCann dropped into his chair and looked up at her. "He got to me a bit," he confessed. He seemed to know just where to push my buttons. I hope I witnessed to the kind of person I am now and not to what I once was."

Tammie Ring was an active member of the small Wesleyan church in Farnsworth. One of the joys of working with Wilson McCann was their shared faith.

"I would never doubt that you did." She said it sincerely, before she turned and walked back to her desk.

In the conference room, Shelly turned her back to Dumas and looked out the window. He could sense her irritation.

"What?" he asked.

"I didn't care for the way you went at him," she said firmly, without turning around.

"What part?" He asked, knowing the answer.

"All the personal stuff…the stuff about his mother and father…I thought it was over the top."

He knew that Shelly had strong feelings when it came to family. Her father and mother were illegal aliens who had come to

California over thirty years ago and settled near Bakersfield. They worked in the produce fields of the San Joaquin Valley. Shelly was born a few years later and both her parents had died while she was young. She had been raised by an aunt and uncle and had worked her way through Fresno State before joining the firm.

"Look, we are being paid to find out what kind of a guy McCann is. I don't know why and I don't care why. You have to admit that, after I pushed him a little, we learned some things," he said, trying to soften her a bit.

"I still don't like it," she said, turning to face him. "Do you believe what he said about his faith?"

"He believes it. It doesn't matter what I believe," he said, starting to assemble his papers.

"I wonder…he seems to have found something that changed his life…for the better," Shelly said.

The man pretending to be Charlie Dumas looked at her with obvious disdain.

"Whatever. If that's what floats your boat, good for you."

Shelly Martinez turned away to keep from saying something she might later regret. She looked out the window and watched a leaf flutter to the ground in the morning breeze. She was looking forward to the next interview with Wilson McCann and meeting his 'trophy wife'…and not for her partner's reasons.

(5)

Liam Colter was tending bar in the dimly lit pub in Gary, Indiana, when Victor Tazlov walked in on a cold and windy October afternoon. The day shift at a nearby plant hadn't let out yet and the pub was empty save for a couple of old men nursing beers in a corner booth and a hard looking woman in her 40's playing solitaire at a table near the grimy front window. Her tattered handbag rested on the edge of the table. Colter was a tall, thin Irishman with a mane of fine white hair combed straight back from a narrow forehead. His eyes were pale blue and, together with a small nose and thin lips gave him the look of a snake that was about to strike.

Tazlov looked around and shed his coat. He carried it to the bar and placed it on one of the stools and sat next to it. Without speaking, Colter took a bottle of Vodka from behind the bar and placed it and a glass in front of his visitor.

Tazlov nodded in appreciation and reached into his pocket. He retrieved a money clip fat with bills, and peeled off a twenty and laid it on the bar. He laid the money clip beside it and proceeded to pour himself a drink.

Colter eyed the money and noted that the rest of the bills showing in the clip were all $100's.

"A cold day, winter is coming soon, I think," he said quietly.

Tazlov downed the drink and poured himself another. "Coming soon for some, not so soon for others," he said, staring straight ahead.

"It's a bitter wind today. That makes it even colder," Colter replied, waiting.

"Perhaps a person could find warmth somewhere else," Tazlov responded.

"One would need money to make the trip," Colter said, picking up the twenty and putting it in his apron pocket.

Tazlov reached into the pocket of the coat beside him and produced an envelope, thick with papers. He placed it on the bar beside the money clip and picked up the glass. "One would need to know where to go and how to get there," he said, as he downed half of the glass. He looked at the remaining liquid as though seeing something far away.

Colter eyed the envelope as he leaned back against the counter behind the bar. "Once one had gone to the new place, he might not want to come back to this weather again," he said. "I've heard that Southern France is nice."

Tazlov held his glass out in front of him and gazed at the clear liquid. "Marseille is nice. I understand that arrangements can be made to live there quite comfortably," he said, and downed the remainder of the vodka.

Colter picked up the envelope and the money clip and placed them under the counter. "Stay warm, my friend," he said as Tazlov rose, put on his coat, and turned to leave.

The woman playing solitaire gave no notice that she had been listening to the conversation but her eyes moved from Colter at the bar to Tazlov as he went through the doorway. Without breaking her concentration, she placed a black jack on a red queen in front of her. Twenty minutes later, she downed the rest of the drink she had ordered, put her cards in the large and rather shabby handbag, and walked out into the cold and darkening afternoon.

THE INVESTMENT

The hard looking woman from the pub walked two blocks before reaching into her old handbag and retrieving a cell phone. She made her call and shuffled forward another half block until an old sedan pulled up to the curb ahead of her. She got in and buckled her seat belt. The young man in work clothes smiled at her.

"You are ravishing! Did you know that?" he said with a grin, as he pulled away from the curb.

"Just get me back to the office so I can change. This wig feels like it is made from hemp and has insects in it," she replied testily.

Thirty minutes later, he stood in her cubicle at the FBI office on West Roosevelt Road in Chicago. She uploaded a combination audio/video file from a small camera that had been enclosed in the side of her handbag. She was transformed to a young woman of thirty with short black hair wearing a dark blue skirt and jacket over a light blue blouse. Her "driver" had shed his worn work clothes for chinos and a white polo shirt.

They watched the film and listened to the muffled conversation between Tazlov and Liam Colter. When it was over, she swiveled her chair around to look at her partner.

"What have we got on Colter?" he asked.

"He is former IRA. He came here about the same time as Tazlov. Has an erratic work schedule which takes him away from the pub at about the same time as some of the events in the cold case files we are sitting on. He's a master of disguise which is why we can't close the loop on him. One time he's a sixty year old stamp collector and another time he's a thirty year old drag queen. We think he is Tazlov's 'enforcer'. A witness, in a murder case that might have led us to Tazlov, was worked over. We think Colter did it."

"Did what?" he asked.

"The witness was found on the sidewalk with a broken forearm and a shattered knee. He said he fell down the steps to a restaurant," she replied, continuing to scroll through the computer's files. Liam Colter's picture and a data file appeared on the screen.

"And…?"

"The witness was found a half a block from the door to the restaurant and the step to the restaurant was two inches above the sidewalk. He said he crawled to where he was found but there were no scuff marks or dirt on his clothing. He clammed up and wouldn't talk after that."

"Colter sounds like a bad dude," he said, running his hand through his hair.

"Maybe this is the time we get him," she replied, turning back to her keyboard and sending the file on Liam Colter to both a flash drive and an adjacent printer.

"Let's put a tail on him and see if it leads to Farnsworth, Michigan," she said.

"I could get you assigned…you could wear your wig," he replied, smiling down at her.

"Yeah, right! Like I'm gonna wear that thing again anytime soon!"

(6)

Camera at the ready, Shelley watched as Ted Lark, Tammie Ring, Kathy Garrety and a rough looking man named Lucas Lindman entered the conference room. They were shortly joined by a tall dark haired woman named Jane Valenkova from Iowa and a young engineer named Jack Rass from Minnesota. The man masquerading as Charlie Dumas welcomed them profusely and asked them to be seated. All except Lindman seemed comfortable as they dropped into the conference room chairs. Lark was Director of information Technology for Tachyons and Kathy was Director of Human Resources for the company. Lindman was an installer/repairman in the company's Wisconsin operations. He was also a union steward. Valenkova was a clerk in the construction department in Iowa. Lindman was obviously nervous with his role as representative of the company's only unionized work forces. All had been briefed on the purpose of the interview and the fact that it would be filmed.

They were an interesting group. Lark, about forty, wore an oxford dress shirt and jeans. Tammie was wearing a gray pant suit and Dumas could sense a bit of hostility as she gazed across the table at him. She was clearly the "gate keeper" for McCann. Garrety was petite and lively in a blue dress jacket and slacks. Her mid length dark hair was immaculate. Lindman wore jeans and a flannel shirt. His work boots were worn. He fidgeted in his chair and looked inquiringly at Shelley. She smiled back, trying to ease his discomfort. He saw the smile and looked away. Valenkova radiated confidence. She smiled at everyone and called them by their first name. This was clearly a woman in charge of herself. Rass, the youngest of the group, was blond and dressed in a suit and tie. His eager expression gave him the appearance of someone seeking both friendship and respect.

Dumas nodded to Shelley and the green light on the camera came on.

"Thank you all for taking time out of your day and coming to do this. Jane, Jack and Lucas, thank you for coming so far. We'll try to get you on your way home in good time," he said, shuffling a few papers in front of him.

"I go by Luke," Lindman said, looking at Kathy Garrety as he said it. Kathy simply smiled and looked right back at him. She was well aware of Luke's confrontational attitude. She also respected his strong desire to represent his fellow workers in the best way possible.

"Yes…fine…Luke it is then," Dumas responded, putting the papers aside.

"Could we get some coffee?" Valenkova asked, looking at Tammie.

"It's on its way, even as we speak," Tammie smiled back, "Donuts too."

A trace of a smile crossed Ted Lark's face. He was notorious around the office for his love of donuts.

"So…let's get started. Why don't each of you tell us your name, your position with Tachyons and how long you have worked for the company?" Dumas said. He already knew this but wanted it recorded on the video camera.

"Jane Valenkova, construction assistant, Knoxville, Iowa, five years."

"Luke Lindman, I and R, Wisconsin, 25 years."

Dumas suppressed a smile. While Tachyons had only existed for five years, the current contract in Wisconsin gave employees credit for previous service with companies acquired by Tachyons. Lindman had worked for Legent before Wisconsin was acquired by Tachyons.

"Jack Rass, Planning Engineer, Edina Minnesota, two years… Go Cyclones!"

"Geez Jack! Does it never end with you?" Ted Lark muttered. Lark had graduated from Michigan State University and the Spartans had lost a football heartbreaker to the Iowa State Cyclones the previous year. Rass was a graduate of Iowa State.

"Give it to 'em Jack!" Valenkova said strongly. Her husband was an Iowa State grad.

"Next," Dumas said quietly.

"Tammie Ring, Executive Assistant, Farnsworth, Michigan, fifteen years counting my time in the service center."

"Kathy Garrety, Director, Human Resources, Farnsworth, Michigan, four years, GO BLUE!" Kathy had finished her degree two years previously, at the University of Michigan, by going to night school.

"I'm glad we got that over with before this meeting turns into a Big Ten vs. Big Eight pep rally," Dumas said. Shelley suppressed a laugh. The group was not going to be easy for "Charlie" to control.

"Big Twelve," Lindman said quietly.

"What?"

Lindman looked at Dumas, the disdain clear on his face. "There isn't a "Big Eight" anymore. Iowa State is in the Big Twelve."

"Go Cyclones!" Valenkova said, quietly.

"Oh," Dumas said, reaching for his papers again. "Ok, let's get started. I know that Tammie, Ted and Kathy work closely with Mr. McCann on a daily basis…"

"Wils," Lindman said quietly, looking down at the table in front of him.

"I beg your pardon?" Dumas said, clearly irritated.

"It's not 'Mr. McCann' to us. We all call him Wils," Lindman replied, looking Dumas in the eye.

Shelley had to bite down hard to keep from laughing. She was really beginning to like Luke Lindman.

"Okay, 'Wils' it is then," Dumas said. "As I was saying, Tammie, Ted and Kathy work closely with Wils here in Farnsworth and probably see him in a different light than Jane, Jack and you do. I would like to get your perspective first. What kind of a leader is Wils? What do you think of him? He has some obvious good points and has had some setbacks in his career. Our article is seeking to show the man within the man."

Jane and Jack looked at each other and at Lindman. Lindman looked down at the table. Jane spoke first.

"I respect him. He isn't always right. He doesn't always do what I might think he should do but he gives me an opportunity to say what I think when he comes to Iowa and he listens to what we have to say about the company and its programs. He is very customer focused."

"How can you say that? He sacrificed service to traditional customers in Iowa to build fiber networks in the Des Moines area," Dumas responded, smiling inwardly. His comment produced the desired effect. The group now knew that he had done his homework.

Valenkova hesitated but was not deterred. She clasped her hands on the table in front of her and leaned forward. Looking Dumas in the eye, she spoke.

"A lot of us didn't agree with that decision. We felt that Wils was going after a fast buck at the expense of our landline customers. I still think that is what he did. But, you know what? It paid off. He came back the next year and poured some of that cash flow into improving and expanding our franchised telephone network. The decision to form the Competitive Local Exchange Carrier paid off and he was up front with us about it and why he did it."

THE INVESTMENT

"He did pretty much the same thing in Minnesota," Rass chimed in. It was clear from his tone that he was an enthusiastic supporter of building broadband networks around the metropolitan areas near Tachyons' existing telecommunications properties.

"You are a Planning Engineer Jack. I presume you have sat in on some of Mr. McCann's…I'm sorry…Wils' budgetary reviews?" Dumas asked, swiveling to face the younger man.

"I wasn't a presenter…I just sat in on the meetings," Rass responded, looking down.

"What were those meetings like?" Dumas asked.

Rass smiled broadly. "They were tough! He asks a lot of tough questions and you had better have your ducks in a row or…"

"Or what?" Dumas probed.

Rass hesitated before responding. "You can get sent out of the room."

"What?" Dumas said it loudly and looked around the room for effect. "That doesn't sound very professional or caring!"

"Mr. Dumas, we are a privately financed company and our investors have a right to a return on their investment. If you are asking to spend millions of dollars, you had better be able to show some return on those investments. Wils makes sure that happens. If you can't show why a project should go forward, you should be sent out of the room…" Tammie Ring began.

"Thank you Tammie, but I was talking to Jack," Dumas replied dismissively.

"It's about doing your job right," Lindman said quietly.

Dumas turned to face him. "What?"

Lindman leaned back in his chair and ran his fingers through his hair. He looked at Rass like a father would look at a rambunctious son. "Wils wants the job done right. If a job is worth doing it's worth doing right," he said, swinging his eyes back to Dumas.

"Yet your union staged a wildcat strike a year ago in defiance to

— 47 —

McCann's…sorry….Wils' service improvement demands," Dumas shot back.

"And we settled our contract in one week this year," Lindman replied evenly. Kathy Garrety smiled at him.

Lindman leaned forward, one hand gripping the arm of his chair and the other, a clenched fist on the table. "Look, two years ago, he came to Wisconsin and fired our General Manager. Our service stunk and management wasn't doing anything about it. Most of them wanted to hob-nob with the big shots in town or the politicos. We in the union stopped caring. Wils brought in new management and set goals and backed them up with money. We thought it was all a show, just like before. When management started disciplinary actions on poor performance, we struck. Wils came back out and sat down with us and showed us that he was serious about three things, service to the customers, a fair return for the investors and fair treatment for the workforce. We took him at his word. Together, we set an overall service performance goal tied to a retroactive wage incentive. We missed the performance goal by one tenth of a percent. He gave us the retroactive wages anyway. This year we didn't get everything we wanted, but we got a fair contract including service related incentives. In my book, he's a man of his word."

A dropping pin would have sounded like a thunder clap in the silence that followed.

Shelley watched as Luke Lindman sat back in his chair and unclenched his hand. She could see the rough skin and the calluses on it. It reminded her of another set of hands, those of her Uncle.

The room was still for a moment and Dumas struggled to regain control of the meeting. At that moment there was a rap on the door and a young man and a middle aged woman entered pushing a coffee cart with two coffee urns and a plate of donuts on it.

Dumas used the next five minutes to re-gather himself while he sipped on a cup of black coffee. He noted that Kathy Garrety stood next to Luke Lindman as they both stared out the window, munching on donuts and sipping coffee.

It was becoming clear to the man playing the role of Charlie Dumas that he wasn't going to get anything out of this group except respect for McCann's leadership of Tachyons. He decided to delve into McCann's personal life and Christian faith as the meeting moved along.

Of the six, only Tammie Ring had given Dumas the feeling that she shared McCann's Christian faith. This, plus her position as McCann's Executive assistant, in Dumas' opinion, cast some doubt on anything she might offer about him as a person.

He was somewhat surprised to find that the others, who disclaimed any regular church attendance or religious involvement, respected McCann's faith and his willingness to live it out in his conduct each day. A few references to times when McCann's behavior had not been exemplary were quickly followed by other examples of when he had gone beyond their expectations in carrying out the second commandment to "love thy neighbor". This was summarized by Ted Lark when Dumas asked him how, as a man well versed in technology and its power, he could give credence to McCann's almost childlike faith in God and His holy word.

"Wils reads his bible and prays every day," Lark said. "I've seen him doing it early in the morning when I come to his office. I've never been a church-goer. I've not read a lot in the Bible. I'm into the cloud and broadband and the latest and best servers, computers and software. But, I don't need to read the Bible to tell me how to live. Wils McCann lives it out in front of me every day."

Shelley Martinez shut down her camera as the meeting came to a close. She was strangely moved by these six people's view of Wilson McCann. She decided to try to learn more about the faith they saw in McCann and talked about so openly. Tomorrow's interviews with his friends and business associates in the community would shed more light on it. Of that she was sure.

The next day was bright and clear with a few white puffy clouds leisurely floating across the sky. At precisely 11:30 a.m., Dumas and Martinez pulled up in front of the Warner mansion. The home had obviously been one of its kind in the 60's and 70's. It still retained its regal beauty, centered as it was on a three acre plot within the village limits. There were other homes more in tune with the current architectural style in Farnsworth. Some of them were part of a development that spread out below the mansion to the west. But, as Shelley shouldered her camera equipment and turned to go up the short entrance walk, she felt like she was walking into history.

Maria, Belle Warner's House Keeper and Personal Assistant greeted them at the door. She turned aside as Dumas walked passed, not bothering to return her smile.

"Buenos Dias," Shelly said quietly, looking into the older woman's dark eyes.

"And the same to you, senorita," Maria smiled back, as she turned to lead them into the interior of the home.

"Belle will join you in the dining area," she said, as she led them into a combination dinette and atrium area. The rich lawn spread out before them through the floor to ceiling glass panels that flanked the doorway out onto a patio.

Maria withdrew and they stood looking out over the village below them as Belle Warner entered.

"Good morning Mr. Dumas and Miss Martinez," she said, extending her hand and grasping Shelley's in both of her own. Shelley felt the firmness of the grip and looked into a pair of dancing blue eyes that belied the owner's years. Belle was dressed in a gray skirt and vest and a white silk blouse. Her matching gray pumps had modest one inch heels.

Shelley sensed a woman possessing a firmness of purpose, coupled with a keen intellect and a loving nature. Belle Warner reminded her of the grandmother who had helped to raise her.

As Belle turned to Charlie Dumas, not a hair on her perfectly coiffed head moved. The blue eyes appraised him carefully as she shook his hand. Dumas, for his part, felt strangely unnerved.

"How long have you been with *Tech Exec?*" Belle asked, continuing to hold his hand firmly in hers. Shelley noted that with Dumas, Belle's handshake was one-on-one with no added warmth.

"I'm actually a free-lance reporter, but I have worked with them for ten years," Dumas responded tentatively.

"Ah! That's a long time. I wasn't aware that they had been around that long," Belle replied, releasing his hand and stepping back while continuing to scrutinize him.

"Well…I did free lance before they formed," Dumas stammered. "I worked with one of the founders."

"How very interesting! Which one?" Belle replied, her gaze unwavering.

Dumas looked away from the piercing blue eyes and knew he was in trouble. He was saved when Maria entered the room, followed by two men of contrasting appearance. The shorter of the two looked amazingly like Andy Devine, the actor who played "Jingles" on the TV show "*The Adventures of Wild Bill Hickok*". He wore a tan corduroy jacket over a checkered shirt and dark brown slacks. The second man was tall and gray haired. He wore steel rimmed glasses. He was dressed in a white oxford dress shirt and dark blue slacks. His black loafers reflected the sunlight.

Shelley knew immediately that the first man was Phil Willard, the owner of the Farnsworth Agway and former Tuscola County

Republican Chairman. She assumed that the second man was Fred Penay, retired former President of the Farnsworth State Bank.

Dumas, seeing his opportunity to avoid Belle's probing questions, quickly stepped toward the two and extended his hand.

"Hi! I'm Charlie Dumas and this is my assistant, Shelley Martinez," he said, as he shook hands with each man. Shelley watched Belle and saw a very brief smile cross her face. She reasoned that Belle knew that *Tech Exec* magazine had been formed six years ago, not ten. Shelley was betting that Belle also knew the magazine's founders, if not personally, then by reputation. Shelley stepped forward and shook hands with both men.

"Hi, I'm glad to meet you," she said. Willard pumped her hand vigorously and Penay regarded her with the cool evaluation of a banker thinking about extending a loan.

Belle moved to the dinette table and rang a small bell that rested there. "I thought we might have a light lunch and get to know each other a bit before Miss Martinez turns on her camera and Mr. Dumas turns on his '20 questions' routine. I hear that you ask some very penetrating questions, Mr. Dumas."

Before Dumas could respond, Maria appeared, carrying a tray with five small salads and two small pitchers containing salad dressing. Belle directed them to their chairs and seated herself. She looked around the table and smiled.

"We usually do what Wils McCann calls 'talking to our plates' before we begin to eat," She said. "If you would, Fred?"

Penay bowed his head and closed his eyes, Willard and Belle did likewise. Charlie Dumas lowered his head but kept his eyes open. Shelley crossed herself and closed her eyes.

"Father thank you for this food and this home and those who are here together. Bless the food to the use of our bodies and us to your service. Amen," Penay said quietly.

As she poured Ranch dressing on her salad, Shelley felt a peace descend around the table. She knew that Charlie Dumas would do his best to stir things up after their meal. But as she gazed around the table, she thought that the three people who were now engaged in quiet discussion were up to the task of answering any questions that Dumas might pose.

(7)

The young woman sitting in the office of Max, McCann's financial advisor, had been recommended by the Department of Employment Security for the state of Illinois. Max handled all of Wilson McCann's personal business affairs, just as he had from the time that McCann had become CEO of Dynacom over ten years ago. He assigned her to opening the mail and arranging it based upon a list of clients that he had gone over with her. He warned her that much of the incoming mail could be classified as "junk mail" and that she should simply discard any that clearly fit into that category.

The problem was in making the determination of what did and did not fit the category. Max represented many clients. His clients were the logical targets for those wanting to sell any number of goods and services. The young woman had little trouble with the envelopes that clearly were trying to interest one of Max's clients in buying a new and improved home security system or a subscription to "the most up to date investment advice available". There were also a number of envelopes containing money saving insurance quotes for everything from life insurance, long term care insurance and property liability and fire, wind and flood insurance.

As she thumbed through the envelopes and dropped the more obvious ones into the small shredder next to her desk, she inadvertently included one containing the final renewal notice for insurance on Wilson McCann's farm buildings.

She had made the same mistake two months ago and had followed that mistake by also shredding the two subsequent reminder notices as well. She demonstrated a consistent lack of effort on specific projects that Max assigned her over the next three months. After two periodic reviews of her performance, Max was compelled to terminate her employment at the end of her probationary period. By that time, the insurance company had stopped sending reminders and terminated the insurance policy on McCann's farm.

The group moved to the spacious family room of the mansion after lunch. Willard and Penay sat on a stylish Chesterfield upholstered sofa. Belle sat in a recliner to their right and Dumas sat opposite her in an overstuffed chair that matched the sofa. Shelly set up her camera opposite Belle. One side chair remained empty as they sat down but was quickly occupied when Jim Marks was escorted in by Maria, who then withdrew, shutting the door behind her.

"Glad you could make it, Jim. You missed a great lunch," Willard said, smiling at his friend.

"I'm sorry, we're getting ready to do the beans and I needed to get things organized," the young farmer replied.

Jim, his wife, Lona, and their two children lived on a farm adjacent to McCann's. Jim worked his own farm, another that McCann had helped him buy and held the mortgage on, as well as most of McCann's one hundred acres. Altogether, he was working close to three hundred acres.

The small town of Farnsworth did not have any motels. It's only overnight facilities were a set of rather seedy condos on the west edge of town and some small apartments above businesses on Main Street that could be rented by the week. The Dunt Center, where Lona Marks was the Business Manager, had been created through economic development funding from the state of Michigan, an investment by Straylin and Co. and McCann's own money. It resulted in a former elementary school being converted into a combination office building for Tachyons' staff, a bed and breakfast facility serving the general public and those who had business with Tachyons, and a senior center.

Dumas cleared his throat and began, "Well, as you all know, we are doing a combination print and video piece on Mr. McCann and we've already completed a good part of the work. We have had preliminary interviews with Mr. McCann and we've talked with some of the folks who work with him. Today, we would like to get your perspectives as neighbors, fellow business people and community leaders."

"And you are?" Marks said, addressing his question to Dumas while looking at Shelly.

"I am Charlie Dumas and this is Shelly Martinez. Shelly will be filming our interviews."

"Thanks, I apologize again for being late," Marks said, sitting back in his chair.

"Not a problem, why don't we begin by going around the room and introducing ourselves and saying how long you have known Mr. McCann," Dumas replied smoothly, nodding at Shelly. The green light on the camera came on. Belle Warner was gazing at Shelly in a way that made the young woman just a little bit nervous. "I'm Belle Warner and I've known Wilson McCann for about six years, give a month or two," Belle said, smiling and turning to look at Fred Penay.

"I'm Fred Penay, I've known Wilson McCann for almost thirty years."

Shelly was struck by the fact that this meant Penay had known

McCann since he was a teen-ager. She caught herself and quickly focused the camera on Willard. His face broke into a broad smile as he looked into the camera.

"I'm Phil Willard and I've known Wils for about the same length of time."

"I'm Jim Marks. My wife and I are Wils' neighbors. We work his farm and we've known him for about the same amount of time as Belle."

"Thank you. We are looking to show the 'man within the man' in this article. We know that Mr. McCann is, by all accounts, a good neighbor and has been very helpful to the community but what about the inner man? He has position, wealth, and a beautiful wife. It all sounds too good to be true. Surely, he has some failings or weaknesses that make him more human. What can you tell us about that?"

There were a few moments of silence as they considered Dumas' question. Belle sat back in her chair, the small smile still playing on her face. Penay seemed engrossed in his shoes. Willard shifted in his seat and looked out the window. Jim Marks smiled.

"He drives an old truck," Marks said. Willard laughed. Penay continued to consult his shoe tops.

"What exactly are you getting at, Mr. Dumas?" Belle Warner asked quietly.

Dumas shifted in his chair and pretended to consider the question while he looked around the room.

"What I mean is…here is this man who is well regarded, wealthy, seems to have the world by the tail and gives all the credit to God. But, perhaps it is easy to credit God when you have everything. If he was stripped of all that influence, wealth, and his wife left him, what would he be like?"

"Like he was when he came back here around six years ago, except he would have Christ," Belle Warner replied, quietly.

"Agreed," Penay said, looking Dumas in the eye.

"And that would be all that matters," Phil Willard added, settling back on the sofa and clasping his hands over his ample midriff.

Dumas made a show of consulting his notes. He looked at Penay. "So, you were the only one who knew, at the time, that Mr. McCann had an illegitimate son?"

"That is true," Penay said quietly.

"You knew him as a teenager." Dumas made it a statement.

"I can't really say I 'knew him'. He worked on his uncle's farm during the summers for several years. I knew his uncle very well. He kept his accounts at our bank."

"What was his uncle like?"

"He was a hard working man. He was honest. He pretty much kept to himself," Penay replied, looking at Phil Willard who nodded his head in agreement.

"So Fred Harms was sort of a pattern for what Wilson McCann became in his career…a hard working man who was honest but sort of a loner," again, Dumas made it a statement.

"You make him sound like he was cold and unfeeling," Belle Warner said, eyeing Dumas.

"As a teen-ager, he liked to have fun. He liked the girls. When he wasn't working he tooled around town in Fred's pick-up and went to the movies and dances in neighboring towns," Phil Willard offered. "I wouldn't say that he was cold by any means."

"I would guess not, he got a girl pregnant," Dumas said, a smile on his face.

Shelly was appalled at the statement. She looked around the room and saw a look of disgust on Fred Penay's face. Phil Willard looked away. Jim Marks lowered his gaze to the floor. Only Belle Warner seemed unfazed.

"Have you made any mistakes in your life, Mr. Dumas?" she asked politely.

"Oh…plenty of them I guess," Dumas replied affably.

"God will forgive them if you come to know him in a personal way, just as he forgave Wils for his mistakes and helped him become the man he is today," she said, looking steadily at Dumas. It seemed to Shelly that the light of love was in her eyes and, for some reason she could not fathom, she was again reminded of her grandmother.

To his credit, Dumas was not deterred. He returned her look and pressed ahead. "My point is that Wilson McCann used people. He didn't invest in people as a young man or as his career progressed. He was not always the 'saint' that you all seem to feel he is today."

"He is not a saint. None of us are. We are all sinners saved by God's grace if we choose to accept his grace," Jim Marks said confidently. Phil Willard nodded his head in agreement and smiled at his younger friend.

"Wils is a far different man than he was as a teen-ager and college student. I can't comment about his life between the summers he lived here with Fred and Ella Harms years ago and when he came back. But I can tell you that the man who came back is not the same as the man who lives here today," Willard continued.

As the conversation continued, Shelly watched as Dumas' attempts to dig into McCann's past were met with confident responses that only served to enhance the image of a man who had changed from what he was into a man who sought God's will in every aspect of his life. He was also a man who had invested heavily in the Farnsworth community. He held the mortgage on one of the farms that Marks worked. He had an interest in the Dunt center, which served the community. He actively supported both his church and other, smaller churches in the community. He had taken over the supervision of the Barnes Loft after Donna Barnes had died and had installed Darcey Hardesty to manage it. He had also invested himself in the operations of the Eastern European Christian Ministries, headquartered in Weaverville, North Carolina as a member of its Board of Directors.

Dumas continued to probe and dig, but the four people he had gathered to answer his questions were steadfast in their support of Wilson McCann as a man who had come to know God in a very real and personal way and who followed the two commandments of loving God with all of his heart, soul, strength and mind and to love his neighbors.

Two hours later, Shelly was putting her camera away as the four men talked in the hallway leading to the entrance to the home. Belle Warner stood just inside the doorway watching her.

"Will you be going back to Saginaw tonight?" Belle asked.

"Yes. We come back tomorrow to finish up with Mr. McCann, his wife and his son," Shelly replied, starting to collapse the tripod.

"May I ask you a question?" Belle asked, stepping toward her. Shelly's pulse sped up as she looked into those dancing blue eyes.

"I guess so...what would you like to know?" she asked, fearing the answer.

"I'm an old lady who has had a good life and I have learned a lot by walking with the Lord. One of the things He has blessed me with is the ability to read people a little," Belle replied, a smile forming on her face. "I've been watching you while you were filming us talking about Wils and his faith. I sense that you have an interest in learning more. Am I correct?"

Shelly felt her heart speed up and she considered what to say and how to say it before she responded. She sensed that Belle Warner was, indeed, someone she could be boldly honest with.

"Mrs. Warner, my mother and father were illegal aliens. They worked the produce fields in the San Joaquin Valley until they died when I was young. I was raised by my aunt and uncle. My grandmother was a Christian. She used to try to teach me Bible verses. I wasn't a very good learner. Now I wish I had listened to her a little better."

It all came out in a rush. Belle could see that the dark haired young woman standing before her was sincere. Her previous misgivings about Shelly melted away. She laid a hand on Shelly's arm.

"Stay the night with me."

Shelly stepped back in surprise. "What?"

"Stay the night and we can visit a bit more about what is important in life. I promise not to inquire into what you and Mr. Dumas are doing although I think there is more to it than what Mr. Dumas would have us think. I would like to get to know you better on a personal level and share some of my experiences. I can provide what you would need to stay the night. Will you?"

Shelly felt as though she were standing on a diving board above an inviting pool of blue water as she looked at Belle. She closed her eyes for a brief moment and when she opened them, she jumped.

"I would love to," she said simply.

Ten minutes later, Dumas drove out of the mansion's driveway, a very concerned man. Shelly had informed him she was staying the night with Mrs. Warner and not to worry, she wouldn't reveal anything. Dumas had argued unsuccessfully, and watched helplessly, as Shelly turned and walked back inside, closing the big door to the mansion behind her.

(8)

"So, assuming the usual reviews and due diligence, and any governmental approvals, we have a deal?" the man in the gray suit asked, leaning back in his chair. His name was Howard Kearn. He was in charge of Mergers and Acquisitions for Mogollon Communications, Inc.

They were meeting in the conference room at Ed Feldman's investment banking firm in New York City. Feldman and Cindy Melzy, CEO of Triad, representing the minority investors in Tachyons sat opposite Kearn. Three people in a room making a decision that would impact the lives of several hundreds of people in four states.

Feldman smiled and sat back in his chair as well. "I think we do," he said, his pleasure unmistakable. He had been trying to divest his firm of its investment in Tachyons for over two years despite the fact that Wilson McCann's well-planned expansion of the company's footprint had increased the value of that investment beyond what it had amounted to initially. Feldman had other investment plans for the cash his firm would receive for a good portion of its fifty five percent stake in Tachyons. The fact that the remainder of Mogollon's payment would be in stock, while of some concern to him, had not changed his mind.

Cindy Melzy, on the other hand, took no pleasure in the consummation of this agreement. She, together with Donald Straylin, had held out as long as they could. They had been amply rewarded for their efforts to keep Tachyons as a separate entity. She firmly believed that, given time, McCann would have brought the company to a point where they could have successfully taken it public and bought Feldman out. Now, that would not happen.

She also knew that Kent Lister, the CEO of Mogollon, held a grudge against McCann for what he perceived as McCann's part in costing him the chance to be CEO of Legent, a much larger and publicly traded telecommunications firm. It was McCann's foresight, along with the financial support of Cindy, Straylin and Feldman, that had led to the acquisition of telecom properties in four states in the Midwest from Legent. Lister had fought that acquisition as COO of Legent and had, in the end, been overruled by Legent's CEO, James Johannson. Later, Johannson had retired. Lister had been passed over as his replacement.

While she was disappointed in the fact that Tachyons would be gobbled up by what she considered to be an inferior company, she took heart in the fact that McCann's strong faith would bring him through whatever lay ahead and that God was still in control of events. That feeling warmed her as she stood and smiled at the two men.

"I must be going, I will look forward to receiving Mogollon's check at the appropriate time," she said, extending her hand to Kearn. Cindy had insisted that Triad, the Warner family and Wilson McCann, who together held forty five per cent of Tachyons, would be paid in cash. She was highly skeptical that Mogollon's stock could hold its value with an increasing amount of debt service and the operational difficulties they were having in certain parts of their operation.

Feldman stood as well and wondered at Cindy's calm demeanor. He had expected her to be difficult. He could only assume that she had finally seen the light of what he considered to be a wise decision on the part of the investors.

"When do you think we can close?" he asked, as Cindy gathered up her papers and began to place them in her briefcase.

"By the first of the year, given that our reviews and due diligence do not reveal any potential snags," Kearn replied, standing as well.

Cindy resisted the impulse to comment. With Mogollon's current issues and their need to successfully issue new debt to help finance the Tachyons acquisition, they would do well to get this deal done by the first of April. She said nothing, continued to smile, wished both men good luck in their future endeavors, and was soon heading back to her office.

"Tell me about your grandmother," Belle Warner said, as she took a sip of decaffeinated tea. It was a little after seven in the evening and she was already in her nightgown, robe and bed slippers. Clad in a set of Maria's PJs and a faded robe, Shelly sat opposite Belle in the mansion's small study. A fire burned in the fireplace and its warmth filled the room. The flickering firelight bounced from the covers of a wall of books behind where Belle sat.

They had eaten their dinner in the same dining area where lunch had been served. Roasted chicken breast, mashed potatoes and string beans were followed by a freshly baked pie. The food was delicious and Shelly had smiled at the thought of the man pretending to be Charlie Dumas alone for dinner in Saginaw. Knowing him, he would be at some chain restaurant. But the best part of dinner in the Warner mansion had been the fact that Maria had joined them. In this household, Maria was more than an employee. As the three women talked over their meal, it was apparent that, to Belle, Maria was a companion of equal value and importance to anyone who might cross her path. Shelley and Maria had spoken Spanish to each other and Belle surprised Shelly by entering into the conversation in their native tongue. It had reminded her of the evenings in the small migrant worker house that she had shared as a girl with her aunt and uncle, their children, and her grandmother.

"She was a happy person. She had a lot of aches and pains from working long days in the fields when she was younger, but she didn't let them get her down. She watched over my two cousins and I while my aunt and uncle worked in the fields. She made sure that we went to school and that we got our lessons done. She often had a hot meal on the stove when my uncle Horacio and my aunt Lucia came in from the fields. Many times, they would bring someone else home with them to eat with us. We didn't have much, but what we had was shared with anyone who had a need."

Belle took a sip from her cup and closed her eyes, savoring the taste of the tea. "You said that she tried to get you to memorize Bible verses. Did she read her Bible?"

"Every morning before we went to school or out to play and every evening before we went to bed she would read us a Psalm or a story liked David and Goliath," Shelly replied, her memory flashing back to those times around the worn kitchen table in the little house they had all shared.

"How old were you when your parents died?" Belle asked, looking at her intently.

"I was four. I don't remember much about them. They worked hard in the fields and it was hot. They drank some water that had been polluted by the weed killer that was used in the fields. Because they were illegal, they didn't go to the doctor."

"And your aunt and uncle…they raised you…did they read their Bible?" Belle asked, gently. She could see the pain that had welled up on Shelly's face.

"No, they just worked hard to take care of us three kids. They respected my Grandma for her faith and I know they loved us all.

They made sure we had a chance at a better life. I'll always be grateful for that."

"And your cousins…what became of them?"

"They both went to college. But, they didn't graduate. My cousin Jose…we call him Joe…has a landscaping business in Bakersfield. My cousin Carmalita…she was named after Grandma…is a Nurse's aide in a hospital in Modesto. She is married with three children."

Belle took another sip of her tea and studied the young woman sitting opposite her. With her dark hair, smooth complexion and flashing dark eyes, Shelly was very attractive even in a set of borrowed pajamas and a well worn terry cloth robe.

"Do you have a boy friend?" she asked, smiling.

"Had…is the operative word. I dated in college. When I moved to Chicago to work, I met someone, but it didn't work out."

"Are you happy in what you do…working with Mr. Dumas?" Belle asked and noted the quick change of Shelly's demeanor as she looked away before responding.

"I enjoy meeting people and doing the filming. I meet a lot of interesting people…like you…and get to travel a little. I miss California," Shelly replied.

"Have you met Wils' son J.W.? He lives in Palo Alto," Belle replied.

"Not yet. We go out to the farm tomorrow to wrap up the interviews with Mr. McCann, his wife and his son."

"You didn't really answer my question about whether you are happy," Belle said, smiling.

"I guess I'm like a lot of people my age. I'm wondering where my life is going. I wouldn't want to be doing the same things ten years from now that I'm doing today. But, I'm not sure just what I want out of life," Shelly responded. She was amazed at how this elderly woman could draw out things from her that she hadn't voiced in a long time.

THE INVESTMENT

"Perhaps I can help you with that," Belle said, setting her cup down on an end table beside her and picking up a small black leather bound book. Shelly saw that it was a well worn Bible.

J. W. Storey arrived at the McCann home around 7:00 p.m. He was tired from a long day of helping a Detroit based client solve a software problem, followed by the one hundred mile drive from Detroit to Farnsworth. The drive allowed him to think and his thoughts inevitably turned to Traycee. By the time he reached Farnsworth, he was in an irritable mood.

McCann and Linda greeted him with hugs and offers of something to eat. He had stopped at a Burger King on the way out of Detroit and wasn't hungry. He gratefully accepted a cup of coffee from Linda and dropped into a chair in the kitchen while she put away the food she had been keeping warm in anticipation of his arrival. McCann went outside to water Linda's horse, Florie, and bed her down for the night.

Linda had a good sense for J.W.'s moods and waited for him to guide the discussion. She didn't have long to wait.

"So, what is this thing we're doing tomorrow all about?" he said, leaning back in his chair.

"Two people from a technology magazine wanting to interview us in connection with a video and print article they are doing on Wils."

"So, it's family, faith and Tachyons and the man who has it all together," J.W. said in a tired voice, taking a small drink from his coffee cup. The coffee had been warmed up pending his arrival and it wasn't all that good.

Linda turned from the cupboards where she had been putting

away a set of salt and pepper shakers. She leaned back against the counter top and hooked her thumbs in the front of her jeans.

"Okay big fella'…what's eating you?" she said provocatively.

J.W. sat his coffee cup down on the table and leaned forward, rubbing his face with both hands. "Its been a long day. I'm tired out. I'm just…just so very…very tired."

Linda came to his side and ran her hand through his hair. He was like the younger brother that she never had. She could feel the misery oozing from him as he sat there looking down into his coffee cup.

"You've been thinking about Traycee again haven't you?" she asked, quietly.

He nodded his head slightly. "Yeah…wonder how she's doing."

"Why not call her?" Linda said, moving her hand from the top of his head to his shoulder.

"No… better to let dead dogs stay buried," he said, standing and moving toward the door to the hallway. He picked up his bag from where he had dropped it and went down the hall to his bedroom.

Linda watched him go and bowed her head. She prayed that God would deal with J.W. according to his will. McCann came in from outside and found her there, her head still bowed in prayer.

"Problem?" he asked quietly, taking her in his arms.

"J.W. is having a bad day. I think he is still having 'Traycee withdrawal'," she said, looking up at him.

"Should I get involved?" he asked.

"Pray. That's the best thing right now," she said, giving him a quick kiss on the cheek.

"She is going to be a great mom," he thought to himself as she moved away and continued to straighten up the kitchen. As he watched her, he breathed a silent prayer that God would give them a child. While he was praying the phone rang.

(9)

Shelly sat on the edge of the king sized four-poster bed in the room Belle had given her for the night. The room was magnificent. The bed, its matching dresser, and the large chest of drawers were what every girl dreamed of. Belle told her that this room had been her daughter Nancy's room before she died tragically years ago. But it was the Bible that she held in her hand that occupied all of Shelly's attention. Belle had shared some of her experiences in her faith walk before giving it to her and suggesting that she consider some of the passages that the older woman had marked especially for her.

"For I know the plans that I have for you,' declares the Lord, 'plans for welfare and not for calamity to give you a future and a hope. And you will seek Me and find Me, when you search for Me with all your heart."

The passage was from the 29th chapter of the book of Jeremiah and was God's message through his prophet to the exiled Jews. Shelly thought of her own family and their migration to the United States to try to find a new life. They were exiles in a strange land. Yet, here she was, a legal citizen of her adopted country and yet she still felt at times as though she was the exile. She felt like she was an alien even now, living in Chicago in a nice apartment with money in the bank, a good job, and the opportunity to live her life as she wished.

She considered the verses again. What was her future and her hope? The verse implied that she could only learn that by seeking God with all her heart. Was she ready to do that?

She turned to the next verse that Belle had marked for her.

"And there is a hope for your future' declares the Lord"

It was another verse from Jeremiah declaring that the work of the exiles would ultimately be rewarded by a return to their homeland. While Shelly had no desire to return to her family's former home in Mexico, she did long for a place that she could call "home" in the real sense of the word. She had always felt that the simple migrant worker's home in the valley had been "home" to her family, they were gone from there. She had gone back once to see it and found it gone. The ground on which it had stood was now part of a field of lettuce. She had wept at the sight.

She turned to the next verse. It was from the book of Isaiah, chapter twenty nine, verses fifteen and sixteen, where God again speaks to his people through another prophet. The last part of verse 15 and the first part of verse 16 were underlined in red.

"I will not forget you. Behold, I have inscribed you on the palms of my hands."

Shelly thought about her life. Her mother and father had been gone for almost thirty years. Grandmother had lived long enough to see her start college fourteen years ago. Her aunt and uncle had been gone for six years. Her two cousins had little interest in maintaining any sort of a relationship. They were busy with their own lives just as she was with hers. As she sat there, she realized that she was, as a Martinez, pretty much alone. That had never bothered her as she started her career and achieved success. Whatever else he was, the man playing the role of Charlie Dumas was a good boss and had given her opportunity to progress and succeed. Yet now, sitting here in this beautiful home, she felt alone. She read the scripture again. A feeling began to build deep within her. She was not alone. God had the name Shelly Martinez written on the palms of His hands!

She turned to the last scripture verses that Belle had marked for her. It was from the book of John which Belle had said provided the best information about Jesus and what it meant to follow Him. She turned to the 14th chapter, where Jesus was comforting his disciples and talking to them about their future and His role in it.

"Let not your heart be troubled. Believe in God. Believe also in Me. In My Father's house are many dwelling places. If it were not so, I would have told you; for I go to prepare a place for you. And if I go and prepare a place for you, I will come again, and receive you to Myself; that where I am, there you may be also. And you know the way where I am going.

Thomas, said to Him, 'Lord we do not know where you are going; how do we know the way? Jesus said to him 'I am the way, and the truth, and the life; no one comes to the Father, but through Me."

Shelly closed the Bible and sat thinking. She remembered the story of her parents' coming across the border at night. They had risked everything they had to have a new life for themselves and, eventually, their daughter. She couldn't remember much about her early life but her grandmother had told her that her father and mother were good Catholics and went to church every Sunday even though they feared that in doing so they might be found out and returned to Mexico. They had found a way to a new life. She was the beneficiary of that love and effort. Now, as she bowed her head, she asked God to open her heart to a new way of life as well, a way of life that would lead eventually to seeing her father and mother and her grandmother again in the dwelling place that Jesus had prepared for them.

McCann put the cordless phone back in its wall cradle and turned to Linda. She could see from the look on his face that the news they had been expecting for the past month had finally come.

"That was Cindy," he said quietly, "They shook hands on the deal this afternoon in New York. Mogollon will acquire Tachyons. They say that they will close by year end but she thinks it will take longer than that…maybe until the first of April."

"I can't believe they did this without you being there. You are the CEO. Couldn't Cindy and Don have done something? Couldn't they have raised the money to buy Feldman's share out?" Linda asked as she slammed a cupboard door shut. The sound echoed through the room. Tessa, their Shetland Sheepdog, sleeping in her bed beside the door to the outside deck, raised her head and looked at them.

"The decision was out of my hands. The majority investor can decide what to do. Cindy and Don did all they could do but they couldn't come up with the right package to satisfy Ed. He thinks Mogollon's stock will go up and he will make a killing," McCann responded. His voice was tired but, as he stooped to rub Tessa's head, he felt some relief for the fact that the two years of uncertainty over Tachyon's future was about to end.

"We need to talk about what we do in the future," he said, coming to Linda and taking her in his arms. She looked up at him and smiled.

"We'll get a cow and I'll sell milk and butter beside the road… remember?"

"And I will write my memoirs about how to lose two companies in less than ten years," he said ruefully as he released her.

"Tomorrow's interview with Charlie Dumas and his pretty assistant will be fun won't it?" he said, as he moved toward the glass sliding door to the deck. He gazed out over the field below the house. The leaves on the brush along the stream that marked the property's east boundary were turning red.

"They won't know if we don't tell them," she said it hopefully.

"Dumas already seems to know about the Mogollon deal. He alluded to it two days ago when he talked to me at the office."

"This is a strange approach to doing a magazine article. I've never heard of a series of interviews just to write an article for a technology magazine…and the videotaping? What's that all about?" Linda's tone showed her skepticism.

"I know. Tammie thinks there is more to it than meets the eye. She thinks Dumas is a fake but we made a couple of phone calls to the magazine and his story was corroborated," McCann replied.

"So…the assistant is pretty? Maybe that will improve J.W.'s attitude," Linda said, as she finished putting things away and wiped off the counter top in the kitchen's center island.

"She is about a year older than J.W. I get the feeling that some of Dumas' questions make her a little uncomfortable," McCann said as he headed toward the family room. "She's staying the night with Belle Warner."

"Spending a night with Belle at the mansion has got to make her a better person. I can testify to that," Linda smiled, following him into the room. She flashed back in her mind to the sunny day two years ago when Belle had showed up at McCann's farm and, over the course of two hours, had led Linda to a saving knowledge of Jesus Christ. Linda was looking forward to meeting Shelly Martinez.

The bright sunlight reflected off the endless field of lettuce. Shelly tried to see where the rows ended but could not. She looked to see the mountains and was surprised at their height and that they were snow capped. It was pleasantly cool as she stood there in the central valley and looked down rows of glistening green.

"Go back Muchacha," her grandmother said. She turned and looked out toward where the voice came from. Her grandmother stooped over the row of lettuce, a broad sombrero partially shading her face. In the distance, Shelly could see two other figures. She strained to make them out, but the rays of the sun seemed to make them shadowy as they bent over the rows of lettuce. She felt that she knew them but couldn't seem to put names on them.

"But, I want to stay with you, Nanina," Shelly said in a pleading voice, using her familiar term for her grandmother.

"You must go back. Your life is not here. It is out there in the world," the older woman replied, gazing down at the lettuce. "You must make a difference."

As she said it, she began to move quickly down the row. Shelly moved to follow her but her legs felt like lead and the older woman quickly began to move away into the sunlight.

"Nanina! Wait for me! I want to stay with you!" Shelly screamed.

A shaft of light fell across her face as she sat up in the bed. Belle Warner stood in the partially open doorway to the room.

"Is everything alright?" she asked quietly.

As Shelly's heart slowed down, she felt a peace she had not known for many years.

"It is now," she said quietly.

(10)

"What time are they coming?" J. W. asked as he poured a cup of coffee and returned to the table in the dinette area of the kitchen. Linda brought a plate of eggs, bacon and toast and placed it in front of him. She dropped into the chair opposite him and sipped from her cup.

"Around 10:00 a.m. This man Dumas stayed last night in Saginaw. He'll pick his assistant up at Belle's and they will come on out."

"Where's dad?" J.W. asked, digging into his breakfast.

"He walked back to the creek," Linda replied.

McCann had risen before her and put the coffee on. He had walked down to the barn and fed Florie and then continued on through the brush to the small stream that flowed across the back of their property. Tessa trotted along beside him.

He and Linda had placed a small wrought iron bench beside a pool where he often sat to pray and meditate and watch the sun come up over the eastern horizon. Linda often joined him there and they listened to the mourning doves call to one another as the sun came up.

Back at the house, J. W. took his first sip of coffee and looked up at Linda.

"How did he take it?" J. W. asked, referring the news that Tachyons was to be sold.

"Remarkably well, he seems to be looking ahead to what the future holds next for him," Linda replied.

"I wish I had his faith," J.W. said, buttering a slice of toast and looking out the window to the east as the morning sun bounced of the red and gold leaves of the brush along the stream below the house.

"You can, you know," Linda said quietly, looking at him with affection in her eyes.

"I just don't get the whole thing of turning my entire life over to God. I'm sorry, I know you and Dad have found that peace that comes from knowing Him but I'm not there yet. I guess you will just have to keep praying."

"I will…we will," Linda said, rising to refill her cup.

Shelly came down the stairs into the dining area dressed in a white blouse and black slacks, formerly belonging to Belle's daughter Nancy. Her dark hair was brushed and fell loosely around her face which shone with happiness. Belle Warner, dressed in a similar white blouse and black skirt, noticed the change in appearance and demeanor immediately.

"I admire your choice in breakfast attire," she said warmly, as Shelly came toward her.

"We could be Muchacha and Nanina," Shelly said happily. She enveloped Belle in an embrace and whispered in her ear.

"Thank you! I have become a follower of Jesus,"

She continued to hold the older woman tightly. Belle squeezed her back and they stood there for a moment. Maria entered with a tray holding a Carafe and two cups. She stood in the doorway, smiling.

"Praise God!" Belle said, releasing Shelly and stepping back while placing her hands on the younger woman's shoulders and looking deeply into her eyes. The joy that she saw in them reflected what she had just heard.

They sat down at the table and Maria placed the carafe and cups before them.

"Bring your cup fiel companero. You must hear this story too," Belle said to Maria and her 'faithful companion' brought her own cup and sat down with them.

Shelly told them about her experience while reading the Bible and her dream after making her decision to accept Christ.

"Your Nanina knows that you are a new person now. She is rejoicing in heaven," Maria said softly.

"And I think my Madre y Padre…my mother and father know too. I think it was them that I saw along with my grandmother in my dream," Shelly said brightly, looking out the window as a bright red male Cardinal flew to a bird feeder in the yard and began to peck at the seed there.

Three hours later, Charlie Dumas arrived. He was astonished to see Shelly not only dressed differently but also acting differently. It began when she cheerfully gave him a chaste hug and said, "Hi Charlie! Isn't this a beautiful day?"

For his part, Charlie Dumas was beginning to wonder what kind of water these people in Farnsworth were drinking. First it was McCann and his Administrative Assistant, then it was Fred Penay, Phil Willard, Jim Marks and Belle Warner and now it was Shelly Martinez.

He was about to suggest that Shelly change back into her jeans, sweatshirt and Cubs cap for the trip to McCann's home but rightly realized that such a requirement would be cheerfully ignored.

He watched from his car as Shelly said goodbye to Belle and her house keeper, Maria, by giving both of them extended hugs and kisses on the cheek. He noted that Belle slipped a worn Bible into Shelly's hands as she moved to come to the car. Shelly looked down at it and gave Belle another hug and kiss. When she got into the car, she clutched the Bible and there were tears in her eyes. Charlie could tell they weren't tears of sadness.

On the way to McCann's Shelly happily told him about her evening with Belle and her life changing decision. As he listened his concern grew.

"Look, I understand that you think you've had some sort of 'come to Jesus moment' but don't do or say anything to jeopardize what we are here to do," he said strongly, as they turned down the gravel road that led to McCann's farm. McCann had asked that they meet at the farm and not his new home.

"Don't worry. I won't tell tales out of school on you but I'm not going to hide my new found faith under some sort of false pretenses either. What you are doing is your business. I'll do my part but I'm not going to pretend to be someone that I'm not…especially now," her tone was not belligerent but he could tell that the old Shelly Martinez had gone the way of the Cubs cap. He would continue his masquerade as Charlie Dumas and hope that Shelly's new openness didn't expose it.

"Okay, just don't mess up this deal," he said sternly, as he turned into the farm's drive.

As they came up the driveway, followed it through the turn-around, and parked, McCann, Linda and J.W. emerged from the house. McCann was dressed in a brown safari shirt and jeans. Linda was wearing chinos and a light blue blouse that accentuated her figure. J.W. wore a white oxford button down shirt and jeans.

Dumas and Shelly stepped out of the car and shook hands with McCann who noticed Shelly's changed appearance and smiled as, out of the corner of his eye, he saw J.W. giving her an approving look.

He introduced Linda and J.W. Shelly was struck by Linda's movie star beauty. J.W. Storey had his father's dark hair and strong chin but his green eyes were clearly those of his now deceased mother.

"Let me give you the ten-cent tour," McCann said as he gestured to the surrounding buildings. As he did so, Nick Hardesty came down the back steps to the house clad in automotive coveralls. McCann introduced him and Dumas quickly asked if he could talk to the young man afterwards. Nick, for his part, looked inquiringly at McCann before nodding and saying, "I guess so…I'll be working in the shed there," as he gestured toward the large hip-roofed tool shed behind them.

"Let's get the camera set up and get some shots of the farmyard, Shelly," Dumas said.

Shelly turned toward their car and J.W. moved up beside her.

"Can I help you?" he inquired, as he moved to open the car's rear door for her. She could smell his cologne and those green eyes seemed to look right through her.

"Sure, there's just a tripod and a camera bag. It's pretty heavy though," she stammered as he moved to reach inside the car, brushing her shoulder as he did so.

"I heard you are a cubs fan…where's your cap?" J.W. said as he retrieved both the tripod and the bag. He lifted them out without seeming to strain and turned to face her.

Shelly realized that McCann had probably given Linda and J.W. a good briefing on herself and Charlie Dumas, including what she had been wearing during the filming in his office.

"Yeah…I was…I mean…I am…but I left it…it's in the trunk," Shelly stammered, inwardly telling herself to get a grip. She was mindful of Dumas' warning and needed to be careful around this very handsome young man.

"So, who's your favorite player?" J.W. asked pleasantly as they moved to the center of the turn-around to set up the tripod.

Shelly busied herself with the tripod while her mind raced. "Ah… Piniella," she said as she began to remove the camera from the bag.

J.W. smiled and gave her a strange look before responding.

"Yeah, but he's the manager. I asked who your favorite player was."

Shelly pretended to be having trouble with the camera. "Yeah, I know but I like 'em all…as long as they are Cubs. Can you move out of the way a bit? I want to get a focus on the barn."

She swung the camera, now attached to the tripod, around and peered through the lens. J.W., for his part, stepped aside and watched her, a smile playing around his lips. He could see she was uncomfortable and decided to ease up a bit.

"It's a beautiful day," he said, conversationally.

Shelly began filming the farm buildings, slowly rotating the camera on its tripod a full 360 degrees as she did so. As she came around to the house, J.W. blocked her view and she retracted the telephoto lens to focus on his face. His smile was genuine and open and she relaxed a little as the camera came to a stop on the small well-house to the right of the drive.

"It really is…it's the first day of the rest of our lives," she said, returning the smile.

McCann watched the two young people with a slight smile. Dumas, clearly irritated by the interplay between them, took a step toward them and McCann quickly interjected.

"It looks like they are going to do their own tour. Come on Charlie," he said, lightly grasping Dumas's elbow and steering him toward the crest of the hill by the barn. They walked past the small shed and the granary and looked out at the fields to the west as McCann explained the crops that Jim Marks had planted the previous summer. All had been harvested except for one six acre field of sugar beets directly below them that stretched back toward the farm's western boundary. By the time they turned toward the barn, with the cattle grazing in the field south of it, J.W. and Shelly were walking side by side across the back lawn towards an old chicken coup.

Dumas kept glancing back as McCann and Linda talked about the beef cattle they were raising and the age of the buildings and McCann's aunt and uncle. They entered the barn through the old horse-stable door on its south side and walked through the feed alley to where the run pens were. By that time, Charlie Dumas was ready to head for the house. Linda nudged McCann surreptitiously and inclined her head slightly toward the barn door.

"Unless you want to go up and see the hay mows, why don't we head on up to the house," McCann said amiably as he turned toward the door.

"Let's," Linda said, stepping out ahead of the two men. "I have some coffee brewing and I baked some raspberry scones to go with it."

"You are quite the farm wife," Dumas said, stepping through the barn yard gate that led back up the slight rise to the turn-around.

"Mr. Dumas, you and I both know that I am not a 'farm wife'. I am an IT integration specialist and I enjoy my work. I made a decision in that house that changed my life forever. I fell in love with the man of my dreams here. He loves this farm and I love him. If coffee and scones make him happy, coffee and scones it is."

Dumas detected a hidden meaning in her comments. It seemed to him that Linda McCann was sending a message that she didn't believe for a minute that Charlie Dumas was a journalist. He looked for Shelly and J.W. but didn't see them. He assumed they were in the tool shed with Nick but he was wrong.

They were walking in the apple orchard on the north side of the farmstead. The apples were pretty well gone from the trees. Their rotten remains littered the ground. J.W. took the opportunity to occasionally steer Shelly away from stepping in them by grasping her elbow lightly.

Each time he touched her, Shelly felt a ripple of excitement and glanced up at him. He was explaining the various types of apples but seemed to be headed in a direction that led away from the orchard toward an adjoining field.

"I thought you might like to see this. You might want to get a picture," he said as they moved out from under the trees. Shelly had taken a small digital camera from her bag and looped its strap around her neck.

She saw the two mounds as they moved closer. There were stones on top of the mounds. Someone had chiseled "Ted" on one and "Wink" on the other.

J.W. pointed to the first stone. "This is where Wils came to Christ…when he buried his first dog," he said quietly. "He told you the story…right?"

"Yes, but I understand it better now," she said, looking down at the stone.

"How so?" he said, looking at her.

She looked off over the field toward the woods beyond and wondered what she should say. She decided to be direct.

"I accepted Christ last night at Belle's home. I understand now what Mr. McCann and Linda have experienced. What about you?"

She saw the reaction and immediately knew that she had gone too far. He looked away before he replied.

"I haven't gotten to that point quite yet," he said it with a bit of an edge and she wondered how she should respond.

"Maybe you will…someday…," she said, turning back toward the orchard.

They walked back toward the house without speaking. As they neared the edge of the lawn, she decided to try to lighten the moment. "The other stone had 'Wink' on it. What's the story behind that?"

"After Dad became a Christian, one of his friends, a truck driver

THE INVESTMENT

named McIntyre, brought him another Border Collie named Wink. She was his constant companion here at the farm for the next two years. She died on the same day that Linda became a Christ follower."

"And Linda and Wils began to fall in love on the day she died," Shelley thought. "That is pretty neat!" She smiled as she thought about it.

J.W. stopped to look back at the orchard. She could see that he was re-thinking the providence of it all. He turned back to her and she asked, "So, anyone special in your life?"

"Are you asking as a photo-journalist?" he said, smiling.

"If you want to take it that way…okay. I was just thinking that a guy like you with a job that takes him around the country probably meets a lot of women who are in the business. You live in Palo Alto…right?"

"Yes. I understand you grew up in the valley?" he said as they crossed the lawn and neared the house.

"Yes, my mother and father worked in the produce fields. Do you like Palo Alto? I would like to go back to that area someday…to live I mean." As she said it, she realized that it sounded like she was linking living in Palo Alto with his love life. Her face felt hot and she wondered if he could sense it.

"I like it fine. My landlady treats me like she's my grandmother," he said, smiling as he opened the door.

She stepped inside to the aroma of fresh coffee and warm raspberry scones.

"Grandmothers are good," she said, feeling Charlie Dumas' eyes on her as she stepped into the kitchen.

The interview was finished shortly after noon. Dumas had probed into J.W.'s relationship with his father, the fact that he hadn't embraced his father's faith, and how it felt to be the illegitimate son of a well known telecommunications executive. He probed into Linda's background and her previous ten-year live in relationship in St. Louis followed by a whirl-wind romance and marriage to McCann and whether she wanted to have children. He asked J.W. what research he had done into Donna Barnes' life and he asked Linda if the shadow of Donna haunted her in any way. He asked McCann how it felt to know that he would, if latest rumors on Wall Street were true, be unemployed while Kent Lister and his team ran what was now Tachyons. By the time they wrapped it up, Shelly was thoroughly sickened by the whole business and glad to turn off her camera. Linda made what seemed to Shelly a half hearted offer to fix lunch. Dumas politely declined, thanked them for their time, shook McCann's hand and promised a "first rate" report on his life and headed out the door to the car. Shelly carefully put away her equipment and followed. As she finished stowing it in the back seat, J.W. leaned against the car.

"If you are ever in or near Palo Alto, please call me or look me up. Here's my card," he said, handing Shelly a business card.

"Same here. If you get to Chicago, call me," she said as he took her hand. She felt heat shoot up her arm.

"I don't have your number…got a card?" he replied, continuing to hold her hand and smiling.

She pulled her hand away and made a pretense of searching in the pockets of her slacks. Dumas had said good bye to McCann and Linda and was opening the driver's side door. He had forgotten to interview Nick Hardesty.

"I didn't bring one…I know! I'll send my contact information to the address on your card," she said lamely, shutting the car's rear door and opening the front passenger side door. She slid into the seat next to Dumas and looked up at J.W. as he bent to shut the door for her.

"I hope you will," he said quietly and she felt those green eyes

THE INVESTMENT

on her. "Good bye and good luck. Remember, it's the first day of the rest of your new life."

As they drove down the drive, Shelly Martinez basked in the warmth of his comment.

Her reverie was broken by Dumas as they pulled off the gravel road and on to the highway. "I'm glad that is over!" he exclaimed loudly.

"They are nice people," Shelly said quietly as she looked out the window at a corn harvester working its way down a standing field of corn.

"Too nice for my money," Dumas replied.

"For the record, I thought you went overboard today. I felt dirty just listening to you," Shelly said as strongly as she could and glaring at him to drive the comment home.

Dumas stared straight ahead as he increased speed. "All those people think that Wilson McCann is some sort of reconstituted saint. They say he is 'God's man'…well nobody I know is that good!"

"Maybe you should change your circle of friends," Shelly said quietly.

She leaned back in her seat and closed her eyes. She breathed a prayer for J.W. Storey, that he would find the same relationship with God that she had found and that had changed his father's life. She also thanked God for bringing her to Farnsworth and exposing her once again to her Grandmother's faith.

McCann, J.W. and Linda stood in the back yard watching the car as it went down the road toward the highway.

"There's something fishy going on," Linda said as Nick Hardesty joined them, wiping his hands on a shop towel.

"What? You don't think she's sincere about her faith?" J.W. said quickly.

McCann looked at his son. He sensed that J.W. had more interest in Shelly Martinez than he did in the interview that Charlie Dumas had conducted.

"No…I mean Dumas…he isn't what he claims to be and what he's doing isn't what he says it is," Linda replied smiling. "I think Shelly is real…at least she is what she says she is. She's pretty isn't she?"

She poked J.W. playfully in the ribs and McCann saw the color rise in J.W.'s face. "She's okay," the young man replied.

"She's more than okay, man!" Nick Hardesty said, joining in on the teasing.

"You're just feeling your oats because you didn't have to sit there and talk into her camera while Dumas asked you embarrassing questions," J.W. responded.

"Hey man, I could look into her camera all day…" Hardesty paused in mid-sentence and looked at Linda who was looking right back at him, a small smile playing on her lips. "…course she can't hold a candle to Darcey!" he finished lamely.

"Good save, young man," Linda said, slapping him on the shoulder.

The good natured ribbing continued as they walked back to the house. McCann was the last to go up the steps. He paused and looked out over his fields where the cattle were grazing. There was something sinister about Charlie Dumas and his behavior. Both Tammie and Linda had seen it and he felt it as well. But, for the life of him, McCann couldn't figure out what or who was behind it.

(11)

The man posing as Charlie Dumas held video conference calls with Cindy Melzy, Donald Straylin and Stu Bailey in New York City upon his return to Chicago. Ed Feldman refused to be interviewed. Dumas was disappointed. He thought Feldman's comments about McCann would have interested his client.

It took a solid week of editing of Shelly's film footage and pictures to produce a well organized film presentation. Dumas worked on the written aspects of the report and, when it was finished, it filled a three inch ring binder. He delivered it to his client on the first Friday in December. When he was ushered into the living room of the big home in Glenview, he found his client in worse shape physically than on the day when he had been given his assignment. Ben had lost his hair and thirty pounds in the intervening time. His eyes, however, hadn't lost their fire and while he moved slowly to the recliner in front of the large television, his eagerness to see what he had paid for was evident. Dumas inserted the disk in the player, handed him the binder and the remote control, and took a seat in an arm chair on the opposite side of the room.

Four hours later, darkness had settled into the room. An older gray haired man had appeared after two hours with a plate of cookies and a carafe of coffee with two cups. Now as the TV screen went black, one cup remained untouched. Dumas had eaten five of the cookies and drank two cups of the coffee.

"Very interesting. I presume your views and observations, together with supporting demographics, biographical sketches and a chronological history of events, are in the binder?" Ben asked.

"They are. If you have questions, I will be happy to return to discuss them with you," Dumas said, waiting.

"I doubt it will be necessary for you to return. I'm quite confident that your work and that of your assistant will be comprehensive and complete. By the way, I understand that the young lady has resigned."

Dumas tensed. How did Ben know that? On the previous Friday, Shelly Martinez had resigned to pursue "new interests". He squirmed uncomfortably in his chair.

"Yes, she says she 'found God' during the trip to Farnsworth. I don't think she knows what she's doing but what can you do?"

"Perhaps you should seek the same God that she has found and that, it appears, many of the people associated with Mr. McCann have found," the old man responded slowly, as he pulled open a drawer in the lamp stand beside the chair and extracted an envelope.

"You will find the balance of your fee enclosed along with what I hope will be considered a generous bonus for a job well done."

Dumas rose and accepted the envelope.

"Does this provide you with everything you need for whatever it is that you plan to do?" he asked. The pale face looked up at him and he shivered at the thought that he was looking into the face of a man who would soon depart this world.

"It may or it may not. If it does not, I shall exert other forces to produce what I am looking to discover. At any rate, your work is done. Thank you again."

As he was escorted to the door by the gray haired old man who had brought in the cookies and coffee, the man who had masqueraded as Charlie Dumas wondered what "other forces" would be brought to bear on Wilson McCann.

THE INVESTMENT

H Forester looked at his reflection one more time before adjusting his tie and turning to the door of the private restroom adjacent to his 10th floor offices on Chicago's north side lake front. It never ceased to amaze him what a good plastic surgeon could do. His name had been Harvey Feurstman for the first twenty five years of his life. He had changed it to H Forester thirty seven years ago. That was when he had started handling Ben's money on a full time basis. The plastic surgery had come two years later when he looked at his personal balance sheet and decided that, with ten million already in his investment account and the assurance of many times that to come in the future, he needed some repair work.

His nickname in college was "Rat Face" because of his small eyes and large nose. He had taken the abuse quietly knowing that those who abused him would eventually see the need of his help. He could name at least three attorneys and two surgeons in Chicago who owed their well being to the little rat faced frat brother who had bailed them out when they were about to fail a course they needed to get into law and medical schools. Ben had been his friend from the moment they met. He often wondered why. Ben trusted his judgment and treated him more as a partner than as an investment advisor. He never quibbled about the way H handled his investments and he had never been stingy with rewarding the diminutive investment banker over and above the customary fees for his services.

In return, H had always listened carefully to Ben's ideas on where and when they might invest Ben's steadily growing portfolio. On a few occasions, he had suggested alternatives and Ben usually went along with them. Yesterday, however, Ben had not listened to his advice. He wondered if the onslaught of the chemotherapy and radiation treatments that Ben was enduring had finally compromised his faculties. But, he would do as he had been told and would make the investment today.

He returned to the elevated leather chair and desk in his luxurious office suite. The chair and desk were elevated three inches above the floor level to compensate for his stature. Those on the other side of the T-shaped desk and conference table were always just a little intimidated by the fact that H seemed to be above them as he sat behind his desk. He never sat at the conference table. The six swivel chairs that surrounded the three sides of the table were at floor level which meant that those sitting in them had to adjust to the three inches in height of the desk in front of them. A few of his longer term associates referred to it as the "throne room". H knew that and it didn't bother him one bit.

He pushed a small button on his desk top and a computer console and three screens activated on his credenza. At the same time, Arleta came in, a file in her hand. She was two years younger than H and five inches taller than he without her three inch heels. They had been married for thirty five years. When he first met her, she was a waitress in an I-Hop near the campus. She weighed in at one hundred eighty five pounds and she had taken him under her wing. He was a Freshman and completely overwhelmed by Chicago, college, and life in general. Before long, he was eating his evening meal there every night except the two nights each week when Arleta wasn't working. As they got to know each other better, she confided in him that she was saving what little she could to go to business school. She came from a farm family without money and lived with two other young women in a flat on the south side.

When he graduated, he asked her to come to his graduation. When he got his first job, he asked her to marry him. It was always said of H that if he was your friend, you had a friend for life. Arleta was H's best friend for life.

He made enough that she could realize her dream of going to

business school at Northwestern and by the time she graduated, he was well into making a fortune. He brought her into the firm as his personal assistant and they never looked back. She had gone on a diet for the first time thirty years ago and the woman she was today, dressed in a well tailored business suit and white blouse was a far cry from the overweight waitress he had met so long ago. He called her "Art" and she called him "Mr. H" except when they were alone. Throughout their forty one year relationship, she had always called him "Harv" when no one else was around. Their one disappointment was that they could not have children. They made up for that by becoming a major patron of a small orphanage in the city. Art spent one of her five "work days" at the orphanage. They spent three weeks each year taking a minimum of six children to exotic places around the world. On Christmas Eve each year, their spacious four bedroom house was filled to the brim with expectant children waiting to see what would be under the nine foot Balsam Fir in their family room.

Art shut the door behind her and came around the desk to drop the file in front of him. He looked up at her.

"He wouldn't listen?" she said, looking down at him.

"Nope. Just said 'do it'."

"It's a basket case. They will be bankrupt inside of three months," she said, moving to the table and dropping into one of the chairs. At her height, she didn't mind the three inch difference.

"I know. He wants us to liquidate all the debt, can the management team and then use it to acquire another company."

"What?" she said, incredulously. "You didn't tell me that!"

"He called me first thing this morning. Said he wanted to start buying shares in this company."

He slid another file to her where she sat. She opened it and began to read. She reached under the lip of the table in front of her and pushed a button. Another computer screen rose from the table in front of her. She took a small stylus from her jacket pocket and began to work with the touch screen. It was the latest technology available and not wide spread in its use yet. H Forester and Associates had invested heavily in its development and had agreed to do the first trial in the Chicago area. He felt that touch screen technology and cloud computing were two technologies that had a real future.

"Well, at least this one has a chance of survival. They've been a lot wiser in their acquisition philosophy. Why not acquire this one first and then use it to acquire the other one when it goes under?"

"The first one is about to close a deal that Ben has an interest in stopping," he replied.

"Why?"

"He hasn't told me anything except that he has a 'personal interest' in it."

She turned to look directly at her husband. "Do you think Ben is beginning to lose it?" she asked quietly.

"He seems even quieter and more reflective since the cancer. I suppose it is only natural. He seems to be just as sharp as ever but he gets tired more easily and his attention span is shorter. But, everything he has done up to now makes sense and has worked…until this one."

"What are you going to do?" she asked, knowing the answer.

"What he told me to do. He's my friend," H replied.

"Who will you use to handle it?" she asked.

He leaned back in his chair and thought for a moment. In situations like this, he usually sent one of his "Associates" out as the representative of the acquiring company. In this case, the acquiring company would be a Singapore conglomerate which owned, among other things, a shipping company. The three tiered ownership structure would, he hoped, shield the acquisition from being tied back to Ben, as he had directed.

I think I'll send Carolyn on this one," he replied.

Art smiled back at him. "You like her, don't you?" she said playfully.

"Not as much as you," he smiled back.

"There's more of me to like," she said, rising and opening the door.

"She's the daughter we never had and I think she has a great future," he said, quietly.

There had been a time when a remark like that would have been hurtful to their relationship.

"And that is why I love you!" she said, as she went out and closed the door behind her.

Carolyn Abbott, thirty two, with an MBA from Harvard and a Doctorate in Business Administration-Project Management from Liberty University, was the kind of young woman that most men only dream about. She was five foot four inches tall with dark curly hair and deep blue eyes. She had all the right curves in all the right places and, to quote H, she had "her heart in the right place and her head on straight". Added to that was the fact that Carolyn Abbott was brilliant.

Carolyn had been with H Forester and Associates for four years. In that time, she had risen to a unique position within the organization. When Ben directed H to make an investment in a firm, it was usually Carolyn who made the initial contact with the firm in which the investment was being made. When a controlling interest in a firm was being acquired, it was Carolyn who was charged with what H called "Re-upping" or "Cleaning Out". In "Re-Upping" a firm, Carolyn would meet with the management team and either re-affirm their mission statement or give them their new one. In the case of "cleaning out" a management team, Carolyn would be the sole determinant of who stayed and who left and would, in most cases, run the acquired firm for at least three months or until a new team was firmly in place.

Carolyn had worked her way through Harvard and, along the way, had acquired not only an MBA but a very liberal view of how the world worked. Then she met Wes Brown, a born-again Christian who ran a ministry to teens in Boston. She had fallen hopelessly in love and within three months had accepted Jesus Christ as her personal Lord and Savior. She was ready to marry Wes and join him in ministry when he was killed while trying to stop a street fight. Devastated, Carolyn searched for an outlet for her new-found faith. She went to Liberty and achieved her Doctorate in less than two years. Along the way, she became impressed with demonstrating how a committed Christian could influence the merger and acquisition business for Christ. She joined a medium sized Chicago investment banking firm and had only worked there six months when she met H and his wife Arleta at a charity dinner. She shared her faith and two days later, H had called and offered her a job. She had risen steadily and now acted as "minister without portfolio" for H, going wherever and whenever he told her to. Along the way, she demonstrated a steely eyed honesty wrapped in loving consideration for the feelings of others. Those who had been given their walking papers by Carolyn went out the door feeling that they had been fairly dealt with. Those who stayed knew that they would be given every opportunity to succeed but they also understood that success was expected.

The digital files on her newest assignment had arrived in her computer from H about an hour ago. She read through them quickly and then gathered additional information from various sources on the Internet.

She looked at the well-worn Bible on her desk. It had belonged to Wes. A piece of red yarn served as a book mark at the place where she had been reading this morning about Gideon and his army of three hundred defeating the Midianites in the book of Judges chapters six and seven.

She bowed her head and said a brief prayer, "Dear Lord, I have been given another task to do. Let me do it within your will and your way. Give me wisdom and strength to represent you well in this task."

She opened her eyes and turned to her touch screen. She tapped it and a keyboard appeared. She tapped out a quick message to H:

Thanks for the opportunity. I'll do my best…but I have to tell you that I feel like Gideon on the Titanic!"

A twenty minute drive from where Carolyn prepared to undertake her new assignment, Shelly Martinez snapped her laptop closed and put it into her travel bag. She glanced around her apartment to make sure she wasn't forgetting anything. She was due at O'Hare in an hour to catch her flight to San Francisco. J.W. Storey had given her a lead on a firm looking to put together a marketing video. The firm was one of his company's clients and she wanted to do well in her presentation. She smiled to herself as she remembered the last time she had seen J.W. The two of them had gone out to dinner together when he came to Chicago on a client visit ten days ago. She was attracted to him and felt that he shared her feelings. There was just one problem. She sensed that J.W. still had strong feelings for the woman he had been in a relationship with and that Shelly's new found faith would present the same problems for J.W. that Traycee Morgan's had.

Since her life changing decision in Belle Warner's home, she had found a peace and contentment that she hadn't known before. Her fledgling faith had taken off. She had joined a Bible study group in a church near her apartment and had made prayer and Bible study a part of her daily routine since leaving her previous employment and starting her own business.

She credited her faith for the fact that she already had five paying clients and the possibility that this new firm in San Francisco could add to those successes. The fact that she would drive on down to San Jose and have dinner with J.W. after her business presentation was an added bonus. She was determined to take it slowly and see where the relationship would lead. She was also troubled by the fact that she had been a participant in a scheme to gather information about Wilson McCann through a programmed lie. She had only honored her employer's contractual terms, but she felt a need to, at some point, confess to J.W. what was really going on.

She realized she didn't have the answers to the questions that would surely be asked of her. When she couldn't give a full explanation, would J.W. break off any possible future relationship? She was determined that, in the future, she would not sacrifice her faith for anything or anyone. From now on, she was only going to engage in totally above board activities.

Forty eight hours later, she walked into Le Papillon on Saratoga Avenue in San Jose. J.W. had driven down from Palo Alto and was sitting at the bar. He rose and greeted her with a hug and a peck on the cheek. At their table, she ordered the grilled swordfish and he ordered the braised duck breast. When their waiter had departed, he sat back in his chair and smiled at her.

"Wow! You really impressed them! I got a call on my cell on the way here."

She blushed as those green eyes locked on hers. "I put a little something together before I came out. I used pictures of some of

THE INVESTMENT

their clients, graphics from their programs, and some of their sponsors' ad material. I tried to make it multi-dimensional."

The client that J.W. had referred her to was a faith-based non-profit in the Bay area. Shelly's presentation had taken her the better part of a week to prepare but she wasn't about to tell anyone that. It was evident, when she finished her presentation, that the client was impressed. When they asked about her personal faith, they had seemed very satisfied with her answers and the fact that, if they hired Shelly, they would be entrusting their promotional campaign to a professional who shared the basic tenets of their beliefs.

"Maybe you will have an answer by the time you get back to Chicago," J.W. said, taking a sip from a glass of water.

"I hope so. It would be neat to have a west coast client. I might be able to make a side trip and see my cousins when I'm out here working," she replied. She would be happy to include J.W. in that side trip as well, she thought.

The waiter brought their salads and she bowed her head to say a silent prayer. J.W. however, smiled and spoke up.

"You can pray for both of us. I'm used to being around people who 'talk to their plates' as Wils...my father says," he said, bowing his head.

"Your father is a good man," she replied, after she asked a blessing on their meal and their friendship.

J.W. looked away before responding. "Yes he is. I admire him for the way he tries to love God with all his heart, mind, soul and strength," he said quietly.

"Yet you don't completely share that same faith," she replied.

"Completely is a good word. I admire his faith and I try to imitate some aspects of it. I occasionally read the Bible and I go to church and I pray at times but I haven't made the 'decision to follow Jesus' in my everyday living. I know you have and I'm happy for you," J.W. responded and she was warmed by the sincerity of his words.

They talked about the progress of her business and his plans to spend Christmas with McCann and Linda as they ate their meal. Shelly had planned to be alone for the holiday but a new friend from her Bible study had invited her to Christmas dinner at her family's home in the Chicago suburbs.

"I'll be heading back to Chicago on the Monday after New Years. I have a client appointment on Tuesday. Could we get together?" J.W. asked, as they prepared to split the bill and leave. Shelly had offered to buy dinner as a way of thanking J.W. for the referral but he insisted that they split the tab.

"I'd love that," she said, hoping she didn't sound too enthusiastic.

Outside the restaurant, they hugged again and she gave him a kiss on the cheek before walking to her car. Perhaps the next time they were together, the hug would become an embrace and the kiss would be more intimate. She hoped so, while at the same time wishing that J.W. Storey shared her faith more completely.

(12)

Wilson McCann looked up at his wife as she stretched to reach the star at the top of the Christmas tree. She was standing on a step ladder to reach the top of the tree, a nine foot balsam fir that dominated the great room in their home. Clad in chinos and a teal satin blouse, Linda was a delight to look at. McCann couldn't resist. He placed his hands on his wife's thighs and slid them upward toward her waist.

"Be careful Molly," he said, using his pet name for his wife.

"Watch it, Machine," Linda said sharply as she retrieved the star and looked down at him.

The nicknames, taken from the Novak and Sinatra characters in *"The man with the Golden Arm"* movie, had started a little over two years ago when they fell in love and married.

"Don't want you to get hurt, especially now," McCann said, keeping his hands in place.

She turned within the circle of his hands and, leaning down, put her hands on his shoulders and dropped off the ladder into his arms.

"You only love me for the baby you think I'm carrying," she whispered into his ear.

"And you only love me because I bought you a BMW for Christmas!" he said, looking into her green eyes and kissing her lightly on the lips. A shiny blue BMW 325-I, wrapped in red ribbon, had greeted Linda when she stepped outside on Christmas morning.

"Are you two at it again? Get a room for heaven's sake!" J.W. said, as he leaned against the archway into the room.

"Good idea!" Linda replied, pulling her husband closer and kissing him again.

J.W. had flown in from Palo Alto to spend the Christmas holidays here in Farnsworth with McCann and Linda. Watching the couple, who were obviously very much in love, brought a pang of remorse as he thought of Traycee Morgan. On the other hand, he was looking forward to leaving the following day for a trip to Chicago where, once his business meetings were completed, he was to have dinner with Shelly Martinez. He was excited about spending more time with Shelly.

"Okay, you two, time to move the tree out of here," Linda said, folding up the step ladder and putting it aside. The big tree stood before them, stripped of all its decorations.

J.W. moved to the front entrance of the home and opened both of the double doors. He and McCann carried the tree out into the softly falling snow and around to the rear of the house. McCann removed the metal tree stand and the two men stood looking out over the fields below the house. In the distance, the brushy creek bed cut a brown slash across the snow covered fields.

"Are you excited?" J.W. asked, knowing the answer.

"You know it!" McCann replied with a smile. "I just wish I could be there when she gets the news!"

"Don't worry, I'll get her there and I know she'll call you as soon as the Dr. confirms it," J.W. said, clapping his hand on McCann's shoulder.

Linda had an early morning appointment in Caro with her Doctor who would, everyone hoped, confirm what a pregnancy self test had shown, that Linda was pregnant with their first child. J.W.

would go with her because McCann had an early morning meeting with the team that Mogollon was sending in to do the due diligence review of Tachyons' operation.

"Thanks. Why don't you go back inside? I'm going down and check on Florie. It looks like this snow is going to last for a while," McCann said, turning to walk down the little hill toward another building that served as a stable for Linda's old mare, Florie, as well as a garage for McCann's old Farmall "A" tractor and his Ranger pickup.

He rolled back one of the big double doors to the stable and stepped inside, pulling the door shut behind him. He switched on the lights and checked the manger and the water tank in Florie's stall to make sure she had feed and water. The old sorrel mare nuzzled his coat pocket, hoping for a carrot.

"Sorry girl, I didn't bring one this time," he said, taking a curry comb from a rack on the wall of the stall. Stepping to the mare's side, he began to brush her.

As he methodically brushed Florie's coat, he thought about the future. As he had on countless occasions, he thanked God for Linda and reflected back over the last several years.

He wasn't bothered by what would come in the future other than an intense desire to place as many of Tachyon's people in positions within Mogollon. Most would have to re-locate but at least they would have an opportunity to remain employed. There would be some layoffs and some downgrades in salaries and he was sure his reputation within the small community would take a hit.

J.W.'s continued resistance to making a total commitment to God bothered McCann. It was a matter that dominated McCann's prayer life. He loved the son that he had not known until five years ago, more than any other living person except for Linda. God had led him to pray earnestly for J.W. and not to push him. As a result their relationship had grown even though they didn't completely share the same faith. He sincerely believed that J.W. was moving closer to making a decision and he had hoped that Traycee Morgan would be the instrument of God's choosing to help his son make that decision. On the night that J.W. phoned to tell them that Traycee had broken off their relationship and was moving to Fresno, McCann had gone into his bedroom and spent a long time on his knees in prayer for his son. Now Shelly Martinez had come upon the scene and J.W appeared to have some interest in her. McCann rejoiced in the fact that Shelley was a new Christian.

J.W. would accompany Linda to Caro tomorrow for her appointment and leave in the afternoon for Chicago and a client meeting the next day. The loss of his son's companionship would not be permanent. The loss of the company he had helped to create would be. By the first of April, assuming all went as currently planned, he would be unemployed. As McCann groomed his wife's horse, he felt God's assurance that all would be well in the future.

He finished brushing Florie and put a horse blanket on her before turning out the lights and walking back up to the house through the falling snow. As he did so, he glanced at one of the trees down in the ravine to the west of the house. Vines had strangled one of its main branches. It looked like the main body of the tree still had life. He had planned to take the dead branch down but hadn't gotten to it. After Mogollon took over, he would have the time to do things like that and a lot of other chores both here and at the farm. He wondered if it would be enough to keep him occupied.

Kent Lister, CEO of Mogollon Communications, fresh from a round of golf at Camelback, stopped at his office in Scottsdale late on Sunday afternoon. He had told Monica that he would be home early

THE INVESTMENT

so they could watch an NFL game before going out to dinner. He didn't enjoy being with Monica as much as he had when he had divorced his first wife and made public his relationship with his former secretary. They had married a year later and Monica clearly enjoyed the role of the COO's wife. When Kent left Dallas and Legent, and moved to Scottsdale as the new CEO of Mogollon, she had spent her time, and Kent's money, building and furnishing an eight thousand square foot home in one of Scottsdale's most prestigious areas. Now she wanted to buy a ski condo in Telluride, Colorado. She was also urging him to consider the lease of an apartment in New York City so she could enjoy shopping when he traveled to the city on business. As he let himself into his office, Lister was thinking that maybe it was time to cut his losses and become single again. One of the hostesses at Camelback was making Monica look like a part of his life that he could do without.

Lister whistled a happy tune as he entered his office. The impending acquisition of Tachyons and his chance to exact some "payback" from Wilson McCann for being part of a failed attempt on Lister's part to become CEO of Legent, had him in an upbeat mood. McCann, and his friend John King, a former VP of Legent, had been responsible for the sale of a significant portion of Legent's telecom operation to Tachyons. In so doing, they had alienated Lister from Legent's CEO, James "Stormy" Johannson. Johannson had begun to question Lister's approach to running the operational part of Legent and, six months after the Tachyons sale, had informed Lister that he was no longer in the running to become CEO when Johannson retired. Lister had left Legent for Mogollon shortly thereafter. Now it would be his pleasure to hand Wilson McCann his walking papers and to tell John King, currently a member of Tachyons' board, that his services would no longer be needed.

Lister turned on his computer and quickly scanned down his e-mail list. He noted that Howard Kearn, the team leader for the

Tachyons due diligence review, had left an urgent message asking Lister to call him. He also noted that Lewis Matsman, Mogollon's Board Chair, had left a similar urgent message. Lister sensed something bad was about to happen and mentally kicked himself for not taking his cell phone with him to the golf course. He had left it behind to avoid Monica's calls and reminders about their late afternoon dinner date.

He decided to call Howard first. Kearn picked up after the first ring.

"Kent, we've got a problem!" Kearn said quickly.

"What?" Lister replied, his sense of trouble escalating.

"We've been called off," Kearn replied. "Lewis called me two hours ago and…"

"What?" Lister said loudly into the handset.

"Lewis called us off. He said something has come up. He needs you to call him," Kearn replied. Lister could sense the confusion in the other man's voice.

"I'll call him immediately. Stay where you are until I get to the bottom of this. Where are you?"

"At the airport, our plane is scheduled to leave in twenty minutes," Kearn replied. Lister heard the stress but knew that the plane was a charter and could be held until he cleared this up.

"Tell the pilots we are on a hold until I get back to you. Do the others know?" he asked. Kearn was leading a team of four who were to be in Farnsworth the next day. They would overnight in Detroit and drive up to Farnsworth in the morning.

"No, I've said nothing," Kearn replied.

"Good. Tell them you're waiting on some last minute instructions from me," Lister responded, hanging up the phone.

He punched in Lewis Matsman's speed dial number. The Chairman answered immediately.

"Lewis, its Kent. What's going on?"

THE INVESTMENT

Lewis Matsman's voice sounded tired. "The Tachyons deal is shelved. There has been a significant change in our financial situation."

———————

The big Dodge Ram pickup roared down the Colwood-Colling Road through the steadily falling snow. Billy DeWalt was late for school. He was late, dad was ticked off, and mom wasn't speaking to him. Billy and Carol Neal had been out late last night. They had parked a mile north of his parents' farm and did what two teenagers ages sixteen and fourteen do at 11:00 p.m. on the first Sunday night of the New Year. Billy's mother and father didn't approve of Carol. They were Baptists and Carol was Catholic. Billy didn't care. He was in love for the first time in his life and Carol Neal was the best looking girl in the sophomore class.

Billy wasn't used to the big Dodge. His car was a ten year old Ford Focus. But dad wanted a load of Lama Feed picked up after school at the Agway in Farnsworth. Lamas! Who raised Lamas besides his father? The DeWalts raised beans, sugar beets and corn on their 700 acre farm west of Farnsworth. They had fattened about fifty head of beef cattle each year for sale. Then, six years ago, Billy's father had purchased a Lama. Now they had fifteen and twice a year they harvested the wool.

Going to the Agway after school meant that Billy would miss the last hour of basketball practice. Coach wouldn't like it. Billy's dad didn't care much about the basketball team anyway. Now Billy was in the doghouse at home because of Carol. Having the Coach ticked at him because he had to leave practice early made it seem like everyone was down on him. Everybody except Carol.

As he approached the intersection of M-81 and the Colwood-Colling Rd, WKYO in Caro aired their morning sports report. One of the commentators was talking about the upcoming game between Farnsworth and Caro. Billy looked for the volume control and realized, too late, that he needed to hit the brake for the stop sign. His right foot came off the accelerator pedal, grazed the brake pedal and came down hard again on the accelerator. The big Dodge leapt forward and slammed into the BMW that was heading toward Caro on M-81, driving it across the highway and into a tree.

McCann arrived at his office a little after 8:30 a.m. on Monday morning. Tammie Ring was already at her desk. The look on her face told him that this day was not going to start off well. She looked up as he entered and didn't waste words.

"They're not coming."

"What?" McCann said, looking down at her before dropping into a chair opposite her desk.

"Mr. Kearn's secretary called me at home. She said they were delayed at the Phoenix airport and then had to cancel their flight. She didn't give me any reasons. She said they would be back in touch and re-schedule."

McCann leaned back and clasped his hands behind his head. Was this Kent Lister's way of playing some sort of mind game? He considered the possibility and quickly discarded it. This was too big of a deal to fool around with. As he sat there thinking, the phone rang. Tammie picked up and her face quickly showed her surprise.

"Yes sir. He is right here. Just a minute and I'll put him on. Thank you! Same to you!"

She punched a button on the phone and put it back in its cradle. "Stu Bailey is on line one. He says it's important and he wished me a Happy New Year!"

McCann got to his feet and walked into his office. He glanced at his watch. For Stu Bailey to be calling before 9:00 a.m. meant something unusual was happening.

He sat down and picked up his phone. "Did you make a resolution to start the day earlier?"

"Don't be so smart. I've got news that you are not going to believe," Bailey replied. His voice was calm which, in itself was a bit of a surprise. Normally Bailey was bursting with energy and excitement.

"Must be pretty dull. You don't sound excited," McCann replied, waiting.

"Mogollon is an acquisition target. Someone bought out all their debt," Bailey replied, his voice a monotone. McCann could tell that he was about to burst forth.

"Come on Stu! It's the first working day of the new year, not April Fool's day," McCann said irritably. It was just like Bailey to call him early and tease him on a day when the next step in Tachyons' eventual acquisition was to take place.

"I'm serious Wils! Mogollon is on the block!" Bailey almost shouted it into his ear. The excitement in his voice conveyed to McCann that this was, indeed, the truth."

"Talk to me," McCann said tersely.

"Okay. I got a call from a guy in the bank that holds a big piece of Mogollon's debt. He said that an outfit in Singapore was offering to pick up all of Mogollon's debt at his bank and several other financial institutions, including any interest payable. He said that, based on Mogollon's current debt load, the acquiring company will have virtually total control over the operation of the company. The shareholders will be so happy that they will be dancing in the streets."

"Have you talked to anyone else about this?" McCann asked, leaning forward in his chair.

"Two other bank reps. Both gave me the 'can't talk about it' response."

"I need to talk to Feldman. Call me if you find out anything more," McCann said, preparing to terminate the call.

"Wils…are the due diligence team from Mogollon there?"

McCann smiled. "No, they cancelled unexpectedly."

"I'd say that's about all the confirmation you need," Bailey said, as he hung up.

McCann immediately put in a call to Ed Feldman's cell phone. He knew the investment banker took the early morning train into the city from his home in Scarsdale. Feldman answered but the connection dropped before McCann could speak. He called again and Feldman didn't answer. He waited five minutes and called again. Feldman still did not answer.

He tried Cindy Melzy's number but went to voice mail. He knew Cindy took her son David to school and didn't take calls early in the morning. He called Donald Straylin but went to voice mail on his number as well. He left "Call me…it's urgent" messages with both and was just about to try Feldman again when Tammie appeared in his doorway. Her face was white and her eyes were wide.

"Wils! You need to go to the hospital now! There's been an accident!"

An EMT who was part of the team that arrived at the accident scene and worked on Linda, J.W. and Billy, was a friend of Jim Marks. As soon as they were done at the hospital, he called Jim and told him about the accident. Jim immediately called the members of the small church group that he, Lona and the McCanns were part of and, twenty minutes after McCann arrived at the hospital, Fred Penay, Phil Willard, Nick Hardesty and Jim walked into the Emergency Room.

THE INVESTMENT

McCann sat on the edge of his chair in the small waiting area. At the other side of the room a middle aged farmer and his wife sat together holding hands, their faces maps of agony. Jim Marks knew that they were Billy DeWalt's parents. Penay, Willard and Hardesty moved to chairs next to McCann. Marks stood beside his friends for a few moments and then turned and walked to where the couple sat.

"Hello Walter…Mary…have you heard anything yet?" he asked, taking a chair next to Mary DeWalt. She dabbed at her eyes and shook her head. Her husband leaned forward and stared at the floor as he spoke.

"Doctor said he would be out as soon as…as soon as they got everything sorted out and…" he choked back a sob and his wife reached for his hand.

"Let's pray together," Jim Marks said as he reached across to take their hands in his.

"Father, I ask that you will watch over Billy and Linda and J.W. and that you will give the doctors wisdom as they care for them. I ask that you take each one in your hands and bring them through this and back to those who love them."

"Amen," Mary DeWalt said quietly as she dabbed at her eyes with her free hand.

Walter DeWalt looked at Marks, the pain etched in his face. "We…Billy and I…we had words this morning before he left…over the girl he was with last night. I never meant…I'm so sorry…I…," his voice trailed off and he looked down again. Fresh tears ran down his wife's face.

Marks squeezed his hand hard. "God understands, Walter. Have faith."

After a few moments, he rose and walked to where the others sat. As he did so, a middle-aged Nurse appeared in the doorway to the Emergency room.

"Mr. & Mrs. DeWalt, please come with me," she said.

The couple rose as one and walked quickly to the doorway. "How is he? Is he going to be okay?" Mary DeWalt said as she stepped through the doorway.

As the door closed behind them, Marks heard the Nurse reply, "Come this way with me please."

"What do you mean you have other, more pressing things to attend to?" Ed Feldman barked into his cell phone as he exited Penn Station. "Is our deal on or isn't it?"

The man on the other end of the call was an attorney for Mogollon sitting in his office fourteen blocks away from where Feldman waited for the next cab to pull up. He tried to keep his voice level and controlled as he worked to placate the angry investment banker.

"Ed, we've got some things to attend to. We want to do the deal but right now we've got to get on top of these other matters. Once that is taken care of, we will get back to you and get things moving again."

"Just answer my question!" Feldman said loudly as his cab pulled up. Are you backing out of our deal? Because if you are, I am going to make you pay!"

"Calm down Ed. We will get back to you as soon as we get these things taken care of. I hope that I can have something concrete to say to you by this afternoon. Okay?"

"See that you do!" Feldman snarled as he snapped off his phone and entered the cab.

Twenty minutes later, he sat at his desk knowing that the call he had demanded would not be good news. Stu Bailey had called and relayed what he had heard. Feldman reached out to his contacts within the investment community and soon knew that Mogollon was indeed in play. The Singapore company had purchased all of Mogollon's outstanding debt plus accrued interest for a whopping two billion dollars. As Feldman searched the Internet for clues as to who was behind the company's bold move, his phone rang.

"There is a Carolyn Abbott on line one," his Administrative Assistant said. "She says she needs to talk to you about Mogollon. She refused to give me anything more."

Feldman quickly executed a search for Carolyn Abbott and, as his Assistant transferred the call, was rewarded with an informative reference.

"What can I do for you, Ms Abbott?" he asked in a very congenial voice.

"Don't worry about your Tachyons investment Mr. Feldman." A soft voice said into his ear. "If Mogollon doesn't buy it, we will. I'll be in touch again shortly."

"And who is this 'we' you are speaking of? Feldman asked.

His answer was a click as the line went dead.

"But, I'm the CEO!" Lister said petulantly into the smart phone he held tightly against his head as he was driven to his office.

"'Was' is the operative word Kent," Lewis Matsman said into Lister's ear.

"Who's going to run Mogollon? What about our deal to buy Tachyons? "Lister barked as his driver turned in to the Mogollon office complex.

"The Board will meet on a conference call in one hour and I'm advised that we will be told who the new investor wants to run the company. As far as I know, the Tachyons acquisition is still to go forward but is on a temporary hold right now," Matsman replied.

"But…I'm on the board!" Lister shouted as he walked past the security desk in the lobby. Three employees, as well as the young woman manning the security desk, turned to look at Lister as he stormed into the elevator and the door closed. The young security guard could tell that Lister wasn't happy. That was fine with her. He had hit on her twice in the last month and she was currently thinking of filing a harassment complaint with Mogollon's Human Resources department.

As the elevator rose to the top floor, Lister heard Matsman's response.

"Again, Kent, the operative word is 'was'. You were on the board until the investor required your termination as part of their debt purchase. I have to go now. I've asked Joyce to meet you in your office and handle your situation."

Joyce was Mogollon's Director of Human Resources. As she headed for Lister's office, she placed a call to the young woman manning the security desk in the lobby and asked her to call for a substitute to man the desk while she herself was needed in Mr. Lister's office .

By noon Phoenix time, Mogollon's board had met by video conference and agreed to appoint Carolyn Abbott as acting CEO. Ms. Abbott had video conferenced with the heads of Mogollon's corporate staff to inform them that they had ten days to submit a new operational plan that would focus on implementing a 20% reduction in General and Administrative costs, an increased attention to improving and expanding service to Mogollon's customers, and their recommendations on other actions that they felt would be critical to improving Mogollon's return on equity. She was asked what the status of the Tachyons acquisition was and responded that while temporarily on hold, the acquisition would ultimately be completed.

THE INVESTMENT

Tachyons would be operated as a separate entity until such time as the board determined that full consolidation would be appropriate.

Ms. Abbott then held a third video conference with selected financial media representatives and presented basically the same information in a form which lent itself to satisfying the media's demand to know what was going on. When a Detroit Free Press business writer, who knew Wilson McCann, asked if McCann might be part of a future management team at Mogollon, Ms. Abbot looked down at her notes, took a deliberate breath and replied, "Should Tachyons become part of the Mogollon operation, Mr. McCann's leadership of the Tachyons operation would no longer be required." A few minutes after the video conference ended, the Free Press business writer was on the phone to Janice DeGroot in the Bay City suburb of Essexville, Michigan. Janice was an award winning free-lance reporter who had followed Wilson McCann for five years. If anyone could get a story on Tachyons, Mogollon and Wilson McCann, Janice could.

(13)

McCann, followed by his four friends, squeezed into Dr. Jonathan Sager's office at the hospital. Sager's Nurse had beckoned to McCann shortly after 10:00 a.m. He, in turn, had asked Marks, Hardesty, Penay and Willard to come with him. Sager was still wearing his scrubs. He stood in the corner facing the five men who ringed his desk. He looked questioningly at McCann.

McCann, sensing the protocol behind Sager's questioning look, quickly spoke.

"It's okay Jon, whatever you have to say, you can say it to all of us."

Sager took a deep breath and looked out the window of his small office before speaking.

"The news is good and not so good," he began. "Linda sustained significant shock to the lower abdomen. From the looks of things, she must have slammed against the steering column. There was significant hemorrhaging. We had to go in and do some lower abdominal repair work. We did a D&C. I'm guessing you knew she was pregnant?"

McCann absorbed the import of what the doctor had already said and what he knew was coming.

"Yes, she was on her way to Caro to see her OBGYN to verify what we believed."

Marks, Penay and Willard exchanged pained looks and Fred

Penay placed his hand on McCann's shoulder. Nick Hardesty turned his face to the wall and leaned his forehead against it. His lips moved silently as he prayed.

"There is some bruising to the ovaries…it's too early to tell, but there may be some permanent damage. Her ability to conceive may be impacted. She has a few minor cuts and bruises to head and thighs but other than that, she will be fine. She should be out of ICU by tonight."

McCann looked down and took a breath. He sensed that the bad news was yet to come. Sager cleared his throat and spoke again.

"J.W. was on the passenger side and took the full force of the impact by the other vehicle. He sustained significant head trauma and upper body trauma. He has a dislocated shoulder and two cracked ribs. We have addressed both but the real issue is the head trauma. We've made an incision in the skull to relieve the pressure on the brain. We have placed him in a medically induced coma. I expect he will be in that state for up to two weeks…"

McCann's sharp intake of breath was coupled with Phil Willard's audible "Dear Lord!" Hardesty, who had turned back to face the doctor said, "Two Weeks?"

"…at this time, I really expect him to recover fully. But, we felt we needed to assure that there was no swelling of the brain. We will keep him in ICU until he comes out of the coma. As of now, our target date for that would be no earlier than 10 days from now."

A short time later, the five of them had moved to a small waiting room near the ICU. One of the Nurses asked if they would like to go to the cafeteria and assured them that she would come and get them if anything changed. No one was hungry but they walked to the cafeteria to get some coffee. As they came down the hall, they passed the room where Billy DeWalt lay in a bed, his father and mother on either side. Billy's right leg was in a cast and his left arm was in a sling. A bandage covered half of his forehead. McCann paused and went inside.

"How are you Billy?" He said quietly. Walter and Mary DeWalt looked at him apprehensively.

"He has a high ankle sprain and he dislocated his shoulder," Mary DeWalt said, her eyes fixed on McCann. "They say he can go home this afternoon."

Billy's expression was one of absolute despair. He looked down at the walking boot on his leg as tears rolled down his cheeks.

"I'm so…so sorry, Mr. McCann…it was an accident. I'm sorry…"

McCann stepped to the side of the bed and laid his hand on Billy's shoulder.

"I know son, I forgive you," he said.

"Thank you," the boy said, wiping away the tears and grasping McCann's hand.

In the hallway outside the door, Nick Hardesty turned away. "I couldn't have done that," he said quietly.

At 2:00 p.m. Tammie came in and, after getting an update on the situation, quietly asked to speak to McCann alone. The other four men respectfully withdrew and she sat down beside him and told him what had happened and what Carolyn Abbott had been quoted as saying. McCann absorbed it and thanked her for coming. He called Kathy Garrety on his cell phone and told her that she was now in charge of Tachyons' operations until further notice. Tammie sat beside him, quietly praying until Jim Marks poked his head back into the room. They both rose and she impulsively embraced her boss.

"I'm praying that God will watch over Linda and J.W. and that he will give you the strength you need to get through this," she said, releasing him.

Tears came trickled down the side of McCann's face. "Thanks Tammie," he said quietly as she turned to leave.

(14)

Farnsworth's leading employer was a manufacturer of ignition and fuel management components for outdoor power equipment, marine & recreational applications. The second shift security guard, a man named Kalechov, entered the office of the firm's Human Resource Supervisor thirty minutes before his 3:00 p.m. to 11:00 p.m. shift was to start, trying his best to look respectful.

"I appreciate your taking the time to talk to me," he said, standing before her desk.

"How can I help you?" she smiled at him. She was busy and didn't offer him a chair.

"I have good news! I have a chance to go to the Bahamas!" His excitement bubbled over and she put down the paper she had been reviewing to give him her full attention.

"That's nice Demitri, when are you going?" she asked.

"That is the problem. I have to go next week for two weeks," he began, and, seeing her frown start to form, hastily continued, "But, I have a replacement lined up...if you approve, of course."

"You know we have our own procedures for maintaining security. I'm not sure we can make arrangements on this short notice..."she began.

"But I have the information right here...please...look!" he extended two folded sheets of paper which she reluctantly took, unfolded, and looked at.

"This is a firm in Chicago. We haven't done business with them before…I can't," she said, handing them back.

"But I talked to one of their people and he will come…look at this…please," he replied, handing her another sheet of paper.

It was the resume of a man named Leonard Clement. She scanned it quickly and was impressed with the background and experience of the fair haired man whose picture was at the top. Ten years of security experience, all in manufacturing plants and references to a clean record were prominent.

"I took the liberty of calling them. Leonard is available and will come on short notice. His rate is less than what you are paying me. He is between jobs and will take the two weeks with no problems."

It came out in a rush and she saw the pleading in his eyes. Clearly the anticipation of a two week sojourn in the Bahamas, away from Michigan's winter, had emboldened this normally quiet man.

She sighed and leaned back in her chair. "All right, Demitri, I'll call them. If he is as good as you think he is, and he can come on short notice, we'll take him."

"Thank you! Thank you! I appreciate this very much!" he reached across the desk to grasp her hand and shook it vigorously.

"I'll let you know by 5:00 p.m. tonight if it is a go," she said extracting her hand from his.

"Thank you!" he said again, backing toward the door.

Once he had left, she called her assistant and asked her to call the firm and check out Clement. She looked out the window at the gray cold day and wished she was headed to the Bahamas the next day.

Demitri Kalechov, for his part, smiled to himself as he headed out the door. It would be nice to spend two weeks on the beach in the Bahamas but even more satisfying was the knowledge that $10,000 had been deposited in a Chicago bank account for him by the man named Leonard Clement. He had never met Clement and suspected that wasn't his real name. Their only linkage was when Clement had said, "Tazlov suggested I call you." Kalechov had been a military policeman assigned to a Russian army unit in Afghanistan.

Liam Colter, alias Leonard Clement, arrived in Farnsworth the following Saturday. He moved into a room over a dry cleaning shop just off Main Street. Suggested by Kalechov, It had a hot plate, coffee maker and small refrigerator. The bath was down the hall and shared with another rented room. That room was empty at the time so Colter had the entire second floor to himself.

Colter's papers, identifying him as Leonard Clement, included a biographical sketch that listed over ten years of security guard experience at three different Chicago firms. Calls to the three firms by the Farnsworth company's Human Resources Department resulted in glowing references as to Clement's attendance, work ethics and experience. They were all answered by the same person in Chicago, an employee of Tazlov, skilled in disguising her voice and accent. Her name was Anya and she had, in 1983, been a Russian Nurse who treated the wounded Peter Zastrow near the Afghan city of Khost. Zastrow was brought in by two of his soldiers, a man named Victor Tazlov and another named Demitri Kalechov.

As darkness spread across the Valley of The Sun, Kent Lister sat in the bar of his country club and watched a business report on Fox 10 News. He took some satisfaction in Abbot's comments relative to McCann. He had received at least ten phone calls from reporters and, in keeping with the severance agreement he had signed earlier in the day, gave no comment.

He was still seething at the way the female security guard had escorted him from the building with a big smile on her face.

At his home in the Scottsdale suburbs, his wife, Monica, looked out at the two television vans parked out in the street and listened to the same TV report. She didn't know why her husband hadn't come home yet, but she was pretty sure that there wouldn't be a condo in Telluride and an apartment in the Big Apple in her future.

Janice DeGroot faced a dilemma. She had been enjoying her second cup of coffee in her Essexville home. She was planning her week when the telephone rang. A source in the Tuscola County Sheriff's office told her about the accident involving Wilson McCann's wife and son. She had called McCann's office and was told that there was no word yet on their condition. As she hung up, another source in New York City called her and told her that Mogollon, which intended to acquire McCann's company, had, itself, been basically acquired through a massive debt purchase by an unknown company operating out of Singapore.

A few minutes later, a *Detroit Free Press* business writer called and told her that Carolyn Abbott, the new acting CEO of Mogollon, had said McCann would be ousted if Mogollon went forward with the Tachyons acquisition. The reporter gave her Carolyn Abbott's resume particulars which indicated that she was a senior executive in the firm of H Forester and Associates, a well known investment banking firm in Chicago. Little was known about their activities but a common thread was that Carolyn Abbott had, on numerous occasions, taken over the management of acquired properties. She had meticulously pruned them and/or refocused them to the point where they were headed toward increased productivity and profitability before turning over the reins to a new CEO. Ms. Abbott had been referred to as a "Wunderkind" by several in the media. Ms.

Abbott's affirmation that Wilson McCann would not be part of the ongoing management of Tachyons if Mogollon went forward with the Tachyons acquisition, would be front page in the business section of Janice's paper, *The Bay City Times*.

"What more can happen to that man?" Janice thought to herself as she packed her laptop into its carrying case and prepared to leave for Farnsworth.

By evening, Janice had gathered as much information as was possible, given that Wilson McCann was still at the hospital and his friends and business associates were surrounding him with an impenetrable wall of support. Kathy Garrety was in charge at Tachyons on a temporary basis and had no statement for the media on the day's events. Billy DeWalt would be charged with failure to stop and excessive speed. Farnsworth Hospital would not discuss medical conditions beyond acknowledging that Mrs. Linda McCann and Mr. J. W. Storey were patients. One of Janice's Farnsworth High School classmates, Joyce Hall, now ran a hair salon in Farnsworth. She told Janice that people in town were saying that Linda's condition was not critical and that J.W. Storey's condition was critical. Carolyn Abbott was not available for comment on the Mogollon situation. Kent Lister, former CEO of Mogollon was in seclusion at his Scottsdale home. Calls to H Forester and Associates were courteously responded to with promises of additional information from personnel close to the situation "at the appropriate time."

To say that Janice DeGroot was frustrated would have been an understatement.

Joyce Hall also told Janice that a technology magazine had been in Farnsworth doing interviews for an article on McCann about 2 months ago. A call to *TechExec* magazine was routed to a man who acknowledged that a team had, in fact, been in Farnsworth to do a story on McCann but he could not say when it would be published. He flatly refused to give Janice the names of the reporters.

Janice already had their names and an Internet search produced no information on a man named Charlie Dumas. Shelly Martinez was listed as a free-lance photo journalist. A call to the cell phone number listed for Shelly went to a recording that the number had been disconnected. A return call to the magazine specifically asking for Charlie Dumas was routed to the same man who again refused to give Janice Mr. Dumas' contact information. When Janice asked if Charlie Dumas was employed at the magazine or if he, in fact, even existed, a friendly "no comment" was followed by the call being disconnected. Janice called a man at another technology magazine that covered the telecommunications industry. He said that he had never heard of Charlie Dumas.

Janice's frustration turned to excitement. She was determined to find out who Charlie Dumas was. She also would work to find out what or who at H Forester and Associates' was involved in the acquisition of Mogollon's debt and, ultimately Tachyons. One of Janice's Editors had called her a "persistent peckerwood" and she intended to live up to the description.

"Not hungry?" the Nurse asked, as she moved the tray aside.

"No," Linda replied quietly, looking out through the window of her room to the darkness.

"The pills will do that to you," the Nurse said, as she took Linda's blood pressure and made a note on her chart. "I'll bring your pain meds in about an hour. In the meantime, try to drink some water. It will help. Is there anything else I can do?"

"No," Linda replied. There was nothing anyone could do now. She closed her eyes and heard the Nurse's footsteps as she left the room.

THE INVESTMENT

She lay there thinking. Her mind traveled back over her life. Her childhood in Estes Park, her estrangement from her family when she chose to go to college far away from Colorado and began her career, her ten year live-in relationship with Matt Walters, a professional football player.

"That was a ten year waste of time," she thought to herself as she lay there.

Matt had broken off the relationship to move from their condo in St. Louis to go to Houston and play for the Texans. She had wanted children and a traditional home and family. Matt wanted to play football.

She had worked for MTD for six years. The first four had built her reputation as an expert in applying the latest information technology to business applications. It had included work she did for Eastern European Christian Ministries. That was when she first met Wilson McCann. Her success on that assignment had resulted in her being named Team Leader for MTD.

The break up with Matt came while she was working on a MTD contract with Tachyons. In the following days, three things happened that changed her life. She became a Christian, she reconciled with her family and she fell in love with the man of her dreams.

She reached for the clutch purse on the night stand beside the bed. She flipped it open and looked at her wedding picture. The two of them were framed against the floor to ceiling window of the Estes Park United Methodist Church. Rainbow Curve on the famous Trail Ridge Road in Rocky Mountain National Park could be seen in the background. Their smiles were radiant.

She and Wils wanted children. For two years, they had hoped and prayed and then it had seemed that their prayers had been answered.

This morning, those hopes and prayers had been denied.

"Why God?" she said to the empty room.

The darkness outside seemed to creep into the room as she

thought about the future. She had given up the opportunity for future promotion when she married Wilson McCann. She had done so happily and willingly. If she had remained single, she would probably be one of Mike Divell's Vice Presidents by now. She would have been able to choose between U.S. and International assignments. She could have traveled to exotic places as she rose in stature within the industry. She had given it all up in her desire for family.

"And you took it…you took it all!" she sobbed as her body shook and the darkness crept nearer.

(15)

The Wednesday after New Years was almost over when Shelly Martinez stopped waiting for J.W.'s call and made one of her own. J.W. had said he would be arriving in Chicago late on Monday afternoon and would call her to make arrangements for dinner on Tuesday. He hadn't called and Shelly had waited. Somehow, she sensed that something had happened to keep J.W. from calling. She could tell that one of the traits the young man shared with Wilson McCann was that of keeping one's word. He had promised to call and he would have called.

She called Tammie Ring. Before Shelly and the man masquerading as Charlie Dumas had left Farnsworth, they had spent one day "wrapping up" as Charlie put it. That included some talks with people on Main Street and a final goodbye at McCann's office. Tammie had taken her aside and shared her happiness in learning from Belle Warner about Shelly's new found faith. Shelly sensed that Tammie was a sister in Christ and they had promised each other to "keep in touch".

Now, as the afternoon shadows deepened into darkness, she sat in her apartment praying silently for J.W. Storey, for Linda and for Wilson McCann. She had resisted the impulse to call Belle. She also had resisted the impulse to pack her overnight bag and head for Farnsworth. What would she say if someone asked why she was there? Would people think it strange that an outsider had appeared at the bedside of a young man in a coma? Would the hospital even let her in if she went? All these questions ran through her mind as she sat there in the darkness.

Finally, she sat back and turned on the lamp beside her chair. As the light drove away the darkness from the room, she lifted her eyes to the ceiling and prayed one final prayer.

"Lord, please restore J.W. to full health and use this experience to lead him into a closer walk with You. Help him to turn his life completely over to You."

With that, she rose and went about preparing her evening meal. She would go to Farnsworth on the weekend and hope that, by then, God would open a way for her to see J.W.

McCann spent most of Tuesday at the hospital. He sat beside Linda's bed for an hour in the early morning and sat beside J.W.'s bed for another hour. The results were almost identical. While Linda was awake, she was not communicating beyond simple "yes" and "no" answers to the questions he asked. When he attempted to draw her out, she said she didn't wish to talk and remained silent despite his entreaties. When he offered to pray with her, she replied that she "didn't feel like praying".

After an hour, he went to J.W.'s room and sat beside his son, watching the respirator do its work and praying silently. He held J.W.'s hand and drew comfort from the warmth of his son's touch that he couldn't get from his wife.

He took a break about 11:00 a.m. and went to the small hospital cafeteria to get a cup of coffee. Dr. Jon Sager walked in as McCann sat at one of the small tables, looking out the window. Sager brought his coffee to the table and sat without being invited.

"We need to talk," he said, his tone businesslike.

McCann sensed that Linda, not J.W., was what was on the Doctor's mind.

"Shoot," he said, before drinking from his cup.

"Linda is doing well physically considering what happened. I'm not sure that she is responding well psychologically," Sager said.

"I know, she was very remote this morning," McCann replied, sensing that Sager had more to say.

"I think I should have a specialist talk with her," Sager said.

"A Psychologist?" McCann asked.

"Yes. I sense that she is not dealing well with the possibility that she may not be able to have children in the future. That, in turn, has manifested itself in a very depressed attitude. That would be normal under most circumstances but Linda has always impressed me as a very vibrant, optimistic person who deals with life in a very positive manner. Before she goes home, I would like to have a colleague of mine talk with her.

"I agree," McCann replied, "Thank you for your concern for us."

"I'll arrange it. Let's talk before she goes home," Sager said, getting to his feet and taking a last drink from his cup.

"When will that be?" McCann asked.

"Probably Saturday, depending on how things go," Sager said, as he turned away.

The Psychologist talked with Linda in her room the following day. Despite his carefully phrased thoughts, questions and advice, she remained coldly unresponsive. When McCann visited later in the day, she was openly hostile to any suggestion of further meetings with the doctor. She was also cold to any attempts on McCann's part to reassure her that a future pregnancy was still possible. She was equally cold to any attempt on his part to pray with her, read her Bible with her or talk about God or faith.

He spent the next two days alternately spending time with J.W.

and Linda and making trips into the office to meet with Kathy and others to assure that things there were not being impacted by his protracted absence.

Late on Friday afternoon, he met with Dr. Sager. The two men sat in Sager's small hospital office. Sager read the report filed by his colleague and put it back in the folder on his desk. He leaned back in his chair and eyed McCann.

"I'm very concerned," he said.

"I am as well," McCann replied.

"I really think she needs help to get past this. The pain medications I have given her do not help the situation, but there is more to it than that. She isn't just depressed. If she were, I would say that is normal and she will get through it. She seems to have given up hope. There is no reason for that on the pregnancy front…yet," Sager said. "But it is deeper than that."

"What do you recommend?" McCann asked

"I'm going to let her go home tomorrow. You should not push her to change her behavior beyond what might be considered reasonable. She is a relatively young woman. She is highly intelligent and is a high achiever. That type of personality may manifest itself in actions that may seem to you to be extreme. If they occur and you feel she is of no danger to herself, let them take their course. Quite frankly, she may vent her unhappiness on you. She may want to make you unhappy and do things or act in ways to achieve that. My best advice is to 'hang in there' and hope for the best."

McCann took it in and sat there, his face in his hands. "I love her very much. I don't want to lose her," he said quietly without looking up.

"You have a strong faith. Rely on that now," Sager said, using his best bedside tone.

"I'll try," McCann replied.

THE INVESTMENT

Linda came home from the hospital on Saturday. The day was cold and gray with a strong wind blowing out of the west as McCann walked from the parking lot to J.W.'s room. He sat with his son for a while praying and thinking. He advised the Nurse on duty that Shelly Martinez would be coming to see J.W. at some time that day or the next and that they were to treat her as family and allow her to be in the room with J.W. Shelly had called his office and spoken with Tammie, requesting permission to visit J.W.

He walked the short distance to Linda's room and he and Linda listened as the Nurse gave them both their instructions on post-hospital activity and a prescription for pain medication that Linda was to take over the next ten day period. He noted that his wife had not combed her hair or put on any make-up. She listened quietly to the Nurse and sat in the wheelchair provided when asked. The Nurse began wheeling her to the exit door and McCann hurried to the parking lot to get the car that Jim Marks had loaned to him to eliminate the need for Linda to ride home in McCann's pick-up.

He drove up to the exit door and put the car in park as the Nurse moved Linda, wrapped in a winter parka, to the car. Linda's expression was unreadable. McCann got out to help her into the car but she opened the door and lowered herself into the front seat with a quiet "I can do it."

The Nurse smiled and said "Take care now," as she shut the door. Linda didn't look at her. McCann got in and drove away. As they drove to their home, Linda looked out the window at the bleak landscape and seemed to shrivel into her coat. McCann's attempts at conversation were met with either one word answers or silence. They drove into the yard and McCann stopped at the entrance to the front door. Florie was outside, standing at the side of the barn.

Before McCann could open the door for her, Linda got out and walked slowly to the door and went inside. He drove the car to the garage apron and parked. When he went inside, Linda's coat was on one of the bar stools in the kitchen. He looked down the hallway. The door to the spare bedroom, which they had planned as the Nursery, was closed. He walked down the hall and rapped gently on the door.

"Everything all right?" he asked.

"I just want to be alone for a while," came the reply from the other side of the door.

He went back to the kitchen and put coffee and water into the old aluminum percolator. He sat it on the stove and turned up the heat. He walked to the patio door and looked out across the cold and dreary landscape. The wind was whipping the dusting of snow that had fallen earlier that morning into drifts along the fence line below the house. He lowered his head and began to pray.

Five minutes later, the steady thump of the old percolator and the smell of freshly brewing coffee filled the room. He poured a cup and took it to the door to the bedroom.

"I made some coffee. Want a cup?" he said against the door.

"Not now. Maybe later," came the dull reply from the other side of the door.

He returned to the kitchen and turned the heat down under the percolator. Linda liked her coffee black. He put creamer and sugar into the cup to fit his own taste and took a sip. The coffee warmed him but didn't erase worry from his mind. He went to the family room and lit the gas log in the fireplace. He sat near it, sipping his coffee and waiting.

After about ten minutes, the coffee was gone. He was just about to return to the kitchen for another cup when the sound of something breaking came from the bedroom. He put the cup down and walked quickly to the doorway.

THE INVESTMENT

"Linda! What's going on in there?" he said sharply.

"Go away!" Came the agitated reply.

"No! I'm coming in," he said, turning the door handle and swinging the door open.

Linda was sitting on the side of the bed, a piece of pink and blue blanket clutched in her hands. More pieces of the same material were scattered at her feet along with the remains of what had been a baby's rattle.

He took in the scene and a deep breath at the same time. He moved to the bed and sat beside her, putting his arm around her shoulders. She slid away from him on the bed and sat there, head down, clutching the blanket fragment.

"Honey, please…" McCann began, "It's going to be all right, just give it time…"

She turned to face him, her green eyes blazing. The look on her face was one he had never seen before. She gripped the torn piece of blanket in both hands and tore it two. As the fabric tore, McCann felt that the fabric of their relationship was also being torn.

"God will see us through this…" he began again.

"God?" she screamed at him. "God? What kind of a God would do this? Don't you understand? We can never have a child of our own! Your son is in a coma in the hospital! What if he never wakes up? I don't ever want to hear about God again!"

He bowed his head as her words rang off the walls and were replaced by silence and then the sound of her sobs. He prayed again for guidance but made no move to touch her. They sat there, inches apart on the bed but miles apart in their feelings. Finally, she wiped her eyes and turned to look at him.

"I want to go away." She said quietly.

"Why?" he looked at her as his heart sped up.

"I need to go away and figure out what to do next," she replied, looking out the window at the wind whipped snow.

"Shouldn't we figure that out together?" he asked quietly.

"Not right now. I need to go away and get my mind right," she replied, coldly.

She stood and retrieved a small waste basket from beside the doorway. Stooping, she began to pick up the pieces of blanket and the shattered rattle and put them in the basket. He watched her, wondering what to say next.

"Where will you go?" he said as she finished and put the basket back.

"Home. I want to go home to Colorado for a while. I just need to get away from Farnsworth and you and all of this…this…hurt," she said, struggling to get the right words.

"Are you sure that you are in shape to travel?" he asked, remembering Sager's caution.

"I'll be fine. I'll take my pain pills," she responded dully.

"I could come with you," he said, looking down.

"No," she said as she turned and walked out the doorway and down the hall.

The next day, she packed her bags, made reservations, and asked him to drive her to the airport. At the curb, she kissed him lightly on the cheek and walked inside the terminal leaving him standing beside the car in the lightly falling snow. He felt as though his world had come to an end and drove back to Farnsworth through the snow, praying for Linda and their future together. While it was Sunday, it was too late to go to church. He stopped at the hospital and sat beside J.W.'s bed in the ICU until darkness fell. The steady rise and fall of his son's chest gave him some degree of relief as he sat there. Finally, he rose, kissed J.W.'s forehead and headed home.

A blue Chevrolet Impala was parked in his driveway when he arrived. He parked and got out of the Ranger. As he did so, a dark haired woman, wearing a parka with the hood thrown back, got out of the Impala. She walked toward him and displayed a leather wallet which she flipped open to reveal a badge.

"Mr. McCann?" she asked in a businesslike tone.

"Yes, what can I do for you?" he said in a tired voice.

"I'm sorry to trouble you sir, but I need to talk to you. I'm Agent Courtney Roberts with the Federal Bureau of Investigation," she replied, her tone unchanged.

A slight breeze was coming out of the west, bringing a few flakes of snow with it. A cold chill gripped him as he looked at the young woman who stood before him in the blurred light from the yard light between the house and barn.

"Let's go inside then," McCann said resignedly, turning toward the house.

Once, inside, he led her to the family room. She removed her parka and sat on the sofa next to him.

She turned slightly to face him and reached into her parka's pocket to retrieve three photographs.

"Do you know this man?" she asked, handing him the first one.

"No. What's this about?" McCann said, looking at the picture of a narrow faced, white haired man.

She ignored his question and handed him the next picture.

"How about this one?"

McCann looked at the picture of a big man with distinctly Slavic features and blonde hair. The eyes in the picture were cold and threatening.

"No. I really would like to know what this is about," McCann replied irritably.

Once again she ignored him and handed over a third picture.

"I think you know this man. Is that correct?"

McCann immediately recognized Peter Zastrow as the man in the third picture.

"It's Peter Zastrow," he said, giving Agent Roberts a hard look.

"What is going on here? Zastrow is in prison…or was. Has he escaped or something?"

Courtney Roberts retrieved the pictures from him and looked at him. Her face was deadly serious.

"The first picture is a man named Liam Colter. He is ex IRA and rumored to have been involved in several unsolved murders. The second man is a Russian named Victor Tazlov. Tazlov is an associate of Peter Zastrow and a member of the Russian Mafia in this country. We think that he has employed Colter to kill someone on the orders of Peter Zastrow." She said it all in a business like tone, watching his reaction carefully.

Despite the warmth of the room, McCann felt a shiver run through him. He swallowed and spoke in a quiet, resigned voice.

"Who?"

"You," Courtney Roberts replied.

It was well into the evening by the time Agent Roberts left. She told McCann that the evidence that supported the FBI's suspicions was weak at best. She further told him that the FBI had set up a watch on Liam Colter and would be ready to act "when and if it becomes necessary".

She did not tell McCann that she had followed Liam Colter to Farnsworth and determined that he had taken up residence in the little community. She encouraged McCann to continue to go about his business and not to worry.

McCann stood in the doorway to his home and watched her drive away. He was tired and beaten down by the events of the last week.

"Don't worry! Ha!" He said to Tessa as they walked through

softly falling snow toward the barn. "My wife has left me, my son is in a coma, I'm about to lose my job and now there is an IRA hit man hired to kill me. What's to worry about?"

The little Sheltie tagged along behind him, wagging her tail. When they reached the barn, she came up to him and rubbed against his leg until he stooped to pet her. Then she turned and trotted to one of his old coats lying in a corner. She lay down on it and began to lick the snow from her paws.

McCann smiled for the first time that day. "You're not worried are you girl?" he said, moving toward the box stall where Linda's horse, Florie, stood.

He fed Florie and Tess and returned to the house. He put a packaged meat loaf dinner in the microwave and heated it. When he went to bed two hours later, most of the dinner was still sitting on the counter in the kitchen.

He lay there in the dark, unable to sleep. Where was God in all this? Once again he appeared to have lost the company he had put so much of himself into. His son was in a coma and no one knew if he would suffer permanent brain damage. He and his wife had lost their unborn child and there was no assurance that they would be able to have children again. Worst of all, she seemed to have lost the faith that they shared. Now, an old enemy from his past had resurfaced with an evil intent. He reached across the bed and touched the pillow that, until tonight, Linda had rested her head upon.

His thoughts ran back over the years that he had wasted without God in his life. He thought of Donna who had loved him enough to keep him at arm's length because of his lack of a saving faith. He thought of Sally McHugh who had loved him unconditionally even though he did not return those feelings. Sally had died holding his hand as, with her last breath, she told him how beautiful heaven was.

He searched in his mind for some reason for this situation. Had he done something wrong? Had he not loved God enough? Had he not loved others enough? Was God, somehow displeased with him?

"God, where are you?"

His shouted words disappeared into the darkness of the room. He switched on the light and reached for the old tattered Bible that had been his Aunt and Uncle's.

"Please, God, speak to me," he said, as he sat up and absently flipped the Bible open.

The Bible opened to the forty second Psalm. The words of the eleventh verse seemed to leap from the page.

Why are you in despair Oh my soul?

And why have you become disturbed within me?

Hope in God for I shall yet praise him,
the help of my countenance and my God.

He closed his eyes and a warm feeling came over him. He reverently closed the Bible and laid it on the night stand. He switched out the light and was soon fast asleep.

———«(●)»———

Shelly stepped quietly into the room. The Nurse at the nursing station had given her a careful examination and had even asked to see her driver's license but in the end, had nodded that it was all right for Shelly to walk down the hall and into J.W.'s room.

His head was swathed in bandages and he was on a respirator. An IV was hooked up to his right arm. A blood pressure monitor was connected to his left arm. His eyes were closed and the steady rise and fall of his chest kept an almost identical beat to the quiet beep of the monitor. She moved around to the side of the bed nearest the window where the light shone on his face. She sat in a chair and took his left hand in hers.

The Nurse had cautioned her that she should make no loud noises and that she would have to limit her stays to fifteen minutes.

Now that she was here, she wondered at the emotion that had made her want to come. She had only been with J.W. Storey on two occasions, once at the farm and once in San Jose. Yet she felt a strange attraction to him. He had been raised by adoptive parents. She had been raised by her aunt and uncle. He had not known his mother. Her memories of her mother and father were few and increasingly dim. He had found his biological father and she had found her spiritual father. They shared a respect and appreciation for the use of technology in business. Beyond that, there was only the spark of friendship that had marked the day at the farm and their dinner together in California.

She thought about her Grandmother and how she had often told Shelly that someday she would find her "hermano del alma", her "major amigo", her "soul mate". Was that what this trip was all about? And what about the fact that she hadn't been totally honest with J.W. about how she had come to be in Farnsworth in the first place? She had participated in a lie paid for by an unknown client of her boss. Shouldn't she confess that?

She sat there, holding J.W.'s hand and praying until she heard the Nurse at the door. Then, she rose and obediently left the room. Belle Warner had offered her the opportunity to stay with her for the evening. She would come back again tomorrow and sit with J.W. for two more fifteen minute periods. Then she would leave to catch her flight back to Chicago.

Each time her prayers were the same, "Lord help J.W. to find You and live for you."

On Sunday afternoon, she squeezed J.W.'s hand one last time

and rose to leave the room. As she did so, an attractive young woman about the same age walked briskly down the hall and paused as she came to J.W.'s room. Shelly took one look and knew instinctively who she was.

"You must be Traycee," Shelly said quietly.

"I don't believe we've met," Traycee Morgan replied, extending her hand.

Traycee Morgan had registered for a two day seminar in New York City aimed at helping Human Resource professionals understand the top ten health care employment issues and how to cope with them. The seminar began on Tuesday morning.

Traycee had maintained her relationship with Wilson and Linda McCann despite her break up with J.W. She called on Friday evening just to touch base and learned of the accident and J.W.'s condition. She immediately asked if she could come to Farnsworth on her way to New York and see J.W. McCann, as he had for Shelly, had arranged for Traycee to be passed through to visit J.W. He also explained to Traycee about Linda's mental state and discouraged her from trying to visit with them at the farm.

Traycee altered her flight plans and flew into O'Hare on Saturday, changed planes and flew to MBS International. She stayed overnight in Saginaw and drove to Farnsworth the next day. She had lunch in Caro and arrived at Farnsworth Hospital in the early afternoon on Sunday. She checked in at the Nurses' station and took no notice of the arched eyebrows of the same Nurse who had cleared Shelly's visits. She walked down the hall and paused at the doorway to J.W.'s room. An attractive dark haired Latino woman was just releasing J.W.'s hand and getting to her feet.

THE INVESTMENT

The two young women sat opposite each other in the hospital cafeteria. The contrast between them was dramatic. Traycee Morgan was five foot two with mid length curly dishwater blonde hair and green eyes. She had a nice figure and the sweater, skirt and low heeled shoes showed it off to good effect.

Shelly Martinez had dressed that morning in preparation for her trip back to Chicago. Her five foot seven inch frame was clad in a hooded sweatshirt, jeans and short western boots. Her long dark hair fell down around her face and over the hood on her back. She had a habit of brushing it back from her flashing dark eyes. She glanced nervously at her watch. She had about twenty minutes before she needed to be on the road if she wanted to catch her short flight from MBS back to Chicago.

"I only learned about the accident on Friday," Traycee said, taking a sip from the cup of coffee in front of her. Shelly's cup contained hot tea.

"They say it may be a week before they remove the medications and he starts to wake up," Shelly said. She had volunteered little when they met. Traycee had spent ten minutes in the room with J.W. while Shelley waited in a small alcove off the Nurses' station. When Traycee came out, they agreed to have a quick visit before Shelly had to leave. Now she was determined to let Traycee lead the discussion.

"So, tell me again how you come to know J.W.? Traycee asked.

Shelly told her about the project she and Charlie Dumas had worked on, without getting into the real motive behind it, and J.W.'s client referral in California which had led to dinner together.

"So, you haven't known him for very long?" Traycee said, quietly.

Shelly tensed at the question. She knew that Traycee had known J.W. for some time but sensed that there was no hidden meaning in the question.

"About three months. You?" she answered the question with one of her own although she already knew the answer.

"Almost three years. But you probably already know that," Traycee replied, looking down. Shelly sensed sadness behind the reply.

"Yes, J.W. told me that the two of you worked together and had dated for some time. He said you moved to Fresno to take a new job," Shelly said, wondering where this was going.

"I moved to Fresno to get away from J.W. before we did something I knew was wrong. The new job was a convenient reason."

Shelly was surprised at the statement and her face must have shown it. Traycee continued. "I loved J.W. …I still do…but he wanted us to live together without marriage and I couldn't do that…you see…"

"You're a Christian aren't you?" Shelly interjected, impulsively reaching across the table and laying her hand on Traycee's arm.

"Yes…" Traycee began.

"I am too! I found Christ the day before I met J.W." Shelly said, withdrawing her hand and smiling broadly.

In that moment, the atmosphere of the moment began to change as the two rivals for the affection of the man in a hospital bed began to converse as two young women of faith. There was still some hesitation and reservation in their manner with each other, like two contestants competing for the same prize, but the iciness of their initial meeting had melted.

The minutes went by quickly as they shared their faith experience and their individual reactions to J.W.'s refusal to make a faith based decision.

Finally, Shelly looked at her watch and knew she needed to go.

"I've told you that I love J.W. Do you?" Traycee asked as Shelly rose to leave.

"I'm still trying to figure out what my feelings are. I plan to come back up next weekend and spend some time with him. Perhaps he will be awake and able to talk. Do you plan to come back again?" Shelly replied, picking up her small travel bag.

"No, I have to get back to work when the seminar in New York is over. I'll be praying for you. Maybe you will be the one who can convince J.W. of his need to make a decision," Traycee replied, taking a last drink from her cup and getting to her feet. She came around the table to face Shelly.

"And if he did...what then?" Shelly asked.

Traycee smiled. "By then, maybe you will have figured out your feelings and J.W. might have to make another decision."

They smiled at each other and hugged, as contestants for the same prize often do, before Shelly turned and strode toward the door. Traycee watched her go. She had walked away from J.W. and now there was a real possibility, given God's will in the situation, that J.W. might walk away from her and into the arms of another.

(16)

The day after Linda left for Colorado dawned as another cold and gray day. McCann rose with the sun and fixed his breakfast. He determined to put the concern about Agent Roberts' visit out of his mind. She seemed quite competent and confident and he was willing to trust the FBI to be in control of the situation. He would not let this situation control his coming and going.

His breakfast over, he drove into Farnsworth and checked on J.W. He sat with his son for an hour and then went to the office to hold a short meeting with Kathy and the staff to assure that things were under as much control as possible, given the circumstances.

That finished, he drove home. It was 10:00 a.m. He considered going back to the hospital to sit with J.W. but decided to wait until the afternoon. He poured himself a second cup of coffee and stood in the alcove that overlooked the fields to the west. One of the trees in the ravine below the house was enveloped in some sort of vine. One of its main branches was dead, the life choked out of it by the vines. If he didn't cut it off, the entire tree would be dead by the end of summer. To McCann, the tree seemed to symbolize his situation. Linda and Tachyons were gone. J.W. was in a coma, and he felt like some part of him was being choked to death. Yet, even as the thought came into his mind, he sensed God's assurance that all would be well in the future. It was the same feeling he had when Ed

THE INVESTMENT

Feldman had announced that he was selling his interest in Tachyons and McCann had faced the eventual loss of his position. He had vowed to love God with all his heart and soul and mind and strength and he wasn't about to turn from that course now.

He returned to the living room and took the Harms Bible from a small table near his big recliner. He dropped into the chair and put his feet up. For the next thirty minutes he read and reflected on Paul's letter to the Philippians, chapter three. As he read the chapter, the seventh and eighth verses seemed especially meaningful:

*But whatever things were gain to me,
those things I have counted as loss for the sake of Christ.*

*More than that, I count all things to be loss in view of the surpassing value of knowing Christ Jesus my Lord, for whom I have suffered the loss of all things, and count them but rubbish in order
that I may gain Christ.*

Putting the Bible aside, he bowed his head and prayed. He prayed for J.W.'s recovery and for Linda. He prayed for the men and women who would be impacted by Mogollon's acquisition of Tachyons and he prayed for each of the members of his small bible study group and their individual prayer requests. Finished, he sat back and closed his eyes and waited. Once again he felt God's assurance that all would be well in time.

Tessa padded into the living room and looked up at him expectantly.

"Time to go out and get at it," he said as he rose from the chair. He stooped to scratch behind Tessa's ears. She pressed her head against his leg and wagged her tail in appreciation.

"Time to fix that tree," he said, pulling on a hooded sweatshirt and his insulated coveralls. He walked down to the barn and rolled back the doors to where the Farmall A was stored. Tessa, after checking out the barn, retreated to the porch on the house and lay down.

He took a length of chain and a double bitted axe from a wall bracket and carried them to the tractor. He backed the tractor out and drove through the frozen snow to the tree. For the next hour he cut away the vines and piled them away from the tree. He gathered some smaller brush from the ravine and threw it onto the pile and set fire to it all. The dry brush caught quickly and he was soon enveloped in the smoke. He moved away, but the wind abruptly changed and he was again in the cloud of smoke. He rubbed his eyes and retreated to the tractor. He checked the tree again and it seemed that the dead branch was fairly rotted where it joined the main trunk. He thought he could save himself some work with the axe by pulling the dead branch away from the tree with the tractor. He looped the chain over the limb and secured it to the A's drawbar and got on the tractor. He put it in gear and let out the clutch slowly to tighten the chain. Then he revved the motor and let the clutch out fully. The little Farmall surged forward and he heard the snap of the tree behind him. He was facing forward and didn't see the entire tree come down. It crashed into the tractor and the man on it and swept him off and down onto the snow. He felt the pain surge through him and then everything went black. The tractor stalled. The main branch of the tree had come to rest on it. If it hadn't, it would have come down on Wilson McCann where he lay unconscious in the snow.

Tessa heard the crash as she lay on the front porch. She rose and looked out over the ravine. She could smell the smoke and her keen eyes took in the downed tree and the tractor. She could see McCann lying in the snow. There were times when McCann would lie on the living room floor and she would come to receive his hugs and petting. She wondered if that was what he was doing now. She stretched and hopped down the porch steps and trotted out into the field.

As she came nearer to where he lay, the smoke became thicker.

THE INVESTMENT

There was something in the smoke she didn't like. She trotted away from it and around it. She came in towards McCann with the wind at her back, taking the smoke away. She put her muzzle down next to his face and smelled the blood that was oozing from his forehead. She licked his cheek and he moaned and tried to move. As he did so, he moaned loudly.

"Ooooooh God!"

Tessa backed away and waited. He was still.

She circled him, sniffing. The smell of the burning wood was in his clothes and on his face and hands. She didn't like the smell and she didn't like the blood. She turned away and trotted towards the house. She stopped, turned to look back, and waited. He didn't move. She turned and continued to the house. When she got there, she went up the steps and waited at the door. There was no sound from within. The woman hadn't been there this morning. It didn't seem to Tessa that she had returned.

The little Sheltie went back down the steps and looked out over the ravine. McCann hadn't moved. She turned and started for the road. She didn't follow the road very far. She didn't like the road with all the cars and trucks. She went into the brush as soon as she could and headed cross country toward the farm where she had lived before. She ran as fast as she could and didn't detour for the brush and the stream with its muddy bank. She plunged through them and up the hillside toward her objective. Thirty minutes later she came up the hill behind the barn and trotted into the farm yard. The cattle were grouped in the barnyard and there didn't seem to be anyone around. She checked the barn and stood at the back door to the house for a few minutes waiting. Then, she crossed the road, went through the swale and headed east towards the Marks farm.

Janice DeGroot had spent the last three days digging into the Mogollon debt purchase. The roots of both companies were easily traced and available to the public through various channels, even though Tachyons was privately held while Mogollon was publicly traded on the American Stock Exchange. The difficulty was in tracing the acquisition of Mogollon's debt. The existing debt had been taken over by a Singapore based shipping company. It was owned by a British Virgin Islands based trust which made it virtually impossible to determine who was behind the purchase of the debt.

The only individual that Janice could find in the myriad of filings by the two entities was a Frenchman by the name of Ryan Pelletier. However, when she began to gather information on Pelletier, she ran across a ten year old photo of him at a party in Chicago. One of the people in the photo was H Forester's wife, Arleta.

That wasn't the real find however. In the background of the photo was another man who, upon further research, was identified as Brendon Vaughn. Vaughn's name was listed as the registered agent in several multi-million dollar transactions involving the sale of materials to companies that had helped to build the Alaska pipeline. Further digging showed that Vaughn had worked as a manager for the pipeline and was now retired and living in Anchorage. Janice got a number for Vaughn and called him. Vaughn's housekeeper answered the phone and said that Mr. Vaughn was sleeping and could not be disturbed. When Janice asked for a more convenient time to call, the housekeeper said that Mr. Vaughn did not take calls from strangers and politely terminated the call.

Janice began to dig into the background of Brendon Vaughn. He was born in Chicago, Illinois and had graduated from high school there. Janice obtained and downloaded a copy of the class yearbook for Vaughn's graduating class and began to go through the list of his classmates. They numbered one hundred and twenty five and had produced two state senators, a respected physician, a judge and two catholic priests. Janice saved the yearbook and continued to dig.

The company that Brendon Vaughn had represented was a Delaware corporation named BJM Enterprises. The company had been dissolved in 1990 and its remaining assets distributed to another Virgin Islands trust. She put in an on-line request for copies of the incorporation and dissolution papers on BJM Enterprises and paid the appropriate fees. Her e-mail receipt stated that the requested information would be sent in photocopy format within the next two weeks. She turned to the second trust and tried to get more information on it to no avail.

She did not know it, but the yearbook file in her computer held the key to what she was looking for. She just hadn't looked in the right place.

Jim Marks was working at the vise in his tool shed when he sensed a presence behind him. He turned and saw Tessa standing there. He knew it was Tessa even though her coat was soaked and muddy and filled with burrs and stick tights. She wagged her tail tentatively and stepped back out into the drive.

"What is it Tess?" he said, putting down his hammer.

The dog came back to the doorway, then turned and trotted back out into the drive. She stopped and turned back toward him.

He walked toward her and she moved away. Finally, he dropped to his knees and waited. She came to him, hesitantly. She smelled of smoke and muddy fur. He reached out carefully and grasped her collar. He picked her up and carried her to his pickup. He put her in the passenger seat and drove out of the yard. Four minutes later, he pulled into McCann's yard. Five minutes later, the EMT's arrived in response to his 911 call.

McCann looked at the six men and women gathered around the conference table. He was so upset that he couldn't see straight. Their heads were bowed over the file folders in front of them.

He moved toward the door and turned to look back. "I was sent here to change things and I'm going to do it, with or without your help!" he said, turning to the door and wrenching it open. As he did so, pain flashed across his back.

"Emmppfff!"

"Take it easy Wils," the voice said.

It was one he seemed to remember but couldn't place. It wasn't one of the people at the table. He tried to open his eyes and the pain came again. This time it was accompanied by a dull throbbing in his head. The dream faded away.

Finally, he was able to open his eyes and fight off the pain to focus them. His face felt like it was on fire and he tried to raise his hand to touch it. The IV line stopped him halfway up and the voice came again.

"Take it easy, don't pull the IV out," Dr. Jonathan Sager said, as he gently restrained McCann's arm.

McCann's vision slowly cleared but the throbbing pain in his head and back continued. As he tried to sit up, a more intense pain, like a shot of electricity, flashed across his back.

"Oh! Man that hurts! What..? Where am I?" His words sounded hollow and far away.

"You're in the hospital. You pulled a tree over on yourself and messed up a couple of disks in your back. You've also got the beginnings of a bad case of poison ivy on your face," Sager responded, looking down at a clipboard a Nurse handed him. She stood to one side, ready to keep McCann from trying to make any sudden moves.

THE INVESTMENT

"What were you doing?" Sager asked.

The fog in his head was starting to clear but the pain wouldn't go away. He checked his other arm and, seeing no tubes hooked to it, slowly raised it to his forehead. He felt the padded bandage there.

"I was getting rid of some vines on a tree and taking down a rotten limb," he mumbled, closing his eyes in the hope that throbbing would stop. It didn't.

"The vines you were burning were poison ivy," Sager said in the tone of a teacher lecturing a dull student. "That's what killed the tree. The whole tree was rotten. You're lucky that the falling tree knocked you off the tractor and came to rest on it instead of you. Otherwise, I would be preparing a cause of death opinion. The oil from the Ivy vine floats in smoke. You probably stood in the smoke and got it all over your face. We need to get that cleared up so we can go to work on your back."

"What…what happened to my back?" McCann responded, opening his eyes again. The throbbing in his head was receding and he guessed that something in the IV had to do with that.

"Like I said, a couple of disks are damaged. Based on the MRI we did on you while you were out, we think one can be repaired. You'll need fusion surgery in your lower back for the other one," Sager said, his tone matter of fact.

"When?" McCann asked weakly, shutting his eyes.

"We'll get the rash under control today and the surgeon will be in tonight to talk to you," Sager replied, turning to go. The Nurse took one more look at her patient and, satisfied that he was drifting back to sleep, left as well.

As his consciousness faded away, a scripture, from a study of the book of Job that he and Linda had participated in, floated through his mind.

I know that Thou canst do all things
And that no purpose of Thine can be thwarted.

ROBERT W. ZINNECKER

The scripture was from the forty second chapter of the book where Job makes his final confession to God

(17)

The day dawned cool. It was another in a string of fairly mild days that had marked the winter to date. The waters of Lake Huron and Lake Michigan were unusually warm for this time of year. The weather forecast for the previous week had devoted a good bit of attention to the potential for a Nor'easter for New England and Upstate New York. However, as the week moved forward, the forecast changed to include the eastern half of Michigan including the thumb area. The expectation was for three to six inches of light snow. That forecast changed dramatically by the time McCann went out to take down the tree limb. Had he tuned in to WNEM-TV in Saginaw, he would have learned that the forecast was now a "storm watch" with the possibility of "significant accumulations of snow with high winds, falling temperatures and blowing and drifting snow."

As the EMT's took the unconscious McCann to the Farnsworth hospital, the forecast was upgraded yet again to a "winter storm warning". The bitterly cold swirling winds out of Canada had shifted further west and came roaring over the Great Lakes to slam into a mass of warm, humid air coming up the Mississippi River Valley. The result was a full scale blizzard, which roared into Farnsworth at 4:00 p.m.

Nick and Darcy Hardesty had been shopping in Bay City. They

returned to Farnsworth just as the storm hit. They picked up their son at Nick's parents and headed to the McCann farm. The last two miles to where the gravel road met the highway were a nightmare. Nick took one look at the rapidly drifting snow at the entrance to the road and turned around to go back to Farnsworth.

"We would never make it to the farm," he said to Darcy as he peered into the wind driven snow.

"What about the cattle?" she replied, leaning forward and trying to see the side of the highway.

"They'll group up in the lee side of the barn. Some of them will go inside the run pen. They'll be hungry but by tomorrow morning, I can get Jim to take me in across the fields on his tractor to feed them if the road isn't plowed."

It took them forty minutes to get back to Farnsworth and the warmth of Nick's parents' home. By that time, the gravel road to McCann's farm was drifted full.

As darkness fell, the winds tore the door off the small shed next to the granary as well as a section of the barn's roof. As the debris from the roof section flew, it encountered the electric line from the house to the barn and tore it loose. Sparks flew and some dropped into the dry hay in the hay mow beneath the exposed portion of the roof. The wind fanned the sparks and the hay caught. As the mow began to burn, sparks and clumps of burning hay were pulled up out of the barn and scattered across the farmstead. Most died out before they hit the ground but one large clump went through the open doorway of the shed and set it on fire. The fire spread to the Granary and more sparks and burning debris were swept up. Most fell on the metal roofed tool shed and slid down into the snow. But pieces of debris landed on the roof of the house and set it on fire.

Jim Marks had crossed the highway from his house to his barn to make sure that the barn doors were securely fastened. He was returning to the house through the driving snow when he saw the

THE INVESTMENT

glow of the burning buildings on the McCann farm against the western sky. He called 911 but it was too late. Even if the fire trucks could have made it up the badly drifted road, the fire had become a roaring monster. The cattle huddled in the run pen below the straw died in the blaze. Those outside ran into the field to get away from the smoke and flames. Only the big hip-roofed tool shed survived as the monster devoured the rest of Wilson McCann's farm buildings.

Because of the storm, the surgeon didn't make it to Farnsworth to talk with McCann about the options relative to his back. Dr. Sager and the staff debated how much to tell him when they learned of the fire. At 10:00 p.m., Sager made the decision to let it go until morning. Wilson McCann had enough on his plate right now. A medically assisted good night's sleep was more important in the Doctor's opinion.

He sat in his dimly lit hospital office thinking about the man lying in the ICU. There weren't many secrets in Farnsworth. The village gossips were quick to pick up on the comings and goings in the small community. He knew that McCann's wife had left for Colorado yesterday. Before he had released her from the hospital, he had advised her to seek some counseling. He could tell that the loss of the fetus and the possibility that she might not be able to conceive in the future had brought on depression that appeared to him to be serious. The fact that she had left McCann while J.W. was still in a coma did not bode well. He also knew that McCann was about to be removed as CEO of Tachyons. The impact of the sale of the company would be significant depending on how the acquisition moved forward. McCann could have been counted on to do all he could to mitigate the impacts. Now McCann had been seriously injured and to top it all, his farm had burned. Sager was not a practicing Christian. He attended church on the average about five times per year. He knew that McCann's faith was a model that most in the community respected. That faith was being severely tested. How much could one man, alone, be expected to bear?

He took his cell phone and a small piece of paper from the desktop and, referring to a number on the paper, made a call.

Earlier that same day, Ed Cantwell, the Chief Operating Officer of Fairfield Communications, opened the door to Cutter Aviation in Colorado Springs and stepped back to allow his boss to precede him inside. Bob Allison, CEO of Fairfield, was fifteen years younger than Cantwell. The two men were as different as their appearance. Cantwell was sixty three, a grizzled forty year veteran of the telecommunications industry. He had risen from the line crew of a small company in the State of Washington to become the number two man of one of the nation's best run telecommunications companies. He was a man of few words and strong action. His manner and appearance were in sharp contrast to the forty eight year old Allison who had come to Fairfield from an investment firm in New York City. Cantwell often wore flannel shirts and jeans to the office when he wasn't scheduled to have meetings with outsiders. Allison always wore a suit and tie. Cantwell's grey hair was a mop that often protruded around his ears. On the "flannel shirt and jeans" days, he didn't bother to shave. Allison shaved at least once a day and twice if he was scheduled to meet with shareholders, investors or potential business partners.

Even more remarkable was the difference in the two men's approach to "down time". On Sundays, Cantwell dressed in his best suit, white shirt and tie and took his wife of forty years to church and out to lunch at one of Colorado Springs' best restaurants. Allison, for all of his reputation as a highly ethical business leader, never went to church. On Sunday, he dressed in sandals, shorts and a tee shirt at home with his wife and two teen-aged children and enjoyed having pizza brought in from Pizza Hut.

Allison was the face of Fairfield and well respected. Cantwell was the muscle of Fairfield and was respected and feared.

"It's storming in the east and into the Midwest," Cantwell said, as Allison handed his carry-all to a Cutter representative who headed out to a waiting private jet.

"I know, but we should be on the edge of it," Allison replied.

"You don't need to go. Pick up the phone and make an offer," Cantwell said in his gravelly voice.

"I can't. The owners are friends of one of our board members. They want the 'personal touch'. I'll be back tomorrow…late."

Allison was flying into New York's Finger Lakes region to make an offer for a small family owned company that a member of his Board of Directors had introduced him to. While it was a small operation, the owners were well-regarded within the industry in the state. A successful acquisition might open the door to future possibilities in the Empire State.

"Lister's out at Mogollon," Cantwell said. He didn't have much respect for Mogollon's deposed CEO. Cantwell had always been glad that he worked with Allison. He had known for several years that being COO was the end of his climb up the corporate ladder. He didn't mind at all working with the man on the next rung above him. Allison 'smooched' the investors, governmental officials and shareholders and Cantwell did the gritty work of managing the operating side of the business. In Nebraska, for example, where Commissioners were elected, Allison had assured them that Fairfield's objective was to provide the best and most comprehensive service possible at the lowest possible cost. Behind the scenes, Cantwell told the commission staff that not another dime would be spent on facilities in the Cornhusker state unless a pending rate increase was approved. One month later, Fairfield was granted its rate increase and service improvement and expansion continued unabated.

"Yep, maybe Carolyn Abbott will turn it around. Their stock is up a tick already," Allison replied, watching through the window as the pilot did his pre-flight check.

"You hear what she said about McCann?" Cantwell asked.

"Yeah, too bad about Wils. I don't understand it. Carolyn is a better judge of talent than that," Allison replied, turning to watch a CNN weather report on a television hanging from a corner of the room. "I would have thought that she would have done her usual thing and cleaned out the dead wood and then completed the Tachyons acquisition, and put Wils in as the new CEO of the combined operation."

"You know her?" Cantwell asked, looking at him.

"Yeah, she works for a guy named H. Forester in Chicago. He runs an investment firm there. He's made a ton of money but no one can figure where his investment capital is coming from.

"Sort of like the Mogollon debt purchase," Cantwell observed, watching the same weather report.

"Who ever heard of a shipping company in Singapore buying the bad debt of a problematic telecom firm?" Allison said, starting to pull on his overcoat.

"Our stock is doing okay though," Cantwell observed, reaching to assist his boss.

"Yup, up ten points in the last month."

"Who's buying?" Cantwell asked.

"Can't really pin it down, it's coming from a lot of sources including a couple of big off shore trusts.

"Anything we should worry about? Cantwell asked, his senses perking up.

"Not yet. We'll keep an eye on it though. Don't want some behind the scenes investor forcing us to put someone on our board that we aren't comfortable with. I'll call McCann tomorrow if I get a minute, and ask him what his plans are."

"Think he would come with us?" Cantwell asked.

"I don't think so. When we talked two years ago, we pretty well understood that there wasn't room for two CEOs in Fairfield."

"He could replace me…in two years," Cantwell rasped.

"Too early for talk about that Ed…well, I've got to get going."

"Okay, I'm meeting with the Regional Managers tomorrow… give 'em their marching orders for 2011," Cantwell replied.

Allison clasped the shoulder of the shorter, older man. "Don't be too hard on them. They are doing a good job for us."

"They should. That's why they get the big bucks and the company car," Cantwell said more gruffly than he really felt. He was proud of the two men and one woman who ran the bulk of Fairfield's operation.

"See you day after tomorrow," Allison said, turning toward the door and the waiting jet.

"Right, have a good trip," Cantwell replied, turning toward the entry door.

Ten minutes later, Allison leaned back in his seat as the jet climbed into the sky. Thirty thousand feet below and already 100 miles to the west, Ed Cantwell was listening to John Denver on an I-Pad in his Land Rover as he drove down Academy on his way to Fairfield's headquarters.

Two and one half hours later, George Hildeburn leaned back into the passenger cabin from his pilot's seat and drawled, "Big storm north of here Mr. Allison, it might get a little rough ahead. I could set down in Jamestown but you would have a drive through snow to where you are going."

"Whatever you think best, George," Allison replied calmly. He had flown with George on many trips and had complete confidence in his pilot.

"I'll make a decision on Binghamton versus Jamestown in about thirty minutes. I'll try to get you into Binghamton if I can," Hildeburn said, turning back to his instrument panel.

George Hildeburn liked flying charter for the CEO of Fairfield. Bob Allison gave his pilot full control of his flights. He had never pressured George to try to do something against the pilot's better judgment, even when it meant that he might miss or be late for a scheduled meeting.

Thirty minutes later, George Hildeburn decided to try to get into Binghamton, New York, to place Allison within a half hour drive of his destination in New York's lower Finger Lakes region. Ten minutes after he made that decision, the jet's port engine quit. With the storm flinging it about the sky, it fell into the back side of the Bristol Hills and Fairfield Communications lost its CEO.

It was 8:00 p.m. in Estes Park, Colorado. Linda had been home less than forty eight hours and she was already beginning to question the wisdom of what she had done. Her sister Laura, and her mother Lucille, had been loving and considerate to her since she had driven in from the Denver airport the previous afternoon. Her father, Quentin, had done little to hide his disappointment in her choice to leave Farnsworth and come running home. A devout man, Quentin McReedy had also sensed that his youngest daughter's Christian faith had been badly damaged. When he attempted to talk with her about the accident and her relationship to God, she had rebuffed his attempt. He sat quietly in his easy chair, reading the *Denver Post* as a fire crackled in the fireplace. The warm fire did little to chase away the coolness between them. Laura and Lucille were at the lodge and wouldn't return until some late night arrivals were checked in and settled.

THE INVESTMENT

She tried to focus on the magazine in her lap to no avail. Regardless of how she felt about God and what He had allowed to happen to her and J.W., she was beginning to realize that she had made a mistake in leaving the man she loved so deeply and running back here to Colorado. She listlessly started turning the pages when "Hail to the Victors" sounded on her cell phone. Quentin had programmed it into the phone as a fun-loving way to needle McCann.

She picked it up and looked at the display. The calling number was a Farnsworth number that she didn't recognize. She accepted the call and said, "Hello".

"Linda?" A familiar voice spoke her name.

"Dr. Sager?"

"I'm sorry to have to bother you but I felt you should know that Wils has had an accident." Sager said in his professional voice.

"What...what happened? Is he alright?" she said, her voice rising. Quentin put down his paper and turned to look at her.

"He pulled a tree over on himself and did some damage to his back. He is going to need fusion surgery on his lower back. But something else has happened," Sager replied. Before he could say more, Linda interrupted.

"What?... what else? Is it J.W.?"

"No, J.W.'s situation has not changed. He is still in the coma. We are watching him carefully..."

"Then what?" She said, rising and pacing toward the window to look out at the mountains in the moonlight. Quentin rose as well and turned toward her.

"We've had a very bad storm here. During the storm, Wils' farm caught fire and most of the buildings burned. Some of the cattle died also. No one was injured but the storm prevented emergency crews from being able to get there in time," Sager said, his tone sympathetic. I have not told Wils yet. We have given him a strong pain medication and he is sleeping. I plan to tell him in the morning."

"Thank you Jon. I'll start back this evening," she said, turning toward the hallway leading to her bedroom. Quentin followed her, a puzzled look on his face.

"You'd best check first. I imagine air travel will be seriously disrupted due to the storm. You may not be able to get here very soon. Is there anything else I or any of our staff can do?" Sager asked.

"No, thank you so much," I appreciate the call," she replied, ending the call. As soon as she put the phone down, she wished that she had asked Sager to tell Wils when he awakened that she was coming home and that she loved him.

As she hurriedly packed her bags, she told Quentin what had happened. He agreed with her decision to leave and suggested that they pray together for Wils.

"You pray dad," she replied quietly, "I'm having trouble talking to a God who lets things like this happen."

Ten minutes later, she kissed her father goodbye and drove to Denver. On the way, she booked a flight to Minneapolis and a tentative next day flight to Michigan's MBS International airport.

(18)

Janice DeGroot was awakened from a sound sleep by the incessant ringing of the telephone. She rolled over onto her side and reached for the phone while glancing at the digital clock next to it. The time read 4:00 a.m.

"Hello," Janice said, still trying to come awake.

"It's me…Joyce. Did you hear what happened?" Joyce Hall's excited voice brought Janice more fully awake. She swung her legs over the edge of the bed and sat up.

"What?" she said, reaching for a pad on the night stand. Janice always kept a note pad at the ready. The pad fell to the floor and she had to reach for it. In doing so, she knocked the clock onto the floor as well. Joyce, meanwhile, continued to talk.

"Stop!" Janice practically shouted into the phone. Silence reigned on the other end of the connection. Janice retrieved her pad and the clock and turned on the light.

"I'm sorry, I dropped a couple of things and I was sound asleep. Please start from the beginning. What happened?"

Joyce began again, this time a little more quietly. "Wilson McCann pulled a tree over on himself yesterday morning. They found him in a field and he's in the hospital. I guess he hurt his back pretty bad. But, last night during the storm, his barn caught fire and burned. The fire department couldn't get to it because the road was blown full of snow. The barn and the house and most of the outbuildings all burned. The barn and the hay are still burning. Some of the cattle died in the fire."

Janice was scribbling rapidly. "What about the young couple that lived in the farm house?"

"The Hardestys…they were away and couldn't get home because of the snow."

"What about Linda? Is she okay?" Janice asked.

"She's in Colorado," Joyce replied.

"What? What's she doing in Colorado?"

"I don't know, she flew out a couple days ago," Joyce said.

Janice sat there on the edge of her bed taking it all in. For a man who was said to walk with God, Wilson McCann now appeared to be a man whom God had abandoned.

McCann awakened at 6:00 a.m. to pain unlike any he had ever experienced. The only way to ease it was to stretch full length and lie still. Any movement caused a lightning bolt of pain to lance across his body and down his left leg.

At 6:30 a.m., Jon Sager entered the room and told him what had happened at the farm. When the Nurse handed him a small cup with two pain pills in it, he laid it on the stand next to the bed and refused to take them. She left with a frown on her face.

The dark cloud of despair that had enveloped him the previous Sunday evening returned and he tried with all of his might to remember the words of the Psalm but he could not. It seemed that a great black wall had risen between him and God and he found that he could not bring himself to pray. It seemed to him that some dark presence sat lurking in the corner of the dimly lit room. He reached for the light cord above his bed and the pain raced through him again as he pulled it. Light flooded the room but the darkness of his soul refused to leave.

Farnsworth began to dig itself out before dawn. County Road Commission trucks cleared the main streets and town trucks began to clean the side streets. Business owners and operators were out early to shovel their walks and entrances. Three members of the Farnsworth Town Council met at the town diner, as they did on most mornings. The diner, formerly owned and operated by Sally McHugh now served a limited menu of assorted coffees, bagels, sandwiches and rolls.

George Whyte, the John Deere dealer, Joe Rambaugh, the Chrysler dealer and Earl Hardesty, Nick's father and operator of the Farnsworth Insurance Agency, were discussing the fire at the McCann farm. As he spread cream cheese on his Cinnamon Twist bagel, Liam Colter, alias Leonard Clement, listened to the three men's conversation at their nearby table.

"So, Nick and Darcy are okay?" Whyte asked Hardesty.

"Yes. They tried to get back to the farm last night before the fire started but the road was drifted full. They spent the night with us," Hardesty replied, the relief obvious in his tone.

"What about the repair shop?" Rambaugh asked.

"The big shed that houses the repair shop didn't burn. It and the old chicken coop on the north side of the farmstead were the only two buildings that didn't," Hardesty said, taking a drink from his cup.

"Did the kids lose much when the house burned?" Whyte asked.

"Most of their furniture is in storage. They were using McCann's furniture and fixtures in the house. They lost clothing and personal items. I'm thankful it wasn't worse," Hardesty said.

"McCann can't buy a break," Rambaugh said, around a mouthful of his bacon, egg and cheese bagel.

"Couldn't happen to a nicer guy," Whyte replied, sarcastically. The implement dealer, dressed in a 'Whyte Implement Co.' jacket, was a thin man with a narrow face and a hooked nose. His features, taken together with the wire rimmed glasses that he wore, gave him the appearance of an unhappy, cornered rat.

"I hear that good looking wife of his left him and went back home to mom and dad," Rambaugh said, washing down the food with a swig from his coffee cup. He was a big man with thinning hair and a ruddy face. His ample stomach bulged out over his belt as the buttons on his shirt strained to hold it together.

Hardesty, whose son had been a prodigal until he went to work for McCann five years ago, sat back quietly, listening. He was dressed in a light blue sweater vest over a button down white shirt. His gray hair and neatly trimmed mustache, coupled with an almost perpetual smile, made a good first impression on most people.

"He's in the hospital with back problems. He pulled a tree down on himself," Whyte said, spreading some jelly on his raison bagel.

"I hear he's out as CEO of the phone company if this rumored acquisition by Mogollon goes through," Rambaugh replied, taking another drink from his coffee and looking over at the young woman behind the counter. He was hoping she would volunteer to refresh his cup but knew she wouldn't. The urns were on the counter beside her. If he wanted a refill, he would have to get it himself.

"His son is still in the ICU in a coma from the accident a week ago," Whyte offered,

"So, 'Mr. Good Guy', who everybody says is 'God's man', has a boat load of problems. Why do you think that is?" Rambaugh asked.

"Bad things happen to good people, sometimes," Hardesty replied, quietly.

"Did he 'sin'?" Whyte asked, sarcastically, with a smirk.

"Maybe he was too puffed up about all the good he does around here," Rambaugh stated, wadding up the wrap from his sandwich.

"Maybe he sinned and didn't go to confession," Whyte replied in a joking tone.

"I like Wils McCann. He has done a lot for Nick and Darcy. I just think he is going through a tough time," Hardesty said in a sincere tone of voice.

"But if man makes God the center of his life and things like this happen to him, doesn't that mean that either he has abandoned God or God has abandoned him?" Whyte asked, giving Hardesty his full attention.

"Look, I go to church. I try to live an honest life. My son and his family are more into this "Born Again" thing than I am. I just know that Wils McCann has done a lot of good in this town since he came here five years ago. He's going through a tough time right now. I guess we will have to see how he and God handle it," Hardesty replied, looking out at a big County plow as it roared down the street.

"He's done a lot of good but he's benefitted from it too," Rambaugh said in a judgmental tone of voice.

"Both of you are still sore because he bought you out of the phone company. He paid you a price that was, in my opinion, more than your shares were worth at the time. George, he paid off all the debts his uncle had run up, including yours," Hardesty said, looking the equipment dealer in the eye.

"That's true," Whyte said, grudgingly. He looked at Rambaugh hoping for some support but the auto dealer got up and walked to the counter to refill his cup. When he returned, Hardesty continued to speak to both men.

"Wils invested in the company and in the town. You both sat on the Town Council five years ago when I was Chair. You both voted against the Dunt Center redevelopment project that, together with the expansion of Tachyons, has been a boon to the town. You can't deny that," Hardesty said, his voice rising. "If McCann was in it for himself, don't you think that the Warners wouldn't have been so supportive when they sold their company to Tachyons?"

Whyte and Rambaugh looked at one another and didn't say anything for a moment. They knew that Hardesty's statements were true. They also knew that Wilson McCann had taken Nick and Darcy Hardesty under his wing and provided the financial banking for Nick's auto repair shop and Darcy's management of the Barnes Loft.

Both Whyte and Rambaugh, as members of the Farnsworth Town Council had voted against the sale of the abandoned elementary school building to HHF, McCann's holding company, when they were members of the Town Council. Hardesty, Phil Willard and Fred Penay had voted in favor of the project which had brought development jobs to the community as the building was renovated and Tachyons expanded its employment.

"Well, we'll see what happens when Tachyons is sold. You just watch! I'm betting that everything you say we gained will be lost when Mogollon takes over and McCann joins the unemployed," Whyte grumbled.

"I still say that McCann has something in his past that God is punishing him for, or he has gotten too big for his britches and God is knocking him down a peg," Rambaugh muttered.

Liam Colter finished his bagel and Nursed his coffee until it was gone. The discussion of McCann interested him greatly. He couldn't explain exactly why. He had always followed a rule of not letting a target become more than just a job to do, a faceless person that needed to be dealt with. Perhaps it was this small town. Farnsworth reminded him of his boyhood in Kenmare, County Kerry.

The memory brought with it the mental image of his mother. The pain that came with that memory was a combination of shame and reverence. What was being said at the next table by Earl Hardesty reminded Colter of his mother's goodness to all, regardless of political or religious persuasion.

Colter rose from his table, zipped up his jacket, and walked out the door and into the street. As he walked back to his room, he thought about what he had heard. He thought about his own life and compared it with what he had heard about Wilson McCann in the diner. If McCann, who some regarded as "God's Man", was being punished for some sin in his past, what could he, Liam Colter, expect in the future?

As Colter walked up the street, he didn't notice a dark haired woman watching him from a blue Chevrolet Impala parked next to the snow covered curb a short distance from the diner's entrance.

Jim Marks called Phil Willard and the two had agreed that, knowing McCann as they did, he was not going to stay in the hospital that day.

The day had dawned to the usual aftermath of a major winter storm. Schools were closed. People who could get out were leaving early for work. Those who commuted from the smaller towns into the cities called in and told their supervisors they would not be coming to work that day.

Marks went to McCann's home and got the key to the front door from its hiding place under a rock behind the garage. He went inside and made sure that everything inside was okay. He had left Tessa in McCann's barn the previous night with plenty of food and water. Based on the situation at the farm, he could only assume that the little Sheltie had perished in the fire. He mentally kicked himself for not having taken Tessa home to his own farm. She could have played with the children and still be alive today. It seemed to Jim Marks that this was just one more blow that McCann would be required to take.

He found a parka, jeans, flannel shirt, boots, socks and underwear and a pair of insulated gloves and stuffed it all into a small suitcase. Locking the door behind him, he put the suitcase in his car and went down to take care of Florie. He made sure she had plenty of water and feed and could enter and leave her stall through the rear barn door. Then, he got in his car and drove into Farnsworth. He picked Willard up at his home and the two men drove to the hospital.

They found a highly agitated McCann waiting. His face was streaked with red welts. He continually flexed his fists to keep from scratching at them. The steroid injection and the Benadryl he had been given made him groggy. When the Nurse told him, for about the third time that morning, that he needed to take the pain medicine that Sager had prescribed for his back pain, he had waved her away. She went to Sager and the doctor was wise enough to tell her not to push it. He said that he fully expected that Wilson McCann would be on his way to his farm within an hour and that she should let him go. She protested that it was "highly irregular" and returned to her station. She glared at Marks and Willard when they came down the hall on their way to McCann's bed in the ICU.

The pain in his back was such that he couldn't sit longer than a few minutes. They helped him dress in the clothes that Marks had brought. He put on the parka and gloves. He walked unsteadily down the hall between them and leaned against the wall at the entrance while Marks brought the car around. He lay back as much as he could in the rear seat and Willard joined Marks in the front seat. Halfway to the farm, they had to stop to let McCann walk around the car to relieve the pain in his back and his left leg. The road had been plowed in the night to allow the fire trucks to get access to the farm. As Marks turned into the road, they could see the black smoke rising from the farm.

The scene that greeted them was one of almost total devastation. What was left of the barn still burned as a contingent of fire fighters watched it closely. The barn walls were virtually gone and the hay and straw inside the barn's smoldering shell was what was still burning. The fire fighters had rightly concluded that what remained could not be salvaged and let it burn. The stench of burned flesh rode the smoke. While the dead animals on the lower level were not visible in the wreckage, the odor of their death was everywhere.

What had been the granary, well house and shed were now just piles of charred wood and metal. The east and north walls of the house stood like skeletons looking down on the smoldering embers below them. The south and west walls were totally gone.

Only the big hip-roofed tool shed and the old chicken house on the north edge of the farmstead had survived. The tool shed's aluminum roof was pockmarked with black blotches where burning hay, straw and wood had come down on it before sliding down the sloping sides to the snow where they died.

Below the barn, small groups of steers huddled together in the cold. McCann tried to count them but his vision was blurred by the medicines he had in him and by the tears that were smarting his eyes.

"I've called the auction barn and they are sending McIntyre with a truck to get them," Marks said quietly, sensing McCann's concern for the remaining animals.

"Thank you, there's no way for us to feed and water them?" McCann mumbled.

"I'm sorry, I can't take them. I'm not set up for cattle," Marks replied.

"I know," McCann replied, as he started walking toward the barn. A fireman turned as he approached and watched him warily.

"There's one more thing Wils," Marks said quietly, laying his hand on McCann's shoulder. "I put Tessa in the barn last night…I'm so sorry…"

McCann turned to face his friend. Tears formed in his eyes and slowly trickled down his ravaged cheeks. He bowed his head and staggered back a step before he responded. The fireman reached out to steady him but he recovered and looked down at the soot mottled snow.

"I know, Jim…you couldn't have known this would happen…no one could. I'll…I'll miss her…"

He turned and started again toward the barn. Marks watched as the wind caught another clump of smoking hay and carried it out into the barn yard. Anger at the situation flooded through him. Wilson McCann was a good man. He, above any man Jim Marks had ever known epitomized what it meant to be "God's man". Why had a loving God allowed all this to happen? It seemed to Marks, as he watched McCann half walk, half stagger, up the slight incline toward what had been the well house, that God had abandoned his friend.

"We're letting it burn out, Mr. McCann. Don't get too close," the fire fighter said, as he moved to intercept McCann.

McCann stopped and stood there amid the now cold ashes of the little well-house looking at what remained of the barn and its contents. His face burned even as the cold wind slapped it. His back ached with a pulsing deadly drumbeat that urged him to lie down in the snow and let the same God who had given him so much and then taken most of it away, take his life as well.

"Why have you forsaken me?" he said quietly as he bowed his head.

The fireman nervously cleared his throat and turned away. The fire continued to burn.

THE INVESTMENT

The same storm that resulted in the devastation at McCann's farm brought light rain during the night to Weaverville, North Carolina, home to Eastern European Christian Missions. The morning, however, dawned with brilliant sunshine. Its rays shone into EECM's conference room but could not dispel the feeling of gloom that held sway among the five people seated around the large conference table. Shirley Jacobs, EECM's Chairperson and CEO, sat at the head of the table. To her left, Donald Straylin, a member of the Executive Committee of the EECM Board and chair of EECM's Development Committee, looked over the papers in front of him. To her right, Charles Hastings, former pastor of the Farnsworth United Methodist Church, who now pastored a UMC church in Detroit, had his head bowed and eyes closed in prayer.

Further down the table sat "Lark" Bishop, a tall African American who served as EECM's general manager and "General Everything" as Shirley phrased it, and John Botek, a rumpled looking man of forty who was EECM's Administrative Manager. Botek, in his role as chief financial officer of the ministry, had delivered the factual information before them. Bishop had supplied the operational analysis and conclusions that went with it.

The financial reports Botek had presented showed clearly that the ministry was suffering a significant downturn in financial support. Bishop's interpretation had included the primary themes that the nation's economy, the competition for the donor dollar brought on by an increasing number of non-profit organizations, and an attitudinal change among younger Christians towards giving to overseas ministries, while so many needs went unmet in the U.S., were the primary drivers behind what the numbers showed.

"I support Lark's opinion," Straylin said, as he shuffled the papers in front of him into a neat pile and rested his folded hands on it.

"There is a real change in attitudes about traditional faith including church attendance, evangelistic methods, liturgy and music,"

Hastings added. "Many people still call themselves Christian but they express their faith in many different ways. They are moving away from traditional institutions."

"So, what is it that you think we should do?" Shirley asked. At five foot two inches, she had her chair elevated as high as it would go. Her short steel gray hair framed a face that, despite her years, was wrinkle and blemish free. She had taken over the CEO and Board Chair responsibilities five years ago upon the death of her husband James. Together, they had founded EECM.

"We need to re-focus the ministry," Lark Bishop said quietly.

"To do what?" she asked without the trace of a smile. Her eyes, however, gave her away.

She loved Lark Bishop like the son she had not been blessed with.

"The needs here in the U.S. as well as those in Eastern Europe. The homeless, those coming out of the prison system, those without jobs, the kids without fathers and mothers, the young people who aren't getting a proper education, I could go on and on," Bishop replied, his voice rising as he ticked off the needs.

"Aren't there already a lot of organizations going after money to serve those same groups?" Shirley asked, knowing the answer.

"Many not in the name of Jesus and many not with the 'hands on' approach that has worked so well for us in Eastern Europe," Hastings interjected.

"And, if we don't?" Shirley said quietly.

"We will need to close our doors and bring our people home within a year and a half," Straylin said.

"I wish Wils were here. I would like to get his opinion," Shirley said, looking out the window at the sunlit sky. McCann's office had called the previous afternoon and informed her that he was in the hospital and would not be attending the Executive Committee meeting. The group had prayed for him, Linda, and J.W., to open the meeting.

"He's got enough on his plate right now with what happened to Linda and J.W., as well as the fact that he probably will be out as CEO of Tachyons in a couple of months," Straylin replied.

"We would need to amend our 501-c-3 if we change our focus wouldn't we?" Shirley asked, indicating the tax exemption granted to EECM by the Internal Revenue Service.

"Yes," Botek replied from his seat at the end of the table.

"We would need to revise our Vision and Mission Statements, our By-Laws, our operational plans…" Shirley began. She stopped and looked again at the puffy clouds that were floating across the sky outside the window. The enormity of it all caused her to take a deep breath before continuing.

"…but I would like to see a plan. Don, will you work with Lark and John to give the Board a proposal at our next meeting? Charles, will you and your church be in prayer for us and would you join Don in talking to Wils to get his perspective?"

"Will do," Straylin replied smiling for the first time that day. He admired Shirley Jacobs as much as any leader he had ever met. She had stepped into the shoes of her more famous husband and hadn't missed a beat as she rallied the organization through the last five years. Men and women, boys and girls in Eastern Europe had found a new life in Christ through EECM's work. He felt that God had a purpose for this ministry. He was looking forward to see where He would take it next.

"Let's pray," Shirley said, bowing her head.

(19)

The closest that Linda could get to Farnsworth by plane was Grand Rapids. The storm's outer edges had reached as far west as Lansing and Midland. She slept fitfully on the flight from Denver to Minneapolis, dozed a few minutes at the Minneapolis/St. Paul airport and again on the flight to Grand Rapids. Now, in a rented SUV, she was driving as fast as the road conditions permitted, to Farnsworth.

The road conditions worsened as she neared Saginaw and it took her an hour to get from Saginaw to Caro. By the time she reached the farm, it was mid-morning. The same scene that had greeted McCann, Marks and Willard, confronted her as she turned in the drive and stopped. She took it all in before she opened the door and got out. McCann stood about fifty yards from the still burning barn. He was bundled in a winter Parka and stood against the wind, his head bowed. Even in the heavy winter coat, he seemed small and frail against the backdrop of the blackened shell of the big barn. She walked through the blackened snow toward where he stood.

She stopped a few feet behind him. The stench of burned flesh mingled with the smell of the burning hay and the barn that had held it. She fought down the urge to retch. Jim Marks and Phil Willard eyed her from the recently plowed turn around in the farm yard but made no move to approach her.

She stepped forward, put her hand lightly on McCann's shoulder, and spoke.

"I'm so sorry," she said softly.

He turned and she was shocked to see his ravaged face. His eyes were dull and red. As he turned toward her he groaned audibly and rubbed one hand across his lower back. She saw the pain etched on his face.

She came to him and took him in her arms and buried her face against his chest. He put his arms around her and heaved a great sigh.

"Careful, I have poison ivy," he said against her hair.

"I don't care…I love you…I'm so sorry…" she squeezed herself closer to him and he groaned.

"My back…it is killing me!" he said, not letting her go.

She stepped back and looked up at him. The pain that she saw in his blotched face was almost more than she could bear. Marks and Willard had approached and were standing a few feet away.

"Let's go home. You need to lie down," she said, taking his arm and leading him toward the SUV.

"I…I'm glad…you came back…" he said, slurring his words as a sob escaped.

"And I'm not leaving again…ever," she said, as she opened the back door to the SUV.

She talked briefly with Marks and Willard and told them to do whatever was necessary. Marks told her that Nick and Darcey were staying with Nick's parents for the time being. The two men would see to the remaining cattle and one of them would remain at the farm until the fire burned itself out. Marks told her that Tessa had been in the barn.

She drove slowly home and helped McCann get inside and onto the couch. She went outside to check on Florie and when she returned, he was sound asleep.

She retrieved the farm's insurance policy from a file in their home office and called the insurance company. She told the representative who she was and gave her the policy number. She related what had happened and listened as the representative keyed in the policy number.

"I'm sorry Mrs. McCann, that policy was cancelled over a month ago for lack of premium payment. We sent your representative several notices and didn't receive a reply. We assumed you had obtained coverage elsewhere. I'm sorry for your loss but there is nothing we can do," the sincerity in the woman's voice did nothing to relieve Linda's shock.

"You might want to call your representative in Chicago," the woman said.

"Yes, I will do that," Linda replied. "Thank you."

She replaced the phone and sat there looking at the now cancelled policy. She raised her eyes to the window and looked outside. Over the ridge line to the east she could see the smoke still rising from the burning barn outlined against the sky.

Charles Hastings and Don Straylin drove to Charlotte from Weaverville and Straylin dropped Hastings off at the airport before heading to his own home. The two men agreed that Hastings would call Wilson McCann that evening and see when McCann would feel up to a conference call to talk about the EECM planning project.

Hastings' flight into Detroit was uneventful and he arrived home a little after 6:30 p.m. His wife Dorothy had dinner on as he came in the door. They prayed and ate before he went to his study to make the call to McCann at the hospital.

When he called, however, he was told that McCann was no

longer a patient, having discharged himself that morning. He called McCann's home and Linda answered. Hastings was surprised to hear her voice. He had spoken to McCann two days ago when Linda had left for Colorado. His friend was greatly distressed with his wife's behavior but seemed to be bearing up as well as could be expected. The news of McCann's accident had been relayed by Shirley prior to the Executive Committee meeting and Hastings had tried to reach McCann but was told that he was sleeping. The fact that McCann had checked himself out of the hospital indicated to Hastings that the accident was perhaps not as bad as originally reported.

"Hi Linda, its Charles," he said into the phone.

"Hello Charles," Linda's voice was cool and restrained.

"I hear that Wils is home. That's good news! I'm assuming things aren't as bad as originally thought?" he tried to keep his tone light.

"No…they are worse," she replied dully.

Hastings immediately went into Pastor Mode. He could sense the dejection as well as some animosity in her tone. McCann had shared with him that Linda was angry with God over the effects of the accident.

"I'm sorry to hear that. What has happened?" As he said it, he bowed his head and closed his eyes, "God help me," he thought, as he waited for her to speak.

"The farm burned to the ground last night. Wils discharged himself to go to the farm. I came back and found him there and brought him home. He's sleeping. He's in a lot of pain. I found out about two hours ago that somehow the insurance on the farm buildings was allowed to lapse and we don't have coverage. Talk about a loving God! He even took our dog! Tessa died in the fire. Isn't God good?"

He felt like someone had punched him in the stomach. Her tone was flat as she recited the situation, but her last three words were said with a bitterness that stung him. His mind flashed back to that sunny summer afternoon when he had first met Wilson McCann and McCann had sarcastically informed him that he wasn't a candidate for getting "saved". Linda's tone was the same.

He spoke slowly and tried to put as much love into the words as possible.

"Yes, Linda, despite what the two of you have encountered, God is good,"

"Well, you can keep your 'good God'. I don't know Him anymore," she said, her voice rising with each word. And the click of the disconnection was like the stroke of doom.

Hastings slowly replaced the phone and sat there as the tears came.

"Oh God! Please help them!" he said, as the sobs shook him.

Dorothy stood in the doorway, twisting a dish towel in her hands. She prayed quietly until her husband's sobs ceased. He looked up at her and wiped away his tears.

"I'm going to Farnsworth," he said, rising from his chair.

By late afternoon, the fire had died down in the barn. What remained was a smoking, smoldering pile with the skeleton walls standing over it. A semi cattle truck was backed up in the lane that led to the barnyard. Jim Marks had plowed the lane out earlier in the afternoon. The plan was to herd the remaining steers into a corner of the barnyard farthest from the smoldering barn and then run them down the lane and into the truck.

In the big tool shed, four men stood looking out at the pile of rubble that, twenty four hours ago, had been a farmhouse. Jim had pushed the remains of the walls down onto the smoldering rubble of the house with his end loader under the watchful eyes of the remaining firefighters. The pile had caught again and had burned itself down as the hours dragged by.

Now Willard, Marks and Nick Hardesty had been joined by McIntyre, the driver of the semi that would take the remaining cattle to a livestock market west of Saginaw.

The four of them discussed the events of the past two weeks. Each had voiced their opinion on what had happened, why it had happened to Wilson McCann, and how he was able to handle it all while maintaining his faith in God's providence.

"Some might say that he is being punished for some past sin," Marks said, looking out as the wind whipped across the yard, picking up soot blackened snow and whirling it out across the road.

"Perhaps he's being tested for some greater good in God's plan," Willard responded.

"Maybe its spiritual warfare," Hardesty said, looking down at his boots.

"Aye! There's wisdom in that, laddie!" McIntyre said, eyeing the younger man.

"I've heard that there is a rumor going around that someone is pulling strings to keep Wils from getting the CEO's job at the new Mogollon," Jim Marks said, gloomily.

"The Devil's at work, lads!" McIntyre said, his eyes piercing under his bushy red eyebrows.

"First his company gets sold out from under him, then the accident, J.W.'s in a coma, Linda leaves, Wils' accident, now the fire… what next?" Jim Marks spoke to the gray sky outside the doorway.

"Do you think there is something in his past that has caught up with him?" Nick asked, looking to the north where the only other building that had survived the fire's rage stood. The old chicken coup, with its slanted roof and row of four windows, stood as a silent observer to the fire's destruction.

"We all have a past laddie," McIntyre replied, looking down. He reflected back on his own drunken rages before he drank from the word of God and traded his thirst for good whiskey for a thirst for a closer walk with his maker.

"It's just so much…so much to try to understand…" the younger man lowered his gaze again as McIntyre's blue eyes bored into his.

"We'd best be getting the beasties into the truck, lads," McIntyre said, turning to head out into the yard.

"Where's the lass?" McIntyre, asked over his shoulder.

Marks, Willard and Nick Hardesty looked at each other before Willard spoke.

"She came home earlier today and took Wils back to their home."

"Nae! I meant the wee lass…Tess!" McIntyre responded in his gruff voice.

"Oh! We think she died in the fire," Hardesty replied. "She was locked in the barn."

"Hae ye tried calling her up?" McIntyre replied, starting to walk out into the yard. As he did so, he reached inside his heavy coat and took a silver whistle from his shirt pocket.

"No…we didn't think…" Nick stammered, as the big scot moved away from them.

McIntyre reached the rise near what had been the well house and blew on the whistle. The tone was so high pitched that the three in the shed could hardly hear it against the wind.

McIntyre turned to the east and blew the whistle again. He repeated the action facing north, west and south. He stood there, the wind blowing the mop of his red hair around his face. He turned three hundred and sixty degrees, looking. As he faced east for the third time, he raised his hand to shade his eyes.

And then he began to run.

Surprised by his actions, the three other men moved out of the shelter of the big shed and into the yard. By the time they reached the point where McIntyre had stood, he was already crossing the road in front of the farm and heading down into the ditch that separated the road from Jim Mark's field. A swale ran up against the ditch. As they looked, they saw a dark object moving against the backdrop of the brush and snow.

McIntyre plunged into the brush and emerged a moment later, carrying in his arms a very sad looking little Shetland Sheep Dog.

"Thank you Lord!" Jim Marks shouted into the wind.

In Farnsworth, another Pastor sat at his kitchen table, his right leg stretched out in front of him. The stainless steel brace that ran from the sole of his shoe up to his knee reflected the light from the chandelier above the table. Elmer Gabbard, Pastor of the Farnsworth Wesleyan Church, listened carefully as Tammie Ring told him what had happened the previous night at McCann's farm. He was already aware of the accident that had placed J.W. in a coma and resulted in Linda's leaving for Colorado. He was also aware of the accident that had put McCann in the hospital. The Wesleyan Church, though small, had an active prayer chain and Tammie Ring was one of its most active participants. The prayer chain had been lifting up McCann and his family together with Tachyons and its employees, and the community of Farnsworth, in prayer, ever since the first day of the New Year.

"So, Linda is back?" he asked.

"Yes, she came in this morning and took Wils home from the farm," Tammie replied, taking a sip from a cup of coffee that Gabbard's rotund wife, Florence, placed in front of her. Florence, clad in a flowered dress and an apron that almost completely covered it, stood at the sink, washing the dinner dishes and listening carefully without entering in to the conversation.

"Have you talked to her?"

"No, I called on her in the hospital one night and she wasn't very talkative. I sense that she blames God for what has happened to them and isn't very open to anyone she feels is a 'God Person'"

"Hmm," Gabbard said as he picked up his cup but didn't drink. He held it up and seemed to sight over the top of it.

"Would you call them?...or maybe go out and see them," Tammie asked, hopefully.

Elmer Gabbard had come to Farnsworth two years previously. He met McCann during his first week in the community. He invited McCann as a representative of EECM to give a "Ministry Minute" talk during his first service at Farnsworth Wesleyan. The following week, he visited McCann at his farm to deliver a contribution from FWC to EECM. While McCann maintained his membership at the Farnsworth United Methodist Church, he remained friends with the Wesleyan Pastor and, from time to time in the past two years, McCann and his wife had secretly given sizable sums of money to the little church to help it cope with various building and ministry needs. The new furnace and air conditioning system in the parsonage was the result of one of those gifts.

"Who has his dog?" Gabbard murmured, still sighting over his cup.

"What?"

"Tessa...who has her?"

"Jim Marks put her in the barn the night of the storm. He thinks she died in the fire," Tammie said quietly, tears forming in her eyes. She brushed them away.

"Wils and I share a love for dogs. I wish I had one," Gabbard said, looking at his wife. "The loss of his dog will hurt him as much as the loss of his farm buildings."

Florence scrubbed a plate strongly and responded without turning her head.

"They steal a person's heart," she said, quietly. They had been married thirty-seven years. During that time they had raised and buried four dogs. She was not ready for another, at least not right now.

"I think I'll pay a call on Wils and Linda in the morning," Gabbard said, taking a long drink from his coffee cup. "The two of you might be in prayer for that and ask our prayer chain to be in prayer as well."

Tammie sipped her coffee and smiled. She loved her Pastor and his wife. Elmer Gabbard was not the greatest speaker on Sunday morning, but his years of experience in shepherding flocks in small towns was his great strength.

"Thank you Pastor," she said.

Jim and Lona Marks stood in their kitchen looking down at the bedraggled and fire singed bundle of brown and white fur that was curled up on a rug in a corner.

To say that Tessa was a mess would have been an understatement. Her long coat was singed in several places and burned through to the skin in two others. The tips of both ears were burned and scabbed over beneath the salve that McIntyre had administered the previous afternoon. Burrs and stick tights from her night in the swamp had been combed out as best they could but there were still many left. Her bushy tail was a mop of burnt hairs and burrs.

"We've got to get her cleaned up before we call Wils," Marks said uneasily, looking at his wife.

"We'll use the hair clippers to trim off the burnt hair and try to comb out some more of the burrs and stick tights. I'm hesitant to bathe her yet. But, she sure needs it. Did McIntyre leave some of the salve?" Lona Marks responded, stepping to the cupboard and reaching up to the top shelf to retrieve a box containing a set of electric hair trimmers that she used to groom their two children's hair.

"Yes, it's in the pocket of my coveralls," Marks replied, going to the entry way and retrieving a small vial of the ointment from the pocket of his coveralls that hung there.

Lona sat on the floor after plugging in the clippers and took Tessa into her lap. The smell of burnt hair rose up as she began to carefully trim the little dog. Tessa, for her part, was quiet until the clippers caught on matted hair and yanked. She swiveled as if to snap at the offending clippers but Lona turned them off and carefully disentangled the clump before proceeding.

"What do you think Wils will do?" she said without looking up.

"About Tess?" Marks replied in a puzzled tone.

Lona looked up. "No silly! He'll be happy to see his little friend. I meant about the farm."

"I don't know. I've got two dozers and a big back hoe coming to start burying remains and leveling as much as we can and piling up what we can't bury. He's in rough shape. He can't sit for longer than five minutes due to the pain. He has to stand or lie down. We had to stop on the way out from the hospital yesterday because of the pain."

"What about Linda?" Lona said, as she took a large metal comb and carefully combed out some of Tessa's fur.

"She was pretty cold yesterday and I don't mean from the weather," Marks replied, looking out the window as a big tanker truck roared by on the highway.

"Don't forget, she is still young in the faith," Lona said, as she turned on the clippers again and began to trim Tessa's tail.

"I know. She's had a big blow with the accident and what happened as a result of it. She was looking forward to being a mom. With all that's happened, she is questioning God's existence. We need to pray for them both."

And, when Tessa had been repaired to the best of Lona's ability, they did just that. Standing together in their kitchen, holding hands while the little Sheltie watched them before putting her head on her paws and going to sleep.

(20)

The pain was like none he had ever experienced. It knifed across his lower back and made every step he took agony. He tried to muffle his reactions to the pain but Linda heard him and sat up in bed as he made his way into the master bath. He sat on the edge of the whirlpool tub and tried to put on his slippers. But, as he did so, another high pitched groan responded to the demon that now possessed him. He forced the slipper on his left foot and took a deep breath before reaching for the other one. Surprisingly, the pain this time was not as sharp and he breathed a silent prayer of gratitude. Linda watched him from the doorway.

The sun was just peeking over the horizon as he made coffee in the old percolator. Linda, still on Colorado time, had gone back to bed. He stood waiting for the coffee and thinking about the events of the past few days. He was warmed by Linda's return and her expression of love for him but he sensed that she was still angry with God.

He tried to see it from her perspective and it wasn't hard to do. The loss of their unborn child, J.W.'s injuries, the loss of Tachyons, his accident, the destruction of the barn, house and outbuildings and the loss of Tessa. Now, through the negligence of someone he didn't even know, there was no insurance coverage on the farm buildings. It all seemed to be a cascade of proof that God, indeed, had turned His back on them.

THE INVESTMENT

He fought off the feelings and decided to go to the farm. He poured coffee into his travel mug and downed half of it before refilling the mug to the brim. Perhaps the coffee would drive away the fog from the pain pills.

He knew that Linda would not want him driving in the condition he was in. He quietly put on his boots, overcoat and cap and eased the door open and shut. Once in the Ranger, the pain came back with a rush. He drove as fast as conditions allowed and was relieved when he pulled into the farmyard and was able to get out and stand, looking out over the scene.

Smoke still rose from the ruins of the barn and house. The stench from the barn was still there although not as bad as the previous day. A bulldozer had pushed mounds of dirt and rubble up against the remains of the buildings to assure that any remaining embers would not generate more flames. The dozer sat silently, well away from the results of its work.

He walked to the edge of the hill and looked out over the snow covered scene to the west. It hadn't changed in the twenty nine years since he had first seen it when, as an eighteen year old "city kid" he had come to work for his uncle. His mind roved over the years. The hot summer days with the never ending work of the farm, the animals and the need to care for them. The haying and the harvests, the uncompromising stubbornness of Fred Harms as he toiled each day and his Aunt Ethel's quiet, resolute manner as she fed her chickens and gathered the eggs and washed, cooked, canned and prepared meals for the three of them.

He thought of Donna Barnes and her rebellious nature as they laughed and loved their way through the summer months. He thought of her as a grown woman, sure in her faith and quiet in her witness to him and her unwillingness to compromise that faith and witness. He thought of Donna's unselfish placement of her new born baby for adoption and how she had kept the secret from him to her dying day.

He thought of Sally McHugh and her willingness to take the place of another in his affection even though she knew there was nothing there for her in his future.

Lastly, he thought of the night during a thunder storm when he had first taken Linda in his arms and kissed her.

All of it had played out against the backdrop of this farm. And now it seemed that, while most of the buildings had been destroyed, the memories lived on.

He trudged through the foot of snow to the place where he had buried Ted and Wink, his two dogs. His gaze swung back to the remains of the barn. Somewhere in that pile of smoking rubble Tessa must be. He would not be able to dig a grave for her and the thought only added to his misery.

He knelt in the snow beside the pile of stones that marked Ted's grave. Five years ago, he had knelt here in the middle of a snowstorm, looking down into the grave where the remains of his faithful Border Collie lay. He had realized that, for forty years, he had lived only for himself and that he needed to change. He had called out to God and God had answered. His life had turned in a new direction with its focus centered on God's will for his life.

"God, have you left me? Are you still there? Please give me strength to live for you despite what is happening to me," he said quietly, as he knelt in the snow.

He heard a vehicle out on the road but ignored it. He squeezed his eyes shut and balled his fists into them as the pain raced across his back.

"I…will…yet…praise you!" he gritted out at the top of his voice. The words were swept away by a gust of wind and replaced by the sound of a truck coming up the driveway.

He painfully got to his feet and turned back toward the drive. Jim Marks was getting out of his truck. McCann slowly made his way through the snow toward his friend.

"Good morning Wils'," Marks said, as he walked around to the other side of his truck.

"Hi Jim, I am not sure how 'good' it is," McCann responded dully.

"It's a good morning! Look who I have with me!" Marks said in a cheerful voice and reached inside the truck to retrieve a twenty pound bundle of brown and white fur.

"Tessa!" McCann shouted as he stumbled to the truck and took the Sheltie in his arms.

The sun, previously hidden by the clouds, popped out and bathed the scene in its glow.

McCann and Tessa returned to the house and Linda took the little Sheltie in her arms and buried her face in Tessa's fur. McCann stood leaning against the door frame watching them with a smile on his face. He moved toward the couch in the family room as Linda put Tessa down on a bed near the fireplace.

McCann lay back against the cushions and gave out a small moan as the pain came rippling back again.

"When do you see the surgeon?" Linda asked, as she moved to the counter in the kitchen to get his pain pills and a glass of water. She had been ready to vent her unhappiness with him for driving to the farm alone, but those feelings had been swept away when he opened the door with Tessa in his arms.

"Not until next Tuesday," he responded, pushing himself erect and instinctively reaching to his lower back to try to rub away the pain.

"Tuesday? That's ridiculous!" Linda fumed.

"He only comes to Farnsworth on Tuesday. Because of the storm, he didn't make it this week. Jon says he is the best there is and he has a pretty heavy schedule. He operates in Bay City and Saginaw as well."

"Maybe we should look for someone else," Linda said, turning toward him with the water and pills in her hand.

"Let's wait and see what he says. I don't want just anyone messing around next to my spinal column," McCann said, resignedly. He took the pills gratefully and downed them along with the water.

Linda returned to the kitchen and refilled the percolator and brought out bowls and glasses. McCann stood to eat his meal and then went to the recliner and stretched out as flat as he could. He had prayed over their meal and thanked God for returning Tessa to them. He noted that Linda had looked away as he did so.

She came to where he was, her mug of steaming coffee in her hand. She placed it on the end table next to his chair and sank to her knees. She placed her hand on his arm.

"Can you forgive me?" she asked, quietly.

"There's nothing to forgive. You were upset and needed time alone. I'm sorry that I made a mess of things and you had to return before you could spend some time with your family."

"I should never have left. I love you and I should not have left. I should have stayed," she said, bowing her head against the chair arm.

"God will take care of us … look he gave Tessa back to us. I thought she was dead in the fire…" he began but, as he did so, she got to her feet and turned away.

"I don't want to talk about God. I don't see how you can continue to love a God, if there is a God, who would let the things happen that have happened to you."

Her words came out hard and flat. The moment of affection vanished as quickly as it had come.

"Linda, God has blessed us. Should we reject Him just because we have suffered a few setbacks?"

THE INVESTMENT

She stood, looking out the window over the snow covered field below the house, her back ramrod straight. She held her mug with both hands and slowly brought it to her lips before responding.

"When I see what has happened over the past two weeks, I just don't want to have anything to do with God."

McCann rubbed his hand across his eyes and reached down to raise the recliner back to an upright position. As he did so, the pain returned and his left leg felt like it had lost its feeling. He levered himself erect and came to stand beside her. Tessa watched the two of them from her bed by the fireplace.

"I'm sorry you feel that way. I don't understand why these things happen but I refuse to stop trusting in God. I believe that, in the long run, He will see us through this. I love you…I trust that you know that."

"I do." Saying it seemed to burst a dam of emotion inside her.

She turned into his arms and buried her head against his shoulder. They stood there not knowing what to say beyond what had been said. The silence was broken by the sound of a car coming up the drive and stopping outside.

"It's been ten days and he seems to be doing well. From what we are seeing, there doesn't seem to be any residual damage. I think we should start the process of bringing him out of the coma," Jonathan Sager said to the ICU team. "I will call Wils and tell him so that he can be here when J.W. wakes up."

As he headed back to his hospital office, he realized that notifying McCann that his son would soon be coming out of his medically induced coma was the "good news" part of the call he had to make. The "bad news" part was twofold. First, he couldn't be sure what lingering or lasting effects of the accident would be present when J.W. wakened. Secondly, the news about McCann's own situation was not good. The surgeon was booked in Saginaw and Bay City for the next two weeks and wouldn't be available to do surgeries in Farnsworth until February 2nd. McCann would have to survive on pain medication until then. Sager had already checked the schedules of two other surgeons and the wait time for surgery in both cases was even longer.

He called up McCann's file on his laptop and entered a prescription for Tramadol and sent it to the local pharmacy. He clicked on one of the tabs on the file and looked at the MRI images. One of the discs was badly damaged. The surgeon would remove it, insert a spacer and grind up the fragments of the original disc and pack them around the spacer. The grafted bone elements would grow or "fuse" the two vertebrae together and a titanium box with screws into the vertebrae would hold it all in place. McCann would wear a brace for thirteen weeks and his activities would be somewhat limited. Sager suspected that the intervening period before surgery and the thirteen weeks after surgery would cramp McCann's style. He also knew that there was a good chance that his patient would eschew the Tramadol which would, in the dose that Sager was ordering, result in McCann being reduced to a zombie like state in order to free him from the pain. He couldn't see someone like McCann being willing to accept that circumstance.

"Well, here it goes, Wils," he said, closing the file and reaching for his phone.

Linda moved to answer the door just as the phone rang. McCann picked it up and, hearing Sager's voice, moved toward the bedroom to take the call while Linda ushered Elmer Gabbard into the living room. The elderly minister walked to where Tessa lay on her mat and bent to stroke her head.

"A miracle wouldn't you say?" he asked, continuing to pet the dog. Linda didn't respond. He finally stood and turned toward her.

Linda was somewhat dismayed when he took off his coat and, stretching his braced leg out before him, settled into the chair most recently occupied by her husband.

"Could I get you a cup of coffee? I'm sure Wils will be out in a minute. I think it was his doctor on the phone," she said.

"That would be fine Linda, I would enjoy a cup. This is the only home that I visit where a percolator is still in use," he said, smiling up at her.

She turned without returning his smile and got a mug from the mug tree on the kitchen island and filled it from the old percolator. She brought it to him and he sipped appreciatively.

"Ahh! That is good!" he said, looking up at her.

Linda liked Elmer Gabbard. It was hard not to. He was like a big old hairy dog who asked for nothing but to be your friend. Yet behind the friendly exterior, she knew there was a keen intellect, honed by many years of service to God and the communities that he had served in the more rural sections of the Wolverine state.

She took her half-full mug from the counter and sat in the chair opposite him.

"It is good of you to come out," she said it matter-of-factly. He chose to ignore her tone.

"I heard about your troubles," he said, smiling at her as he raised his cup and took another sip.

"Well, we appreciate your friendship," Linda said, hoping her tone of voice would speed up his departure.

For his part, Gabbard continued to sip his coffee and smile, his bad leg stretched out in front of him.

"How are you doing Linda?" he asked, quietly.

McCann, having finished his conversation with Dr. Sager, had started down the hall to tell Linda that they needed to get dressed and go to the hospital. When he heard Gabbard's question, he turned and went back in the bedroom. He sat on the edge of the bed but the pain came again and he stood to relieve it. He glanced at his watch. It wouldn't hurt to wait a few minutes to let Gabbard's unexpected visit play out. He was quite sure that visit was aimed more at Linda than it was at him. He pulled a pillow in against the headboard and lay down on the bed.

Down the hall, the atmosphere was almost as cool as the atmosphere out in the fields below.

"I'm fine," Linda said, tightly.

"Somehow I doubt that," Gabbard responded amiably.

"All right, I'll just say it…I'm angry with God for what he has done," she said it strongly, hoping to provoke him. He smiled and took another sip from his mug.

"I don't blame you. Your accident, then Wils' accident, J.W.'s situation, the fire, the Tachyons situation…Tessa…it's a lot to bear," he said, conversationally.

"How could a just God let all that happen? I can't believe in a God like that," her tone was aimed at ending the conversation but it didn't work. Gabbard wiggled his shoulders and settled more deeply into his chair.

"Do you know who is thought to be the most despicable woman in the Bible?" he asked, over the rim of his mug.

"What?" she said, the surprise evident in her voice.

"Take a guess," he encouraged.

"I don't know…Rahab the prostitute? Hagar? The woman taken in adultery?…what's that got to do with anything anyway?" She made her answer more petulant than necessary but she was, never the less, intrigued by the question and where this was going.

"Many scholars agree that it is Job's wife," Gabbard said, looking her squarely in the eye.

The answer hit her full force. She knew the story well. Job, God's man, had suffered the loss of everything. He had sat in the gateway to the city, covered with sores and wailed at God for the loss of his children and his wealth. The parallels to her husband's situation were striking. The truth of Gabbard's implication hit her like a punch in the stomach.

"She told Job to curse God and die," Gabbard said quietly, "Is that your role in this Linda?"

Linda McCann bowed her head and the sobs came as another dam burst. Elmer Gabbard sat quietly, his head bowed and his eyes closed. He had done what he felt led to do. The rest was up to God.

(21)

Carolyn Abbott had arrived in Phoenix the previous Monday. The Mogollon executives were into their second week of trying to meet her directives to come up with a revised plan for the company. Her arrival had been anticipated for several days. When she actually arrived, she did so with little fanfare. When the executive office staff arrived shortly after 9:00 a.m., Carolyn had already been in Kent Lister's old office for two hours. She had obtained the necessary security information to access Mogollon's information systems the previous week. She had combed through the construction and operating budgets and results and had developed her own set of planning strategies. She reviewed them one last time before calling H in Chicago to see if he had any last minute instructions.

H, for his part was pleased with the uptick in Mogollon's stock and the reaction of the stock market to new leadership. He suggested she get someone new involved in trying to straighten out Mogollon's information system problems and Carolyn made a note to call Mike Divell at MTD. She smiled to herself at the thought that Mike might even assign Wilson McCann's wife to the job. She wondered, given H's peculiar instructions to her regarding McCann, how he would react to that.

She was bothered by what she had been told to do. It was unusual for H to give specific instructions relative to an individual and more so when the instructions seemed to conflict with both his and Carolyn's ethical approach to such things. H had directed that Mogollon, once she had a feasible plan, should reinstitute the Tachyons acquisition. The bothersome part was his insistence that she was to remove Wilson McCann from consideration to replace her as head of the combined organization once the acquisition was completed.

It just didn't make any sense. McCann was clearly one of the best CEO's in the industry. Tachyons was in better organizational and operational shape than Mogollon. That was due to his leadership. The news of Bob Allison's death two days ago had brought immediate speculation on the street that Wilson McCann would be a top candidate to replace him. The fact that Fairfield's Board had installed Ed Cantwell as acting CEO had done little to ease that speculation. Cantwell was viewed in the investment community as an operating man. Fairfield's stock, which had been rising on the wave of increased investor activity, had dropped five points since Allison's death.

"It's non-negotiable Carolyn," H said into her ear as she once again raised the issue of McCann.

"But why?" she asked again.

"The investor in Mogollon does not want him as CEO," H replied. His voice sounded weary.

"But why?"

She heard the sigh. She could visualize H, sitting at his elevated desk as a high school English teacher grown weary of a student who just didn't seem to grasp the nuances of the language.

"Okay, forget it. I need to go walk around…let them know I'm here," Carolyn said, trying to end the conversation on a more encouraging note. H had often said he envied her for her ability to inspire people by simply employing her "MBWA" theory, which stood for "Management By Walking Around."

"Carolyn?...I just don't know," H said quietly.

"Got it...I'll be in touch," she said. She felt better knowing that she wasn't the only one puzzled by the mysterious investor's detest for Wilson McCann.

J.W. had been climbing for what seemed like forever. His knees and hands hurt from scrabbling over rocks and sand to reach the top of the hill. Finally, he heaved himself over the crest and lay there looking across the canyon. It was unbelievable! The city on the other side of the canyon stretched for as far as his eyes could see. The turrets and spires of the buildings seemed to reach the sky and beyond. They glittered like gold and silver in a sunlit panorama without shadow. As his heart quieted and he stopped panting for breath, he heard the music. It seemed to radiate up from and over the city. He felt that he could lie here and listen to it forever but he knew he must reach the city.

He looked to his right and saw a path which led to a narrow bridge across the canyon. He got to his feet and walked toward the bridge. The canyon was not wide. It seemed no more than two hundred yards across. But, as he neared the rim, he looked down and could not see the bottom of the abyss. It seemed to fall away forever into darkness. Even the light from the city could not reach the bottom.

He reached the narrow bridge and looked across. As he did so, he saw a beautiful woman coming toward him on the bridge. He walked to meet her. As the two of them neared the center of the bridge, the woman became clearer. He knew instinctively that it was his mother. Not his adoptive mother but his birth mother. As she drew near, she stopped and smiled at him. Behind her, another woman appeared and stopped just beyond the beginning of the bridge. She too was smiling. He sensed that she was Ellen McCann, his Grandmother.

THE INVESTMENT

"Hello James Wilson. I'm so glad that we could finally meet," Donna said. Her voice was light and melodic. He felt that his heart would burst from the emotions that were running through him.

"Mother! Please hold me!" he said, moving toward her.

"I cannot. I'm sorry," she replied. "You must go back."

"Why? Why can't I go to the city with you?" he cried out, continuing to move toward her.

"You cannot come to the city yet," she said. He felt the love that came from her.

He was almost up to her. Only a few feet separated them. "Not even for a few days?"

"There are no days in the city. There is only forever," she replied, continuing to smile.

He reached out to her and his hand came against a glass pane that separated them. The light was so bright around her that he couldn't see the glass. He placed his hands against it and she put hers against them on the other side of the glass.

"You must go back now my son but I will be here if you return. I love you," she said, looking into his eyes. He could feel her gaze penetrate to the very core of his being. As she did so, the bridge began to move beneath his feet and he felt himself falling into the canyon. As he fell, he looked up and saw his mother looking down at him with love.

"Noooooooooo!" he screamed as he fell.

The Nurse had her back turned to the bed when J.W. moved and moaned. She punched the call button to summon the charge Nurse and the doctor.

"He's waking up!" she said, as they entered the room.

McCann had waited as long as he could and finally joined Gabbard and Linda in the dinette area. Linda was in tears and Gabbard was quietly letting her cry it out. He stood in the doorway watching until she looked up. She wiped away her tears and stood. He moved to take her in his arms.

"I don't understand it…why is God letting this happen to us?" she, said, as she buried her head against his chest. He was encouraged by her choice of words. Before Gabbard had arrived, she would have said "Why is God doing this to us?"

"I don't know but we will continue to trust him…won't we?" He said, as he kissed her hair.

"I'm going to try…I promise," she said, turning to smile at Gabbard.

"The call was from the hospital. They say J.W. is waking up and they want us to come as soon as we can," McCann said.

"Let me pray for you before I leave," the elderly minister said, rising from his chair and putting his coffee cup on the kitchen bar.

They stood there, holding hands, the minister favoring his crippled leg, the beautiful woman trying to regain her faith and McCann with his blotched face and throbbing back, trying to understand what was happening to him.

"Dear Lord, I pray you will bless this house just as you have in the past. I pray that you will help us to understand your will and your ways and to continue to give ourselves to you with all of our hearts, souls, minds and strength. I pray for J.W.'s complete recovery," the old minister prayed quietly. As he did so, a ray of sunlight shone through a crack in the rolling clouds above the home in which they stood. It briefly illuminated the room in which they stood and then vanished as quickly as it had come. Their eyes were closed in prayer and they didn't see it.

Linda put the second and third row seats in the rented SUV down and spread three blankets in the expanded area. McCann had walked slowly down to the vehicle and climbed into the back and lain down for the trip into Farnsworth. Elmer Gabbard had hugged each of them and left five minutes earlier.

Now, as they drove over the snow packed roads, McCann's cell phone rang. He fumbled in his coat until he retrieved it.

He listened carefully and then spoke.

"Absolutely, let him in. We are on our way. We should be there in about 10 minutes."

Linda pulled the rear view mirror down to see her husband lying in the back of the SUV.

"Who was it?"

"Dr. Sager. He says J.W. is awake and that Charles Hastings is asking to come into his room and talk to him," McCann replied, a note of wonder in his voice.

Linda put the mirror back in its proper position and stepped on the gas. The SUV started to skid on the snowy road and she over corrected in bringing it back. The memory of the crash flashed through her mind and she hit the brakes hard. The SUV did a one eighty and bumped up against the snow bank at the side of the road. McCann gritted his teeth as his body came back to rest on the blankets.

He reached up over the back of the driver's seat and squeezed her shoulder hard. She was holding her head against the steering wheel with both hands.

"What say we take it a bit easy? Right now, you're our family's only healthy driver," he said quietly, continuing to hold her shoulder despite the pain in his back.

"Right," she said, leaning back in the seat and slowly turning the SUV around to head toward Farnsworth.

Charles Hastings had driven up M-53 as fast as he dared, sticking to the speed limits in the towns along the way and exceeding it when the road ahead was clear. He turned west onto M-81 and arrived in Farnsworth shortly after 10:00 a.m. Once in the little village, he had to make a decision as to whether to go to the hospital and see J.W. or go to McCann's home and see McCann and his wife. He chose the former and parked in the hospital parking lot.

Once inside, he was directed to the ICU and stopped at the Nurse's station. The Nurse on duty gave him a cool gaze.

"Are you family?" she asked.

"No, I'm a Pastor," Hastings smiled back at her.

"I'll need to see if the family is willing to let you see him," she said.

"That's fine, can I wait over there?" he asked, indicating a small waiting area opposite the station.

"Yes, just have a seat. I'll try to contact them. They have had a lot of bad luck lately," she said, turning to the phone.

"I understand. Thank you," he said, retreating to the waiting area as she lifted the phone.

A few moments later, she motioned him to the counter. "I spoke to Mr. McCann. He and Mrs. McCann are on their way here. He said to allow you to go in. It is the second door on the right. You need to be aware that Mr. Storey awakened earlier this morning. The doctor has left instructions that any visits be short and quiet."

Hastings thanked her again and walked down the hall. He opened the door and went in. A Nurse was checking J.W.'s chart and turned to face him, a look of irritation on her face. He raised his hand, palm out.

"I am a Pastor. Mr. McCann gave permission for me to visit the patient," he said quickly.

She stepped aside and he got his first clear look at the young man on the bed. J.W. Storey was slightly elevated in the bed and his eyes were closed. The Nurse eyed him from beside the bed.

"Please keep it quiet and don't stay too long," she said, as she prepared to leave.

As she spoke, J.W.'s eyes popped open and he smiled broadly.

"Pastor Charles! I'm so glad to see you!" he reached for the minister's hand, his arm restrained by the IV tube attached to it. Hastings stepped to the bedside and grasped his hand.

"J.W., God bless you. It is wonderful to see you awake and..." Hastings began.

"...and recognizing people too," the Nurse finished for him, a big smile crossing her face as she opened the door.

"God has blessed me! I need to tell you about it," J.W. Storey looked up into his face as he continued to grip the minister's hand. The joy on his face was unmistakable.

And, as Charles Hastings dropped into a chair beside the bed, J.W. continued to grasp his hand and his story bubbled forth. He told of the moment of the crash and how he saw the big Ram pickup bearing down on them and how, at that moment, he recognized that he needed God.

"...just before it hit us and everything went black, I remember thinking, 'God help us!', and he did, didn't he?" he said, his eyes shining.

Dr. Sager stood in the doorway listening.

"I was going to ask you if you remembered what happened. It is clear that you do," he said, looking at his patient.

"I saw my mother and my grandmother...in my dream I mean..." J.W. said, as Sager looked into both of his eyes with a pen light.

"It was beautiful...the city I mean...you can't believe how beautiful it was...and the music that I heard...it was unbelievable," J.W. finished as Sager, having listened without expression, completed his examination. He and the Nurse exited the room.

"So, how do you feel about all this?" Hastings said, conversationally.

ROBERT W. ZINNECKER

"I've waited too long to do this. I want to turn my life over to Jesus Christ and live for him," J.W. said in a firm and quiet voice.

(22)

"Just thought you might like to know. I guess his chickens are coming home to roost," George Whyte said from his office in the Farnsworth John Deere dealership.

In Chicago, the man who was known in Farnsworth as Charlie Dumas thanked the implement dealer and hung up the phone. He leaned back in his chair and looked at the ceiling. Whyte had just filled him in on the latest problems to befall Wilson McCann. Dumas had cultivated a relationship with both George Whyte and Joe Rambaugh, the Chrysler dealer in Farnsworth. The two men felt that McCann had cheated them out of their investment in the Farnsworth Telephone Coop. and had been more than willing to provide a lot of negative information about McCann during Dumas' interviews with them in the fall.

It hadn't taken much work on Dumas' part for him to come to the conclusion that McCann's purchase of their shares in the family owned company had been more than reasonable. He sensed that what really bothered the two of them was that their sale of the shares had left them with no stake in the new Tachyons or any positions of influence on its board of directors. Nevertheless, they were a good source of gossip, both factual and hearsay.

He thought it all over for a few minutes and then placed a call to the old man. He recited what White had told him about the crash,

McCann's wife's sudden departure from Farnsworth, the statements about McCann's future if Mogollon acquired Tachyons, his accident, hospitalization and the fire at the farm.

The voice on the other end of the line was tired but resolute. "I want to be kept advised as to what happens, every detail of it. If you need to go back to Farnsworth, do so. I'll expect weekly updates until I tell you to stop. Your fees and costs will be deposited in your account. If you require anything additional, call me."

The line went dead and Dumas asked himself the question that had been nagging at him for almost four months. Why was a man who would be dead inside of six months so interested in Wilson McCann?

McCann stood against the wall trying to ease the pain in his back. Linda sat next to J.W.'s bed and Charles Hastings stood on the opposite side of the bed, his gaze fixed on McCann. He had never seen his friend looking this bad. His blotchy face and tired eyes gave witness to the physical pain he was in. Yet Hastings had just witnessed a joyful reunion between a father and son and the son's declaration of a new found faith.

J.W. had recounted his story of the moment of the accident and his vision while in the coma as all three listened, Hastings for the second time. J.W. told of seeing his birth mother and McCann's birth mother and the beautiful city. His father's eyes filled with tears for the second time.

J.W. had prayed the sinner's prayer emphatically while still clasping Hastings' hand. When McCann and Linda had arrived at the room, he had immediately told them that he had accepted Christ as his savior and intended to live a new life in Him. Tears had flowed down McCann's ravaged face and he had embraced his son as best he could, given the tubes and IV still connected to J.W. and McCann's own painful situation. Linda had smiled and planted a kiss on J.W.'s cheek but Hastings sensed some reservation remaining in her demeanor. Hastings wondered if it was J.W.'s description of his birth mother or something more.

After about fifteen minutes, the Nurse and Jon Sager appeared in the doorway.

"I'm afraid that I must ask you to give J.W. a little rest now," Sager said, looking into J.W.'s eyes with a small pen light. "He's come out of the coma really well but he needs to rest."

"When can we come back?" McCann asked, moving away from the wall and taking his son's hand.

"Give him the rest of the morning. Let's say about 2:00 p.m. Okay?" Sager responded, making some notes on J.W.'s chart. He looked at McCann carefully. "How are you doing? Should I re-admit you?"

It was said with just a touch of humor but the meaning was clear. Sager was not at all happy with McCann's abrupt departure from the hospital the previous day. While he understood the motivation, he also was concerned for his patient.

"I'll be alright. I'll take my pills. There isn't anything more you can do for me here than Linda can do at home," McCann replied, his voice reflecting the pain he was in.

Sager looked at Linda. "You okay?" Sager's question was more than a query about her physical well-being and she knew it.

"I'm getting there. I'll take good care of Wils. You can count on it," she replied and he could see the determination in her eyes.

"Alright then. Come back this afternoon if Wils is up to it." Sager turned and went through the door, the Nurse following.

McCann turned to say good bye to his son but J.W. was already asleep, a smile on his face.

Sager was waiting for them at the Nurse's station.

"How much of what has happened did you tell him?" the doctor asked.

"Just that I had gotten into some poison ivy at the farm," McCann replied, leaning against the counter.

"Good, it's best not to hit him with too much until we see how he is when he is fully off the meds," Sager said, eyeing McCann closely.

"When will we know…how…he…whether…?" McCann began. Linda's green eyes were fixed on the Doctor.

Sager nodded. "He'll be in and out today. By tomorrow we can tell a little more. We'll run a scan and some reaction tests and then we can begin to think about letting him go home. I don't want him going back to California yet though."

"He can stay with us," Linda said.

"I'll talk to you tomorrow. Wils, I suggest you go home and lie down. Linda and the Reverend can come back this afternoon," Sager's tone was firm, but he really didn't expect McCann to stay away from his son.

The three of them went outside and McCann invited Hastings to come to their house for lunch. The minister noticed that Linda said nothing as she opened the rear of the SUV and helped McCann crawl in and lie on the blankets. His painful gasp made Hastings cringe.

He followed Linda's vehicle out of the parking lot and headed toward the McCann home. For a moment, he toyed with the idea of driving past the farm but decided against it. He sensed that he was needed more at McCann's side right now. He also wanted to judge whether or not he should discuss the EECM situation with his friend.

THE INVESTMENT

McCann had gone immediately to their bedroom and lain down. Linda and Hastings were left in an uneasy silence in the kitchen. Hastings went to the old percolator and touched it. It was warm and he poured himself a cup of coffee and put it in the microwave to heat it.

"Help yourself," Linda said from in front of the window where she stood looking out over the fields below the house.

"I'm sorry, I haven't had anything since leaving this morning," Hastings replied a little self consciously. He was buying time, waiting for Linda to make the first move toward some sort of discussion.

"I'm sorry...for how I acted last night..." she said, without turning.

"Not a problem. I understand. You folks have had a rough couple of weeks," Hastings replied, removing the cup from the microwave. He took a sip and found it just right.

"Yes...I'm having a hard time with it...I'm sorry...," She turned toward him and he saw the hurt in her eyes. "Please...sit down. Can I get you anything else?"

"This will do for now," Hastings replied taking a chair opposite the window. She sat at the end of the sofa.

"Tessa looks a little the worse for wear," Hastings said, looking at the little Sheltie where she lay asleep on her mat.

"Jim brought her to the farm this morning. Mr. McIntyre found her in the swamp yesterday. We thought she had died in the fire. Jim and Lona cleaned her up. I guess she looked even worse when they found her," Linda's voice seemed more relaxed as she talked about their dog. "Rev. Gabbard said it was a miracle."

"Ah! Was Elmer here then?" Hastings asked. He had met the elderly Wesleyan minister on several occasions and had grown to like him.

"Yes...this morning...he...we...talked about Job's wife," she finished lamely, looking away.

— 209 —

Hastings took a moment to mentally process what she had said. He smiled inwardly as the point hit him.

"And...how did that go?" he said conversationally.

She smiled at him for the first time. "You preachers have a way of getting inside someone's head without irritating them too much," she replied.

"That's good. We go to school to learn how to do that," he said, smiling back.

She took a deep breath and leaned back against the cushions. She looked up at the ceiling before returning his gaze.

"Charles, I am struggling. I don't want to be Job's wife. I want to be supportive but it is tough. I wanted children. Now they say I may not be able to have them. I'm happy that J.W. seems to be okay and that Tessa was found but Wils doesn't have a job and it seems so unfair how that was handled and now the accident and the fire and the screw-up on the insurance...it is just so hard," She looked away again.

"Hard to...?" he said quietly.

"...hard to believe in a God who would allow all this to happen to someone who loves Him as much as Wils does," she said, her tone anguished.

"Yet Wils seems to be continuing to trust...doesn't he?"

"Yes, he is so strong in his faith but I think even he at times questions the 'why' of it, but he seems to rise up to the occasion every time," her tone satisfied Hastings that the love between this man and woman was still strong.

"So...this is about you and God," he said, matter-of-factly.

"I guess so," she lowered her gaze as she said it.

"You spoke of Job's wife...have you read the book of Job?" Hastings asked.

"Yes...we studied it in our small group," Linda responded.

"So you know about all the advice that Job was given by his

friends and all the logic they applied to his condition and all the criticism they heaped on him?"

"Yes…some friends they were!" Linda replied sarcastically.

"And in the end…what happened?" Hastings probed.

Linda thought for a moment before responding. As she did so, Hastings took a long drink from his mug and watched her. She was truly a remarkable young woman, a combination of brains and beauty that was a tribute to God's creation.

"Well, Job yelled at God and God sort of yelled back at Job and asked Job if he knew or did the things that God had done and in the end I guess Job realized what his relationship with God should be and returned to it," she said thoughtfully, like a student reciting a paper to her teacher.

"So this is between you and God…right?" Hastings asked again.

She smiled at him. "And you and Elmer are the voice of God yelling at me?"

"I didn't yell," Hastings said, smiling. "I doubt that Elmer did either."

"I think I need to ask for God's forgiveness and that he let me back into his service," Linda said quietly, bowing her head.

"Good idea," Hastings replied, putting his mug down and bowing his head to pray.

(23)

Liam Colter, alias Leonard Clement, sat in his room carefully cleaning the rifle. It was a Dragunov SVD Sniper rifle, capable of killing accurately over a distance of up to fourteen hundred yards. For what he had been paid to do, that would be more than adequate. A PSD-1 telescopic sight lay on the bed beside him.

As he worked, he thought about the man he had been hired to kill. Colter had been in Farnsworth for a week. He needed to be gone a week from today. He had carefully observed his target and researched the best possible places to shoot from. He had also spent a reasonable amount of time becoming acquainted with the community and the various comings and goings of its people. The village employed a Town Constable as its only police officer. The Tuscola County Sheriff's Department patrolled on a regular basis as did the Michigan State Police. The time frame of his shift at the plant enabled him to monitor the community in both broad daylight and in the darkest hours of the night. He needed little sleep and usually caught a couple of hours in the early afternoon before his shift began.

He had learned a great deal about his target. A prominent man in the community was easy to research. In this case, the activities of the past week amplified the buzz surrounding him. Colter frequented the eating and drinking establishments and listened carefully as he ate his meal or Nursed his beer. He also listened carefully to the few workers assigned to the second shift during his shift breaks in the plant break room.

Colter was fifty six years old. He had been inducted into the IRA at the age of twenty six. His first major action had come four years later when, as a member of the South Armagh Brigade, he had been on the fringe of the attack on the police station at Corry Square.

When the troubles in Ireland subsided, he hired himself out to various rebel groups and slowly honed his skills and saved his money. He had come to the United States ten years ago and for the most part had been involved in minor jobs such as roughing up a cheating drug dealer or persuading a witness not to testify. Three years ago, however he had been hired by Tazlov to assist in eliminating a prospective witness in a securities case against Tazlov's boss. Tazlov had done the killing and Colter had helped dispose of the body. Tazlov hired him again last year to rough up a potential FBI witness on the streets of Chicago. Now, Tazlov had come back with a more serious request and more serious compensation.

Colter thought about what he was to do and the man who would die. He found himself thinking about simply throwing the rifle and scope into the Cass River and leaving. He had connections in Barcelona who could provide him with new identification papers and a new face. He would pay but he could afford it. The money that he had so carefully put away in a Swiss bank account would see him through the remainder of his life if he was careful with it.

He had never bothered to think much about the men and women who had suffered because of his actions. He was simply a workman practicing his trade and collecting his paycheck like any other workman. But this situation was different. With the exception of the two men he had overheard talking in the diner the day following the snow storm, he had heard nothing but good about the man he had been sent to kill. Even those who didn't particularly share the man's way of life spoke well of him.

Colter knew all about Tazlov and those he represented. Tazlov was a mid level operative in the Russian Mafia or "Bratva" in the United States. The reason Tazlov had given Colter for this job was that the subject had killed the son of Tazlov's employer. Colter's research satisfied him that this was a lie. Tazlov was working for the jailed Russian hedge fund manager, Peter Zastrow. Peter Zastrow's son had killed himself. Colter surmised that Peter Zastrow's treatment of his son had more to do with the son's death than any actions by the man Colter had been hired to kill.

Colter had received one half of his fee and the remaining half would be deposited in an account he had designated in France. As a skilled workman, he placed a high value on keeping his word and carrying out an assignment. His IRA training had given him a sense of loyalty to causes and the need to keep one's word.

Yet, as he sat there in his room, the rifle in his lap, he wondered if this was a cause he should remain loyal to.

In Fresno, Traycee Morgan sat at a table with four other young people she had just met. She was still trying to adjust to the time change from her trip to New York City. She had returned the previous evening and worked a full day today. This was her first attempt at trying to meet some of the other young adults who were part of the church she had begun attending on the east side of Fresno.

A trio, made up of two young men and a young woman were playing and singing at the front of the room. The music began with a lively praise chorus that got the group of twenty or so young people clapping. The trio followed it with a traditional hymn and now with another, more subdued praise chorus. The lead guitar player was the Assistant Pastor of the church. A tall dark haired young man with the trace of a beard on his friendly face, he played beautifully and sang the chorus with his eyes closed as if he was praying it. Traycee found herself unable to take her eyes off him.

After a short devotional, the group stood and formed a circle around the room holding hands for the prayer before they enjoyed some refreshments laid out on two tables at the rear of the room. Traycee was standing near the Assistant Pastor as he led them in prayer. When he finished, most of the group headed for the refreshment table. The young man shed his guitar and turned toward her.

"Hi. I'm Caleb. You're new aren't you?" he said, extending his hand.

"Hi. I'm Traycee…two Es and no Y…I…this is my first my first time…I mean…I've been coming to church but not to this group," she stammered, looking into his brown eyes. She felt like a silly school girl with the school's star quarterback.

"Two Es? A bit unusual. So, let's see, that would be T_R_A_C_E_E_Y then?" he said, smiling and continuing to hold her hand in his.

"Y before C," she smiled back disengaging her hand before she spoke. The warmth of his touch lingered.

"Aha! Tray-Cee…I get it. That's a different spelling. I went to college with a girl named Trace with no Y and only one E but she pronounced it the same way. Are you new to Fresno?" he asked, putting his guitar on the nearest table.

"I've been here about six months. I went to several churches before I found this one. Like I said, this is my first young adult meeting," she said, feeling a little more relaxed.

"Well, it's great to have you with us. Let's get some cookies and something to drink and you can tell me more about yourself," he said, motioning towards the refreshment table.

They helped themselves to paper plates and Styrofoam cups and took some cookies and soda, although Traycee would have rather had a strong cup of coffee to help fight off the jet-lag she was feeling.

They found seats at a table with three other young people who were busily engaged in conversation and who, after saying hello to Caleb and exchanging names with Traycee, returned to their conversation. She was glad to have his attentions to herself.

She told him about her job at the medical center and he asked about what she had done previously. Telling him about her time at Trinity brought back memories of J.W. and she wondered how he was doing. She had meant to call when she returned to Fresno but hadn't gotten around to it.

Caleb told her that he had come to the church a year ago from a smaller church in Bakersfield where he had been a Youth Pastor. She sensed that this position was a step up for him and probably paid better. As a Human Resource professional, she found herself often thinking in terms of salaries and benefits. She wondered what the "package" for an Assistant Pastor would be.

Just then, a little girl in a Winnie The Pooh jumper and her hair pulled back in a pony tail came into the room and ran up to him.

"Hi Punkin'!" he said, as he pulled a chair out for her. She didn't sit however.

"Daddy, can I have a cookie?" she asked excitedly.

"Sure! You can even have two!" he replied with a smile. The little girl skipped to the refreshment table and took a plate from the stack.

Traycee was a bit disappointed. She had assumed that he was single. She watched as one of the other young women poured the little girl a glass of punch.

"Is that your wife?" she asked, and immediately regretted being so blunt.

His smile came quickly but faded as he watched his daughter head back to the table.

"My wife passed away two years ago from pancreatic cancer.

This is my daughter, Sarah. Sarah, this is Traycee. She is new to our church," he said, as he took the cup of punch from his daughter and placed it on the table before helping her into the chair next to Traycee. Sarah turned to Traycee and extended her hand.

"Hi Traycee. Did you have some cookies?" she said cheerfully. "You can have one of mine if you want."

Traycee's jet-lagged mind and emotions spun as she looked into Sarah's happy face. Caleb was a single father! Why did that make her feel so good?

The smell of the chicken and dumplings that Linda had prepared for their dinner still pervaded the kitchen and family room as the three of them enjoyed the late evening fire in the fireplace. Hastings sat in the easy chair with a mug of coffee in his hands. McCann lay on the sofa, his head in Linda's lap. Tessa was curled up on his stomach, her back to the sofa. Hastings looked at them from behind his mug and wished that he had the nerve to take a picture on his smart phone. The scene before him was one of contentment and joy.

He and Linda had returned to the hospital earlier in the afternoon and spent an hour with J.W. who was, in one moment, animated and alert and, in the next, drifted off to sleep. The Nurse told them this was natural. J.W. had expressed a desire to call Traycee but that was nixed by the nursing staff. His desire was whetted by being told that both Traycee and Shelley had visited him while he was in the coma. Hastings knew about the relationship between J.W. and Traycee and had been praying that the young woman would lead J.W. to the Lord. Linda filled him in on Shelley and her transformation while staying with Belle Warner. He wondered how this situation, involving three young people of faith, would work itself out.

He had been prepared to leave for Detroit when they left the hospital but Linda had begged him to stay the night. That, together with his desire to talk with McCann about the EECM situation persuaded him to do so. He had walked down to the barn when they returned to the McCann home and called Dorothy to tell her that he would be staying the night and that Linda's faith had been restored.

"And you are God's instrument," his red haired wife said, on hearing the news.

"I think Elmer Gabbard was as much an instrument as I," he responded.

Now as they sat there, he decided to wait until morning to talk with McCann about EECM. The mood this evening was one of happy contentment in the Lord and he didn't want to do or say anything that might change that.

They rose early the next morning and had breakfast with McCann standing at the counter to ease his back. After they each had their first cup of coffee, Hastings sat back and looked at his friend. The blotches on McCann's face were beginning to fade but his face reflected the pain he was in and the stress he was under.

"How are you?" Hastings asked simply. McCann understood the meaning of the question immediately.

"The Lord gives and the Lord takes away. Bless His name," McCann said, his voice level and without emotion.

"Do you still bless His name?" Hastings asked.

"It has tested my faith, that's for sure. But, I still praise His name. I spent too long without Him in my life to reject Him now. But, I have to confess, there have been times when I cried out to Him to ask Him where He was in all this."

"And...did He answer?" Hastings asked.

"His word says that I will yet praise him. I take comfort in that assurance that He is still with me," McCann replied, his voice strong.

Satisfied that McCann's spiritual health was as good as it could be in the circumstances he faced, Hastings broached the subject of EECM's need to re-focus or begin the process of shutting down.

McCann was thoughtful as he listened to what Hastings told him. He walked to the window and looked out over the fields and then returned to the counter.

"I would like to be part of the group putting together a new plan for EECM. I'm confident that we can continue to do God's work with not only a different focus, but one that will expand the ministry and its support across the country," he said.

"You're not going anywhere until you have the surgery on your back," Linda said from her seat at the end of the counter where she had been sipping her coffee and listening to the two men.

"I know. We can do some conference calls and lay out the framework and Lark and John can do the legwork and send us drafts that we can work on from our locations. If necessary, the group can meet in Weaverville or Charlotte and I can conference in by Skype or Facetime," McCann said, his tone confident.

Linda smiled. She was glad to see him focusing on something that might draw his attention away from Tachyons, Mogollon and the fire. She vowed to herself that she would sit at his side and help where she could and make sure he didn't go beyond what his current physical situation dictated.

The two men continued to talk about the approach when the phone rang. She took the phone from its cradle and went to the living room to take the call. When she returned, she was smiling. McCann looked at her questioningly.

"That was Max. He says his liability insurance will cover the impact of the farm losses caused by his employee's negligence. He said you were too good a customer to lose! He also said you should relax and not worry. He is going to work with Jim Marks to get things going."

"Praise the Lord!" McCann said, a smile spreading across his face.

Tessa rose from her mat by the fireplace and walked to his side and rubbed herself against his legs. Some of the ointment on her burns came off on his pant legs. He took her hint and walked her to the sliding door to let her outside. They watched as she rolled in the snow that was up to her shoulders.

"Things are looking up!" McCann said enthusiastically.

"Amen to that," Hastings replied.

"We're agreed then? Ed, you are okay with this?" the Chairman of Fairfield's Board of Directors asked from his seat at the head of the table. The eight men and three women, including Fairfield's acting Chief Executive Officer, Ed Cantwell, nodded their agreement, several muttering a "yes" for added emphasis.

"There is the issue of Mr. McCann's health which, if he is amenable to our offer, will need to be checked out by our medical people," the Chairman reminded them. Again, several heads nodded.

"I believe that concludes our business for today. I will keep you apprised of our actions and results as we move forward. In the meantime, any operational questions should be directed to Ed. He has my full confidence and support."

Having said this, the Chairman rose and picked up a folder from the table. The others left their folders on the table as they exited the room. The folders contained only one document, an eight page summary of Wilson McCann's background, experience and other relative information which had enabled them to approve moving forward with an offer to McCann from Fairfield to become its Chief Executive Officer.

THE INVESTMENT

The Chairman had arranged for a limo to take him to the Broadmoor Resort for the evening. He had just settled into the rear seat when his cell phone sounded. He answered the call to hear a cheerful voice on the other end of the line.

"Good evening, Mr. Chairman, I understand that Fairfield intends to make an offer to Wilson McCann to make him its next CEO."

"You have exactly fifteen seconds to tell me who you are and what you want," the Chairman replied, leaning forward and shutting the sliding glass window that separated his seat from the driver.

"Gladly. My name is H. Forester and I represent a group of investors who control about three percent of your common stock. You may have noticed that Fairfield's stock has been quite active lately and the price has gone up. I'm sure that makes you and your fellow directors happy," the voice didn't lose its pleasant tone.

"What exactly do you want?" the Chairman asked again, sinking back in his seat as the Limo turned onto Academy.

"We don't 'want' anything per se. I need to advise you that tomorrow morning we will complete the necessary filings with the SEC to notify them that we intend to pursue the purchase of an additional seven per cent of Fairfield's stock. We expect that ownership of ten per cent of your stock would justify a seat on your board and would also provide us with an opportunity to participate in the selection of the next CEO."

"But you said you understood that we were interested in Wilson McCann. I'm not confirming or denying that and anything I might say is off the record," the Chairman responded, his mind racing as he digested what he had just been told.

The voice on the other end of the line lost its cordial tone. "The interests I represent would not look favorably on Mr. McCann as CEO of Fairfield. You certainly have the right and duty to do what you feel is in the best interests of Fairfield and its shareholders. As the representative of a shareholder group with a significant holding, and one which intends to expand its influence on Fairfield's operation, I must clearly state that we would not be comfortable with Mr. McCann as its CEO. I suggest you hold off on any action in that regard until things become clearer to you. In the meantime, we are very comfortable with Mr. Cantwell as acting CEO."

"But…" the Chairman sputtered as the limo turned right onto the US 85 ramp.

"We'll be in touch. Thank you for your time. Enjoy the Broadmoor!" The phone went dead.

(24)

Carolyn Abbott flew back to Chicago from Phoenix on Monday morning. She arrived at the offices of H. Forester and Associates at 10:30 a.m. and went straight to H's office. He smiled benignly at her as she entered and leaned back in his chair. He could tell by the determined look on her face that she wasn't feeling good about her latest assignment.

"So, how are things in Phoenix? Mogollon's stock is up another five points this morning!" H said, continuing to smile.

"I'm sure your investors will be happy," Carolyn replied, looking him in the eye and not smiling.

"Our investors," H leaned forward, his smile fading. His meaning was evident. He was still the boss and she was still the employee.

She leaned back and sighed, "I'm sorry. The management in Phoenix is trying, but they are behind the curve in today's application of business principles. They are still trying to run Mogollon as though it were a 1980's telephone company. And when I think of what McCann could bring to the table…"

H waved his hand to cut her off. "Let's not go there. It's not our call. The people who are putting up the money have other plans."

"Like what?" she asked, in a tired voice.

"Mogollon is going to be acquired very shortly," H replied, his smile returning.

"By who?" Carolyn asked, the consternation plain in her voice.

"Fairfield Communications," H said quietly. "I need you to go to New York City. I've got a couple of meetings set up for you there."

While Carolyn and H were meeting in Chicago, Stu Bailey was on the phone in New York City. Money was moving and rumors were flying. Stu was working his contacts to put his finger on what was going on. "Jeanine! Get me…" followed by the name of the person he wanted had become the phrase of the day as his beleaguered assistant placed one call after another and, at one time had three calls of hold at the same time. Bailey talked to money managers, merger and acquisition experts and three of his prime contacts, who were usually "in the know".

Finally, as the morning drew to a close, he began to assess what he had learned. He started thinking about how he could capitalize on it. At that moment, Jeanine reversed the process and spoke loudly from her desk outside his door.

"Stu! Pick up line one! Cindy Melzy!"

Jeanine leaned back in her chair and allowed herself to think about where she might go for lunch. It had been a rough morning. She decided on Sinigual, a Mexican restaurant just two blocks north of their offices.

"Hi Cindy, what's happening?" Bailey said, leaning back in his chair.

"I was about to ask you the same thing," the CEO of Triad replied.

"There are rumors flying, that's for sure," Bailey said, hoping Cindy might add to what he already had heard.

"Would our friends at Mogollon and Fairfield be part of those rumors?" Cindy asked in a quiet voice.

Bailey smiled to himself before responding. It was obvious that she was hearing the same things he had been hearing.

"Could be. What do you know?" he said, coyly.

"I know Carolyn Abbott is coming to see me tomorrow morning and I think she is going to tell me that Mogollon is on the block," Cindy replied. Her tone implied that she assumed that Bailey didn't know about Carolyn but did know about MoGollon. Bailey realized that she was offering a bit of information with a possible string attached.

"Let me guess," he replied carefully. "She's going to tell you that MoGollon's debt investors want to sell it and she's coming to you because those same investors are the ones buying Fairfield stock. I hear that tomorrow morning a filing will be made for plans to purchase up to ten per cent of Fairfield's common. Those investors will be looking for board representation. A new board member could institute an effort by Fairfield to acquire Mogollon. That board member would need to have a consortium backing him or her to add a few other investors to the main investor so that people wouldn't start putting two and two together to get five. Am I right?"

"That board member would need the help of someone below the radar screen but with their finger on the pulse of the way things work," Cindy replied. Her voice conveyed that she knew who that person would be.

"We should do lunch," Bailey replied, leaning back in his chair. "How about the Bull and Bear in about an hour?"

"See you there," Cindy replied, hanging up.

"Jeanine!" Bailey yelled.

Jeanine picked up her note pad and turned to go into his office. He gave her a list of things that he needed done "right away". As she returned to her desk, she thought, "So much for thoughts of a nice lunch out". She would be doing lunch at her desk again.

At noon, Bailey walked the six blocks from his office to the Waldorf and entered the Bull and Bear. Cindy was already seated at a table near the rear. After they had ordered, Bailey got right to the point.

"So…I'm thinking that to acquire Mogollon, Fairfield would need about two billion."

"Somewhere in the area of one point five to two point five," Cindy replied, smiling. Stu was always working the numbers. "Prices are not what they once were. We're recovering from a significant downturn, remember?"

"Yeah, some recovery!" Bailey retorted. His lack of confidence in the current administration in Washington was no secret to those who knew him.

"What's their EBITDA?" Cindy asked. Earnings before income taxes, depreciation and allowances were one of the multiples that could be used in valuing a potential acquisition.

"I don't know. You can't base it on historical because Carolyn Abbott is cutting costs and restructuring and refocusing faster than Sherman went through Georgia," Bailey said, taking a long drink from his coffee.

"What's she like? Do you know her?" Cindy asked.

"I've never met her. I only know what I read and hear. She works for H Forester and Associates out of Chicago. They represent a group of investors that no one seems to know much about. The routine is that H buys a company and sends Carolyn in to turn it around. She has done that on several occasions very successfully," Bailey replied. "You would like her. She thinks like you do."

"What's that supposed to mean?" Cindy asked, puzzled.

"You know…she's a Bible thumper just like you and Don Straylin and…Wils," at the mention of McCann's name, Cindy looked away. Bailey looked down, considering whether to go on or not. Cindy sensed that he had more to say and waited.

"I heard something this morning…about Wils I mean," Bailey said quietly.

"What?"

Bailey looked away and cleared his throat before speaking. His discomfort was obvious.

"Someone told me that the Fairfield board voted to ask Wils to be its new CEO and then changed its mind."

"Why?"

"The rumor is that H Forester's investor group nixed the idea," Bailey replied, looking down at his plate.

"Why?" Cindy asked again.

"I don't know. Someone with a lot of money doesn't like Wilson McCann," Bailey replied, as their salads arrived.

(25)

Carolyn Abbott flew into New York City on Tuesday morning. She had taken an early flight out of O'Hare. She arrived at the Triad offices shortly after 11:00 a.m. Cindy Melzy greeted her warmly as she was ushered into the Triad CEO's office.

Cindy gestured to the conference table and the two women sat opposite each other and exchanged pleasantries while Cindy's assistant brought in coffee and Danish. When the young man left and closed the office door behind him, Cindy leaned back in her chair and eyed the younger woman.

"So, what's this all about?" she said quietly.

Carolyn reached for a Danish and put it on a small plate beside her coffee mug. She hadn't eaten since having a bagel at O'Hare early this morning and her stomach was grumbling.

"I've been asked to approach you about something that, for the moment must remain confidential," Carolyn replied. She broke off a small piece of the Danish and popped it into her mouth as she waited for Cindy's reaction.

"That depends of course, on what it is," Cindy replied, taking a sip from her mug. "Let me be totally open with you. The word on the street is that someone or some group of investors is buying a significant stake in Fairfield Communications. That same someone or group also holds Mogollon's debt and the rumors are that they plan to offer to sell Mogollon to Fairfield. The Mogollon shareholders would love that because they would make back everything they had lost prior to your taking over as CEO. How am I doing so far?"

Carolyn smiled and took another bite of her Danish. Cindy Melzy was every bit as sharp as H had said she was. The fact that she shared Carolyn's faith was an added plus. Cindy was about ten years older than Carolyn and had been CEO of Triad for the last two years. She was the protégé of Malcolm Shaw, Triad's Chairman. Rumor had it that she had once been romantically interested in Wilson McCann before he met his wife Linda. Carolyn sensed that, before this conversation was over, Wilson McCann would be a part of it.

"You are spot on," Carolyn replied, taking a sip of coffee. She put the mug down and leaned forward.

"We need someone on the Fairfield board who would be willing to advance the idea of acquiring Mogollon. My employer feels you would be an excellent candidate to do that and, if you are agreeable, our investment group would put your name forward as early as tonight to take a seat on the Fairfield board as representative of our interests. We intend to have acquired at least ten per cent of the Fairfield stock by then."

"Who is 'we'?" Cindy said, her blue eyes boring into Carolyn's.

"H. Forester and Associates," Carolyn replied. She knew this wouldn't satisfy Cindy and she was right.

"I know who you work for and I'm well acquainted with the investment community in Chicago. But that doesn't tell me who is really buying all this debt and stock. And don't give me the name of the Singapore shipping company that bought Mogollon's debt."

Cindy's tone had an edge to it but it was a friendly edge and Carolyn appreciated it. She thought for a moment and made a decision before she spoke.

"Cindy, I work for H. He tells me to go run an operation that his firm has invested in and clean it up and turn it over to someone else. Then he sends me somewhere else and I do it all over again. That's what I'm doing at Mogollon. I don't know who or where the money is coming from. I know that sounds almost unbelievable but it is true."

"So...who would I be representing on Fairfield's board if I accept?"

"H would put your name forward." Carolyn replied.

"Why is Wilson McCann being blackballed by H. Forester and Associates?"

The room was suddenly a lot colder and quieter. The question had been asked in a level tone but Carolyn Abbott could sense the intensity of feeling that lay behind it. She found it very difficult to look Cindy Melzy in the eye.

"I honest to God don't know," she said meekly.

Janice DeGroot hadn't won journalistic recognition by sitting back and letting the news come to her. Those who knew her would, if asked to use one word to describe her, would have said "tenacious".

She had checked for a Charlie Dumas living in Waco, Texas and could only come up with a Fritz Dumas of the same general age as the man who had been in Farnsworth, based on Joyce Hall's description of him. She called her contact in New York City and asked for names of people in the journalistic fraternity who covered technology in general and telecommunications in particular. One of the names provided worked for *TechExec* magazine. She wangled some travel money from her Editor and flew to Dallas to talk with the woman. The result of the interview satisfied Janice that there

THE INVESTMENT

was no story in process or planned on Wilson McCann. There was also no one named Charlie Dumas on the payroll or under contract to do any such story.

(26)

It was late afternoon of the day following her meeting with Cindy when Carolyn Abbott boarded a flight from New York City to Phoenix. She was exhausted. Her meeting with Cindy had been followed by a meeting with Fairfield's Investor Relations Director at the law offices of one of Fairfield's board members. That meeting was followed by a call to H to advise him that Cindy had accepted the opportunity to become his appointee to the Fairfield board. By that time, the street had heard that a consortium of investors, led by H Forester and Associates had purchased a ten per cent interest in Fairfield in the open market and was seeking a seat on Fairfield's Board to be filled by Cindy Melzy, CEO of the Triad investment banking firm.

This morning, Carolyn had met with Mogollon's Executive Committee of the Board and participated in their deliberations as to how to best handle the negotiations with Fairfield to offer Mogollon to the Colorado Springs based aggregator.

At noon, she had lunch with Arleta Forester followed in the afternoon by a lengthy meeting of Mogollon's board. In addition to presenting a status report on her progress in turning Mogollon's operations around, she listened in as the Executive Committee presented the situation relative to a possible acquisition by Fairfield. As expected the board was unanimous in its feeling that

THE INVESTMENT

such an acquisition would be in the best interests of Mogollon's shareholders.

Arleta, in the role of the representative of a Fairfield investor, had gone from the Mogollon board meeting to meet with Cindy. They discussed the makeup of the investment consortium that would put together the financing of an offer by Fairfield to acquire Mogollon. Arleta had called Carolyn to brief her on that discussion.

Now, as she headed back to Phoenix, Carolyn knew that she would have to deal not only with the uncertainty among the management of Tachyons over their future, but the management team atMogollon as well. At times, it seemed that it was almost too much.

As the plane lifted off and banked to head southwest toward Phoenix, she opened a small Bible that she carried in her brief case. For several years, she had followed the practice of reading through the Bible in a year. She was into the book of Exodus and had reached chapter three where God calls Moses out of Midian to lead his people out of Egypt. As she read, the words on the page seemed be directly for her:

"Therefore, come now, and I will send you to Pharaoh, so that you may bring My people, the sons of Israel, out of Egypt."

But Moses said to God, "Who am I, that I should go to Pharaoh and that I should bring the sons of Israel out of Egypt?"

And He said, "Certainly I will be with you, and this shall be the sign to you that it is I who have sent you: when you have brought the people out of Egypt, you shall worship God at this mountain."

Carolyn leaned back in her seat and closed her eyes. She immediately thought of the fact that Fairfield was located in Colorado Springs, beneath the shadow of Pikes Peak. A small smile crossed her face as the thought ran through her mind that, ultimately, the people of Tachyons and the people of Mogollon would be part of a firm whose headquarters was next to the Colorado mountain. She felt reassured that, if this was God's will, he would be with her through it all.

Rather than fly back to Michigan, Janice spent some of her own money to change her ticket and fly to Chicago. She met with two of her Chicago contacts and asked how she could find a photo journalist named Shelly Martinez. Provided with some trade group material, she combed through it and found that a Shelly Martinez had just launched her own business and had already lined up a few clients. Janice arrived at Shelly's apartment building as the sun was dipping below the horizon.

She rang the button for Shelly's apartment number 220 and was rewarded with a female voice asking, "Who is it?"

"My name is Janice DeGroot. I'm a reporter from the *Bay City Times* in Bay City, Michigan. I'm here to talk to you about a certain Charlie Dumas and a fictitious magazine article about Wilson McCann of Farnsworth, Michigan. I'm about to blow the lid off this story and if you don't talk to me, I can't guarantee that you won't look bad in what I report." She said it with as much bravado as she could muster, hoping it would be enough.

There was silence that seemed to last a very long time. Finally, the door entry buzzed and Janice opened it and went in. The apartment was on the second floor. She climbed the stairs rather than taking the elevator and turned to see an attractive dark haired young woman standing in the doorway of number 220.

She held out her hand and the young woman ignored it. "What do you want from me?" She asked quietly.

"The truth, for starters," Janice replied. "Can I come in or do you want to talk in the hall where others can hear?"

"Come in," Shelly said, stepping aside.

The apartment was neat and well decorated. A partially eaten meal was on the dinette bar between the living room and the kitchen.

"I'm sorry, I've interrupted your meal," Janice said, trying to ease the tension.

"No you're not. What is it you want?" Shelly motioned to a chair in the living area. Janice sat down and took a small pad from her brief case. She usually used a recorder but knew that wouldn't be helpful in easing the tension between them. She glanced at the pad as if looking at a question list. The pad was blank.

"Who is Charlie Dumas?"

Shelly sat down on the sofa opposite her and took a deep breath. "If I tell you, you cannot use my name."

"Agreed," Janice said quickly.

"His name is Allen Gates. He owns and operates a private investigation agency here in the city."

"What is…was your relationship with this Allen Gates?"

"I worked for him. I helped him on work where he needed photo journalistic assistance," Shelly said quietly, looking down at her feet.

"So…let me guess…someone hired Allen Gates to investigate Wilson McCann and he masqueraded as Charlie Dumas and you went along to help him," Janice said, speaking rapidly. She was rewarded by the dark eyes fixing on her.

"Yes," came the simple reply.

"Who hired him?" Janice asked.

"I honestly don't know," Shelly said. Her eyes didn't waver and Janice knew instinctively that she was telling the truth.

"Had you done work like this before?"

"Quite a few times but we…Allen never lied about who he was before."

"Did Allen… and you do other work for the same person who hired him to investigate Wilson McCann?"

"Yes," Shelly replied, squirming a little on the sofa.

"What kind of work?" Janice pressed.

"That is confidential. I can't tell you that. You should talk to Allen."

"Fair enough. What were you and Allen supposed to gain from this work…the interviews with McCann and others?"

"All I know is that we were supposed to learn about what Allen called 'the man within the man'…what he was like…things that others thought about him…what his family and friends were like."

As she said this, Janice noticed something in her demeanor that changed.

"You came to like Wils McCann didn't you?" she asked.

Shelly looked away. Janice sensed something personal had impacted the young woman sitting opposite her.

"What happened in Farnsworth?" Janice urged.

"I…stayed one night with Belle Warner…she is a very nice lady…she…I became a Christian that night."

Janice leaned back in her chair. She knew all about Belle Warner and Phil Willard and Fred Penay and others in Farnsworth who were committed to their faith. While she didn't necessarily agree with all of their beliefs, she had always admired them. The fact that Wilson McCann was committed to the same faith had been fairly reported in any news items she had done previously.

"So, you embraced the same faith that your subject possessed… he and his family?" Janice asked quietly.

"Yes,"

"Then why didn't you be honest and tell them what you were up to?" Janice tried to keep her tone reasonable.

"I just couldn't. Allen warned me about that."

"So, you came back to Chicago, finished the job and resigned." Janice said it matter-of-factly.

"Yes,"

"But you won't tell me anything more about Allen Gates and who his client was or what else you did for that client?"

"I can't," Shelly's replay was firm.

Janice put her pad back in the brief case. The only thing she had written on it was the name of Allen Gates.

"I could use Allen Gates' address and phone number," Janice said, getting to her feet. "I'll understand if you don't want to provide it."

Shelly rose as well and went to a small desk. She opened the center drawer and removed a business card with her name and the address and phone number of Allen Gates Private Investigations. She handed it to Janice.

"Could I ask you a question?" Shelly said as she opened the door to the apartment.

"Sure," Janice replied, stepping out into the hallway.

"How is J.W. Storey doing?"

Janice turned and looked at Shelly. Mentally, she heard a second shoe drop. Shelly was interested in McCann's son!

"The last I heard, he was still in a medically induced coma," she replied, watching Shelly closely.

The attractive young woman seemed to relax a bit. "Thank you," she said as she closed the door in Janice's face.

(27)

Colter drove his rented sedan west from Farnsworth for the second time that week. As he did so, he watched in his rear view mirror as a dirty farm pickup pulled in behind him. His warning senses kicked in and he slowed to see if the pickup would pass. It did and he relaxed a bit as it widened the space between them. He glanced in the mirror again and this time, his senses went into overdrive.

The dark blue Impala framed in the mirror was the same one he had seen two days ago when he had left the village. He hadn't given it much thought then. Now, as he watched it keep pace, he remembered that he had seen it parked on the main street of Farnsworth near his room and near the plant when he got off work at 11:00 p.m.

There were lots of familiar cars and trucks on the main street of Farnsworth and he had attributed most of them to regulars within and without the community who had daily business there. There was no parking limit on the main street and he had observed some cars that remained parked for most of the day.

This car, however, bothered him. He couldn't really say why. The driver appeared to be a woman although he couldn't tell her age. The Impala kept pace when he sped up or slowed down. Finally, he pulled into a farm drive and let it pass. He waited until a woman appeared on the back porch of the farm house, looking at him questioningly. He pretended to be consulting a map and backed out onto the highway and headed back towards Farnsworth. He hadn't gone a mile when the Impala was once again in his rear view mirror.

Liam Colter felt a cold chill despite the warmth from his car's heater. He was being watched.

Janice spent more of her own money in making another change in her flights and renting a room. She spent a restless night and was lingering near the entrance to the Bradley Business Center on Chicago's North Side when Allen Gates came to work. She knew it was Allen Gates because she had spent an hour the previous night on her laptop researching Gates and his firm. In addition to the biographical information she had gained, she also read through several civil and criminal cases where Gates or a member of his small firm had given testimony. It was quite evident from these cases that Allen Gates' operations could be considered "high end" and "boutique" in their client services.

She entered their offices and was greeted by an attractive receptionist in a tight fitting blouse who evidently served as a common receptionist for several of the small firms who occupied offices in the building.

"Who may I say is calling for Mr. Gates?" the young woman asked.

"Janice DeGroot. I'm a newspaper reporter," Janice replied, handing the woman a business card.

"Do you have an appointment?" the woman asked, looking at the card and reaching for the phone.

"Yes," Janice lied.

Five minutes later a full bodied woman of about forty with short gray hair walked into the reception area. She didn't smile as she approached.

"Good morning. I'm Vera Haskell, one of Mr. Gates' associates. I'm afraid we don't show any appointment for you. Perhaps I can help?" Her tone carried a strong indication that she wasn't really interested in helping Janice in any way.

"I'm afraid there must be some mistake. I need to see Mr. Gates. It is very important," Janice responded in her best businesslike tone of voice.

"I'm afraid Mr. Gates is not in," the woman replied.

"I'm afraid you are mistaken. He came in about four minutes ago," Janice replied evenly, looking at her watch.

"I think you should leave," the woman replied, folding her arms across her ample breast.

"I will but would you be kind enough to give Mr. Gates a message?" Janice said, letting a small smile cross her face.

"What?"

"Tell him that I will be visiting with the authorities to determine if investigating people under a false name and business reference in an attempt to gather both personal and business information in violation of their personal privacy rights is against the law. The primary person involved in what could be an illegal activity is the CEO of a privately held Telecommunications company in Farnsworth, Michigan. I can do that with or without his cooperation. I would like to do it after having talked with him," Janice said, letting her words run out like a steady stream of bullets from a machine gun.

The woman took a step backward and dropped her arms to her side. When she replied, her tone was slightly milder.

"Please have a seat. I will speak to Mr. Gates and ask if he will speak with you,"

Janice turned and dropped into a chair. She looked up as the woman walked away.

"Thank you for your help," Janice said loudly in a pleasant tone of voice.

Fifteen minutes later, the same woman ushered her into Allen Gates' office.

"Ms. DeGroot, what can I do for you?" he said, without rising from his chair.

"Good morning Mr. Gates…or should I call you Mr. Dumas?" Janice replied.

"Either will be fine. There's no sense in my denying that I posed as Charlie Dumas. I'm sure a reporter with your obvious investigative skills could expose any such denial. Perhaps you would like a job with our firm," he smiled as he said it and gestured to a chair opposite his desk. She sat and leaned forward.

"Anything I say to you is off the record," Gates said conversationally.

"And why is that?" Janice countered.

"Because I assume you are going to ask me questions that would be harmful to my client if I were to answer them truthfully."

"Ok…for my satisfaction…who is the client that hired you to investigate Wilson McCann?"

"I cannot answer that," he said, smiling.

"Why did your client hire you to investigate Wilson McCann?"

"I can answer that question. I can even answer it on the record if you wish," he replied, leaning back in his chair.

"Please do," Janice said.

"I don't know," he replied.

(28)

Five people jammed into Dr. Jon Sager's small office at the Farnsworth Hospital. In addition to Sager, McCann, Linda and J.W., a distinguished red-haired man with glasses and an intimidating demeanor was seated at Sager's small desk. He spoke in a very abrupt and cold manner as he described what he would be doing to McCann one week from that day. When he finished his short description of what was involved in removing the damaged disk and fusing the two vertebrae, he sat back and looked McCann directly in the face.

"Do you want to do this?" he asked, rather coldly.

"I want to do whatever you think needs to be done to get rid of this pain I'm in," McCann replied rather meekly from where he stood against one wall. The pain from the drive in this morning was still with him.

Dr. Ralph Maxwell sat forward, smiled broadly for the first time and extended his hand. "You'll do fine!"

Shelley Martinez had flown into San Francisco two days ago. She rented a room at the San Francisco Marriott Waterfront near the airport. She got a good night's sleep and presented her program

THE INVESTMENT

to her San Francisco client the next morning. The client was ecstatic about Shelley's work and signed a three-year retainer over lunch. That success was added to the news that J.W. was well and out of the hospital. Her spirits were high as she went back to her motel. Her belief that God had a plan for her future was strong.

After she had another good night's sleep she intended to fly back to Chicago. As she walked into the airport, she decided, on the spur of the moment, to go to Michigan instead. After a short debate with an agent about whether it was better to fly to Chicago and book a new flight to MSB or change her Chicago flight to go to Detroit instead, she chose to change her return ticket and fly to Detroit. She intended to drive up to Farnsworth the next day.

She booked a room at the Detroit Metro Airport Marriott and rented a car. After another good night's sleep in Detroit, she drove north to Farnsworth and arrived at McCann's home at 11:00 a.m. the next morning. She rang the doorbell and knocked but no-one answered. She drove to the farm and saw, for the first time, the results of the fire. Most of the debris from the fire had been cleared away and work had already been completed to restore the small well house. Work was beginning on what looked to be a restoral of the barn foundation in preparation for re-building. The doors to the big tool shed were closed and no one was there. Disappointed, she got in her car and drove back to McCann's home.

She pulled in just as McCann, Linda and J.W. were returning from their meeting with Dr. Maxwell. J.W., smiling broadly, gave her a long hug while McCann and Linda stood to one side watching.

"I want to thank you for coming to the hospital," he whispered to her as he held her close. "It meant a lot to me." She felt the warmth of his embrace flow over her.

He released her and stood aside as both McCann and Linda greeted her warmly. They all went into the house and Linda immediately went to put the coffee on. McCann lay down on the sofa in the family room. Shelley was shocked at his appearance. He was obviously in a lot of pain. She sat in a chair opposite the couch. J.W. sat in a recliner close to her.

"How are you doing?" Shelley asked, looking at McCann.

"The bad news is I'm in a lot of pain. The good news is that surgery is scheduled and they tell me it should take the pain away," he replied with a brief smile.

"What kind of surgery," Shelley asked, looking at J.W.

J.W. gave her a brief rundown of their meeting earlier in the day with Dr. Maxwell. When he finished, he looked at McCann. Shelley followed his gaze and saw that McCann was asleep.

"The pain meds do that to him," J.W. said, with a brief smile. "Let's take a walk. You didn't get to see this place when you were here with good old Charlie Dumas!"

For a moment, she felt a touch of anxiety as she thought of the lie she had been part of when she first met J.W. She had to set that right!

"Let's do that! I need to tell you about my trip to San Francisco this week and what has been going on in my life," she said, getting to her feet.

They walked down the little hill to the barn and spent a few moments with Florie before moving down the path toward the stream. Tessa followed along behind them, darting off at various intervals to follow a scent. As they walked, she filled him in on the results of her trip and about her growing business.

J.W. for his part, told her about the dream he had while he was in the coma. "I saw my birth mother, plain as day," he said, the amazement he had felt then still present with him now.

"You are so fortunate. Try as I might, I can't remember my father and mother, my 'Padre' and my 'Madre'", she said, wistfully.

He turned to face her. "They died when you were young?"

"Yes, I don't even know where they are buried," she said, looking down.

THE INVESTMENT

"What were their names?" he asked, reaching out for her hand. She felt the warmth of his touch run up her arm as they continued to walk on.

"Roberto and Felina," she replied.

They came to the stream and sat together on the bench. As they watched the water flow by, Shelley turned toward him and looked into his eyes.

"J.W., I need to tell you something," she said, her heart racing.

When she had finished, he stood and walked a few feet away. He bent and picked up a small stone and tossed it into the little pool in the stream before them. The ripples in the water ceased before he turned back toward her. She could feel his steady gaze on her and she tried to look him in the eye but failed. She lowered her head and waited.

"Where do you stand with God?" he asked quietly.

She looked up and saw warmth in his eyes. In that moment, she knew that whatever the future might hold, they would always be friends and that there might be hope for even more.

"I've asked for forgiveness when I came to faith and I am walking in the assurance that I have been forgiven," she replied, not taking her eyes from his face.

"You need to make it right with my dad and with Linda," he said, in a reassuring tone of voice.

"I intend to do that before I leave today," she replied.

He turned back toward the stream. "It's nice here isn't it? He asked. She felt relief at his obvious move to change the subject and move on.

"It's very nice. Do you come here often?"

"Since I've been laid up, I do. Dad comes here a lot to talk to God. He and Linda sit here towards evening a lot. It's one of their special places."

She sensed that his thoughts were going somewhere else and to someone else. The question rose within her before she could stop it.

"How are you and Traycee doing?"

She regretted it the minute she said it but, at the same time, she felt like a barrier between them had been crossed.

"I haven't talked to her yet…since coming home from the hospital. I'm going back to California after dad has his back surgery and is home again. I plan to go to Fresno and see her."

"Well, good luck," Shelley said, as she stood and began to walk back toward the house. He fell into step beside her. As they walked together, Shelley felt that she had done all she could to open the door to whatever type of relationship with J.W. that God intended. It would be up to Him to guide J.W. to whatever lay ahead.

McCann was awake when they returned to the house and Shelley told him about her role in the deception with Charlie Dumas. To her relief, neither McCann nor Linda reacted negatively. Beyond asking a few questions about who had employed them and what she knew of the unknown employer's motives, they were quick to forgive her for her role in the situation.

They were very interested in Shelley's new career and accomplishments. J.W. sat quietly, smiling at her as she told them about her growing business and her latest customer contract.

"So, you will be going out to California often?" Linda asked as they sat down to lunch.

"At least four times a year. I hope to land other clients in the area to develop more of a base there," she replied. She felt her face redden as she realized what they might read into this.

McCann, standing by the kitchen counter to eat his lunch because of the pain in his back, smiled at her.

"Is this where you see your career going forward?" he asked.

She thought about it for a moment. "It is now, until the Lord leads me in a new direction. Ultimately, I would like to be doing something for Him."

"There are a lot of opportunities in ministry for a young person with your talents," McCann replied, walking around the counter and refreshing his coffee from the old percolator.

"I'd appreciate any guidance you would want to give me," she said sincerely.

"I'll think on it. I've got to get this back fixed before I'm much use to anyone," he sighed, as he took a sip from his cup.

Later, after exchanging hugs all around, Shelley got in her rental car and drove back to Detroit. A great weight had lifted from her shoulders. She had confessed her part in the deception of the previous year and had come away with a renewed friendship with Wilson and Linda McCann. Depending on what happened in Fresno, her friendship with J.W. might remain just that. She hoped for more but found it hard to hope for something selfish that might hurt Traycee, J.W. or both.

"Lord, I'm praying the 'prayer that never fails'" she said aloud as she drove down M-53. "Never-the-less, not my will, but thine be done!"

Liam Colter sat alone in his room as darkness descended on Farnsworth. The rifle and scope lay on the bed. The envelope that Tazlov had given him in Gary lay next to it. Colter was thinking about his mother.

She had passed away two years ago. He hadn't gone to her funeral. She had told him many years ago not to come back to Ireland. She knew what he had done and she knew that if he came back she would soon be attending his funeral.

His mother had been a devout Catholic. She had demonstrated the two greatest commandments that Jesus had affirmed. She had loved God with all her heart and she had loved others, even those who hated and lived out their hate in her troubled homeland. Liam Colter thought that his mother would have gotten along famously with Wilson McCann.

He now knew who the woman in the blue Impala was. He had driven rapidly out of town earlier that day, turned onto a gravel road into the brush country south and east of Farnsworth and driven into a lane in the brush and turned his car around. The blue Impala had appeared and from his vantage point in the lane, he got a clear look at the driver, a dark haired woman in her 30's.

He waited until the Impala had disappeared down the road and then drove back to Farnsworth. He spent the rest of the day thinking. His mind carefully sifted through every person he had come in contact with since the day that Tazlov had come to the bar. Ultimately, his mind came back to that day. The two men in the bar were regulars. They came in every other day or so to drink their beer and talk sports. The only other person in the bar that day, a rough looking woman, was a stranger. He concentrated on what he remembered. She had ordered a scotch and soda, sat at her table playing solitaire, while nursing her drink. When he had asked her if she need anything else she declined. She paid him in cash, including a generous tip, and continued to play. She had left the bar shortly after Tazlov.

He concentrated on bringing to mind her appearance. Colter was well acquainted with disguise. He had used elaborate disguises on many occasions in his line of work. The woman had appeared to be older than her eyes. Colter always concentrated on the eyes. That was what triggered his recognition. The woman's eyes were those of a much younger woman than her hair and clothing presented. Colter leaned back and squeezed his eyes shut, trying to match the woman to the woman in the impala. He had seen the woman in the car in profile. The nose was the same. The chin was the same. The woman in the Gary bar was the woman in the blue Impala! Something told him that she was a law enforcement agent.

"Probably FBI," he said to the darkened room.

"He's made me," Courtney Roberts said to the Tuscola County Sheriff, Dean Wilson. "He drove out into the country south of town today and I lost him. I think he was watching me when I followed him."

Wilson leaned back in his chair and sighed as he looked at the well dressed dark haired young woman on the other side of his desk. Special Agent Courtney Roberts had first approached his office over a month ago. She told him that the FBI suspected that a former IRA operative and reputed "hit man" was thought to be coming to the Farnsworth area for the purpose of killing someone. She hadn't told him who the target was. She hadn't asked for any assistance although Wilson had offered it. She stated that she simply wanted him to be aware that she would be working in the area and might, on short notice, need to involve the Sheriff's office and possibly the Michigan State Police. Wilson had made careful inquiry at the State Police offices and they had confirmed that special agent Roberts was, indeed, working on a case that they were aware of and that they were prepared to assist on, if called.

Now, Wilson stifled the urge to tell this young FBI agent that, if she had involved either the State Police or his offices in the case from the beginning, she wouldn't be in the situation she was in now.

"If you need our assistance, I need to know all the details," Wilson said, putting his hands behind his head and leaning even further back in his chair.

Fifteen minutes later, Wilson had what he wanted and a deputy was dispatched to cruise Farnsworth for the next several days. Special Agent Roberts took up residence in a back room of the Sheriff's offices and would monitor the situation from there.

Unfortunately, the deputy assigned to Farnsworth was sidetracked on the second day to deal with a family conflict at a farm west of the village. During the three hours he was away from the community, Liam Colter disappeared. Two days later, an envelope addressed to "The FBI Agent" in care of the Tuscola County Sheriff's office, arrived in the morning mail. The envelope contained all of the money and other information that Tazlov had given Colter in Gary. A yellow post-it note stuck to the packet of money contained a handwritten message that read, "I'm sorry we couldn't meet personally. I hope you won't think me rude to leave without saying good bye but I need to get on with the rest of my life. Give my regards to Mr. McCann. I would have liked to have met him. I've left a gift for you in the closet of my room in Farnsworth."

When Courtney Roberts, Dean Wilson and a deputy arrived at Colter's room, they found the rifle, scope and ammunition in the closet. The room had been carefully sanitized. Beyond the rifle, scope and ammunition, they found no traces that Liam Colter had ever been there. By the time an APB was issued, Liam Colter was in Barcelona.

Janice had spent the week following her trip to Dallas and Chicago on other assignments and in trying to sort out what she had or had not learned and how the pieces all fit together. In Janice's mind, there were two story lines. One was the mysterious investment in Mogollon which indirectly had given the unknown people behind that investment control over the acquisition of Tachyons.

Now, that same group of investors, represented by H. Forester and Associates of Chicago, had acquired a significant minority holding in Fairfield common stock. Her contact in New York City told her that there were rumors that the investors would recommend that Cindy Melzy, a minority investor and board member of Tachyons would be nominated by the investment group to take a seat on Fairfield's board.

At the same time, there were rumors that Wilson McCann had been blocked from becoming CEO of the new Mogollon and that an undisclosed plan by Fairfield's board to ask him to take the same position at Fairfield had been blocked as well. Word on the street was that the mysterious investment group had made it clear that McCann was not favored by them. Meanwhile, the stocks of both Mogollon and Fairfield had surged on speculation by one of the investment "gurus" in New York City that Fairfield would soon make an offer to acquire Mogollon.

Calls by Janice and many others to the offices of H. Forester and Associates had yielded nothing. The firm's spokesperson, H. Forester, and his wife, Arleta, smiled in public and issued "no comment" replies to questions.

As she sat in her kitchen, her third cup of coffee in hand, she looked out the window and saw the mail carrier stop at her mailbox and exit his vehicle. He came up the drive and deposited the morning mail, including a rather large manila envelope outside her front door. She put down her coffee and went to the door to retrieve it.

The brown envelope contained the incorporation and dissolution papers for BJM enterprises. She sorted through them looking for the names of the principals in the firm. There was only one. His name was Bennett Joseph McCall.

Janice took a final drink from her coffee cup and opened her laptop. She put the McCall's name in the search engine and when the screen refreshed, she sat there, amazed.

The small conference room at the plant of Farnsworth's leading employer was small to begin with and the eight people crowded into it made it seem even smaller. On one side of the table sat Sheriff Dean Wilson, Lieutenant McBride from the Michigan State Police, FBI agent Courtney Roberts and another FBI agent named Orto. On the other side of the table sat a profusely sweating Demitri Kalechov, the head of the plant's security service, the Human Resources Supervisor and an attorney for the company. "I know nothing!" Kalechov said for the fourth time.

"But you do know Ivan Tazlov," Agent Roberts replied.

"Yes! Yes! I've told you…we served together in the army in Russia years ago…he is a friend," Kalechov's voice was almost a wail.

"A friend who gives you expensive gifts to set up a man sent to kill someone," Sheriff Wilson said sternly.

"No! No! I know nothing about anything like that. Ivan gives me a gift. He wanted me to be happy in the new year!" Kalechov began to sob and wiped his eyes with a bandana that he continued to twist in his hands as the others sat back and watched.

"And Liam Colter…the man you knew as Clement, he told you that Tazlov had sent him," Roberts said methodically as she checked the notes on her tablet computer.

"Yes! That is true…you checked him! You hired him!" Kalechov almost shouted at the Human Resources Supervisor who appeared almost as nervous as he was.

"I've checked the records, Mrs. Robbins followed proper procedures, the references checked out," the attorney for the company interjected. It didn't seem to help the woman who continued to look down and fidget in her chair.

"There are no letters of reference. There are only internal telephone interview forms. We've checked the phone numbers in Chicago and they have all since been disconnected and they all had the same billing address. The people who occupied that address left a week ago," Agent Orto responded in a matter-of-fact tone.

"You screwed up! All of you! Wilson said, his voice rising. "You let a killer come into my county and live among us for two weeks…"

He stopped as Roberts laid her hand on his arm. But he continued to glare across the table at the attorney and the woman sitting next to him. Kalechov blew his nose loudly into his bandana.

McBride looked at Roberts and spoke quietly. "I think we have gathered about all we can here. Either we charge Mr. Kalechov with being an accessory to a conspiracy to commit murder and take him in or let him go for the time being. I suggest you pay Mr. Tazlov a visit."

"Mr. Kalechov, I'm warning you not to leave the county for the next month. You will surrender your passport and limit your travel. You will check in with Sheriff Wilson each day until notified to the contrary. We will be talking with you again," Roberts said, turning off her tablet and putting it into her briefcase.

"Demitri, I must inform you that you are suspended without pay until this is resolved," the company attorney said to Kalechov who covered his face with his hands as he sobbed.

(29)

The evening prior to his back surgery, Wilson McCann and his wife ate their dinner together quietly. J.W. had gone to the Marks' farm for an evening with Jim and Lona. He would go with them to the hospital in the morning.

Their meal was interrupted by the sound of a car coming in the drive. When Linda opened the door, she faced a dark haired woman in a parka with the hood thrown back.

"Mrs. McCann? Is Mr. McCann in?" the woman asked in a business like tone of voice that Linda found a bit unsettling.

"Yes he is but who are you?" Linda replied, standing in the doorway as if to prevent any unauthorized entry.

The woman reached into her pocket and produced a leather wallet which she flipped open, revealing her badge.

"Agent Courtney Roberts with the FBI," she replied firmly.

Linda's face revealed her shock but, before she could respond, McCann spoke from behind her.

"It's okay Linda, Agent Roberts and I have met before. Come in Agent Roberts," he said, taking Linda's elbow and gently moving her aside as the woman entered. Linda's face took on an even more questioning look and she turned it on her husband.

"What is going on here?" She asked, in an icy tone.

Five minutes later, McCann and Agent Roberts had brought

Linda up to speed. Linda, for her part was visibly upset with her husband for not telling her about Roberts' last visit to the home.

"You're telling me now...weeks later...that this gunman has been sent to kill you? Unbelievable! How could you do this?" Linda's green eyes blazed at McCann.

"I'm sorry...perhaps if I brought you up to date on where things stand..." Roberts interrupted.

"Yes. Please do! I'm so glad I'm here this time to learn what is going on about some mad man's attempt to have my husband killed," Linda responded loudly, turning her fierce gaze on the FBI agent.

"Simply stated, the man...Liam Colter...the man sent to...we think..." Roberts began lamely as she wilted under Linda's hostility.

"...to kill my husband? Go on!" Linda interrupted.

"He's gone," Courtney said, looking at McCann for help.

"Gone? Gone where?" Linda retorted loudly. McCann moved to his wife's side and attempted to put his arm around her shoulders but she shrugged it off and turned away. She stood with her back to the fireplace and continued to glare at them. Agent Roberts took a deep breath before responding.

"We don't really know. We think he may be in Europe."

Two hours later, Roberts was gone. Linda sat in the recliner next to the fireplace and McCann lay on the sofa, easing the pain in his back.

Linda had calmed down and looked across the room at the man she loved. She felt like slapping him and kissing him hard at the same time.

"What were you thinking?" she said, for the third time since Roberts had left.

"So many things happened all at once. You were gone. I didn't know if you would come back, J.W. was in a coma. The company was gone. Then the accident happened and then the fire, and Tessa was gone. I just figured that if the FBI somehow didn't stop him, he would just put me out of my misery," McCann said, trying to inject a little humor into it.

"It's not a laughing matter Wils," Linda replied even as she marveled inwardly at how the man on the couch, in obvious pain, could be so matter-of-fact about something this serious.

"I know. I'm sorry. I should have told you. I promise that if anyone is ever sent to kill me again and I know about it ahead of time, I'll tell you. Okay?" he said, cracking a small smile.

Linda got out of the chair and went to kneel beside him.

"I love you so," she said as she took his head in her hands and kissed him.

At 7:00 a.m. the next morning, McCann gripped the hand of the man he hoped would eliminate the physical agony he had been going through for the past five weeks. He was impressed by the change in manner by the Doctor. The cold, regimented personality displayed before McCann had agreed to the surgery had been replaced by a friendly encourager. McCann found himself wishing that Ralph Maxwell could do something to remove his emotional pain as well. The doctor, having checked in with his patient, left to "suit up" as he put it, for the day's activity. Elmer Gabbard came, had prayer with them, and left.

The small pre-op room at Farnsworth Hospital was cold. A Nurse's Aide assured him that she would bring a warm blanket once he was changed and on his gurney. There was only one other patient in the area when McCann, Linda and J.W. arrived. McCann completed the usual paperwork and changed into a gown. He climbed onto the gurney and the Nurse's Aide returned with a warm blanket. She was followed by a Nurse who would insert his IV. The Nurse asked the usual questions as to his name and birth date.

"Fred Zwick…January 3rd, 1990," he said forcefully.

"Ah! A wise guy eh? Do you know what we do to wise guys Mr. McCann?" the Nurse replied, smiling. He knew the face but couldn't place where they had met. Her name tag said "Julie".

"A pre-surgery colonoscopy?" he said, playing along while still trying to place her. Linda looked away, embarrassed. J.W. smirked.

"Pre-surgery circumcision," she said, wrapping a rubber strap around his upper arm in preparation for inserting the IV needle.

"Ouch!" J.W. said, grinning.

"Okay you two," Linda said, sitting in a chair beside the gurney and glaring at both McCann and J.W. McCann was still trying to remember where he had met Julie when Dr. Maxwell came in.

"Are you ready to do this?" he said, reading down through a form attached to a clipboard. He scribbled his name at the bottom and hung the clipboard at the end of the gurney. He then proceeded to mark the surgical site on McCann's back.

"I've been ready for five weeks," McCann said, shifting a little on the gurney to relieve the pain.

"Okay, let's get to it. I'll see the two of you in about four hours," the Dr. said, turning to Linda and J.W. "Kiss your man good bye… for now anyway!"

Linda bent to touch her lips to his. J.W. squeezed his hand. "New day, new back, and a new man!" he said encouragingly before they walked out.

Julie returned, this time in scrubs with a surgical mask draped below her face. It was then he remembered her. She was the Nurse who had taken him in to see J.W. on the day of the accident. Together with another Nurse, they rolled the gurney into the operating room. An Anesthesiologist came to the side of the gurney and introduced herself.

"What are we doing this morning?" she said through her mask.

"A partial hysterectomy," McCann replied, looking up at her. She turned toward Julie and McCann wished he could see her face behind the mask.

"He's a wise guy…but he's a good guy!" Julie said from behind her own mask. Let's put him to sleep so we don't have to listen to him anymore for four hours. I've got some Mantovani on this morning."

"One more time, Mr. McCann, what are we doing this morning?" came the muffled question as she inserted a needle into the IV line port.

"A back fus…," he began and then she was gone and the music began to play.

Janice stared at the screen in front of her in open mouthed amazement. Bennett James McCall was one of the richest men in America according to Wikipedia. Born in Chicago and educated at Northwestern University, his wealth had come initially from the 1976 sale of production rights to an oil pipeline valve that had been used extensively in the construction of the Alaska pipeline. In 1981, he sold the patent rights for millions of dollars and had invested in other businesses associated with the pipeline.

The article stated that he had shown an amazing ability to sell these businesses at the height of their earnings and reinvest the proceeds in subsequent ventures that had doubled and quadrupled his wealth. The article's introduction concluded with a statement that a definite dollar figure of his current wealth could not be estimated but that it was rumored to be in the area of twenty billion dollars. The introduction concluded by citing his involvement with many other businesses and investments.

She scrolled down to the personal section, which described McCall as being reclusive in his advancing years. She was not surprised to see that he had attended the same high school as Brendon

Vaughn. She opened up the high school year book that she had stored on her laptop and looked for his name and picture in Vaughn's graduating class. It wasn't there. She scrolled back two pages to the rows of pictures under the "Juniors" class heading and received her second surprise of the day.

McCall's picture was there. He was a dark haired teenager with a cocky grin on his face. The students were arranged in alphabetical order. Under each picture, the person's nickname was given. McCall's was "B.J."

But, what caused Janice to sit back and gape at the screen, was the picture to the immediate right of McCall's. Another dark haired young man looked straight into the camera with a faint smile on his teen-aged face. Under the picture was the name James McCann! Under McCann's name was the nickname "Jimbo". The resemblance to Wilson James McCann was striking!

McCann was in the Recovery Unit of the hospital until 3:00 p.m. He was moved to his own room and, at 5:00 p.m., he was sitting up and eating his dinner. It was the first meal he had eaten without needing to stand in several weeks.

As he pushed the tray to the side and lay back against the pillows, the Nurse came in.

"Let's walk, Mr. Zwick!" She said with a smile.

McCann grinned back at her. Obviously, the word about the "smart guy" had spread in the small hospital.

He swung his legs over the side of the bed and, trailing his IV pole behind them, he walked out into the hall and back.

"Good job!" she enthused as she tucked him in. "I'll be back at 7:00 p.m. and we will do it again."

"I can't wait," he said, closing his eyes. The large back brace that wrapped around his body wasn't the most comfortable for lying in bed. But, five minutes later, he was fast asleep.

The Nurse returned as promised and they repeated the same process. As they walked out into the hallway, he said, "I can walk farther this time."

"It's up to you…but don't overdo," she said, looking up at him.

They walked down the hall to the Nurses' station and around it. Dr. Jon Sager watched their progress from the doorway to one of the patient rooms. As they completed their circuit and headed back to McCann's room, Hager smiled broadly.

"Look at you! You are amazing!" he said enthusiastically.

"When can I go home?" McCann replied as he turned into his room and headed back to his bed.

Sager smiled. He expected as much from McCann.

"You don't like our accommodations? You don't like our personable staff? What's the hurry?" he asked. He checked the brace to make sure that it was in proper place as McCann sank back against the pillows.

"I miss my wife and my dog," McCann said, looking up at him.

"You saw them less than a day ago. I think we will keep you for a day or so more and then maybe you can go home. Dr. Maxwell will make that call," Sager said, as he turned to leave. Wilson McCann would be fine, of that he was sure.

Victor Tazlov sat back and stared at the two agents sitting opposite him at a table in the FBI's Chicago offices.

"So, let's go over this again. You say you gave Demitri Kalechov a two week vacation in the Bahamas but you know nothing about a man named Clement who told Kalechov that you sent him to take Kalechov's place at a plant in Farnsworth, Michigan. You further say that you know a man named Liam Colter only as a bartender in a bar that you seldom go to. Is that correct?" Agent Courtney Roberts asked.

"Da," Tazlov said confidently.

"And, you don't know anything about a plot to have Liam Colter, posing as the man named Clement, kill Wilson McCann?" Roberts said again.

Tazlov was well aware that all of this was being recorded. He smiled back at her. "Nyet" he said quietly.

"Then how do you explain this?" Roberts said, reaching into a thick binder in front of her and pulling out a well stuffed white business envelope.

The blood drained from Tazlov's face as she slid the envelope across the table to him.

"I want to talk to my attorney," he said, his voice less confident.

McCann came home on the morning of the third day after his back surgery. He wore the custom made back brace that covered almost all of his back. Two Velcro straps wrapped around to the front over a large pad and held the brace firmly in place. He could now sit for extended periods of time until the brace became uncomfortable and he stood or lay down to relieve the discomfort. He immediately began a regimen of walking the length of the house and back fifteen times, four times per day. Linda watched him carefully and was quick to forestall any activity that she thought not in his best interests. As early February brought a warming trend and two sunny days to the Michigan's Thumb, they were able to put on winter parkas and sit on their deck to enjoy the sunshine. When McCann wanted to walk down to the barn, Linda quickly ushered him back inside just as the phone rang. They let it ring and listened as Janice DeGroot left a message indicating she was working on a "significant news story" that she thought McCann would have an interest in and that she needed his perspective. They decided to call back later.

By Friday, McCann was walking to the road and back and down to the stream without problems. Linda took him into town for his post-operative check up with Dr. Sager. Once that was completed, they went to McCann's office to say good bye to his staff. McCann had requested no "going away party" but Tammie Ring disregarded her boss's desires and McCann and Linda were greeted in the conference room by his immediate staff and as many from the office as could attend. When the goodbyes had been said and, in a few cases, the tears had been shed, he went to his office to do a short video conference with Carolyn Abbott in Phoenix. Mogollon's official acquisition of Tachyons would be effective at 5:00 p.m. that evening. Carolyn would come to Farnsworth on the weekend and meet with the staff on Monday morning. Tammie had cleared out McCann's office of any personal belongings and arranged for them to be brought to his home.

McCann sat in his chair and looked around the office. The bareness of his surroundings matched the barrenness that he felt inside. Linda decided to wait for him outside his office with Tammie.

"I'm not sure what to say, Wils," Carolyn said from the screen on his desk.

"Not much to say," McCann replied, trying to force a smile. He liked Carolyn Abbott. The circumstances he found himself in were not of her doing. He felt some satisfaction in knowing that she would provide good leadership to those who had supported him for so long and so well.

"Is there anything you would like me to do? Anything you need?" she asked.

"Can't think of anything. I know you will take good care of the folks here," he replied, trying to keep his tone light.

"Your severance will be deposited at 5:00 p.m. this evening. I've checked and everything is in order," Carolyn said. McCann would receive a substantial severance payment under the terms of his employment agreement with Tachyons. The agreement provided that, in the event of the sale of the company, the acquiring company would have to offer a similar position to McCann. In the absence of such an offer, McCann's "golden parachute" had deployed.

"Thanks Carolyn. I appreciate that. Is there anything I can do for you?"

"No, I am sorry this has to end this way. I hope you know that, in some areas, I am just following orders," she said. She looked down as she said it and he couldn't see her eyes. He sensed that Carolyn Abbott was not enjoying this any more than he was.

"Okay then, good luck and take care," he said in a tone indicating that, for his part, the conversation was over.

"Okay Wils, you too," Carolyn Abbott said and the screen went blank.

In Phoenix, Carolyn Abbott sat back in her chair and closed her eyes.

"Why is this happening? Why did I have to do this?" she thought as she sat there.

In Farnsworth, McCann took one more look around and stood. The brace held him stiffly erect and he was grateful for that. He stifled the urge to ask himself "why?" again and moved to the door. Tammie Ring and Linda both stood as he came through the doorway. Tammie gave him a quick hug and brushed away a tear.

"Bye boss," she said, as she turned away.

McCann and Linda left through a side door and got into the Ranger. Tammie stood there, watching the old familiar truck as it slowly pulled out of its parking space and drove away with Linda behind the wheel.

ROBERT W. ZINNECKER

"I don't understand it," Ted Lark said from the doorway.
"Neither do I. Maybe we will learn why they did this to him on Monday," Tammie said, as she sank into her chair.

(30)

Tachyons used two conference rooms at the Dunt Center. As the sun climbed higher in the sky, giving promise of a beautiful late winter day, technicians began to place microphones at a podium at one end of one of the rooms. At the sides of the room a pair of TV crews from two competing channels were setting up their cameras. Other than a PR representative from Tachyons, the only people in the room were from print, radio and TV.

Fifty feet down the hallway from where the media activity was taking place, a group of twenty people sat looking at Carolyn Abbott as she rose and took her place behind a similar podium.

The group was comprised of the top eighteen management people from Tachyons and two people from Mogollon in addition to Carolyn. As she moved to the podium, she could feel the tension in the air and the room became deathly quiet as she spoke.

"Good morning ladies and gentlemen. As most of you know, I am Carolyn Abbott. I am the acting CEO of Mogollon Communications and, as of this morning, I am also the CEO of Tachyons. Also, as of this morning, Mogollon's acquisition of Tachyons became final. We have met all of the governmental and regulatory stipulations associated with the acquisition and I am pleased with the job our people have done to accomplish this almost two months ahead of schedule. Mr. Kearn, Mogollon's Director of Legal and Regulatory Affairs, is here with us today and can answer any questions relative to the legal and regulatory aspects of the acquisition."

She nodded to a gray haired man seated in the front row. He nodded back nervously.

There was a noticeable murmur in the room. She noted several heads looking down. She waited a moment and continued.

"I am here to announce several things that will, in some way impact all of you. First, the integration of Tachyons into Mogollon will move forward as quickly as possible."

"Second, we will be moving the headquarters of Tachyons to Phoenix as quickly and expeditiously as possible. However..."

The murmur in the room was a little louder this time and she paused until it subsided.

"As I was about to say...we will, however, make every attempt to re-focus the workforce located in Farnsworth so as to do our best to maintain employment levels close to what they currently are. There will, however, as in most situations of this type, be re-locations, transfers, re-assignments, promotions and, in some cases demotions and separations. That leads me to my third announcement."

The hush had resumed as the group focused on what was about to be said.

"I'm sure that many of you have heard rumors as to the condition of Mogollon's information systems. They are traditionally based Information Technology systems and, quite frankly, they have not handled some of Mogollon's most recent acquisitions and integration attempts. Tachyons, on the other hand, has based its information systems on state-of-the-art cloud based technology. Most of you are familiar with that approach which was championed by your previous CEO, Mr. McCann."

She noted several heads nodding in agreement but the looks on the faces were not friendly.

"It is our plan to expand that cloud based platform and migrate

Mogollon's information systems to it. Farnsworth will be the new Mogollon's technology hub for that migration. I've asked Ted Lark, Tachyons' IT Director to take charge of that migration. Ted will be working with existing Mogollon IT staff and representatives from our consulting firm, MTD, to accomplish that mission as quickly and efficiently as possible."

Many of the eyes in the room turned to look at Ted Lark who was sitting in the rear of the room. He kept his face serious and his gaze fixed on Carolyn.

"As a part of that transition, I used the term 'hub'. I want you all to become familiar with that term. We will apply it often in our shared future. Tachyons operates a service center in Edina, Minnesota. Five miles from that center, Mogollon operates its Midwest regional operations. We will merge those two operations and Edina will become the customer service hub for the new Mogollon."

The murmur came again and she let a brief smile cross her face.

"Mogollon has a small operation in Indiana and one in Illinois. Tachyons has a fairly good sized operation in Michigan. Farnsworth will become the operational 'hub' for those three states under the direction of Doug Warner."

There were brief smiles on some of the faces and eyes turned to Doug who was seated beside Ted Lark. He nodded his head and smiled briefly.

"Lastly, Mogollon's Human Resource Department is located in Phoenix. Its Director of Human Resources, Gerald McNeary, is nearing retirement. He will retire before the end of the year. I'm pleased to announce that Tachyons' Director of Human Resources, Kathy Garrety, who has done an excellent job of filling in while Mr. McCann was incapacitated, will become the Director of Human Resources for the new Mogollon upon Mr. McNeary's retirement. I have given Kathy the option of remaining here in Farnsworth or moving to Phoenix."

Again the eyes moved to Kathy who was seated at the end of the second row next to an older man who most assumed was Gerald McNeary. Kathy smiled briefly and looked down at a folder in her lap.

Carolyn shifted on her feet and stood to the side of the podium. "Are there any questions?"

A hand rose in the middle of the group.

"Yes?" Carolyn said. She thought she could guess what the question would be.

"What about Mr. McCann?"

The hush returned. Carolyn let her gaze sweep her audience as she prepared to provide the answer that she hadn't wanted to give.

"As I am sure you all know, Mr. McCann, as of last Friday evening, is no longer with the company."

Six miles from where Carolyn Abbot was speaking to the Tachyons management team, Wilson McCann stood looking out the window of his home at the slowly melting snow in the field below him. The late morning sun was erasing much of the last few months' accumulation. He smiled to himself. The sun and Carolyn Abbott were a lot alike. They were warm and pleasant while at the same time, they destroyed the past.

Linda sat at the kitchen bar, enjoying a late morning cup of coffee. The aroma from the old percolator filled the room.

"I can't believe she didn't even ask you to attend," she said. Her tone was reflective with a little bitterness mixed in.

He didn't turn. "I would have done the same if I were in her shoes. It's a new beginning. I would have been a distraction."

"I'm glad for Kathy, Doug and Ted. They are good people," Linda said, eyeing her husband's back. The big black wrap-around brace was prominent in the sunlight flooding in through the window. He was getting stronger and was walking two miles each day.

"She is doing everything she can possibly do to mitigate the impact of the acquisition. This technology hub thing could be a real boon for the community. If more companies are acquired in Doug's states, that could add employment as well," McCann said. His tone was slightly wistful.

He turned toward her. She was wearing a denim shirt and jeans. His heart lurched again as it had over three years ago when he had first held her in his arms. Their love for each other had survived a rough spot and was back in full force.

"I think you should do it," he said it as forcefully as he could.

"Don't you think I would become a distraction?" she replied, looking up at him as he came to the bar and sat on the stool next to her.

"You won't let that happen. And, besides, Ted and his team know you and respect you and you have experience that will drive this project through as quickly and successfully as possible," he said, placing his hand on her arm.

"Al would be working with me," she said, looking out the window as a hawk swooped down on the hedgerow.

"I'm glad he's happily married with two kids," McCann smiled. He knew that, in the years before he and Linda had fallen in love, Al Prince had been hopelessly smitten with Linda. Al had worked shoulder to shoulder with her on many projects including the revitalization of EECM's information systems.

"We're all getting old," she said quietly, looking down at her coffee cup.

"Not too old," he said, squeezing her arm. He knew where her mind was going. Al Prince had two children and they had none. "God is faithful," he said quietly. A month ago, that statement would have brought on, at best, a stony silence.

"I know. I just have to trust Him more," she said, turning and kissing his cheek.

Mike Divell had called two days ago. Carolyn Abbot had signed a contract for MTD to work with Tachyons and Mogollon personnel to migrate Mogollon's information systems to Tachyons' cloud based technology. Mike had asked Linda to lead the team to do it. The work would involve activity in Farnsworth and in Phoenix over the next three months. The positive aspects were working in Farnsworth. The negative aspect was traveling to Phoenix and working there. She didn't like to be away from McCann while he was still rehabbing from his back surgery.

"I'll be fine. I can work on the EECM plan with the committee and Lark and John," he said, trying to reassure her.

"No planning trips to North Carolina though!" she admonished, giving him a firm look.

"Yes ma'am!" he smiled back at her. "Now, make a decision!"

"Okay, I'll do it," she said, taking a final drink from her cup, getting up and reaching for the phone.

McCann smiled but at the same time felt a little envy. Linda would be busily occupied for the next three months. The challenge would help to renew and revitalize her. He would be limited in what little he could do around here and the committee work for EECM. He would have a lot of time on his hands. He turned again to the window. Brown grass was emerging from the snow. The seasons were beginning to change and advance. He would need to change as well. But would there be a 'springtime' of renewal and revitalization for him?

Linda paused, phone in her hands, "Have you heard from J.W. since he left?"

J.W. had left a week ago. He had spent four days in the hospital after coming out of the coma and then over two weeks here with McCann and Linda. Dr. Sager cleared him to return to California a week ago and he had left the previous Friday morning. McCann was slightly bothered by the fact that his son hadn't called but attributed it to J.W.'s excitement over stopping to see Traycee on his way back to Palo Alto. McCann sensed that his son planned to "pop the question" when he saw her in Fresno. Both McCann and Linda cautioned him to let the young woman know that he was coming but he had replied that he wanted to surprise her.

"I haven't heard from him. It's a little odd. I'll give him a call tonight when I know he's home from work," McCann replied.

A week earlier, J.W. Storey sat in his rented automobile, parked just down the street from Traycee's condo in Fresno. He had arrived in Fresno, by way of Los Angeles, that afternoon. He drove directly to Traycee's condo and found her car in the drive but no one answered the door. He retreated to his car to wait. The street was lined with cars as the condo complex's small parking lot was filled. He assumed that Traycee was working late or having dinner with friends. He chided himself for not having called her from the airport but he had wanted to surprise her. Daylight turned to dusk and then to darkness and the streetlights came on. The entrance to Traycee's condo was lit up by one of the streetlights but J.W.'s car sat in the shadows.

An hour later, a car came down the street and parked opposite the entrance to Traycee's condo. The driver's side door opened and a tall dark haired young man got out. The passenger side door opened a moment later and Traycee emerged. She reached back into the car and pulled the seat forward. A little girl about four or five emerged and Traycee picked her up and kissed her. The young man came around the car and took the child from Traycee after giving her a hug and a kiss. As she mounted the steps, Traycee turned and blew a kiss to the two of them. The young man put the child back into the car, got in, and slowly drove away.

J.W. Storey absorbed what he had just seen and his heart sank. He sat there in the darkness as he considered what to do. Finally, he started his car and slowly drove away.

Janice DeGroot had spent the weekend calling everyone she could think of who might shed some light on Bennett McCall and his activities. She called H Forester and Associates and was told that Mr. Forester was "unavailable". She called Shelley Martinez and left a message asking if Shelly knew Bennett McCall. She called Allen Gates and, when told that Mr. Gates was also "unavailable", she told the receptionist to "tell him that Janice DeGroot called and I know about Bennett McCall". She hoped that would make Mr. Gates more "available".

Now, as Monday dawned, she sat in her kitchen drinking coffee and putting the pieces together in her mind. Bennett McCall and James McCann had been classmates. Bennett McCall had made a lot of money. Bennett McCall's money was somehow tied to the debt purchase at Mogollon and Mogollon's subsequent acquisition of Tachyons. Now, it seemed that someone, possibly McCall again, was buying into Fairfield and pushing Fairfield to buy Mogollon. From a financial standpoint, with the way the market as reacting to all this, it seemed like a perfectly logical set of business moves.

She scribbled on her yellow pad. She drew a flow chart of her thoughts and wrote in the boxes. Janice liked to think things through and create a flow to her thinking that would ultimately result in an orderly, well-written piece of journalism. As she scribbled, she had trouble connecting the one box in the flow that dealt with Wilson McCann's relationship with Bennett McCall. Why would McCall, if in fact it was McCall who hired Gates and Martinez to build a file on McCann, be barring McCann from playing any role in Tachyons or Mogollon?

Impatient, she called her contact in New York City. She talked with him for ten minutes and another unanswered piece of the puzzle presented itself. Her contact related that there was a rumor going around that Fairfield's Board of Directors had made a decision to hire Wilson McCann as their new CEO but that decision had been turned back by the "new investor" in Fairfield's common stock. He further told her that Cindy Melzy had been elected to Fairfield's Board at the insistence of that same "new investor".

Janice put the phone down and called Cindy. Cindy had not arrived at her office. Janice accepted the offer to leave a message on Cindy's voice mail.

"Hi Cindy! Its Janice DeGroot from Michigan. I hope you remember me from when I wrote about the formation of Tachyons. I just learned that you are going on Fairfield Communications' Board as the representative of a new investor in that company. I wonder if you know why that investor, whom I suspect is, in reality, Bennett McCall, wants to keep Wilson McCann, your friend and former CEO of Tachyons, from becoming Fairfield's new CEO? I would appreciate a call back. Here's my number."

Janice gave her number and hung up the phone. She sat back with a smile on her face. She called this "stirring the pot" and it had served her well in the past. As she sat there, she thought of one more "pot" that she could "stir".

She glanced at her watch. It was just after 9:00 a.m. She was due in Farnsworth for Carolyn Abbott's press conference at 10:30 a.m. The roads, on this relatively worm February morning would be clear. She could be there in forty minutes easily.

Both McCann and Linda were upset. Repeated calls to J.W. had not been returned over the weekend. Finally on Monday morning, Linda called Traycee at her office. After the preliminaries of inquiring about each other's health, Linda got to the point.

"How did things go with J.W. on Friday?" she asked.

"What?" came the puzzled response.

"Didn't J.W. see you on Friday?" Linda asked, her voice rising slightly.

"No. I haven't seen him and he hasn't called," Traycee replied.

"I'm sorry. J.W. left for California early Friday morning and he was going to come to see you and surprise you. He didn't come?" Linda asked again, realizing that she was sounding redundant.

"No. I haven't seen him, I told you," Traycee replied, a little impatience creeping into her tone.

"Traycee, we haven't heard from J.W. since he left and he isn't returning our phone calls. Were you home on Friday?" Linda asked, realizing she was being impertinent to ask.

"I worked until after 5:00 p.m. and then went to a young adult meeting at my church with a friend. He brought me home about 8:00 p.m.," Traycee replied.

Linda thought for a moment as what Traycee had said registered.

"I'm sorry for being so nosy but you said 'he' brought you home. Your friend is a man?" Linda said, as quietly and politely as she could.

There was a pause on the other end of the call. Finally Traycee replied.

"Yes. Our Assistant Pastor and I have gone out a few times. He brought me home. Why do you ask?"

"Traycee, is it possible that J.W. was waiting when you came home and he saw you?" Linda asked.

The reply came after a long pause and was barely audible. "Yes."

Linda promised to call back after she or McCann had spoken to J.W. and hung up the phone.

McCann, sitting in the big recliner with Tessa on his lap, looked at her, concern registering on his face.

"What?"

"I think J.W.'s surprise for Traycee may have turned into a surprise for J.W. I think we had better try to get in touch with his boss or his landlady…or both," Linda replied.

(31)

Carolyn Abbott dropped into the chair in McCann's old office and heaved a sigh of relief. Since morning dawned in Farnsworth, she had held the meeting with the management team and then met with the press. The meetings had gone well with the exception of several questions concerning McCann's departure from Tachyons by the press. Her description of a "mutual agreement" between Mogollon and McCann was accepted but she doubted the question would die there. She suspected that several of the reporters, including the woman from the *Bay City Times,* whom she knew to be a friend of McCann's, wouldn't let it drop there. She was puzzled that the woman had not asked one question during the press conference.

She was about to check her e-mail when Tammie Ring came to the doorway.

"I'm sorry to interrupt, but one of the reporters from this morning's press conference is back. She wants to talk to you and she gave me this to give to you."

Tammie handed a small envelope across the desk.

"Which one is it?" Carolyn asked, not opening the envelope.

"Janice DeGroot from the *Times,*" Tammie replied.

Carolyn leaned back in her chair and held the envelope while she looked out the window. Finally, she opened the envelope. Inside was a small slip of paper, torn from a yellow legal pad. The neat handwriting seemed to jump from the paper.

Why would Bennett McCall keep Wilson McCann from becoming CEO of Mogollon and now of Fairfield?

Carolyn took a deep breath and leaned forward toward her laptop computer, resting on the desk. She opened it and spoke to Tammie at the same time.
"Give me five minutes and then show Ms. DeGroot in."

In New York City, Cindy Melzy played Janice DeGroot's message through for the third time. She knew Janice from her coverage of the formation of Tachyons. She admired the woman's persistence. She knew that Wilson McCann also liked her. They had joked on several occasions that if they could ever get Janice to accept Jesus Christ as her savior, the cause of Christianity would gain a noble warrior.

She knew a little about Bennett McCall. Unlike many of the other "raiders" who bought into companies for the purposes of either re-shaping them or forcing them to shed unprofitable operations or even to put themselves up for sale, McCall, a reclusive, shadowy individual who lived behind the scenes, was more interested in operating the businesses and usually did so through a surrogate or group of surrogates.

She called her mentor and Chairman of Triad, Malcolm Shaw, and asked for more information. Shaw, a Wall Street veteran, and twenty years her senior, would know McCall. Of that she was sure.

"I've only met him on a couple of occasions. Before he made

his first fortune, he was quite a gregarious fellow. Once he began to make some serious money, he became a recluse and disappeared into the background and used others to handle things for him. He has a network of people all around the world who act on his behalf and are amply rewarded for doing so. Why do you ask?" Shaw responded to her question about McCall.

"I have reason to believe that he is behind the purchase of the Mogollon debt, Mogollon's acquisition of Tachyons and now the investment in Fairfield that resulted in my seat on Fairfield's Board. Does H. Forester work for McCall?"

"I don't know, but I wouldn't be surprised. H and Ben traveled in the same circles in Chicago and, if memory serves me, they both went to Northwestern," Shaw replied. Is H involved in this too?"

"Carolyn Abbott, the acting CEO of Mogollon, works for H. She told me that H was one of those behind the investment in Fairfield," Cindy replied.

"…and you are interested in Ben McCall…why?" Shaw asked.

"Because, for some reason, Ben McCall doesn't want Wilson McCann to have a job," Cindy said firmly.

"Very interesting," Malcolm Shaw replied, in his cultured British accent.

J.W.'s landlady, Helen Loree, eighty five years old with hearing and vision problems, was very concerned about him. Her niece, Margaret had moved in to stay with her during the almost two months that J.W. had been away. She loved her niece dearly but Margaret tended to be a little impatient with her elderly aunt. J.W. was kind and patient with her. She loved having him in the upstairs apartment over her living quarters. When J.W. had returned in the middle of the night on Friday, Margaret had gotten up and checked on him. The next morning she told Helen that J.W. was back but that he seemed very quiet and distant. Perhaps his recovery from the accident hadn't gone as well as she had been told by his father when he had phoned her about two weeks ago.

When she wanted to go up and say hello to him, Margaret cautioned her to let him rest. He had had a long flight and then driven all the way from Fresno last night. Helen couldn't understand why he had been in Fresno until Margaret reminded her that his former girlfriend now lived there.

Helen's concerns mounted when J.W. appeared late in the day on Saturday, unshaven and with dark circles under his eyes. He had only visited with her for a few minutes before going back to his apartment. He had remained there during the day on Sunday and had left early this morning for his office. Margaret had also gone to work after telling Helen that she would pack up and move back to her own home that evening.

Just a little after noon, the phone rang. Helen assumed it was Margaret telling her that she had a real estate client and would be late tonight. She was surprised when Wilson McCann's voice was on the line.

"Hello Mrs. Loree," McCann said. "How are you this morning?"

"Well, I'm concerned about your son," Helen replied directly. Before she could say anything more, McCann interrupted her.

"J.W. is there? Is he all right?" Even with her hearing problems, Helen could detect the anxiety in his voice.

"He's here but I'm not sure he's all right," she replied, trying to adjust her hearing aid as she did so.

"What do you mean?" McCann quickly responded.

She told him quickly about J.W.'s return and his behavior. When McCann asked if she knew whether J.W. had been in Fresno, she said he had.

"Did he see the young woman he was sweet on?" she asked.

"We don't know but we assume that something happened there that may have resulted in his behavior," McCann replied. "Will you tell him I called and ask him to please call us?"

"I will and I'll get to the bottom of this. I want you to know that I love this boy like he was my own and if he has a problem, I'll put my prayer power to work on it," the old lady said, firmly.

"Thank you Mrs. Loree, we appreciate that," McCann replied.

Tammie ushered Janice DeGroot into the office and Janice seated herself comfortably in the chair opposite Carolyn. She dropped her brief case beside the chair and took a yellow legal pad from it. The two women eyed each other for a moment before Janice broke the silence.

"Thank you for agreeing to speak with me. I didn't want to ask my questions during the press conference. I hope you understand why."

"Yes, thank you for that. It might have been a bit unsettling to say the least," Carolyn replied, eyeing her.

"I trust you have taken a few minutes to familiarize yourself with Bennett McCall…that is in case you weren't already familiar with him," Janice said in a friendly tone.

"I did…although I'm still not sure why you are asking about him and what it is that one of the world's richest men has to do with Mogollon and Fairfield."

"At present, I'm not really too interested in the business aspects of either company but when a man of Wilson McCann's capability is not part of the future of either company, and rumors persist that someone with money is keeping him from being part of that future,

I'm interested in that. After all, Mr. McCann and his family are part of the community which my paper serves…a very positive part I might add."

"What makes you think that this Mr. McCall is involved in Mr. McCann's future…or the lack of it?" Carolyn asked in a guarded tone of voice.

Janice reached into her brief case and extracted a page of paper with rows of pictures on it. She handed it across the desk to Carolyn who gave it a confused glance.

"This is a copy of a page from a high school year book from a high school in Chicago. Take a look at the fourth row, fifth and sixth pictures," Janice said, leaning back in her chair.

Carolyn did so and put the paper down. "So?" she asked.

"Come on, Ms. Abbott! The boys in the pictures are Ben McCall and James McCann, Wilson's father. I have reason to believe that Ben McCall hired a private investigator, named Allen Gates, working under a fictitious name, to spend over a week here in Farnsworth last fall investigating Wilson McCann. This was done under the guise of doing an article for a technology magazine that has since denied the existence of authorization for such an article. If that is true, that borders on criminal activity."

It all came out in a rush and Carolyn found herself struggling to keep up with all that this woman was throwing at her. She needed to talk to H Forester.

She leaned forward and tried to speak as forcefully and honestly as she could.

"Ms. DeGroot, I don't know anything about this. I can promise you that I will consider everything that you have told me and, if I have anything to say that would help you, I will contact you. Now, I must ask you to leave as I need to catch a plane back to Phoenix and I have a few calls to make before I leave."

Janice rose and put her pad back in her brief case. She pointedly left the copy of the year book page on the desk between them. She smiled briefly down at Carolyn.

"Thank you for your time, I'm sure we will talk again in the future," she said, as she turned toward the door.

As she exited the building, she smiled to herself. She was certain that she had "stirred the pot" in Carolyn Abbott's world.

H Forester picked up the phone, ready to withstand another of Carolyn's complaints about the treatment of Wilson McCann. Arleta had taken Carolyn's call and then called H. She told him that Carolyn was on the phone and sounded upset. H. could only assume that the meeting in Farnsworth had once again raised questions about why McCann was not part of the Tachyons-Mogollon transition.

"Hi Carolyn, how did things go?" H said, as cheerfully as he could.

"I want to talk to Ben McCall," Carolyn Abbott said into his ear. "I want to hear him tell me what he has against Wilson McCann."

H felt as though someone had punched him in the stomach. How had she found out about Ben? His mind raced as he tried to think of how to respond.

"What are you talking about?" He said lamely.

"Come on H! Pick up your smart phone. I just sent you a message with a picture of Wils McCann's father and Ben McCall in it. I got it from a reporter. She says Ben McCall is the one who is keeping McCann from being CEO of Fairfield!"

H Forester had always respected Carolyn Abbott for her intelligence and integrity. He knew that it was useless to try to duck this issue. Carolyn wouldn't buy that.

"And what if he refuses to see you?" he asked, matter-of-factly.

"Then you will have my resignation on your desk by the end of the day," Carolyn Abbott replied.

(32)

Linda had driven into Farnsworth to do some grocery shopping. She wanted to assure that McCann had food to eat without the necessity of driving while she went to Phoenix along with Ted Lark to get their first look at the Mogollon information systems and assess what kind of effort would be required to transition them to the Tachyons cloud based systems. McCann was sitting back in his recliner with Tessa in his lap. The worst of the burn spots on the little Sheltie were beginning to show signs of new fur and, except for them, she looked and acted like her old self. He heard a car drive into the yard and resisted the urge to leave his chair. He assumed it would be Jim Marks, coming to report on the progress of restoration and construction at the farm. For the time being, just a new barn and well house were being built.

When the door bell rang, he shouted.

"Come on in Jim! The door is unlocked!"

The door opened cautiously and Janice DeGroot stuck her head in.

"I'm not Jim but can I come in anyway?" she said, to the empty foyer.

McCann remembered that he hadn't returned Janice's recent "urgent" phone call and kicked himself mentally for not having done so. Now, he would be forced to deal with Janice on a face-to-face basis. While he liked and admired Janice DeGroot and had benefitted from her positive coverage of both Tachyons and himself, he was in no mood to put up with questions about Tachyons, Mogollon or why he didn't have a job.

"Come on in Janice. I'm in here," he said, adjusting the recliner and lifting Tessa down to the floor where she checked out the newcomer and then retreated to her bed by the fireplace.

"Good morning Wils! You didn't answer my phone call so I took a chance and came on out. I just was at the press conference and had a meeting with Carolyn Abbott," Janice said cheerfully as she shed her jacket and dropped her brief case on the floor near the sofa.

"It's always good to see you," McCann lied. "But any Questions you have about Tachyons or Mogollon would need to be handled by Carolyn or one of her staff. I'm not able to make any comments."

Carolyn seemed unfazed. "Can I sit down?" she asked in the same cheerful tone.

"Of course, can I get you a cup of coffee?" McCann asked, making no move to do so.

"No. I've had a taste of what comes out of that tin pot you call a coffee maker and I prefer what comes out of my Keurig," Janice replied with a smile, as she dropped onto the sofa and began to extract things from her briefcase.

"Well, you media people that make the big bucks can afford fancy coffee makers but we unemployed and burned out farmers can't," McCann said, trying to match her jovial tone.

"I heard about the farm. I'm sorry. It looks like your little friend there survived with only a few minor problems," she said, riffling through her papers and sending a glance toward Tessa who was stretched out and fast asleep.

McCann smiled back and chose to say nothing. He would leave the direction of this conversation to Janice.

She laid her papers beside her and pulled her laptop from the bag and turned it on.

"This'll take just a minute. I want to show you something," she said as she waited on the machine. When she had clicked on a few keys, she stood and turned the lap top around in her hands and laid it in McCann's lap.

"What?..." McCann said as he grasped the laptop and squinted at the screen.

"See anyone you know?" Janice asked, standing in front of him.

"No...I don't understand what this is...what...?" he stammered as he looked at what appeared to be a page from a high school year book.

"Fourth row, sixth picture from the left," Janice said quietly, continuing to stand above him. "Recognize him?"

McCann's gaze swung to the designated picture and it was as if someone had punched in him the stomach. He blinked and looked again. It was as if he were looking in a mirror thirty years ago.

"It's...it's...my dad! Where did you get this?" he stammered.

"It's your father's high school yearbook. Had you never seen it before?" Janice asked, her tone one of unbelief.

"No...never...," he moved his finger to the picture as if to touch the real person it represented.

"He...he died when...when I was seven," McCann said, continuing to gaze at the picture. "This is amazing! But I don't understand why you...," he stopped and looked up at Janice.

"...why I have your dad's yearbook from the year he was a junior in high school? I'll tell you why. Look at the picture to his right. Do you know who that is? Have you ever seen him?"

"No...I seem to remember the name from somewhere but can't remember where...who is he? What does he have to do with me or my father?... Bennett McCall...is he someone I should know?" McCann's befuddlement satisfied Janice that he had no inkling of what she was about to tell him.

"You probably have seen his name and maybe his picture in

Fortune or some other business magazine. He is now one of the richest men in the country, if not the whole world. They say his fortune is north of twenty billion dollars," Janice replied, sitting back down on the sofa as McCann continued to hold the laptop and gaze at the photos.

"And why is that of interest to you…or to me?" McCann asked, looking up for the first time since taking the laptop.

"Because, for some reason, your dad's classmate doesn't like you!" Janice replied, sitting back against the cushions.

The old man moved slowly to take the phone from his Butler. The Butler retreated from the room. "What is it?" he asked, his voice raspy.

On the other end of the connection, H Forester spoke carefully and firmly.

"Carolyn Abbott knows about you and your role in the investments in Mogollon and Fairfield. She is demanding to meet with you because of the McCann situation."

"Can you deal with it?" the old man asked.

"She is threatening to resign if you don't agree to meet with her in person," H replied.

"Let me think it over. I'll get back to you," the old man said, disconnecting.

The Butler reappeared, a concerned look on his face.

"Another call sir," he said, indicating the phone. "I put them on hold. I believe it is Mr. Gates."

The old man sagged into a chair and punched a button on the phone.

"What is it?" he said, his voice cold.

"The woman from the newspaper in Michigan knows about you and about our work in Farnsworth." Allen Gates' voice sounded nervous.

"Damn!" the old man said.

"What do you want me to tell her?" Gates asked, his voice a little steadier.

"Can you buy her off?" the old man asked.

"I doubt it. I could try. I've checked her out and she is a career journalist who has a lot of scruples," Gates replied, firmly.

"Stall her. Tell her I will meet with her but not this week," the old man said, his voice becoming more resolute.

"Will do, I'll get back to you," Gates said, and the line went dead.

Ben McCall summoned his Butler. The old man looked up at him from his chair and the resolution was plain on his face.

"Call Mr. Forester back and tell him that I want to talk to him and him alone…here…this very day." He said, looking into the fire that burned softly in the fireplace near his chair.

The butler turned to go and, as he did so, his employer spoke again.

"We will be having several visitors over the next few days. We will need to assure that they are welcomed in the most hospitable manner."

The Butler closed the door to the room behind him. Visitors to this home had been few and far between during the last few years. His employer had been visited mostly by those whom he paid to do his bidding. He wondered who would be coming of such import that Mr. McCall wanted them to be treated hospitably.

———※———

McCann had moved to the sofa and sat next to Janice as she

went through the papers. By the time she had finished, he had a clear picture of Bennett McCall's involvement in the buyout of the Mogollon debt and the investment in Fairfield that had now led to Cindy Melzy's election to the Fairfield Board. Janice had also brought him up to date on the rumors, currently floating through the financial community, that someone, probably McCall, had blocked Fairfield's consideration of McCann as its CEO. McCann was shocked to learn that this was even being considered. She also told him that she believed that McCall was behind the fictitious *TechExec* article and Charlie Dumas who she had discovered was a Chicago Private Investigator named Allen Gates.

McCann had, in turn, gotten on the phone to Cindy in New York City and quizzed her about her meeting with Carolyn Abbott. Cindy, while divulging little of what Carolyn had discussed with her, expressed the same questions concerning the motive behind McCall's opposition to McCann. McCann pointed to another cordless phone on the wall in the kitchen and indicated that Janice should pick it up and join the conversation. While she moved to do so, he told Cindy that Janice would be coming on the line.

"Well, Ms. DeGroot, you have given us something to think about haven't you?" Cindy said, her voice businesslike. "I take it that I won't have to return your call from earlier this morning?"

McCann shot Janice a questioning look and she nodded her head indicating that she had, indeed, called Cindy before coming to see him.

"No, that won't be necessary," Janice replied.

"Where are we going with all of this then?" Cindy asked.

"Good question. I'm still a bit confused about it all," McCann replied.

Just as Janice was about to answer, her cell phone rang. She grabbed it and looked at the screen as the phone continued to ring. She covered the cordless phone with her hand and whispered to McCann.

"It's Allen Gates…the guy who pretended to be Charlie Dumas."

Clicking off McCann's cordless phone, she dropped it onto the sofa and put the cell phone to her ear as she moved out into the foyer.

"What happened?" Cindy asked.

"Janice just took a call from Allen Gates…the guy that pretended to be Charlie Dumas," McCann replied.

"Who…? What are you talking about?" Cindy's confusion was obvious.

Just then, Janice re-entered the room.

"Allen Gates says that Ben McCall has agreed to meet me some day next week," she said, a big smile on her face.

"Cindy, I'll call you back. I need time to think," McCann said, looking up at Janice.

"Okay, talk to you later," Cindy said, and the line went dead.

McCann was about to replace the handset in its cradle when the phone rang. He picked it up and said "Hello".

The voice on the other end of the line was raspy, but authoritative.

"Mr. McCann, this is Bennett Joseph McCall. Your father, James McCann, was my best friend and I need to talk to you. I live in Chicago and will send a plane to pick you up and bring you to my home. It will bring you back when we have finished talking. I would like you to come tomorrow or the next day if at all possible. Please say yes."

(33)

Shortly after 8:00 p.m., J.W. Storey climbed the steps to his apartment. He was surprised to find the door unlocked. When he cautiously opened it and turned on the light, he was equally surprised to find his landlady asleep in one of his living room chairs. When the light went on, Helen Loree woke with a start and looked about, trying to orient herself. Her eyes centered on J.W. and clarity came to her countenance.

"Helen! What are you doing?" J.W. asked, his voice concerned. "Is anything wrong?"

"You tell me, young man!" the old woman shot back, straightening her glasses which had slipped down her nose. "Why haven't you called your father? What is going on?"

J.W. dropped his brief case into a vacant chair and sat down opposite her.

"Did he call?" he said quietly.

"What?" Helen asked as she tried to adjust her hearing aid.

"Did my dad call?" J.W. asked again, more loudly.

"Yes he did! You have not been returning his calls!" she said, equally loudly.

J.W. hung his head before replying. "I've been busy…a lot to catch up on at work…,he began.

"Not this weekend you weren't! You were up here all weekend. I want to know what is going on! What happened when you went to see Traycee?"

J.W. fought down the urge to tell her to mind her own business. He knew that it was her nature to be abrupt and that she really cared for him. She had been like a grandmother to him since he had moved here almost five years ago. He heaved a sigh and looked at her.

"Can I get you some tea?" he asked. "How long have you been up here? Did you have supper?"

"Stop ducking the question!" Helen retorted. "And, yes, I would like to have some tea along with some answers. I've been here since six and yes, I've had my dinner, thank you!"

"Okay…okay…I've got to tell somebody. It might as well be you. Let me put the tea on first," he said, getting to his feet and moving to the small kitchen where he put a tea kettle on to boil and took two tea bags from a tin on the counter top.

After the water had heated, he brought her a cup and saucer and one of the bags. He poured water into the cup and did the same for himself. Once they had dipped their bags in the hot water to their satisfaction, he sat back and took a sip before beginning.

She watched as he took a deep breath. Obviously, something had affected him greatly.

"First, I want to tell you that your prayers have been answered. I've given my heart and life to the Lord," he said quietly.

"Praise the Lord! I am so happy!" she said as she clapped her hands together and then dabbed a tear from her eye. "Tell me about it!"

J.W. related the dream he had while in the coma and the impact it had on him. Helen continued to interrupt with "Praise the Lord" comments and to dab her eyes as he talked. Her joy was contagious and he found himself smiling for the first time in three days.

The mood turned somber as he told of going to Fresno to see

Traycee and tell her about his new found walk with the Lord only to see her with another. Helen considered what he had said before speaking.

"I believe God has a plan for each of us and has invested Himself in that plan through Christ's blood on the cross. I have prayed that you and Traycee would find happiness together in serving Him. But, perhaps that is not His plan. You don't really know what the relationship between Traycee and this man is, do you?"

J. W. admitted that he didn't and that he had probably overreacted to the scene by driving away without giving Traycee a chance to explain.

"Then, perhaps you owe it to her to share with her your feelings and to listen to what is in her heart now," Helen said in a kindly voice.

"I am afraid to. I am afraid that she has found someone new and that God will take her away from me. Why would He do that Helen?" The anguish in the young man's voice was difficult for her to hear.

"J.W., I'm eighty five years old and I have had a lot of ups and downs in my life. But one thing I know for sure because I've tested it countless times. God loves us and he wants the best for us and sometimes, when it seems that He has taken someone or something from us in a way that hurts, it is, in the long run, the best for us. We just can't see it at the time. With God's blessing, oftentimes we get to see it later on. Sometimes we never get to see the 'why' of it. I believe we will see those unanswered 'whys' when we sit at His feet in glory."

J.W. looked across the room at his elderly landlady. What a rock of faith she was! He put his cup down on the end table beside his chair and rose. He stepped across the small space between them, bent and kissed her on the cheek. His lips came away wet with her tears.

"Thanks Helen. God loves you and I love you," he said quietly.

Almost two thousand five hundred miles to the east of where J.W. and Helen sat, Wilson McCann sat beside his fireplace with Tessa in his lap. His brow was furrowed and his eyes were closed. His fingers drummed restlessly on the arm of his chair.

Linda was curled up on the sofa opposite him, her legs tucked up under her. She had been reading some e-mails on her laptop. She paused and looked at her husband. She thought about his favorite scripture and how it was reflected in his life. She mentally recited the verses from Second Samuel, chapter twenty two, verses two and three:

The Lord is my rock and my fortress and my deliverer;
My God, my rock in whom I take refuge;
My shield and the horn of my salvation, my stronghold and my refuge.

"What are you thinking about?" she asked quietly, breaking the silence.

His fingers stopped drumming and he rubbed his eyes before replying.

"I've been trying to remember my dad and his relationship to this man McCall," he said.

"Any luck?" she asked.

"I remember my dad having a friend who seemed a contrast," McCann began. "I've tried to forget those years and it is hard to go back to them. My father was a quiet man. He was a hard worker. He worked in a plant and came home tired and dirty. He was good to me and my mother. He drove an old pick-up…"

"…Just like his son!" Linda interjected.

McCann smiled at the memory.

"He took me to a Northwestern football game once. It was at Ryan Field...that was before they renamed it Dyche Stadium...I was five years old. They were terrible. People call the period from 1972 to 1994 'the age of futility' or something like that...they only won two games that year. I saw one of them...they beat Iowa... but I really didn't understand much of what was going on."

"What does that have to do with Ben McCall?" Linda asked.

"I think my father got the tickets from him. I looked him up and he went to Northwestern. I think he gave my father the tickets. It was the only time my father and I went to a game of any kind."

"They must have been good friends then," Linda commented, trying to draw him along in his thinking.

"I seem to remember a man taking us to dinner one time. He was loud and boisterous and dressed in clothes that were the style of the day. My parents, by contrast were pretty plain and quiet," McCann said, rubbing Tessa's head as she slept in his lap.

"Anything else?" Linda prodded.

"Yes, even though he was a loud, happy person, there was an edge to him...his eyes weren't happy," McCann said, closing his eyes as if visualizing the man he was talking about.

"What do you mean? His eyes weren't happy?" Linda asked, leaning forward and putting her feet on the floor.

McCann thought for a few moments before responding.

"I seem to remember my mother teasing him about not having a girlfriend and he stopped laughing and his face was grim and he said something about never letting someone hurt him again," McCann said slowly.

"What do you think he meant?" Linda asked.

"I don't know, but I was sitting across the table from him and his eyes were cold and hard. I remember that it kind of scared me and I moved closer to my father," McCann replied. "I was seven. A little while after that, my dad died."

As he said this, the sound of a big truck coming up the drive way interrupted his reverie. Linda saw its headlights pass across the windows next to the front door.

McCann picked Tessa up and put her carefully on her bed in front of the fireplace before moving toward the foyer. The quiet of the evening was broken a few moments later by someone pounding on the door.

Traycee Morgan was getting ready for bed when the phone rang. She answered on the third ring and her heart leapt at the sound of J.W.'s voice.

"Where have you been? I haven't heard from you lately," she said, as she sat on the edge of her bed.

"I came back this last weekend. I had a lot of catching up to do," J.W. replied.

"Linda called me, she…and your dad…they were concerned that you hadn't called. They said you were coming here," Traycee said it as a statement and not question.

"I did…you weren't home…when I came, that is, so…I waited…," his voice tailed off as though he didn't know what to say next.

"Was it Friday night?" Traycee asked, knowing the answer but wanting him to say it.

"Yeah…I knew you were busy so I…I left." The words were strained.

"I was at a young adult program at church," Traycee replied. "When did you leave?"

"I saw you come home with someone and I didn't want to…" he didn't finish.

"Didn't want to what? Didn't want to talk to me because I was with someone else?"

She tried to say it calmly because she felt as though they were both on thin ice here and she was afraid of what might happen next.

"Are you…are you seeing someone?" His voice was almost a whisper.

She hesitated before she spoke. She wished with all her heart that he was here so she could see him, could touch him; could try to help him through what she knew would happen next.

"Yes." She said it quietly.

There was a long pause before he spoke again. When he did, she was glad that his voice was stronger and more positive.

"That's good. I have some news as well. I gave my heart and life to the Lord about a month ago. I'm a fellow believer now!" His voice had regained its passion.

"I'm so happy for you!" Traycee responded. Her mind flashed back over the many times that she had encouraged him to make that decision.

"I…I'm sorry that I didn't see you the other night. I shouldn't have left. Maybe we can get together some time in the future," J.W. said.

"Yes, maybe we could. That would be good. But, don't forget to call your dad," she said, unsure how to reply.

"Will do. Good luck with the new guy. Tell him for me that he's a lucky man. Keep in touch," J.W. said, and the line went dead.

In Fresno, Traycee Morgan sat on the edge of her bed, her phone still in her hand, and prayed that she hadn't hurt a man she had once loved.

In Palo Alto, J.W. Storey bowed his head and asked God to give him strength to get through this and do whatever it was that God wanted him to do.

Both of them were crying as they prayed.

McIntyre, clad in a red and black checkered Mackinaw and matching Tam, filled the doorway when McCann opened it.

"We have a doorbell…you don't need to knock the door down!" he said, as he grasped the burly Scotsman's hand.

"Aye! I ken ye do but 'tis a wee thing and I dinna see it," McIntyre said as he came into the foyer and stomped the snow off his boots.

"What brings you out at this hour?" McCann asked as he led his friend into the family room where McIntyre enveloped Linda in a bear hug before removing his Tam. He then bent to caress Tessa as she lay on her bed. The little Sheltie wagged her tail and licked his fingers as he crooned to her.

"Ah! I see! You came to see my wife and my dog!" McCann said, watching with a smile on his face.

The big Scotsman turned and reached into the pocket of his coat and removed an envelope. He handed it to Linda.

"The Laird of this house does not offer me a drink to warm my being so I will give you this and not himself," McIntyre said with a smile, as he began to remove his coat.

"What is it?" Linda asked, looking at the envelope.

"Tis the check for the sale of the beasties," McIntyre replied, throwing his coat onto the end of the sofa.

"Would you like some coffee Mr. McIntyre?" McCann asked, bowing to the scot.

"Aye! That I would and dinna pollute it wi your sweets!" McIntyre replied feigning a scowl.

"Coffee black…coming right up for your worship!" McCann said over his shoulder, as he turned to the kitchen. He returned a moment later with a mug of steaming black coffee which he handed to McIntyre. The big man turned and sat down on the sofa next to Linda while McCann returned to his recliner.

"Thank you for bringing the check from the sale of the cattle. It's good to see you." McCann said, after McIntyre had taken a sip from his mug.

"Aye, 'tis the least I could do. Sorry I am that it has come to this," he replied. "And how is it with you?"

"I'm much improved, thank you. I can sit to eat a meal or to read a book. I don't have to stand or lie down to be without pain. I am walking two miles each day," McCann replied.

"He's even flying to Chicago, although I'm opposed to it," Linda interjected.

"And what's in Chicago that would draw ye out so soon after a surgery?" McIntyre asked, taking another sip from his coffee.

"A man named Bennett McCall who says he was a friend of my father," McCann replied.

McIntyre's whole demeanor changed in an instant. He looked long and hard at McCann.

"A bad one, that man. I'd stay clear of him were I you," he said coldly.

(34)

J.W. sat for a moment thinking about what had just happened. He wiped his eyes with his handkerchief and then went to his small kitchen and refilled his tea cup. He could hear Helen's TV in the rooms below him. Because of her hearing problems, Helen tended to turn the volume up and sit close to the television in the evenings. Over the years, he had grown accustomed to it and hardly noticed it anymore.

He walked back to the living room and sat down. After taking a drink from his tea, he picked up his phone and called his Father.

Linda answered on the second ring. "J.W.! We've been concerned!" She said, her voice a combination of excitement and relief.

"I know…I apologize…there are some things…and I was busy at work and…is dad there?" J.W. finished lamely.

"I'll put him on. He may want to take the call in the bedroom. Mr. McIntyre is here," she replied. "Here he is."

J.W. could tell that his father was walking toward the bedroom as he answered.

"Hi! I was worried. I called several times and waited for a call back. What have you been up to?" McCann said into his ear.

"I had sort of a bad weekend…," J.W. began.

"What happened?" McCann came back, his voice concerned.

"I went to Fresno to see Traycee and she wasn't home and I

waited and she came home and…she was with someone else," J.W. said, pausing to take a breath before continuing "…and I talked to her tonight and she is seeing another guy."

"How are you?" McCann asked. His voice was both firm and concerned.

"I'm okay dad," I prayed about it and I feel like maybe it is God's will."

"I'm sorry son. I wish I could be there with you," McCann replied earnestly and J.W. felt the love and the encouragement behind the words.

"Thanks dad…it means a lot to me to know that you and Linda are there for me. Traycee is a great person and I just waited too long to make the decision she needed me to make. But, I've turned my life over to God now and I have to move forward according to His plans, not mine," J.W. said, his voice strong and steady.

They talked for a few minutes more before McCann said that he had to go.

"I understand McIntyre is there. Give him a slap on the back for me," J.W. said. "Are you feeling okay?"

"I'm okay. I'm going to Chicago tomorrow," McCann replied.

"So soon! Is that wise?" J.W. questioned in a concerned voice.

"Private jet will pick me up and bring me back. I'm going to see a friend of my father. It should be interesting," McCann replied.

"Sorry I am to hear it!" McIntyre said, when McCann had finished telling him and Linda about J.W. and Traycee.

"J.W. seems to be dealing with it well," McCann replied.

"He's a good lad, that boy!" McIntyre said forcefully. "And now he's God's man for a fact!"

"You were about to tell us about Ben McCall," McCann said, as he refilled the big Scotsman's mug from the old percolator.

"Aye, that I was. A bad piece of the Devil's handiwork that one!" McIntyre said, taking a long drink from his coffee.

"How so?" Linda asked, leaning forward, her cup clasped between her hands.

McIntyre closed his eyes, as if he was deep in thought, before he spoke.

"Ye ken my story? I was an accountant and a good one in my younger days. I came to work for a trucking company with ties to the grand adventure in Alaska with the pipeline and all. Ben McCall bought the company that owned the company that I worked for. 'Twas just a wee company…but then we began to change!"

He paused and McCann could see that the memories were painful.

"Was it something illegal?" he asked.

"Nae! Ben McCall, if anything good can be said on his behalf, it is that every nickel he has made has been made honestly. The man is as honest as the day is long," McIntyre replied, looking up at him.

"What then?" Linda asked, her green eyes intense as she considered the man beside her on the sofa.

"The pressure! We grew like topsy! We expanded and diversified and at every step more money flowed and the pressure increased. I was working fifty hours a week and then sixty and then eighty…" his voice trailed off.

"Couldn't you have quit?" Linda asked. McCann shot her a glance from across the room and she sat back, cradling her cup in her lap, and waited for McIntyre to continue.

"Aye! I could have walked away but the money…the money was too great!" McIntyre said sadly.

McCann thought back to the day five years ago when he had first met McIntyre as the burly scot had delivered a load of beef cattle to his farm. McIntyre had shown him how his Border Collie, Ted could herd them. When Ted was killed, it was McIntyre, pretending to try to find a home for a rescue dog, who had delivered a fully trained replacement named Wink. Of all the men he had met during his life, this bigger than life Scotsman represented all that was good about the redemptive power of God.

"Is that when the drinking started?" he asked quietly.

"Aye," McIntyre said softly, dropping his eyes to the floor. I lost my job, my family...almost my life...I was living on the streets when I found Jesus."

"So... McCall was a hard master?" McCann asked.

"Aye but 'twas more than that...he is a maister of the board of life," McIntyre responded, his voice regaining some of its strength.

"A maister?" Linda's face showed that she was mystified.

"The man is a chess maister...a 'master' at maneuvering people to do his will. It was like we were all pawns in this great game that he was playing," McIntyre replied. "And at every move, more money flowed. He bought and sold companies like ye would sell cattle on your little farm. He maneuvered people to points where they couldn't say 'no' to him. And, he was a cold, hard fish."

McCann reached to the end table beside his recliner and retrieved a printout, a page from the year book that Janice DeGroot had shown him earlier in the day. He leaned forward and handed it across to McIntyre. The big man looked at it long and thoughtfully. The picture was one of two teen aged boys with a pretty blonde girl standing between them.

"The one on the left is my father," McCann said as McIntyre continued to look at the picture. "The one on the right is Ben McCall. They were juniors in high school when that was taken. The girl's name is Ann Meister."

"Aye! She must be the very one!" McIntyre replied, his voice rising.

"What do you mean?" Linda asked, leaning in from his left to look at the picture which she had first seen about two hours ago.

"They said that, somewhere early in his life, Ben McCall was hurt by a lass he intended to marry. They say that, from that day on, the pursuit of money and success became his God and that he vowed that no one would ever hurt him again." McIntyre's voice seemed to fill the room with its somber tone.

"Apparently he succeeded. They say He's worth over twenty billion dollars," Linda commented, leaning back on the sofa.

"And nae a lass to bring a wee bit of cheer into his life," McIntyre replied gloomily.

"Well, tomorrow should be interesting," McCann observed, taking a drink of his lukewarm coffee.

"Dinna let the man place ye on his chess board," McIntyre advised firmly.

(35)

The Dassault Falcon 50 drifted down out of the clouds and touched down at MBS International Airport right on time at 9:00 a.m. the next morning. As it taxied to the private jet terminal, Linda turned to McCann, her face showing her concern. The black brace that virtually covered his white shirt under his suit coat only added to her angst.

"Are you sure this is okay?" she asked, laying her hand on his arm.

"He sent a jet big enough for a couple of stretchers and a few EMTs if we need them," McCann smiled into her flashing green eyes.

"Don't joke! This whole thing bothers me," Linda replied, as the door to the jet opened and an elderly gray haired man descended the steps. The plane's engines continued to purr as he made his way to the doorway.

"Mr. McCann? I'm Walter, Mr. McCall's assistant. Please come with me and we will be on our way," He said, not bothering to close the door which he held open. He smiled at Linda as McCann walked past him onto the apron.

"We'll have him back this evening ma'am," he said in a friendly voice before turning and following McCann back to the jet and up the stairs. Ten minutes later, the jet roared down the runway and lifted into the air. As it vanished into the cloud cover, Linda stood at the window and watched it go.

"Please watch over him," she prayed quietly, before turning to go back to her car.

In Palo Alto, J.W. was having breakfast with his landlady. Helen had roused him from sleep an hour earlier and virtually demanded that he come down and eat breakfast with her. It was evident that two things were driving the elderly lady this morning. One was her grandmotherly interest in J.W.'s well being and the other was her curiosity as to how his calls to his father and Traycee had turned out.

J.W. had to admit that the scrambled eggs, bacon and hot cornbread were a big improvement on the cold cereal he usually fixed for himself before leaving for work. That fact alone made him more willing to satisfy her curiosity.

"Traycee is seeing someone else. That's the bottom line," he said, between bites of his food.

Helen, who was having smaller helpings of everything, along with her tea, took this in and replied quietly.

"And how are you handling that?"

J.W. paused and leaned back in his chair. He looked out the window of Helen's small kitchen and then back at her.

"It hurts. I missed my opportunity. I know that. But, I've turned my life over to God and He knows what is best for me. If this is His leading, then I'll just have to pray for the patience and strength to get through it. If Traycee and I are meant to be together, It will work itself out," he said.

"It is always best to trust in the Lord and wait upon him," Helen said, a smile crossing her face.

"I know that now. I wish I had known it a long time ago," J.W. replied wistfully.

"The Lord's timing is always best. We don't understand it at times but I know it is true," she said, taking a sip from her tea. "Have you heard from the other young lady?"

THE INVESTMENT

J.W. smiled at her. He had told Helen about Shelley after the two of them had dinner together in San Jose the previous year.

"She came to visit me in the hospital and at dad's home. I have not heard from her since then."

"Maybe you should call her," Helen replied, taking a small bite from her eggs.

"Let's not rush things," J.W. replied, wiping his mouth and drinking the last of his coffee. He pushed back from the table, stood and came around to Helen. He bent and kissed the top of her head.

"Thank you for caring so much," he said. "I've got to get to work."

Helen's eyes welled at his tenderness. She dabbed them with her napkin.

"I'd call her!" she said loudly as J.W. went out the door.

An hour later, J.W. was plodding through the accumulated list of client technology issue reports on his computer. They had been left for him during his absence. Most of them had been dealt with by his team and he needed to get up to speed on the status of each client. As he sent another report to the "reviewed" file in his computer, his phone rang. When he answered, a familiar voice filled his ear.

"Hi there! I see you are back and hard at it!" Shelley Martinez said in a playful tone.

"You just saved me a phone call and made my landlady happy," J.W said, as he sat back in his chair.

At the same time that the Dassault was taxiing out for takeoff at MBS, FBI Agent Courtney Roberts was sitting opposite her supervisor's desk in Chicago.

"Good news and bad news," her supervisor said, giving her a hard look.

Roberts shifted in her chair and remained silent. "The good news is that Tazlov has gotten his lawyer involved and has clammed up. We think the lawyer may tell him to cut a deal." He said it without a trace of a smile.

"The bad news is that, due to your mishandling of the Colter situation, we don't have a key witness that could have put Tazlov away for a long time and broken the Bratva in the Midwest. We have the three people linked to Tazlov and Colter that operated here in Chicago and they appear willing to testify for us in return for slaps on the wrist. That will help with Tazlov but we would have liked to have had Colter."

He leaned back and looked out the window. Courtney took a deep breath and waited.

"What were you thinking?" he said, as he turned back to her and glared at her.

"I was watching Colter…I had advised the target of the situation…" she began.

"But you didn't involve local authority until it was too late and you didn't put the target under surveillance and you botched your surveillance of the subject. I ask you again…what were you thinking?" His voice rose as he continued to glare at her.

She dropped her eyes to the floor and didn't respond.

"Until further notice, you are assigned to desk duty here in the office. That is all Agent Roberts," he said firmly and pointed to the door.

As she trudged back to her cubicle, Courtney Roberts wished that she had never heard of Liam Colter.

"Can I get you anything? Are you comfortable?" Walter asked, as the big private jet waited at the end of the runway prior to takeoff.

THE INVESTMENT

The pilot, an attractive brunette, had just told them that they were holding for five minutes to allow a couple of commercial airliners to land.

"I'm fine, thank you," McCann replied from one of the jet's big overstuffed chairs. He held a three ring binder in his lap that Walter had given him as he entered the plane.

"Mr. McCall requested that you review the contents of this prior to your meeting with him," Walter had said.

The brace was digging into his mid-section so he loosened the Velcro straps a little and shifted his position in the chair. His seatbelt caught the bottom edge of the brace and he carefully eased it up over the edge. Walter watched him, a look of concern on his face.

"Are you sure you are comfortable? Would a pillow be of assistance?" Walter said as he leaned forward from his seat next to the cockpit door.

"No, I'm fine…just getting settled in. The brace is a bit of a nuisance," McCann replied with a smile.

"It's only been ten days since your back fusion. Once we get through the clouds, we should have smooth flying to Chicago," Walter replied in a reassuring tone.

McCann smiled inwardly. The old man knew that he had back surgery ten days ago. What else did he know?

Ten minutes later, the big private jet shot out of the cloud cover and into bright sunshine. McCann loosened his seat belt, put the tray table in front of him down, and began to read through the contents of the ring binder. Walter went to the rear of the plane and returned shortly with a tray containing a ceramic mug of steaming coffee and a matching cream pitcher and sugar bowl.

The coffee was delicious and McCann sipped it slowly as he reviewed the contents of the binder.

The first section traced a series of investment transactions dating back over forty years. From an initial investment of fifteen thousand dollars, they reflected the transition of that investment to holdings of over twenty billion dollars.

As McCann slowly reviewed the pages before him, the sheer genius of the investment growth was staggering. Every purchase and sale seemed perfectly timed as the mountain of money continued to build.

The second section contained three fold out organization chart pages. The first page presented the holdings of various investment vehicles with Bennett J. McCall at the top of the chart. The following pages broke down the investment vehicles into individual trusts, funds and portfolios and the final pages converted these charts into actual companies owned by the enterprise. The charts were staggering in their breadth and interplay. They reflected substantial ownership of oil and gas companies, supplier organizations to them and transportation companies that were involved in the movement of both oil and gas and the supplies and equipment needed to operate them. Another page showed significant investments in utility companies including telecommunications and internet based development and monitoring companies. On the final page, the investments in both Mogollon and Fairfield were highlighted in yellow.

McCann drained the last of his coffee and sat back in his seat. His mind was digesting all that he had just read. The contents of this binder traced the birth of an empire and displayed it in all its financial breadth and depth. The term that his friend Stu Bailey often used came to mind. This was truly "mind boggling!"

"More coffee, Mr. McCann?" Walter said, as he stood beside McCann's seat, coffee carafe in hand. "We will be landing in about ten minutes."

"Yes, please," McCann replied, his head still spinning from what he had just seen.

"It really is quite something isn't it?" Walter said, as he poured the dark aromatic liquid into McCann's mug.

A black Cadillac Escalade drove out to meet the plane when they landed. Walter preceded McCann down the steps.

"We shall see you this evening. Have a good day!" The brunette pilot said to him as he left the plane.

Walter was holding the rear door to the Escalade for him. The driver, a man in his mid-fifties, was wearing sun glasses and a smile as McCann entered the vehicle.

"This is George. He will be driving us to Mr. McCall's home," Walter said, as he closed the rear door and climbed into the front seat beside the driver.

George turned to him and extended his hand over the seat.

"Is there anything you need before we leave? Are you sure you will be comfortable? I have some pillows in the back if you would like one," he said, gripping McCann's hand firmly.

McCann smiled back at him. "George probably knows how many stitches are in my incision," he thought to himself.

"No, I will be fine thanks. How far is it?"

"About a thirty minute drive…depending on the traffic. If you need to stop or take a break, just let me know," George said, as he shifted the big SUV into motion.

As they drove through the gaited entry to the large home in Glenview, McCann checked his watch. Exactly thirty minutes had elapsed since they had driven off the airport apron. He thought again of the contents of the binder that he held in his hand.

Walter quickly got out and opened the door for him. "Right this way," he said, gesturing to the massive double door entrance. He moved ahead of McCann as they neared the door and held it open for him.

"You will be meeting Mr. McCall in his study. There is a

bathroom for your convenience just outside the room," he said, as he led McCann deeper into the home.

McCann had been in larger, more grandiose homes during his life but this one radiated efficiency and the latest technology. The fixtures and furnishings were expensive and perfectly coordinated. As they moved down the hall, the blinds on the windows automatically adjusted to let in more light. McCann sensed that motion detectors were sending signals to some sort of control that automatically adjusted them for occupancy.

Walter was waiting when he emerged from the restroom. He held the heavy door to the study open.

McCann stepped inside. At the end of the room, a fired burned brightly in a great stone fireplace that spanned the width of the room and reached up into the second story. On one wall, six wall mount TV screens, each at least five feet wide, were dark as they awaited a command from the desk that occupied the opposite side of the room. Between the desk and the TV screens a dark mahogany table and six matching swivel chairs took up a good portion of the floor space. To the left of the doorway, a built-in book case held books, pictures and various sculptures and figures of owls. McCann counted at least thirty different sizes, shapes and types of owls on the shelves. He also noted a familiar framed picture by itself on a shelf at eye-level. It was the same one Janice DeGroot had given him. His teen-aged father and his friend Bennett McCall with Ann Meister smiling back at the camera between them. He took it from the shelf and looked at it.

"Those were happy days…I wish I could go back to them," the quiet, raspy voice surprised McCann. He turned toward it.

In the wall of the room, behind the desk, a sliding door, hidden to the casual observer, had opened. The man who stood there was a far cry from the smiling youth in the picture.

Bennett McCall was completely bald and his eyebrows were

gone. The ravages of his disease were on display in his emaciated body. He leaned into a wooden handled walker as though he would fall to the floor if he let go.

"Please…sit down…we have much to talk about," he said, pushing the walker with one hand toward the table and gesturing with the other toward a chair at the side of the table. He shuffled slowly to its counterpart at the head of the table and Walter moved quickly to roll it out and swivel it to help the old man ease into it. As McCall did so, he took two deep breaths and leaned back for a moment, his eyes closed. McCann, still holding the picture taken in 1967, took the indicated chair and placed the ring binder on the table in front of him.

"So, you've read my little book, have you?" the old man asked. His voice was like a hiss. Walter exited the room.

"I did. It is quite amazing," McCann responded, looking down at the binder and placing the picture beside it. "What does it have to do with me?"

"Everything," the old man said, looking up at the ceiling. The door that McCann had just walked through opened and Walter re-entered the room with a tray containing a water pitcher and glass and a coffee carafe and cup.

Walter poured McCall a glass of water which the old man quickly drank. McCann suspected that the room had a hidden camera and that everything was being watched by Walter, George and unknown others.

"Coffee Mr. McCann? Or should I call you Wils? I can assure you it is every bit as good as what you get from your old percolator at home," the old man said, as he poured himself another glass of water. Walter retreated through the doorway and closed the door after him.

"Thank you," McCann replied, reaching for the carafe and filling the cup. "Your man, Allen Gates, or should I call him 'Charlie Dumas', didn't miss a trick did he?"

"Allen Gates is very good at what he does. I commend your friend Ms. DeGroot for her persistence. I plan to visit with her next week. She obviously has briefed you on her findings," McCall said, a thin smile playing across his pallid features.

"Why am I here?" McCann asked bluntly, taking a sip from his coffee. McCall was right. It was delicious.

"Ah! Cut to the chase! I like that in a man," McCall replied, continuing to smile.

McCann took another drink from his cup and waited, saying nothing.

"You look a lot like your father," McCall said quietly, looking him over appraisingly. "Do you remember me at all?"

"I remember eating lunch at a diner when I was about six or seven with you and my father and mother," McCann replied. "I'm sorry, beyond that, I don't remember much."

"Do you remember your father's funeral?" the old man asked as his eyes bored in across the table.

"Vaguely."

"I was there. It rained. You wore a cheap little overcoat and your mother carried an old umbrella," the raspy voice said, matter-of-factly.

McCann said nothing, letting his mind go back to that gray rainy day on the south side of Chicago when his young life had changed forever. Try as he might, he could not remember much about the day except the tears his mother had shed and the look of despair on her face.

As if anticipating his thoughts, McCall spoke again. "Your mother was a good woman. She was much stronger than your father."

"How would you know that?" McCann replied, the heat in him rising.

"He was a plodder. He had no vision beyond working in a plant," the old man said, dismissively.

"If you brought me here to insult my father, I think I will leave,"

McCann said tightly, as he began to shove his chair away from the table.

"Wait! I'm sorry. I should not have said that. He was a good friend to me," the old man said. McCann could detect both the truth and the despair in McCall's voice.

McCann eased back in his chair and waited. McCall gestured toward the ring binder.

"Do you remember the first page of the first section?" he asked. McCann saw that his outstretched hand was shaking.

"Yes. You started with fifteen thousand dollars. As I said, it is quite remarkable what you have done with that initial investment over the years. But what does that have to do with me?" McCann asked.

"Half of it was your father's money," the old man said, dropping his hand into his lap.

(36)

Six days later, Janice DeGroot sat in the same chair opposite McCall.

"That's quite a story," Janice said. While she had the reporter's natural ability not to show surprise at the story she was involved in, what the old man had told her and the surroundings she found herself in, had shaken her professional composure.

"And now you and I must decide how much of it we can put on the record and how we will tell it," McCall said, as he leaned back in his chair and gazed at her intently.

McCall had stipulated immediately that what he was about to share with her that went beyond what she already knew, was off the record until he placed it on the record.

"Let's start with the end and end with the start," Janice said, looking at her notes which now occupied the better part of her yellow legal pad.

"Help me with that?" the old man replied.

"We'll start with how you are turning over the direction of your financial holdings to the son of your best friend in high school. We'll end with how you came to have that best friend and how you put all this financial empire together," Janice said. She was winging it and hoped the old man wouldn't notice.

"And…what about my treatment of Wils' father?" McCall asked, looking into the fire that burned brightly at the end of the room.

Janice looked away and took a deep breath. Everything in her reporter's instinct told her not to do what she was about to do.

"We'll just say that he was supportive of you until his untimely death and not get into what 'support' means," she said quietly, turning to look at him.

"And hope no one asks more questions…aren't you violating some sort of journalistic ethic?" he said, a faint smile on his lips.

Janice looked down at her pad. "I'm not interested in heaping blame on someone for a mistake made over thirty years ago. I'm interested in how a man became a success and found it in his heart to make the son of his boyhood friend the beneficiary of that success."

"He hasn't agreed to anything yet," McCall replied. Wilson McCann had made it very plain a week ago that he was not willing to step into the role that McCall had created for him.

"We'll cross that bridge when we get to it, won't we?" Janice said lightly. Now that she had gotten by the initial decision on how to frame this story, her creative juices were flowing. McCann had studiously avoided her since his meeting with McCall. However, he had agreed to meet with her upon her return from Chicago and before his next meeting with McCall, which was scheduled in two days.

"I'll draft it and you can review it. The parts that I gathered from others can't be contested. Anything I attribute to you is open for discussion. Deal?" She gave McCall a hard stare.

The old man smiled. "You are a remarkable woman, Ms. DeGroot. When this story breaks, you are going to be getting some offers. I would be prepared, if I were you. Yes, we have a deal. I'll await your story of my life."

The next day, Walter ushered H Forester and Carolyn Abbott into the room for their meeting with McCall. As she extended her hand to the old man, she wondered if she had overstepped in her demand to meet him. H, for his part was completely relaxed and quick to pour himself a cup of coffee from the carafe on the table.

"I'm pleased to finally meet you," McCall said, gazing into her eyes.

"Thank you sir. I apologize if you think me rude for demanding to see you," Carolyn replied nervously. "I just needed to understand…that is…why…"

"Why I was blackballing Wilson McCann? Totally understandable my dear, please sit down. Would you like some coffee? Mr. McCann told me last week that it was very good," McCall replied with a trace of a smile as he gestured to a chair directly opposite the one he was standing behind.

Carolyn, still trying to get a grip on her nerves, sat quickly and poured herself a cup of coffee. McCall took a chair and Walter, who had been standing aside, poured him a glass of water from a pitcher beside the carafe. McCall took a long swallow and sat back in his chair.

"First, I want to thank you for your hard work these past few years," he began, smiling at her. "Mr. Forester has kept me informed of your work and I think it is only fair to say that our collective successes, both his and mine are due in large part to your abilities. Having said that, how would you like to become CEO of Fairfield Communications?"

For the first time since they had walked in, H showed surprise. McCall turned briefly and smiled at him. "It's time for Ms. Abbott to have something to run that isn't just a 'get in and get out' type of position. She has demonstrated a unique combination of intelligence, integrity and…may I say it…beauty that is not often found in today's top executives. I think we should reward the work that she has done for you and our collective interests. Don't you agree?"

THE INVESTMENT

H took a quick sip from his cup and glanced at Carolyn. "Of course," he said with a smile.

McCall turned his gaze back to Carolyn. "I assume you accept?"

Carolyn looked at the old man who would soon be gone from this world. There was something in his demeanor that told her he could be trusted after all.

"Yes. Thank you," she said with a smile.

"Good! Now, let's talk about why Wilson McCann didn't get the job and why you might be interested in what he might be doing in the future," McCall said, draining his glass.

The May sun beat down on her as she stood before the two plots with their faded headstones. She held the two small bouquets that J.W. had taken from the trunk of his car when they arrived. Tears rolled down her cheeks. J.W. wisely stood a few feet off and let her experience the moment.

Shelley had flown into San Francisco two days ago. Her success with her original client had led to two new opportunities, one in Oakland and one in San Jose. She arranged to meet J.W. after meeting with the San Jose prospect and they had dinner together the previous evening. She had the next day free and was hoping to spend some time with J.W. Her hopes were met when, during dinner, J.W. announced that he had a surprise for her and was taking her for a drive the next day. He had resisted all of her attempts to pry his secret from him. She had risen early this morning in anticipation of spending a full day with him. She wasn't sure of how deep his feelings were but she had hoped that this trip would give her some indication as to where their relationship was headed.

They had driven into the San Joaquin valley and had finally

arrived at this little graveyard, south of Bakersfield and well off the beaten path.

"I've been doing some research in my spare time," he said, as he parked before the little burial site. "This is where your mother and father are buried."

She stared at him in disbelief. She had never known where her parents were buried. Her Grandmother was buried near Merced. The fearful culture of the illegal immigrant community had resulted in great secrecy surrounding her parent's burial place. When pressed about it, her Grandmother and her Aunt and Uncle had merely responded "In the valley."

The two small headstones were faded slabs of gray. All evidence that they had ever contained the names of Roberto and Felina Martinez was gone. Yet, as she stood there, she resolved to never forget this place or the love for their future daughter that had brought them to this land. She would buy new headstones and bring them here.

She knelt and placed the little bouquets gently by the headstones. She let the sobs take her and braced both hands against the ground. After a few moments, she stood and wiped away her tears. She turned to J.W.

"Thank you…I hardly knew them and yet I miss them so much. I can't believe that you did this for me," she said, earnestly.

"I know the feeling," he said quietly, "I'll never know my birth mother in this life but I will see her in heaven. Based on what you have told me about them, I believe that you will see your Madre and Padre there too."

She took a step toward him and he took her in his arms. They stood there in the sun as the emotion of the moment washed over them.

"Sometimes I feel alone," she murmured.

"I will always be there for you, if you will let me," he said, holding her close.

THE INVESTMENT

She looked up into his eyes and all of her questions about the future of their relationship were answered in what she saw there.

(37)

Wilson McCann spent a good part of April traveling back and forth between Farnsworth and Chicago as he worked to organize the results of his first meeting with Ben McCall.

The initial outrage he had experienced was gone. He had come to realize that anger at an old man near death because of a terrible injustice to his father and mother would serve no purpose. He no longer engaged in mental "what ifs" concerning how his life and that of his mother would have been different had McCall been honest in his dealings with them and allowed them to share in the fortune that had been amassed from James McCann's unrewarded trust in his boyhood friend.

He met with McCall four times in the following weeks. Each time, the old man had deteriorated from the previous visit. Yet, even to the end, his mental prowess had stayed with him as the two men, united in the memory of someone long gone, worked to set in place the financial future of the legacy that McCall would leave behind.

Over the course of the time that they spent together, the relationship between the two men had blossomed into an easy camaraderie. McCall for his part felt a growing kinship for the son of a man who had been his best friend and who had died long ago.

McCann's initial dislike for McCall as a person who had defrauded his family, coupled with his grudging respect for the old man's business acuity had changed as well. He found McCall to be much like the father he had lost. After their third meeting, he began to call the old man "B.J." and McCall for his part, had occasionally slipped up and called the younger man "Jimbo".

McCall had grown increasingly reclusive over the years as his financial empire multiplied and he had few close friends. He insisted that, upon his death, those few, in addition to H Forester, who had been faithful to him over the years, Brendon Vaughn, Walter, a Frenchman named Pelletier and George, his driver, should be taken care of financially for the rest of their lives. He had also added Ann Meister, now Ann Hoff, to the list who should receive a substantial amount of money. Within the next thirty days, all would become multi-millionaires.

McCall admitted to blocking McCann from becoming CEO of Mogollon and Fairfield but justified it by his intention to make McCann CEO of the various enterprises that controlled his empire. He was content that he had made the right decision in making Carolyn Abbott the new CEO of Fairfield. McCann, for his part agreed totally with that decision. He knew she would carry on the good business tradition that Bob Allison had begun. As representative of the McCall interests in Fairfield, McCann would be a permanent member of Fairfield's Board of Directors.

Recognizing what the accumulation of money had done to McCall, Wilson McCann refused to be put in control of it. The two men spent the better part of an afternoon in April debating the issue. McCall's fervor to right an ancient wrong clashed with McCann's equally strong refusal to become the captive of a twenty billion dollar monster that would be his master and not his servant.

In the end, they went back to that day in 1970 for the solution. James "Jimbo" McCann and Bennett J. "BJ" McCall had each put in $7,500. While McCall had spent the intervening forty years amassing the fortune, he insisted that, without his boyhood friend's trust and commitment of his savings, there would have been no fortune. They finally agreed to split the enterprise into two equal parts.

Two separate foundations were established after provisions were made to satisfy the substantial tax burden on the estate. One, in McCall's name, would be administered by H Forester and Associates and would be devoted to the continuation of the business ventures McCall owned either outright or in part. The other foundation, named for James and Ellen McCann, would be administered by a Board of Directors Chaired by McCann. The board included Cindy Melzy, Donald Straylin, Stu Bailey, Fred Penay, Shirley Jacobs and, for as long as she cared to, Belle Warner.

Janice DeGroot's story about McCall and his relationship to Wilson McCann had been an outstanding success. It had been picked up by the wire services and follow up stories had run in **Barrons**, **The Wall Street Journal** and **Fortune Magazine**. A few reporters attempted to dig deeper into the relationship between McCall and McCann's father but were politely stonewalled until they gave up.

McCann felt sure that Janice was well on her way to another Michigan AP Journalism Award. She had fielded several offers from larger newspapers including the **New York Times** but, with McCann continuing to live in Farnsworth, she said she didn't want to leave the **Bay City Times** and the opportunity to continue to cover her "favorite newsmaker".

McCall, at first, resisted any attempts on McCann's part to talk about his relationship with God. He insisted that he had not done anything which would earn God's favor and that he was prepared to meet the consequences of his life. He told McCann of the bitterness he felt when Ann had broken their engagement. He had vowed that no one would ever hurt him again and that he would devote his life to achieving such success that he, and not others, would determine the course of events in his life. The fortune he had amassed stood as testament to both his resolve and the bitterness that had driven it.

THE INVESTMENT

As the two men talked, McCall confessed that the great injustice he had done to James McCann had festered within him. He had scrupulously done business in ways that assured no one else would ever be able to say that he had cheated them. He knew that he had a reputation as a hard man to work for but was resolute in his belief that he had, in all but one instance, treated others honestly.

The diagnosis of his cancer and the realization that his life would be cut short had driven him back to the one who had hurt him. He told McCann of his visit to Ann and of her urging that he make right the great wrong that he had done to James McCann and his family.

Their discussions of McCall's relationship to his maker culminated on a cold spring day in late April. He and McCall sat together in the small drawing room. McCall was now using a portable oxygen tank periodically and it sat between their chairs as they sat before the fire. McCann knew that Walter was watching on the mansion's closed circuit TV system and would appear in a moment if McCall needed anything. The end was near. The thought that he was being watched no longer bothered him. Walter's sole focus was to make sure that his employer was as comfortable as possible as he prepared to leave this world.

Having dispensed with the work that had brought them together this day, McCann attempted once again to direct his father's friend's attention to the subject of preparation to meet the end of his life.

"Do you know the parable of the talents?" he asked.

"Are you going to quote the Bible to me again?" the old man asked in a quiet voice. McCann didn't sense any great resistance so he removed the tattered old Bible from the brief case beside his chair and opened it.

"Where did you get that old thing?" McCall asked.

"It was my Aunt's…my uncle gave it to her," McCann responded, flipping through the pages to get to where he wanted to be.

"I never knew him. Your mother was a gem," McCall placed the oxygen mask over his mouth and nose and inhaled deeply.

McCann sensed an attempt at diversion on the old man's part and smiled as he found his place in the Bible.

"Listen to this. You might find it interesting. It deals with investments and returns."

He began to read:

For it is just like a man about to go on a journey,
who called his own slaves, and entrusted his possessions to them.

And to one he gave five talents, to another, two, and to another, one,
each according to his own ability, and he went on his journey.

A small smile crossed McCall's face. "Like me, I suppose. I'm about to go on a journey and I'm working with you to pass out my money," he said, returning the oxygen mask to its cradle at the top of the portable tank.

"Maybe, but hear the rest," McCann said, continuing to read.

Immediately the one who had received the five talents went and traded
with them, and gained five more talents.

In the same manner the one who had received
the two talents gained two more.

"I could have used those two working for me," McCall said, leaning back in his chair and closing his eyes. McCann could tell, however that he was listening intently.

"I think you must have had some folks like them working for you, based on the results we've been discussing," McCann said, smiling.

"H. Forester for one," McCall said, smiling back.

THE INVESTMENT

"Keep listening," McCann said, turning back to the Bible.

But he who had received the one talent went away and dug in the ground, and hid his master's money.

"Some people just don't get it," McCall said, opening his eyes and looking into the fire. "You have to invest in order to grow."

"Let's see how it ends," McCann said quietly.

Now after a long time, the master of those slaves came and settled accounts with them.

"Ah...here comes the 'we'll all have to give an account of our lives speech!" McCall said, but McCann could tell that his humor was slightly feigned. He ignored the comment and read on.

And the one who had received the five talents came up and brought five more talents saying, "Master, you entrusted five talents to me; see, I have gained five more talents.

His master said to him, "Well done, good and faithful slave; you were faithful with a few things, I will put you in charge of many things, enter into the joy of your master.

The one also who had received the two talents came up and said, Master, you entrusted to me two talents; see, I have gained two more talents.

His master said to him, "Well done, good and faithful slave; you were faithful with a few things, I will put you in charge of many things; enter into the joy of your master."

"That's good! Risk and reward! I love it!" McCall croaked. McCann smiled at the old man's enthusiasm and read on.

And the one also who had received the one talent came up and said, "Master, I knew you to be a hard man, reaping where you did not sow and gathering where you scattered no seed.

And I was afraid, and went away and hid your talent in the ground; see, you have what is yours."

"He needs to can this guy!" McCall growled.

"Is that what you would have done?" McCann asked, looking at him.

"I had to do it on several occasions. But, I always gave them a severance package," McCall's tone seemed to seek appreciation for his actions. McCann chose to ignore it.

But his master answered and said to him, "You wicked, lazy slave, you knew that I reap where I did not sow, and gather where I scattered no seed.

Then you ought to have put my money in the bank, and on arrival I would have received my money back with interest.

Therefore take away the talent from him, and give it to the one who has the ten talents."

"For to everyone who has shall more be given, and he shall have an abundance; but from the one who does not have, even what he does have shall be taken away.

And cast out the worthless slave into the outer darkness; in that place there shall be weeping and gnashing of teeth."

McCann closed the Bible and placed it back in his brief case.

THE INVESTMENT

The silence between them was broken only by the crackling of the fire.

"And…who…who am I?" McCall asked quietly.

"Good question," McCann replied, "Who do you think you are?"

"I could be the master in the story," the old man said it more as a question than a statement.

"Could be," McCann replied, "Any other ideas?"

"I could be the guy with the five talents. Look what I did with fifteen grand in forty years."

"Very true. There are others in this world with more money than you have. Maybe you are the guy with the two talents," McCann replied conversationally.

"I suppose. Maybe if the guy upstairs, that you worship, had given me more time, I could have become a five talent kind of guy," McCall said, somewhat petulantly.

"How much more time would you have needed," McCann asked, smiling.

"I'm going on seventy one. If I could have made it to eighty… who knows?" McCall's voice trailed off as he said it.

"What about the one talent guy? Are you him?" McCann asked.

"No way!…what are you getting at?" McCall pushed himself up to a more erect position in his chair.

"Suppose the master in the story is God and you and I are like the slaves. God invests in us and allows us to live our lives and then, as you have rightly said, the day comes when we must give an account. If we live for Him, according to his direction in our lives, much like the two slaves who went out and invested their talents for their master, we will be rewarded. If we reject God's ways and don't bring in a return on his investment in us, we will see Him take back that investment he made in us and we will be, as the parable indicates, cast out into 'outer darkness'."

McCann stopped and the silence descended on the room again.

After a moment he turned to look at McCall and saw a tear roll down the old man's cheek. The old man's face was inscrutable as he stared into the fire. Finally, without returning McCann's gaze, he spoke.

"Why do you care about me, Jimbo? I've cheated you, and your family, in the worst possible way and you have every right to hate me and yet you don't."

"B.J. you are a good man! Even those who don't like you or your approach say that you are honest and fair. Sure, you treated my father and my family in a dishonest way. You made a big mistake. I forgive you. I've probably made more mistakes in my life than you have and God forgave me and gave me a new life. He will do the same for you in the time you have left," McCann said it with all the conviction he could muster.

"I don't have much time left for a new life," McCall said quietly.

"You have all the time there is," McCann replied.

The old man sat quietly for few minutes until McCann prepared to leave. As he was closing his briefcase in preparation to depart, McCall asked him to mark the story in the Harms Bible and leave it behind.

McCann hesitated. The Bible meant a lot to him and he had never left it with anyone since the night he had given it to Linda in Minneapolis when she was about to end a ten year live in relationship and was looking for new meaning in her life. That had eventually led to Linda coming to faith in Christ and the two of them falling in love. He handed the Bible to the old man and promised to pick it up the next time they met.

"If there is a next time," the old man replied.

McCann arrived home late in the evening. Linda was in Phoenix working on the Mogollon IT transition. Jim Marks had been there earlier, fed Florie and Tessa and left. The house was quiet and he stretched out in his recliner with Tessa in his lap and was soon asleep.

THE INVESTMENT

His phone rang loudly again and again as he roused himself from sleep and grabbed for it.

"Hello," he said in the darkness of the room as Tessa raised her head. Having determined that it wasn't necessary for her to jump from his lap, she went back to sleep.

"Will you pray with me?" the raspy voice on the other end of the call said into his ear.

A flood of joy overwhelmed him as he thought of what the words meant. He resisted the urge to shout into the darkness, took a deep breath and said with all the love he could muster, "I would be honored to, B.J."

That night, one of the richest men in the world gave what remained of his life to the Lord. Eight days later, he would be welcomed into his savior's loving arms.

Bennett J. McCall died in his sleep with his faithful Butler, Walter, by his side. In those intervening eight days, he had done more good than many men do in a lifetime. The high school where he had graduated received enough money for a state-of-the-art science lab. Northwestern University received a grant of twenty million dollars to its business school. The orphanage where Arleta Forester spent a day each week received ten million dollars to bolster its programs and increase the number of at risk children it could take care of. A fund was established to provide college scholarships for up to ten high school seniors who had gone through the orphanage's programs. Two missionary programs that served in Southeast Asia and Brazil, where McCall had significant investments, received enough funding to ensure their continued work for a minimum of twenty years. A small church about a mile from McCall's home received three million dollars to completely replace a leaking roof, revamp its heating and air conditioning systems, and put in a new parking lot. With what was left over, they were asked to start a day school for the surrounding area. McCall had never darkened its door but the eight day period from his transformation to his passing demonstrated that a man with a lot of money and a lot of passion could achieve quite a lot in a short time.

That same little church near McCall's home was where the short service was held. It was attended by only a few close friends and associates. McCann noticed a woman dressed in black, her face covered by a veil, who came forward prior to the service and laid a single rose on the casket. He knew immediately that this must be Ann, the girl who had broken McCall's heart but who, in the end, had been the motivator of his desire to right a wrong that had been done years ago.

McCann spoke briefly and the elderly pastor read the parable of the talents and gave a short homily. The interment was in a small cemetery behind the church. A brief rain shower ended as they stepped outside the church. The sun broke through the clouds and bathed the scene in springtime warmth. The woman in black was gone.

Tomorrow, McCann would catch a flight to Charlotte and drive up to Weaverville to chair his first meeting as CEO of Damascus Road Ministries, formerly Eastern Europe Christian Ministries. He would announce a major redirection of the ministry according to the plan that Donald Straylin, Charles Hastings, Shirley Jacobs and he had put together with the guidance and assistance of Lark Bishop and John Botek. The ministry would essentially become a worldwide ministry and its primary focus would be expanded to meet a growing list of needs in the U.S. and around the world.

Programs would be established to fight human trafficking, assist the homeless, re-start the lives of those coming out of the prison system, finding work for those without jobs, providing a proper life for children without fathers and mothers and young people who weren't getting a good education. All of this would be done in the name of God.

The engine for this redirection would be fueled by a fifty million dollar infusion from the James and Ellen McCann foundation which would become the bed rock for the expanded ministry. That infusion would be supplemented by a twenty five million dollar challenge gift from the estate of Bennett McCall. What only McCann and H. Forester knew was that, in the event that the challenge was not matched from other donors in total, an additional contribution from the McCall estate would assure its success.

H. Forester had suggested that Carolyn Abbott be added to the Damascus Road Board of Directors.

"Consider it done," McCann had replied. Carolyn Abbott would, he knew, be an excellent board member.

At the same time that Wilson McCann was adjourning his first Damascus Road board meeting in Weaverville, Shelley Martinez placed her powder blue golf ball on the green carpet at Golfland Hills in San Jose, California. She looked at the slowly turning wind mill that fronted the small water hazard and the carpet on the other side that led to the hole.

"No pressure!" J.W. Storey said quietly, from behind her.

"Shut up!" she said with a smile, not looking at him.

She waited, counted to three in her mind and tapped the ball. It rolled down the carpet and up the small ramp that led to the windmill. It hopped between the slowly turning blades and across the water. It landed on the other side and slowly rolled into the hole.

"I win!" She shouted loudly enough for the young couple and their two children playing the hole behind them to look up. When they did, they saw an attractive young Latino woman locked in the arms of a tall dark haired young man in what appeared to be more than just a celebratory embrace.

"What do you think?" The husband asked his wife as he prepared to address his ball.

"I would say that those two are head over heels for each other," she replied, watching as J.W. and Shelley walked away, hand in hand.

The eight acre field of wheat glistened in the May sunshine as Wilson McCann stood at the crest of the hill near the brand new barn on his farm. He looked out over the fields to the west and watched Linda, riding Florie, gallop through the adjacent pasture field. Her blonde hair flying in the wind, she turned the mare and headed back toward where he stood.

He thought back over the previous nine months. The sale of Tachyons, the accident that nearly took the life of his wife and son, the loss of his unborn child, the accident on the farm, the fire and its destruction, the emotional and physical pain he had endured. He had felt, at times, that God had abandoned him. Yet now, as he stood beside a new barn and watched the love of his life and helpmate in his faith ride toward him, he was filled with a great sense of God's enduring and unchanging love.

A car drove into the yard behind him and he turned to see who it was. J.W. and Shelley got out and came toward him, hand in hand. He sensed that they had something to tell him and he could guess what it was. Once again, God had answered prayers and given him the blessing of a new member for his family. That blessing might be multiplied again if Linda's visit with the doctor in Caro resulted in the news that they had prayed and hoped for. If that prayer was answered, he intended to make sure that she wouldn't be galloping across the fields on Florie for the next eight months.

He had been tested. In God's strength, his faith had not only survived but had been strengthened. Linda rode up and dismounted. She came to him and put one arm around his waist and encircled J. W. with the other. The four of them stood there looking out over the fields. McCann had learned much over the last few months. A breeze out of the west caused the green wheat field to shimmer in the sunlight as his mind ran through what he now knew more strongly than ever before. There is nothing God cannot do. It is impossible to frustrate God's purposes. God's plans are beyond our understanding and too deep to explain. Only through God's instruction are we able to humble ourselves and rest in His will. When the day of reckoning comes, God is always fair. No one can be compared to God when it comes to blessings. Only God can fill our lives with divine music that frees us to live above our circumstances.

As he stood there with those he loved so deeply, a portion of his favorite scripture from the twenty second chapter of Second Samuel came to his mind.

In my distress I called upon the Lord.
Yes, I cried to my God.
And from His temple, He heard my voice.
And my cry for help came into His ears.

Epilogue—
Barcelona, Spain—
2012

McCann looked out over the audience before him in the Catalonia Hotel's ballroom. The audience represented those who had generously responded to the McCall challenge here in Spain. Several of the Damascus Road board were seated in the audience at tables near the speaker's podium.

He could see Linda seated towards the rear of the room, holding one year old Ellie on her lap. What a joy his daughter was to them. She was beginning to walk and that was the reason for Linda's position near the rear of the room so his daughter would not be a distraction during his speech. He noted a dark haired man standing just inside the door with his sunglasses still on. McCann assumed he must be a member of the hotel's security team.

Shelley Martinez, camera at the ready, sat off to the right. She was Damascus Road's new Director of Public Outreach with particular emphasis on the Latino population. The Board had given unanimous approval to her employment even though, in one month, she would become McCann's daughter-in-law.

"Thank you all for coming," McCann began. "God has blessed us. You, through your support, are a blessing to others. Your participation in the McCall Challenge is greatly appreciated."

Twenty minutes later, his speech concluded, he mixed with the crowd and enjoyed the refreshments that had been brought in by the hotel staff at the conclusion of his speech.

As he poured himself a cup of punch, he watched Eleanor Lucille McCann. She was "Ellie" to her parents and named for his mother and Linda's. Now, she made for the door, her mother in hot pursuit.

"Welcome to Barcelona, Mr. McCann," the voice interrupted his thoughts and he turned to face the dark haired man in sunglasses. Clad in a green jacket and gray slacks, the man extended his hand. McCann noted the Celtic cross showing through the open neck of his oxford shirt. He also noted the bulge under the left side of the jacket.

There was something in the man's features that bothered McCann. The hair didn't seem right for the facial features and the facial features looked as though they had been altered. It was then that McCann realized that his mind was comparing the face to a picture he had seen two years ago. But, as he struggled to place it, the stranger grasped his hand and squeezed it strongly.

"I enjoyed your talk. You have done a good job since you took over two years ago," he said, smiling.

"Are you familiar with our work then?" McCann asked.

"Not so much your organization as I am with you." The stranger smiled back, and there was something in the smile that was unsettling.

"I don't believe we've met," McCann said, releasing the stranger's hand.

"Not personally, but I've followed your career for some time," the man replied, smiling at McCann's obvious confusion. "You've done a good job as CEO of Damascus Road since you took over. Do you ever wish you had stayed in the Telecommunications business?"

"No, I feel that the Lord has called me to the right place at the right time. Are you in the telecom field here in Spain?"

"No, I've traveled a bit in my previous profession. I spent some

THE INVESTMENT

time in the States. I even passed through Farnsworth one time. I had some business there but it wasn't completed. I came here two years ago," the man said, his smile a knowing one. "I've brought you something that is long overdue."

The reference to Farnsworth bothered McCann but before he could respond, the stranger reached inside his jacket with his right hand. McCann's heart jumped until he saw the fat brown paper envelope that the man now held.

"I'd like to make a contribution to Damascus Road's future. It's in my mother's memory. She would have approved of the work you are doing," he said, extending the envelope.

McCann's eyes moved to the envelope. It was stuffed with a wad of Euros.

"Thank you, that is very kind of you. May God bless you and your family for your generosity," McCann said, as his heart slowed down. "Was your mother a Christ follower here in Barcelona?" He switched the envelope to his left hand and reached out with his right to shake the stranger's hand a second time.

"Yes, she talked with God often and no…she lived in Belfast until her death four years ago," he replied quietly.

"And you? Do you know the Lord?…I'm sorry…I didn't catch your name…" McCann said hesitantly.

"My name doesn't matter. I'm working on my relationship with the Good Lord. My mother's name was Maura. You can consider this an investment on behalf of her memory and my relationship with the Almighty."

With that, the stranger turned and walked away.

"Wait!" McCann took a step to follow him but was intercepted by Linda, holding Ellie.

"Who was that man?" she asked.

"I don't know, but I have a feeling I should," McCann said, his eyes searching the crowd for the green jacket. But the man was gone.

Later that evening, as he sat holding his daughter, and reflecting on the one hundred thousand Euros that were now safely stored in the Catalonia's office safe, the picture he had been searching for earlier popped into his mind.

"Liam Colter," he said quietly as he kissed his daughter on the top of her head. "He called it an investment."

ALSO BY
ROBERT W. ZINNECKER

ACQUISITION

Wilson McCann, the CEO of Dynacom, tried everything to save his firm. But, when a rival gobbles up the telecom giant for a lower than expected share price, McCann is vilified in the business press. He decides to escape the rough and tumble corporate world for a new challenge, rescuing his dead uncle's debt-ridden farm.

It's in the small Michigan village of Farnsworth that McCann meets three women from his past who want to be a part of his future. Each has a decidedly different objective. Meanwhile, old associates seek to draw him back into the telecom industry even as new friends urge him to find God's plan.

Problems multiply when McCann gets involved in an acquisition scheme that would restore him as a CEO. A prominent politician may turn the deal into a disaster, and a series of personal tragedies drives McCann to his knees. It is there that he begins his greatest acquisition, and his future opportunities collide with the results of his past.

Acquisition is the provocative story of one man's search for meaning amidst Wall Street raiders and small town farmers…and the surprising revelations about what matters most.

Learn more at:
www.outskirtspress.com/acquisition

ALSO BY
ROBERT W. ZINNECKER

SELL OUT

High-powered CEO Wilson McCann embraced a new relationship with God after moving to the small Michigan village of Farnsworth. Now, the nation's economic deterioration impacts his friends' livelihood and the investors in Tachyons, the telecommunications company he leads, threaten to sell out.

A national telecommunications firm vies with an unscrupulous hedge fund operator to acquire McCann's company. He comes face to face with the need to make a total commitment to his faith, his company and the beautiful woman God has sent to stand beside him.

Set against the backdrop of greed-driven corporate espionage, the potential collapse of the nation's financial system and misplaced personal priorities, **Sell Out** is the compelling story of a man seeking to know what it means to love God with all of his heart, soul, mind and strength.

Learn more at:
www.outskirtspress.com/sellout

CPSIA information can be obtained
at www.ICGtesting.com
Printed in the USA
FFOW01n1632100516
23951FF